Hollywood GIRLS CLUB

Hollywood
GIRLS CLUB

a novel

MAGGIE MARR

 THREE RIVERS PRESS • NEW YORK

Copyright © 2007 by Six Mile Ridge Productions, Inc.

Excerpt from *Secrets of the Hollywood Girls Club* copyright © 2008 by Six Mile Ridge Productions, Inc.

All rights reserved.
Published in the United States by Three Rivers Press, an imprint of the Crown Publishing Group, a division of Random House, Inc., New York.
www.crownpublishing.com

THREE RIVERS PRESS and the Tugboat design are registered trademarks of Random House, Inc.

Originally published in hardcover in the United States by Crown Publishers, an imprint of the Crown Publishing Group, a division of Random House, Inc., New York, in 2007.

This book contains an excerpt from the forthcoming book *Secrets of the Hollywood Girls Club* by Maggie Marr. This excerpt has been set for this edition and may not reflect the final content of the forthcoming edition.

Library of Congress Cataloging-in-Publication Data
  Marr, Maggie.
  Hollywood girls club : a novel / Maggie Marr. — 1st ed.
    1. Women in the motion picture industry—Fiction. 2. Motion picture industry—Fiction. 3. Hollywood (Los Angeles, Calif.)—Fiction. I. Title.
  PS3613.A7687H66 2007
  813'.6—dc22   2006020626

ISBN 978-0-307-34630-8

Printed in the United States of America

DESIGN BY ELINA D. NUDELMAN

10 9 8 7 6 5 4 3 2 1

First Paperback Edition

This book is dedicated to the entertainment community,
a place where genius thrives,
creativity flourishes,
and dreams really do come true.
M.M.

Hollywood
GIRLS CLUB

1

Celeste Solange and Her Fifteen-Thousand-Dollar Shoes

CELESTE SOLANGE NEEDED SHOES. AND NOT JUST ANY KIND OF SHOES—SHE needed Manolos, Choos, and Versaces. Shoes with price tags containing a minimum of three zeros. Shoes that made salesclerks salivate and Beverly Hills trophy wives green with envy. Damien would pay. She'd make sure of it. He'd blanch at the sight of his credit-card bill. Celeste glanced into the rearview mirror of her midnight blue Porsche Boxster convertible. Although she wore oversized Gucci sunglasses, she knew that behind the shades her turquoise eyes were red-rimmed and swollen (the same gold-flecked catlike eyes for which she was famous). Her signature blond hair, usually expertly coiffed and styled, whipped in the California wind. A cross between Michelle Pfeiffer and Marilyn Monroe, Celeste was *the* sexpot screen siren of the century (or at least the last five years).

Who did Damien Bruckner think he was? Celeste wondered. She pressed her perfectly pedicured toes onto the accelerator, feeling it sink to the floorboard as she took the tight turn on Mulholland Drive. When Celeste met Damien five years before, he was, perhaps, the most prolific film producer in Hollywood, and Celeste the hottest star. But five years (in an industry where the power brokers changed every ten years) was a lifetime.

Celeste crested a hill and looked at Los Angeles lying at her feet. She could almost see the Pacific if it weren't for the haze. L.A. had been beautiful in the forties. As a child, she'd seen pictures in her grandmother's old movie magazines—orange groves, mountains, beaches, and waves all visible from the top of Mulholland and the Hollywood Hills. The very beauty those pictures promised had captivated a young Celeste, drawing her from a trailer court in Tennessee to the land of movie stars. Now, with the exhaust and pollution, the view was tarnished. It was dirty and gray. Just like Damien Bruckner.

Damien believed he'd satisfy Celeste by giving her a five-carat diamond and his last name. But after what Celeste had found, neither the diamond nor the name was enough. None of it was. *The fucker*.

For five years, Celeste fucked him and blew him. Even fucked a few of his friends, and why? Why? Good question. Celeste thought she'd known the answer. For the fulfillment of a promise. That once Amanda Bruckner, Damien's first wife, was gone, she—Celeste Solange, superstar—would be Mrs. Damien Bruckner. And finally, in the perfect Malibu wedding just six months ago, Celeste had gotten her wish. Or what she thought was her wish. Fulfilling Celeste's desire to be one half of "the" power couple in the movie business. It had been a grandiose event. Everyone was there. Tom, Kate, Will, Bruce, even the ever-reclusive Robert. The press was phenomenal. Helicopters whirling overhead, paparazzi sneaking through the bushes. (Damien and Celeste had been smart enough to get tents.) The picture of her dress, Celeste heard, had sold for more than a hundred grand.

And then, almost immediately after the wedding, the rumors began. The rumors and the questions. What about Celeste's career? Was it over? She hadn't worked in close to two years—was she leaving film to become a domestic diva? Perhaps a little Bruckner was soon to follow the Malibu wedding ceremony. Or perhaps, as the most popular tabloid rumors implied, Celeste was already pregnant with what was sure to be the perfect Hollywood child. None of it was true. Celeste's sabbatical from film was at

Damien's behest, causing, he believed, the public's hunger for her next picture to swell. Because Celeste's first film in two years was scheduled to be the next film Damien produced, an action adventure entitled *Borderland Blue*.

Celeste pulled hard on the steering wheel of her Porsche. Amanda Bruckner was brilliant. Barely forty-five and set for life. She sat in a stunning $15 million home in Nice overlooking the ocean, and Damien threw gazillions of dollars at her just to keep her quiet and to stay the fuck away from Los Angeles. Amanda kept his name and a huge chunk of his money (in addition to the $50,000 a month in alimony Damien paid). Amanda would have laughed at this scenario. Thrown back her head and cackled with glee. How could she not? The irony was absolute.

Black lace panties. It seemed Damien liked them on all his women. Because the black lace panties that Mathilde (Celeste and Damien's housekeeper) had found in Damien's suitcase this morning weren't all that different from all the pairs of little black lace panties Celeste wore when Damien was sleeping with Celeste and still married to Amanda.

"*Señora, es tu?*" Mathilde had asked, holding up the crotchless undies as she unpacked the suitcase Damien had brought home from New Zealand late last night.

Emerging from the bathroom sauna, Celeste froze at the sight of Mathilde waving the panties over the couple's king-size bed. Her heart pounded. *Those are* not *mine.* Even from a distance she could tell. The offensive black polyester lingerie that Mathilde held was cheap and shoddily made. It had been a decade since Celeste had felt anything but Agent Provocateur against her skin.

Celeste put on her Hollywood game face (she was a Golden Globe–winning actress, after all) and smiled at Mathilde. "*Sí. Un presente for Señor Bruckner.* To remember me by, while he was away on set."

No need to have the help talking, Celeste thought. If Mathilde found out that Damien was having an affair, everyone in town would know. All the hired help rode the same bus—how do you think everyone in Hollywood found out that Steven Brockman was gay?

Celeste flinched at the memory, swerving around her rapper neighbor's Escalade attempting to turn onto Mulholland in front of her. It wasn't the fucking around that pissed her off. (She could be jealous, but why? She'd had special friends on the side.) They were a liberal sort of Hollywood couple. Celeste had been aware of Damien's fling with this little cocktease of an actress Brianna Ellison for months. But the trip to New Zealand, to a film Damien wasn't even producing (executive producing only; he might as well be a grip), combined with this little tramp getting the lead in *Borderland Blue,* that was enough to make Celeste burn.

Damien didn't even have the integrity to tell Celeste that she'd been bumped from the lead role (and the sneaky bastard hadn't left the trades lying around this morning—he'd taken *Variety* and *Hollywood Reporter*). But Damien wasn't clever enough. Much like finding crotchless panties in the hands of their housekeeper, Celeste learned of her public disgrace via another employee—this time her publicist, Kiki Dee. There in the fax machine, just like every morning, lay copies of all the articles (*Us, People, Star,* the *Enquirer, Variety . . .*) that mentioned Celeste. But this morning there'd been a hissing cobra on the second page of Kiki's twenty-page fax. BRUCKNER BLUE FOR BRIANNA screamed the headline in *Variety.*

The humiliation was horrifying. Celeste had spent the last two years prancing around town talking about nothing but her next big part in Damien's next big film. For two years, through script rewrites, changes in director, and changes in locale, Celeste had held off doing any other film, waiting for Damien and *Border-land Blue*. She'd been offered other roles. Roles for which other actresses were nominated and even won awards, fulfilling what was Celeste's dream—to have an Oscar to sit next to her Golden Globe. But no, Celeste waited. She waited for Damien's film, because he'd promised.

And now Brie Ellison was getting the lead. Brie was an eighteen-year-old wannabe who hadn't even starred in a film.

Sure, her breasts were perky and she had great hair, but so did Celeste. Celeste had paid twenty-five grand just three months ago to have her breasts re-perked (a little maintenance in preparation for the bikini scenes). It wasn't pleasant having stitches around your nipples.

How had this happened? Where the fuck was Jessica and why hadn't she told Celeste? It was Jessica's job, as Celeste's agent, to protect her business interests and to never let Celeste get blindsided in the trades like this. She obviously couldn't trust her husband to look out for her best interests (at least whenever his cock was involved). *But her agent, one of her closest friends? What was going on?* Jessica had to have known about this deal; she was the president of CTA, the most powerful agency in town. Agents knew everything, every bit of business, gossip, and intrigue that went down, usually before all the players. And Jessica was the best.

Celeste flipped open her cell phone.

"Jessica Caulfield's office," answered Kim, Jessica's number one assistant.

"It's me," Celeste said, trying to contain the bitchiness in her voice.

"One moment, Celeste. I'll get her."

They'd better recognize her voice. She'd paid enough in commission to CTA over the last seven years to buy a Third World country. Ten percent of her $20 million quote combined with ten percent of first-dollar gross was big bucks.

"Cici—"

"What the fuck is going on, Jessica?" Celeste screamed, the bitchiness roaring over the phone line. Fuck it. She knew she sounded shrill and high maintenance, but she didn't care. This was her life, her career!

"Cici, the deal closed late last night, one A.M. I didn't find out until two."

"You could have called."

"Someone leaked it to the trades; it wasn't supposed to run today. I'm sorry, Cici. I swear we just didn't get in front of it fast enough."

"It looks like I was bumped for someone younger and by my own fucking husband!"

"Cici, there are at least a dozen producers who want you in their films. I have three full-quote offers right now—pick one. We'll run it tomorrow; it'll look like it was your decision, not Damien's. That *you* stepped off of *Borderland Blue* for a better film."

"I don't like them. I've read them," Celeste whined, her anger deflating. She wanted sympathy from her agent. And coddling. And a fucking good script.

"What do you like? What do you want to do?"

I like Borderland Blue, Celeste thought, *and I want my husband not to be such a backstabbing bastard.*

"What about Lydia's film?" Celeste asked. Lydia Albright was a close friend of both hers and Jessica's and a mega-producer. One way to get back at a bastard was to do the film of his biggest competitor.

"She can't make your deal," Jessica said.

"What about a trick deal?" Celeste asked. "SAG minimum and more gross points?"

Celeste thought she heard Jessica swallow hard. It was a big gamble. Celeste, who hadn't worked in two years, forgoing her $20 million fee on the possibility of Lydia's film, *Seven Minutes Past Midnight,* becoming a success. The risk was obvious; did the public still love Celeste enough that she could open a blockbuster action film and earn her fee on the back end?

"If that's what you want, I'll call right now," Jessica said.

Good girl! Celeste thought. *Jessica has balls of steel.* "I'll call Lydia. You call the attorneys and start drafting the deal."

"Anything else?" Jessica asked.

"I want a producer's credit, too," Celeste said, the wind whipping though her hair.

"Not a problem. Call me after you talk to Lydia."

"Got it," Celeste said, and clicked her phone closed.

Celeste smiled. There was one more call to make before she dialed Lydia. Another call to make Damien pay. Celeste knew that aside from taking the role in *Seven Minutes Past Midnight,* there was one other thing that would force Damien to experience the same anger and pain that now made Celeste burn.

For the second time, Celeste clicked open her cell phone. This number, like Jessica's, was on voice recognition.

"'Allo; Frederick."

"Lover," Celeste purred.

"Oh, my Cici! I wondered if I might hear from you today," Frederick said, with a hint of a question.

"It is a very big day." The anticipation warmed Celeste's skin.

"'Ow big?"

"Black Card big," Celeste answered, referring to the limitless credit card that Damien kept locked in his safe. A card, Damien mistakenly believed, of which Celeste knew nothing.

"Oooh!" Frederick moaned into the phone. It sounded as if he'd come all over himself. "We just got some fabulous Christian Louboutins this morning."

"Perfect. I'll take twenty pairs."

"He must be in very big trouble, your Damien," Frederick cackled. "Back from New Zealand?"

"Last night."

"You know, my boyfriend's ex-lover is doing makeup on that set. For the actress, Brianna Ellison. You know her."

Celeste felt the rage run through her body. Of course Frederick knew. Everyone knew. The film industry was a small town in a huge city. Everyone's boyfriend's ex-lover did makeup, set design, acted, wrote scripts, produced, gaffered, gripped, agented, or directed. It was six degrees of separation minus five degrees.

"She's lovely," Celeste hissed. "I hear she likes girls."

"Interesting," Frederick cooed. "I hear she likes cock."

If Frederick were a woman, she'd rip his eyes out for that. But being a member of the catty-effeminate set, Frederick could say whatever he wanted, and both he and Celeste knew it. It was fair. Frederick would pay Celeste back with a juicy tidbit of Brie gossip once Celeste finished dropping fifteen grand in his store. And if Frederick really wanted to help, he'd start spreading some wonderfully salacious lie about little Miss Brie Ellison—perhaps something in the gonorrhea or methamphetamine family?

Celeste clutched her phone tighter.

"I should be there in twenty minutes."

"Darling, for you I'd wait forty. Ciao."

Celeste tossed her phone into the passenger seat and then balanced the steering wheel with her knee. The vial had to be in her Chanel bag somewhere. She just needed a teensy weensy sniff to keep her alive. There wasn't a Starbucks on the way, and with so much shopping to do and so little sleep (silly her, she'd cried into her Egyptian cotton towels for three hours), she just needed a jolt. She dug into the powder with her pinky nail. *Sniff. Sniff.* Celeste wiped under her nose and glanced in the rearview mirror. Still perfect.

2

Lydia Albright and Her Alexandra Neel Pumps

LYDIA ALBRIGHT'S MOVIE WAS FALLING APART. HER STAR, BRADFORD Madison, was incarcerated; her director, Zymar, was in Bali stoned on Thai sticks; and the studio, Worldwide Pictures, was pulling the plug, stopping the money—shutting her down. Lydia was *the* biggest producer in Hollywood, with more than a billion dollars in box-office ticket sales and an overall deal at Worldwide. But the box office hadn't been kind to Lydia's last film, *Until the End.* The movie had cost the studio more than $175 million to make, and the ticket sales grossed only $125 million worldwide. The studio would make another $100 million in DVD sales, but still, these were not the numbers that Worldwide considered a success. And in a town where "How much money have you made for me lately?" was the mantra, Lydia knew that her next film, this film, *Seven Minutes Past Midnight,* had to be a hit.

She slid off her Alexandra Neel pumps and paced barefoot in front of the wall of windows in her office bungalow on the Worldwide lot. She glanced in the mirror on the north wall of her office (placed there to help her chi). Her fair skin looked exceptional for thirty-eight (ahem, forty-two). So far no cuts or stitches, just some chemical peels and a weekly micro-derm. Lydia's thick mahogany hair was pinned back in a chignon, a style that accentuated her high cheekbones. Jane Russell, circa 1953 *Gentlemen Prefer*

Blondes—that was whom the old old-timers (mostly put out to pasture but still breakfasting at Nate 'n Als) told her she looked like. A frown creased her forehead, and under her blue eyes were traces of dark circles that she'd tried desperately to conceal this morning with Laura Mercier's thickest formula. She hadn't slept well last night. *How was this happening?* The last forty-eight hours might have ruined *Seven Minutes Past Midnight*'s chances to ever make it onto the big screen.

With Weston Birnbaum dying suddenly and Arnold Murphy taking over as president of production, Lydia knew it could not only be the end of her film, but also the end of her career at Worldwide. She slumped into her chair. The warm earth-toned art and deep-red walls that Lydia's interior designer had promised would keep Lydia calm were not working.

Fucking Murphy. How could they name Arnold Murphy president of production? Arnold was Lydia's staunchest enemy, and an insufferable pig. "The little leprechaun" was the term Lydia had originally coined for Arnold, and it fit: He was short, fat, and balding, with wisps of red hair. It would be tit for tat now, wound for wound. This time, Lydia knew, Arnold was in the ideal position to deal her the deathblow.

Six years. For six years Lydia had worked on getting *Seven Minutes Past Midnight* into production. Finally she had the right director (albeit he was currently incommunicado in a Balinese brothel), the right actor (he'd make bail), and the right studio head. Surprisingly, finding the right studio head had been the trickiest piece of the puzzle. Nobody wanted to make this film— well, nobody but Lydia and Weston Birnbaum. Weston was the executive who'd finally said yes and gotten the accounting department at Worldwide to start cutting checks. God bless Weston.

Lydia glanced at the *Daily Variety* lying on her desk. Well, that Weston Birnbaum, whose cock Lydia had sucked (and it was a big fucking cock) at the Four Seasons two months ago—not an unpleasant experience, although Lydia rarely sucked cock anymore, at least not to get her movies made (she'd discontinued fellatio for film when she stopped being an actresss)—now that wonderful man was dead. A massive heart attack. Lydia's best friend, Jessica Caulfield, had called Lydia at four A.M. yesterday morning.

"Two of them," Jessica said. "Asian twins. I think you've seen them. Did you see *Dancing Dog, Hidden Windmill?*"

"Shit." Lydia sighed. "Who will get it?"

"At the same time. One sucking his cock, the other sitting on his face."

"There's no way they'd bring in Arnold, is there?" Lydia asked, horrified at the prospect of her nemesis heading up the studio that funded the majority of her films.

"Fuck no," Jessica said. "He lost more money than any of them. Can you imagine? She was sitting on Weston's face, and he had a massive coronary. Jesus and the police," Jessica continued.

"I'm fucked if it's Arnold," Lydia said, alarm bells ringing in her ears. Just when all the pieces for her film were finally in place, why did Weston have to die?

"It won't be Arnold."

"I'm so fucked." Lydia sighed again.

"Not as fucked as Weston."

And there it was in today's *Daily Variety*. Proof that short men with Napolean complexes could run movie studios. Lydia skimmed the headline again: WORLDWIDE MAKES MURPHY MOVIE MOGUL. *And now,* Lydia thought, *my movie is soon to be in the shitter.* She spun her chair around, looking out the windows at the tower of power, Worldwide's corporate headquarters, a thirty-six-story structure of glass and steel dominating the Worldwide Pictures lot. Arnold might already be in the top corner office, looking down at Lydia, knowing the fate of her film. He was savoring it, the prick, toying with her like a cat would a dead mouse.

"Arnold Murphy on one," called out Toddy, Lydia's faithful first assistant. There were three assistants total: Number one, Toddy, answered phones and took care of scheduling; number two took care of everything Toddy didn't have time for; and number three, Lydia's personal assistant, took care of every detail of Lydia's life, including scheduling her yearly mammogram, her monthly spa retreat, her weekly micro-derm, her biweekly therapy, and her almost daily mani-pedi.

Lydia put on her headset and smiled. You could always hear a frown over the phone. "Murph, congratulations! So sad about Weston, but so thrilled to be working with you."

"Cut the bullshit, Liideeeaaa," Arnold said through the static of his cell phone.

Lydia cringed upon hearing Arnold's voice. She loathed his insistence on always dragging out the pronunciation of her name, the way one might speak to a small child.

"Such a charmer. Murph my love, did someone forget to fill your flask before your morning commute?" He wasn't even in the fucking office yet and he was calling to shut down her movie.

"We are not making this movie," Murphy said.

"Yes you are." Lydia felt her heart start to beat fast.

"No."

"Listen, you little redheaded prick, you've already spent twenty million in preproduction alone. You've made pay-or-play offers to the star, the director, and to me, the producer. If you do not make this movie, you are going to be seventy million dollars in the hole before you even walk onto the lot to start your first day of work at this studio. Not the best first impression for the board of directors, now, is it?"

Murphy let out a small snicker. "Liideeeaaa, your director's high, your star is in jail, and your luck has run out."

Fuck. Fuck. Fuck. He was shutting down Seven Minutes Past Midnight.

"You and I both know that it pains my heart to make this—"

"Celeste Solange on line two," Toddy called out.

Lydia pressed the mute button on her phone. "Celeste is in New Zealand."

"What, they don't have phones in New Zealand?"

"Murph, hold on a second," Lydia said, leaving the leprechaun and switching to line two.

"Cici?"

"Lyddy."

"Cici, where are you? You sound so close. I thought you were in New Zealand," Lydia said.

"I am close—well, relatively speaking. I can see the ocean and I'm on this side of it."

"What happened?"

"Have you seen *People* yet?" Celeste asked.

"No, I'm still working on today's *Daily Variety*."

"Damien is fucking the eighteen-year-old," Celeste said. "Seems he was much too cozy on set to want me around."

"Interesting. Damien is fucking a child and I'm getting fucked by a leprechaun."

"What?"

"Have you seen the trades today? *Variety, Hollywood Reporter?*"

"Just the part about me getting bumped from my soon-to-be ex-husband's film," Celeste snapped.

"Guess who got the Worldwide gig?"

"Fuck if I know. I'm just an actress, hired help. Marsala, or Walter? Aaah. Wait, a leprechaun . . . no fucking way, Lydia. It isn't Murphy, is it?"

"Bingo. He's holding on line one. Shutting down *Seven Minutes Past Midnight*. First call of what I am sure will be his illustrious tenure as studio head. Little fucker is still in his car, hasn't even made it into his office yet, and he's shutting down my film."

"But I was calling to tell you I'll do it," Celeste said.

"What? Cici, I love you and you've always been my first choice, but I don't have it in the budget. Jessica and I discussed it ages ago, but I can't make your twenty-million-dollar quote—I can't even make half your quote. Besides, this is Murphy. He's shutting me down, and it's got nothing to do with the script or the film."

"We could travel, take it to another studio? What about Summit or Galaxy?"

"Cici, you're a gem. But Murph isn't going to let any studio buy this project out. It's not about the money or the movie. This one is personal. It's about Murph and me."

"No worries. I've got Robinoff."

"What?" Lydia set down the *Daily Variety* she'd been flipping through. God, she loved Celeste. Ted Robinoff was the ever-elusive CEO of Worldwide Pictures and Arnold Murphy's boss, a virtual recluse. Some thought Robinoff had a direct line to God and others thought that the only direct line to Robinoff was through God's office. "How?"

"Lyd, I'm telling you I can deliver this. Just get your director sober and your star bailed out and don't tell Murph who did it. We'll get it done through Ted before Murphy gets into the studio. Just get off the phone with him. Have your assistant do it. Have Toddy tell him you had to run out, some sort of emergency."

Lydia looked through her office door at her three assistants, all listening in on her line (there were always at least eight ears on a call, most times more: the caller, the callee, and both assistants. First rule of Hollywood: There are no secrets). "You heard the lady. Toddy, get off this line and get on line one. Tell the leprechaun to take a leap."

"Cici, I'm sure glad you're on my side. You must have some heavy-duty shit on Ted."

"Nothing like that, just pulling an old favor. I need a change and there's no one I'd rather do a movie with than you. Besides, I hear your star boy is a pretty good actor, and when he's not in the slammer or on set, he likes to be in bed. It's a great script, Lyddy. I'll do a really good job for you."

"Like I said, you were always my first choice; I just knew that Jessica and I could never come to terms on a deal. Just not in my budget."

"This film isn't about the money. You're getting Celeste Solange at bargain-basement prices. All I want is a producer's credit and a piece of the back end."

"Just tell Jessica this was all your doing, otherwise she'll never let me book any talent out of CTA again."

"I already told Jess."

"And?" Lydia asked.

"She didn't flinch. It'll be the easiest deal you'll ever make. Give her a call. My attorney is drafting a deal memo right now. Jessica will fax it to you and to Worldwide Business Affairs. It's pretty sweet."

"I owe you big."

"We're friends. Let's go make a film."

3

Jessica Caulfield and Her Balenciaga Sandals

JESSICA CAULFIELD LOUNGED ON THE PATIO AT THE IVY IN BEVERLY HILLS WITH one of her many movie star clients, her brown lizard sandals pinching her toes. You hadn't "arrived" in the film biz until you could get patio seating at the Ivy at one P.M. Reserved for the deal-makers, power brokers, and stars, the Ivy sat on a nondescript Beverly Hills street. The patio, whitewashed brick with a picket fence and white roses, provided no view for the patrons, feasting on crab cakes and chopped salads. But the view from the street—that was something else entirely. Aston Martins, Bentleys, and Jaguars continuously pulled up to the valet, and exiting from these pristinely polished automobiles were the rich, the famous, and the beautiful.

Behemoth SUVs with dark tinted windows, home to the ever-annoying yet ever-needed paparazzi, sought out the parking meters across the street. The valets, clean-cut, crisp-looking young men with the short haircuts and high cheekbones of prep school graduates, lined the sidewalk in front of the patio seating, trying to obscure shots taken with the giant telephoto lenses. Jessica knew it was all part of the dance. If privacy was truly the desire, why not raise the fence? Or enclose the outside area with a hedge? No, this spot was the place to be seen. A statement, made by anyone who entered, that you did in fact belong within the confines of Hollywood and the Ivy. You were a member of the club.

Jessica leaned her head forward and sipped her iced tea, her auburn hair falling in waves around her Dior sunglasses. Jessica had been dining at the Ivy for close to seven years. She was one of the most powerful talent agents in town and easily commanded lunch on the patio. And this lunch was to finish a deal with one of CTA's hot young stars, Holden Humphrey.

Jessica had discovered Holden five years before. She'd just begun her career as a talent agent at CTA when a publicist, Kiki Dee, had begged Jessica to attend an actors' showcase. Jessica had resisted, knowing that other agents fended off these requests, and if she went, she'd be the only agent in attendance. But she owed Kiki a favor (everyone at some point in their Hollywood career owed Kiki a favor). So she went.

When Jessica arrived, the desperation in the air had been palpable. Mostly old actors (anyone over thirty-five) doing scenes from old films, all hoping (as was the case at every actors' showcase) to be "discovered." Sure, some of the actors were brilliant and many had talent, but, Jessica thought miserably, these people were in denial about the reality of the film industry. Hollywood was the Calcutta of entertainment, hundreds of thousands of actors starving for work. The odds against them were staggering; they'd have a better chance of winning the lottery than becoming a superstar. But there had been one not particularly gifted young actor who possessed a spark. The "It" factor. "It" was an indefinable quality, a quality for which casting directors, agents, and managers searched. Not necessarily talent or bravado, "It" was a gift from God, Jessica believed, that very few people received. Or perhaps everyone had "It," but only a couple of people in the world truly knew how to tap into their "It" reserve. Either way, Jessica knew Holden had "It," even if he couldn't act.

And now, five years later, Jessica sat across from Holden Humphrey at the Ivy, the Los Angeles sun burning her scalp. They were discussing any last-minute desires Holden might have before she closed the deal for his next film, *Money for Love,* with

Galaxy Pictures Business Affairs. Sure, these details could be hammered out over the phone, but a little face time with Holden (a $15-million-per-film star) was part of Jessica's job.

"Jess, forget the Dom. I want Cristal. Cristal is off the hook," Holden said between bites of his specially made double cheese-burger (just for Holden the Ivy added an oregano-garlic spice mix and extra cheese). "No one drinks Dom. I hear that Cristal is a deal-breaker for Tarantino."

Jessica bit her tongue, gritted her teeth, and tried to smile. A Harvard-educated lawyer, Jessica had spent the last five years (her most fertile years) negotiating deals for actors, and she was going to spend the next thirty-six hours (while she was ovulating) arguing with the head of Galaxy Pictures Business Affairs for Holden Humphrey's million-dollar perk list (in addition to his multimillion-dollar fee and profit participation).

"And I want the trailer that Costner gets. You know the one, right, Jess? There are only two in the world."

Jessica did, in fact, know the trailer to which Holden referred. It was the same trailer that Jessica had spent three days arguing with Summit Pictures' head of Business Affairs for Holden to get on his last feature, *Purple Racer.* At least on this picture there was a precedent. The expansion of a star's perk list was all about "the precedent." If one studio gave a star the biggest trailer or cases of Cristal versus Dom, then every other studio had better pony up if they expected a star to do their film. Stars wanted the best, the most elusive, the most expensive. Jessica glanced over at Holden, chewing a bite of his twenty-five-dollar burger. *Twenty-five dollars for a cheeseburger?* Jessica thought. She remembered when she was fresh out of law school with student loans to pay and intern-ing for free at the studio; twenty-five dollars had purchased her groceries for a month.

But even with ketchup dripping down his chin, Holden was gorgeous. Honey-blond hair, sultry blue eyes, cheekbones that could cut steel (Johnny Depp and Brad Pitt rolled into one), a jawline that was solid—and that flawlessness was all above the neck. Holden's body . . . it was just as extraordinary. Yes, he was a specimen of physical perfection. And even for Jessica, who'd known him before he was a star, it was difficult to concentrate when Holden flashed his stellar smile. But the one thing Holden could not do, at least not yet, was act. He could barely deliver a line (he wasn't the sharpest knife in the drawer, either).

Jessica prayed that Holden's business manager was smart about Holden's money, because the gravy train that was Holden's career wouldn't last forever. Holden's $15 million acting quote wasn't going up anytime soon, and if the ticket sales from *Purple Racer* were any indication, then Holden's core audience (preteen girls and middle-aged gay men) was growing tired of paying twelve dollars a ticket to watch him wiggle his ass and grin. Holden's career, Jessica feared, was cresting the hill on the entertainment roller coaster and poised for the stomach-piercing descent.

"Holden, did you talk to Gary Moises?" she asked, hopeful that Holden had taken her advice and started studying his craft with the best and most exclusive acting coach in Los Angeles.

"I'm not down with an acting coach," Holden said, taking another bite of burger.

"He's the best in L.A.," Jessica countered.

"Jess, I want to feel natural. My fans want me; they don't need that Mizel/Method crap. They want me to do my thing. Viève agrees," Holden said, putting his arm around the babe du jour to his left.

Jessica glanced at the tiny elfin creature now ensconced in Holden's embrace. She'd almost forgotten that Viève was there; the girl had barely moved. For the past hour Jessica had been calling her Bev, and nobody had noticed or cared—not even Viève. A connoisseur of exotic tail, Holden always seemed to have a particularly unusual woman with him. This tiny creature looked as though she weighed perhaps two pounds. She didn't speak or eat and ordered nothing, preferring to sip Pellegrino with lemon.

"Viève acts, Jess. You should take a look at her reel," Holden said, patting the tiny creature on the head as if she were a pet.

Doesn't everyone, Jessica thought. She curled the sides of her mouth upward. For the ten percent of $15 million and gross profit participation he threw her way, Holden deserved at least the semblance of a smile. *Thank God for sunny days in L.A. and patio seating at the Ivy,* Jessica thought. Both required that she wear sunglasses. Otherwise at this very moment Holden would see *the look.* And if he saw *the look,* then he'd know the contempt that Jessica felt for having to smile at the tramp Vième and argue for three days for Cristal as opposed to Dom Perignon so that Holden could get paid beaucoup bucks to do the one thing millions of people would give their left leg to do: stand in front of a camera and smile.

"Is that Josh Dragatsis over there?" Holden asked, sipping his Pellegrino.

Jessica glanced to her left. Josh Dragatsis, a young talent agent from ACA, stared at Holden like a Doberman Pinscher eyeing a raw piece of meat.

"He's been leaving me ten messages a day about some indie film, *View of Sunshine.* Like I want to do an independent film? What a dumbass," Holden said, frowning. "I've got to get a new cell number."

"Yes, you do," Jessica said, reaching across the table. "Give me your cell. I'll have Kim cancel the service and messenger a new phone to the house this afternoon." She'd dodged that bullet. *Josh, that little prick, calling a CTA-represented star ten times a day!* Jessica knew that Josh had only five clients of any value on his roster, and to teach him a lesson, Jess would make sure that by this time tomorrow, her cadre of CTA agents had stolen three of Josh's five. There was no way she'd let a junior agent get away with hitting on Holden.

"You know, Vième is in my Transcendental Meditation class," Holden said, clasping Vième even tighter. "Every Tuesday and Thursday. It grounds me."

"I guess fifteen million dollars three times a year isn't grounding enough?" Jess asked, a wry smile playing around her lips.

"Jess, you crack me up. I want Vième to be on set as my TM coach. Will you add it to the perk list? Try to get her a grand a week," Holden said.

"And your dad? Is he going to be your driver again on this film?" Jessica asked, knowing that this was the beginning of a long list of unemployable family and friends Holden wanted to see paid.

"You know it. I think he got fifteen hundred a week last time," Holden said.

"And Tommy?"

"Can't leave out the little bro. He's my rock, my trainer. Just like last time, two thousand a week."

"What about Cubby?" Holden had somewhere in his rise to fame acquired Cubby, a nondescript hanger-on with no ambition for his own life but to carry Holden's bags and fuck Holden's left-over girls.

"Personal assistant again."

"That usually goes for five hundred a week, but I'll try for seven-fifty."

"Jess, you rock!" Holden said.

Jessica arched her eyebrow, a sardonic grin crawling across her face. Magna cum laude and editor of *Harvard Law Review* and she "rocked," here at this very moment. *Yippy skippy, her life was complete.* Holden was almost half her age, and definitely had half her brainpower, but he had ten times her bank account, and Jess's bank account wasn't half bad. Her annual salary as president of CTA was well into seven figures. It paid for a house in the Hollywood Hills, a trainer, and everything that she thought she wanted.

Well, almost everything. Lately, Jessica felt an emptiness clutching at her insides each night as she pulled up to her quiet home. Her fiancé, Phil, was a software designer, a career that demanded he live in San Francisco during the week. It allowed her Monday through Friday to relentlessly pursue all her Hollywood ambitions, ambitions that until recently had fueled her to work harder and longer hours than any other agent in town.

She had nothing to fall back on. Sure, a law degree (if she wanted to sit in an office and read corporate contracts all day). But

Jess's dream was entertainment. Unlike Lydia (second-generation Hollywood, the late Mr. Albright having been a producer), Jessica had climbed her way up Mount Hollywood through sheer wit and dogged determination. She had no familial connections to the movie industry on which to rely, and without family connections, the only way into entertainment was from the bottom up. Immediately after law school, Jessica had pushed a mail cart and interned at Worldwide, assisted and finally been promoted to executive at I M FOX Productions, and finally, *finally* summited as president of CTA. It was only in the last three months she'd allowed herself a view of the landscape that was now her Hollywood life, and although it was shiny, she found it lacking, like a six-carat cubic zirconia. She wondered if it wasn't her biological clock sounding some sort of evolutionary alarm.

While her girlfriends from high school and college were off marrying, buying houses, and filling those houses with children, Jessica was working seven A.M. to midnight pursuing her Hollywood dream. Her friends in Oregon stared at her slack-jawed when they met (maybe once a year), drinking in her stories of celebrity and fame. Incredulous at her tales, perhaps on the inside bemoaning their lot in life: paunch-bellied husbands approaching middle age, carpooling in their Dodge minivans, PTA, sticky fingers, croup, spilled syrup, laundry, unmade beds. Although they were still friends (you couldn't turn your back on the girls who held your hair while you puked your guts out after getting drunk on tequila for the first time), their lives were irrevocably different from Jessica's. And in part it was that very difference from them and the similarity to Cici and Lydia that had begun and cemented Jessica's entertainment friendships. Who else would understand her frustration today while sitting at the Ivy across from one of the world's biggest stars, but another member of the Hollywood club?

Jessica tossed her auburn curls and inhaled. *Enough.*

"Okay, so the perk list is pretty much the same, with the addition of the Cristal and, of course, Viève. Great. I'll speak with

Business Affairs after lunch. I'm sure they are going to hate the private-jet miles."

"What is it with these studios and their private jets?" Holden asked. "Why do they have them if they don't want their stars flying around in them?"

"Holden, it's not that they don't want you to use them. It's how you use them. Flying from Belize to Chicago at two A.M. because you want a hot dog? It doesn't sit well with Accounting." Jessica smiled; she'd learned that she could say anything to anyone as long as she punctuated the statement with a smile.

That was her job: Take ten percent and smile. For now, Holden Humphrey was a star, one of Jessica's many. There were ten stars in Hollywood who could get any movie going anywhere, and Jessica currently represented seven of them. Plus a slew of writers and directors. It was an amazing thing. She, like all the giants before her (Wasserman, Ovitz, Berg), was an über-agent.

It was as if she'd been struck by lightning. Signing the first star had been luck. The second's career was in the toilet when Jessica found him an amazing small character piece, an independent film for which he won a "little gold man." The award turned his career around, and once he was on top again, the big money offers started pouring into Jessica's office. The third was a referral from the first, and once Jessica had three, it was a party. Everyone loved a party, especially stars. The getting was easy. Signing the star, developing their career, finding them the right role, had always been easy for Jess. It was the keeping that was tough. Jessica glared at Josh Dragatsis, who was still staring at Holden and salivating over his chopped salad. *Poaching. Always someone trying to snatch her success away from her.* Actors, Jessica knew from experience, were mercurial creatures. Anyone craving the spotlight enough to want to see themselves twenty feet tall in front of the entire planet had to have some sort of complex. Jess loved them for their boldness, their bravado, their bravery, their childlike love, and their belief that the entire world was their toy box and everyone was meant to be their playmate.

Jessica had only two clients she truly trusted, two who were her friends. Second rule in Hollywood: There are no "real" friends, only business associates. But Cici and Lydia defied that rule, and were two of Jessica's closest friends. It was a bond forged through time, shared loss (you hadn't worked in Hollywood and not lost something), and trust. Their troika had yet to be tested by the making of a film together, but it appeared this was about to change.

If Cici hadn't called Jessica first, she never would have believed the news. Celeste Solange working for free. Well, practically free: SAG scale plus ten percent. In any other circumstance Jess would have called Lydia and ripped her apart because, close friends or not, this was a business. Granted, Cici got a huge piece of gross profit participation, but *Seven Minutes Past Midnight* wasn't a small independent film strapped together with tiny bits of financing that stars would work on for practically no money (often to the abject horror of their agents, who lived on their ten percent of the stars' fees) because the roles were so juicy and could garner rave reviews and an opportunity to appear in front of a billion eyeballs on an awards show. No, *Seven Minutes Past Midnight* was a studio-backed blockbuster of a film. But this film, Lydia's film, wasn't about money for Cici. It was about payback and pride.

Jessica could hear the indignity in Cici's voice. *Damien Bruckner was a dumb fuck,* Jessica thought. First Amanda, then Cici, and now this Brianna Ellison? *Like she was going to be a star?* Damien was really thinking with his dick when he cast Brie in the lead role instead of Cici. And so public! It was splitsville for Damien and Cici. *Good riddance,* Jessica thought. Besides, Cici worked more when she was between men. Once *Seven Minutes Past Midnight* wrapped, Cici's next film would pay her $20 million fee. Plus, with her profit participation, Cici stood to make more money on *Seven Minutes Past Midnight* than she'd ever made on anything if it turned out to be a hit (and it damn well could be with the cast and director Lydia had managed to put together).

"Jess," Holden said, breaking Jessica's reverie, "don't forget my mom. She wants to be the production photographer again."

Jess smiled at Holden. "Of course. That was fifteen hundred a week, right?"

"Yeah. And don't worry, this time she won't forget to put film in the camera."

4

Mary Anne Meyers and Her Fuzzy Bunny Slippers

MARY ANNE MEYERS CLICKED THE SAVE ICON ON HER COMPUTER SCREEN. Finished. For now. She glanced out the window in her home office and watched the sun creep up over the Hollywood Hills. It'd been a long night. But the script was good, solid. The story was tight. Mary Anne had incorporated every one of Lydia Albright's story notes for *Seven Minutes Past Midnight,* and they were good notes. Lydia was smart; she definitely understood story structure and what made a good script.

Mary Anne leaned back in her chair and sipped her Earl Grey tea. What a view. What a life. What a miracle. An eight-week miracle. Had it only been eight weeks? She was growing so accustomed to this new life (despite the nagging fear that it was all a dream and she'd awaken soon). The life with the Mercedes, the home in the Hollywood Hills, the housekeeper, the full bank account. It felt as though years had passed since Mary Anne was: broke, with $11.87 in her checking account and an overdraft looming because of the $15.79 she'd coughed up at Ralphs to buy groceries; unemployed, having lost her second waitressing job in three weeks; and evicted, forced to sleep on her friend Sylvia's couch. Mary Anne had called her sister, Michelle (the responsible one, according to their mother, Mitsy), and begged her to wire money so she could come home. The dream was dead.

After nine years of bartending, selling shoes, answering phones, walking dogs, and finally, her miserable attempt at waiting tables, Mary Anne Meyers had dreamed her last Hollywood dream, written her final word, and accepted her fate of returning to the safe (if frigid) confines of her hometown, St. Paul, Minnesota. She'd hocked her computer four weeks before to cover rent, and now the computer, the money, and the apartment were gone.

As Mary Anne lay on Sylvia's pea green couch staring at the cracks in the ceiling, her mind drifted to thoughts of her first week in L.A. Not much had changed since then (except her age)—nine years before, she'd been homeless and broke, too. Then the phone rang. Not Sylvia's phone but Mary Anne's cell phone; she still had service for one more day.

"Mary Anne Meyers, please," said a crisp voice on the other end of the line.

"This is Mary Anne."

"I have Lydia Albright for you."

Lydia Albright? *The* Lydia Albright? Mega-movie-producer-with-over-one-billion-dollars-in-box-office-grosses Lydia Albright?! Mary Anne sat up, bumping her head on the oversized thrift-store lamp and knocking her water glass onto the floor.

"Please hold one moment," the crisp voice continued. "Lydia will be right on the line."

There was a brief pause. Mary Anne's heart pounded against her chest.

"Mary Anne, this is Lydia. How are you? Nice to meet you over the phone."

"Yes," Mary Anne exclaimed breathlessly. "You, too. Fine. Thank you."

"Listen, I read *The Sky's the Limit* and I loved it."

"You did?" *How had Lydia Albright gotten a copy of her script?*

"I think you have an amazing voice on the page. You're able to capture the essence of what is real in a story. Your writing, well, it's just extraordinary."

Mary Anne was floored. *How was this happening?* "How did you—"

"We get everything," Lydia answered before Mary Anne could complete her question.

"Everything," Mary Anne whispered.

"Mary Anne, I have this script, and if you're not too busy, I was wondering if you'd give it a read. See if you can come up with a take for the story. It's close, but still needs a little work. I had dinner at the Four Seasons with Weston Birnbaum last night, president of production at Worldwide, and I told him that I think you're the writer to fix it. It's called *Seven Minutes Past Midnight*. I think you can make the script work. Weston and I would like to go into production once this draft is complete."

"Too busy . . . ," Mary Anne mumbled, in shock.

"Dammit, you are? Because I really—"

"No! No. Yes, send it. I'm not too busy. I'd love to see it, read it, help. Please, yes."

"Great! Where should I send it? I'll messenger it over now."

"Um . . ." Mary Anne scrambled over the cat and the couch cushions to the desk by the front door and grabbed the Wells Fargo envelope with Sylvia's address. "It's 6615 Franklin, apartment 303."

"Fantastic. You'll have it in an hour. Listen, Mary Anne, if you want it, the rewrite job, it's yours."

"Yes. Oh, thank you, Lydia. Thank you."

"No problem. You're the one with the talent. I'll have Worldwide Business Affairs call your agent to get your writing quote."

"Okay," Mary Anne said. *Her agent? She didn't have an agent!* She paused, thinking. *Could she get an agent? Would Lydia still hire her if she knew that she was unrepresented?*

"Mary Anne?" Lydia interrupted Mary Anne's scrambled thoughts. "Who does your deals? Who represents you?"

"Oh, aah . . . My, aah, I, aah . . ." Mary Anne hung her head; so close, but the dream was still dead. "Lydia, I don't have an agent," Mary Anne said, sounding defeated.

"For fuck's sake! I cannot believe someone with your talent is sitting out there in the world without an agent. I'll take care of it; I know a few. What dumbasses. No wonder the movies are for shit."

"Oh, thank you, Lydia," Mary Anne said, again beaming. "No wonder."

"Okay," Lydia said. "So script in one hour, agent in two, Worldwide Business Affairs after that. And do you think we could sit down tomorrow? Talk about the script? Is your schedule clear tomorrow?"

"It's clear."

"Great. I'm going to jump onto this other call, but Toddy, my assistant, is on the line. She'll schedule a time with you for tomorrow. I'll see you then."

"See you then," Mary Anne said.

It was *the* call. The call that the hopes and dreams of every Hollywood busboy, bartender, and waiter (also known as struggling actor, writer, and director) were built upon. And after Mary Anne had gotten *the* call from Lydia Albright just eight weeks ago, everything—*everything*—in her life had changed. One-point-five million dollars would do that (Mary Anne had sent the bus money and a celebratory bottle of champagne to Michelle in Minnesota after her first writing check cleared).

Kim, the assistant to Jessica Caulfield (Mary Anne's new agent), messengered Mary Anne ten copies of the *Daily Variety* announcements that ran two days after Lydia's call. MEYERS MEETS *MIDNIGHT* read the headline. Mary Anne sent five copies to her family in St. Paul. For the first time, she felt that her parents, Mitsy and Marvin, were proud of what she did. The story of Mary Anne's success ran on the front page of the St. Paul paper, the *Pioneer Press*. Her father actually started telling people his daughter was a writer. Strong praise from a man who'd never read anything Mary Anne had written. Maybe Marvin would even see the movie? Of course he'd see the movie; she'd invite him to the premiere.

Mary Anne was living her dream. She was writing. For the first time in her life, she was writing and someone was paying her for it. Jessica handled the deal. First Worldwide paid five hundred thousand dollars against one million for *The Sky's the Limit* for Lydia, because she wanted to produce that film as soon as *Seven*

Minutes Past Midnight was finished. The numbers were confusing to Mary Anne at first, until Jessica explained that she would get five hundred thousand dollars now and five hundred thousand more if and when *The Sky's the Limit* went into production.

Then Worldwide paid Mary Anne another $350,000 to rewrite *Seven Minutes Past Midnight,* and an additional $175,000 to polish the script. (A polish was meant to be less work than a new draft, but it was really the same amount of work.)

First, Mary Anne spent four weeks rewriting *Seven Minutes Past Midnight* for the director, Zymar—no last name, just Zymar. That was before Zymar disappeared to Belize. Or was it Bali? Then Mary Anne did more character work for Bradford Madison (the star) before his drunk-and-disorderly arrest. Finally, she'd spent the last seventy-two hours making the Raphaella part bigger and sexier, now that Celeste Solange had signed onto the film.

How had this happened? Mary Anne Meyers from St. Paul, Minnesota, was writing a bigger and sexier role for the biggest star in the world, Celeste Solange. From homeless to millionaire with one phone call. Only in Hollywood.

Everyone in this town was a gambler, an addict, only the stakes were much bigger than in Vegas. In Vegas you gambled your money, but here, in this town, you gambled with your dreams. Mary Anne was now one of the winners. She'd hit the jackpot; she was one of the success stories that fueled the never-ending fire. And now Mary Anne was finished with the script.

She glanced at the clock; it was six-thirty A.M. She needed some sleep. Lydia's office would call by ten and they'd want her to come in so that she and Lydia could go over the new draft this afternoon. The start date for shooting the film was only a week away (assuming Zymar returned from overseas and Bradford completed rehab). Lydia wanted Mary Anne on set every day. She needed her there for production writing. That was another seventy-five thousand a week to add to Mary Anne's flourishing bank account.

Mary Anne padded down the hall past the guest room (she had a guest room!). She glanced in the mirror hanging in the hall.

Her green eyes looked tired. Her light brown hair, earlier pulled into a ponytail, now stuck out at odd angles (she had a habit of pulling on her hair while she wrote). Dark under-eye circles were evident even through her freckles. "You look like the girl next door!" Celeste Solange had exclaimed yesterday, the first time they met, flashing her effervescent world-famous smile.

Mary Anne had been starstruck; it was the first time she truly understood the word. How did you speak to someone you'd watched on a twenty-foot screen since you were twelve years old? This woman had won a Golden Globe! What could *she*, Mary Anne Meyers from Minnesota, possibly have to say that could interest Celeste Solange?

"Just be yourself," Lydia had whispered into Mary Anne's ear prior to Celeste walking into the room. "She's a person. Think of her like you would your neighbor or a cousin. Don't treat her differently; they get tired of that."

Some cousin! was all Mary Anne could think. But she tried. Tried not to be speechless, flounder her words, gush, stare, beam . . . all those things Hollywood newbies and tourists were guilty of doing. She tried to call Celeste Cici, as the star had insisted. She also tried to focus on the person Celeste was, not the persona she presented. Mary Anne guessed that there was a piece of Celeste that she held back, that wasn't for public consumption, that couldn't be or else there wouldn't be any of her left. When everyone wanted a piece of you, didn't you *have* to retain something for yourself?

Mary Anne walked into her bedroom. Painted lavender, the room was calming. Her giant king-sized bed, draped in a paisley-flowered duvet, called to her. Mary Anne sat on her bed and slid off her fuzzy bunny slippers, placing them next to the three-foot pile of scripts that Jessica had messengered to the house. Every screenplay sent from a producer clamoring for Mary Anne to rewrite his or her script.

"Lydia must have a lot of faith in you," Jessica had said. "First-time writers never do production work. I know Lydia thinks you're talented."

Mary Anne lay back and tried to soften her mind for sleep; all she needed was a couple hours. But her mind wouldn't stop spinning. Once you worked for Lydia Albright, you could work for any producer or studio in town. Mary Anne couldn't believe the writing offers that were beginning to come in to Jessica.

It was difficult for Mary Anne to wrap her mind around her success. She'd spent almost a decade trying to break into the film business, thinking that nobody wanted her and that she wasn't very talented. And now, with just one phone call, just one person believing, the whole town was banging on her door. *Where had they been the past nine years?*

"Basically, it's an industry full of lemmings," Jessica said. "Point them to the sea and they'll go. Even if there's a big cliff."

Mary Anne shut her eyes. *Enjoy it,* she thought, drifting off to sleep. *At least you're not a rodent.*

5

Chanel Sandals by the Pool

"A DIVORCE?! CELESTE, YOU DO NOT WANT A DIVORCE," DAMIEN SAID.

Celeste lay on a chaise lounge next to their Olympic-size swimming pool, sipping fresh-squeezed guava-mint-orange juice. Damien dried the droplets of water off his silver-haired torso. She'd watched him complete fifty laps (his morning ritual for twenty years) and wondered at each turn how she might successfully drown her philandering husband without ruining her new Chanel pool sandals. Now Damien stood before her, glistening and blocking the morning sun. At fifty, he still had a phenomenal body. Tall, lean, and tan. Damien was vain, priding himself on his physique. He could easily pass for a man in his thirties.

"Like hell I don't," Celeste said.

"You're overreacting. It was a prank by the crew on set. Those panties are not Brie Ellison's."

A prank? That was bullshit and Celeste knew it. But bullshit that a part of her (the part of her that still loved the prick standing before her) wanted to believe.

"We just got married, for God's sake," Damien said.

"I know, I was there—the one in white."

"Yes." Damien paused. "White. That was a stretch, even for you." A lascivious grin lit up his tan face.

God, he had the most magnificent smile. He was an ass, but he had perfect teeth.

"Yes, and marriage, the monogamy bit, seems to be a stretch for you," Celeste shot back bitterly.

"We are not getting divorced." Damien sat on the edge of her lounge chair. "I just spent half a million dollars to marry you. A wedding you begged me for. We're not getting divorced. There is nothing going on."

"Really?" As if throwing down an ace, Celeste tossed the *Enquirer* she'd been reading into Damien's lap. There, on the cover, were Brie Ellison's surgically enhanced lips sucking Damien's earlobe. Damien glanced down at the cover and smiled.

"A picture is worth—"

"A thousand words," Damien finished. Leaning in, he rubbed his strong body against her tensed arm. "Come on, Celeste," he whispered. "You know it's fake. What if I believed everything this rag printed about you? Isn't there a two-headed baby in Roswell that some alien fathered when you were abducted by a UFO?"

Celeste fumed. He was right. The *Enquirer* wasn't enough to go on. But the *Enquirer,* the crotchless panties, and the fact that Brie Ellison was starring in Damien's next film, well, *that* was plenty of proof.

"Cici. I love you." He leaned in and nuzzled her neck. "You still drive me wild. You know how film sets are; they're like high school. And they've gotten worse. You haven't been on one in a while." Damien lifted the strap of her Chanel bikini and kissed her shoulder.

His kisses made her feel warm. God, she wanted him and hated him both at the same time.

"I was supposed to be on one this fall," Celeste snapped. "Or have you forgotten?"

"So that's what all this is about. I told you the other night, the studio won't make your deal. They don't want to pay your quote. Twenty million is too much for this film, and Brie is only getting paid a million." Damien slipped his finger under the clasp of her

swimsuit top. "God, I've missed you." He pulled up th᷈
and started kissing her breast. "Let's go to the pool house.
voice was husky and his eyes had that vacant look of lust that a
men's take on when they're hard.

Her body, at that very moment, wanted to give in. Even as their
marriage soured, she knew their sex life would never wane.
Catching herself, Celeste pulled away from Damien's embrace.
"Can't," she said, pulling her swimsuit top down. "I have to get
to the studio."

"Studio? What studio?" Damien looked surprised.

"Worldwide."

"Who are you meeting for lunch at Worldwide?"

"It's not lunch. It's business."

"Yeah, right," Damien said, and playfully tried to pull her
down on top of him. "Come here."

Celeste again pulled herself away from her husband. "We start
shooting in a week."

"*We* who? What the hell are you talking about?"

"Damien, my love, don't you read the trades? *Daily Variety?
Hollywood Reporter?* Or are they also just rags printing lies?"

He glared at her. *Score one for Celeste.*

"It's a little Lydia Albright film. *Seven Minutes Past Midnight.*
Perhaps you've heard of it?"

"What?! Since when? Lydia's career is over with Arnold running Worldwide."

"Since three days ago. If you weren't on set pulling high-school
pranks with the crew, maybe you'd know what's going on in the
movie business."

Damien leaned back on the chaise lounge. "Worldwide won't
meet your quote. They've already spent twenty million on Bradford Madison plus gross points in profit participation and ten
million for Zymar to direct."

"Deal's done. Funny you mention Bradford. Yes, hmm . . .
Now, there is an interesting actor I haven't worked with yet."

"If you like them wet behind the ears and fresh out of rehab."

r Damien, letting her nipples graze his arm.
no, I just like them fresh."

She'd chipped the enamel surface of his exte-
Age was a sore spot for anyone in Hollywood;
at least anyone over twenty-five. No one willingly told you how many years they'd lived. Best guess was to take whatever they said and add five years; that generally put you within seven years of the real number.

"Celeste, I know *you* do. But I guess the real question is—does Bradford?"

Fucker.

She wouldn't let him win. Or at least *know* that he had. She turned toward the house.

"We're having a script read-through," Celeste called as she clipped across the flagstone to the back entrance. "Not sure what time I'll be back."

"No worries. I fly out at ten," Damien called.

Celeste stopped and turned to face her husband. He was loung-ing on the chaise like a snake soaking up sun.

"New Zealand again," Damien said, and smiled. "Problem on set."

"How long?"

"Couple of days, maybe a week. They only have ten more days to shoot." He sipped his juice and reached for the *Enquirer.* "Great picture of Brie, don't you think? Good publicity for the film."

Celeste's eyes were tearing, but she didn't want him to see her cry. She had to get away from him.

"Have a safe trip," Celeste said, and turned toward the house. The largest, most luxurious house in the Hollywood Hills; twenty thousand square feet of unhappy home.

Celeste sat alone at a table on the patio behind Factors Deli. Not her first choice, but she knew Lydia had an affinity for this spot (her father often brought her here for lunch when Lydia was a little girl and he was still producing), and it was close to Jessica's

Beverly Hills office. Only for these two women would Celeste Solange wait. Her days of waiting for anyone had ended the same time her acting quote rose to eight figures.

The waiting was mildly irritating but the alone she didn't mind. She'd never acquired the usual set of gadflies and hangers-on that some celebrities collected. *People as trinkets* was how Celeste thought of them. She had her "team": agent, stylists (makeup, clothing, and hair), publicist, attorney, business manager, accountant, and trainer—but everyone had a job, a place in her life, each contributing to their part in the multinational corporation that was Celeste Solange. A corporation that in a good year could gross upward of $100 million (although she hadn't had a "good year" in almost two; thank you, Damien).

Not a bad climb from poor, white Tennessee trailer trash to multimillionaire (she didn't even have a GED—few people knew that). Thanks to her brilliant business manager, Jerry Z, her assets were many—real estate, stocks, jewels, a restaurant in Tribeca, two clubs in L.A. Who knew (other than Jerry) what on any given day Celeste actually owned? Her overhead was low (well, relatively; compared to most celebrities, she spent like a pauper). She'd never rented a private island or purchased a jet. Damien had his own money and he paid for their living expenses—the house, the cars, the staff.

The one luxury she did indulge in was shoes, very expensive shoes. This past month she'd gorged herself with twenty pairs of Louboutins, five varieties of Choo stilettos, and a limited-edition pair of Prada mules encrusted with diamonds that easily cost thirty thousand. Celeste's eyes sparkled. She would pay nothing; but Damien? She couldn't wait until he opened *that* Black Card bill.

Celeste's personality (she could barely admit to herself) was just as multifaceted as her holdings. You didn't get to the top in Hollywood without stepping on some fingers and toes . . . perhaps throwing a few elbows to the ribs. But the softer side of Celeste, the gentler interior, was there, too. The little girl who grew up without a mother (no one ever mentioned her father) still existed; Celeste had just hidden her away for safekeeping.

Very few souls witnessed that vulnerable girl; she could think of two total: Jessica and Lydia.

Celeste glanced at her unopened menu. There was no need to read it; she was having greens with lemon and a side of tuna for protein. The studios paid her *not* to eat. She'd never subscribed to the idea that the waiflike, heroin-addicted look was sexy. In fact, some of her counterparts might even call her full-figured (if you thought five-foot-seven, one hundred eighteen pounds with a thirty-six-inch bust was fat). No, Celeste had curves; great, full, rounded, luscious curves. No fat, not an ounce, but definite curves. Still, she stuck to the tuna before films to keep the curves in proportion.

Celeste sipped her tea (super sweet—some things from the South you never gave up) and looked around the patio. Two tables to her left sat one of her (many) former lovers, an actor, with Brad Grey, the former manager and owner of Brillstein-Grey and now the head of Paramount. That actor had a penchant for asses, Celeste remembered, and not just cupping them. She'd wondered if it didn't suggest a latent desire, as he'd never seemed particularly interested in her breasts, either. But who in Los Angeles didn't swing the other way, at least on occasion? Her dead grandmama in Tennessee must have rolled over in her grave at least a thousand times since Celeste had moved to Los Angeles. The things she'd seen? And done?

Celeste heard the slapping sound of the screen door between the patio and the restaurant slamming closed, and she looked up to see Jessica scanning the patio and tucking her BlackBerry into her Chanel purse. Celeste was always impressed by just how powerful and put together Jessica appeared (even if her personal life was messier than Celeste's). Wavy auburn hair with loose curls framed Jessica's face, and she wore an Armani suit, Dior high heels, and Dior sunglasses that covered her emerald green eyes. *A modern-day Katharine Hepburn,* Celeste thought, *but with a better nose.*

Celeste knew that Jessica was one of her true friends (a rarity in life; all but extinct in L.A.). Jessica had seen the best (infectious laugh, wicked sense of humor, and talent) and the worst (bitchiness, rage bordering on mania, and insecurity) that Celeste had to offer and still Jessica loved her. The first time they'd met, years before, Celeste remembered being unimpressed. She wasn't sure she liked the look of this hungry young agent. It was Ezekiel Cohen, Celeste's first agent and former owner of CTA, who introduced them, just after Jessica landed at CTA. Ezekiel was a brave man, lunching with two alpha females. Ezekiel, Celeste learned, wanted to add Jessica to Celeste's "team" of agents at CTA, a proposition that had it been made by anyone but Ezekiel, Celeste would have flatly refused. The lunch had been less than smooth; Jessica talked too much and seemed too brash. But Celeste trusted Ezekiel's business judgment. He'd found Celeste, worked with her, and at that lunch seven years later, Celeste's career was just starting to take off when he requested that Celeste at least return one of Jessica's fifteen calls.

Thank God for Ezekiel Cohen, Celeste thought as she leaned forward and air-kissed Jessica on both cheeks.

"So how'd it go?" Jessica asked, taking off her sunglasses.

Celeste cocked her right eyebrow (a signature Celeste Solange look that could stop men dead). "Aside from no director or costar, I'd say pretty good."

"No," Jessica said, horrified.

"As I live and breathe, I swear this girl is not telling a lie."

"Lydia must be pissed."

"Pissed is an understatement." As if on cue, Lydia arrived, pulled out the chair next to Jessica, and sat. "Do you know where my director is? Have you heard?" Lydia's voice crested near a decibel that caused other diners to glance toward their table.

"Still in Bali," Jessica said.

"I need him back here now," Lydia said.

"Zymar always goes to Bali between films," Jessica said, reaching for the bottle of Pellegrino and pouring some into her glass.

"Between Arnold, Zymar, and Bradford Madison, there won't be a film. What the fuck is wrong with these guys? Isn't Zymar repped at CTA? Doesn't one of your hotshot lit guys have him?"

"I'll get you an address," Jessica offered, "but I don't think he takes his cell."

Lydia looked toward the heavens. "How do these people function?"

"They don't, that's why they're here," Celeste said, a smile creeping across her lips. The land of broken toys, wayside waifs, and dysfunctional divas; some talented, most not. They all made the pilgrimage to movieland seeking to fill the void within.

"Order?" Lydia asked, skimming the menu.

"Done," Jessica said. "I had Kim phone it in."

"How do you know—"

"She called Toddy," Jessica said, interrupting and silencing Lydia. "And she"—Jessica nodded toward Celeste—"if I'm not mistaken, is on her preproduction greens-with-lemon-juice-tuna-on-the-side diet?"

Celeste smiled. "Am I that predictable?"

"Only with your diet. With everything else you're still a surprise."

It was good to be known so well. These two were perhaps the only two left who didn't blow smoke up Celeste's rear (even her family in Tennessee was a bunch of ass kissers).

"So the director and the costar were a no-show. How's our baby writer holding up?" Jessica asked, taking a bite of bagel chip. "You know, Lydia, you're putting a whole lot of faith in a first-timer."

"She can hang." Celeste eyed her agent. "She won't crack."

"Really?" Jessica leaned back in her chair. "That's strong praise from one Ms. Solange, who has in fact seen it all."

"I have, and she'll be good. Today she even called me Cici."

"Only took four meetings, but yes, we have broken Mary Anne of the habit of calling you Ms. Solange," Lydia said as the waiter set down her chopped Cobb salad with blue cheese dressing on the side.

"What?" Jessica asked.

"Starstruck," Lydia said. "No more than normal, right, Cici?"

"She's a pro. A little Midwestern, but a pro. Hasn't asked me for an autograph."

"It's early. Just wait till the family in Minnesota wants something signed."

"She's sweet and genuine and as yet unjaded. Do you remember your first gig in this town? How exciting that was?" Celeste asked, squeezing lemon over her undressed salad and looking at her friends. She knew from experience that transplanted optimism withered quickly in the Southern California sunshine.

"I do. It was Mike Fox," Jessica said.

Celeste watched as Jessica's eyes drifted past her in a faraway gaze Celeste was sure was reserved for long-ago travels or lost loves. Mike and Jessica's torrid love affair had left a big mark on Jessica. A mark, Celeste believed, that affected Jessica's current choice of mate. It's not that Phil was a *bad* guy; he was easy for Jessica. He was gone all week, letting Jess concentrate on work, and then on the weekends he provided her with a dinner date. Phil for Jessica, Celeste believed, was not a love match but a convenience.

"Learned a lot there," Jessica said, her tone hardening.

"You?" Celeste asked Lydia.

"It's all a blur. I've been going to movie sets since I was six months old. For me it's just a way of life. Preproduction, production, postproduction; preproduction, production, postproduction, like spring, summer, fall, spring, summer, fall."

"You're forgetting winter," Jessica said.

"Jess, who does winter? We're in L.A."

Celeste smiled. "I remember mine. It was two lines in a De Palma film."

"Two lines. That's pretty good for a first gig," Lydia said.

"Thank you, Ezekiel Cohen," Jessica said.

"Until Ezekiel it'd been cattle-call auditions, absolutely nothing. He got me working in two months—real work. A good agent can work miracles."

"Yeah, but Cici, you had some God-given talent there, too," Jessica said.

"These?" Celeste asked, arching her back and pointing to her breasts.

"Not just those." Jessica laughed. "Real talent! I remember watching your acting reel, all those student shorts you did. You were good. You lit up the screen. Still do."

Listening to Jessica, Celeste started to tear up. *What the fuck is wrong with me today?* she wondered. *That's twice in less than an hour and three times in one day.* She never cried; she'd given up the luxury of free tears on her third film (she'd cry for a role but never for herself). It was a waste of time and energy, and nothing was *that* important. She still wore her sunglasses; she hoped neither Lydia nor Jess would notice.

"Cici?" Lydia extended her hand. "What is it?"

Fuck! She hated emotional pity parties; it wasn't her style.

"Nothing, I'm fine, really."

Jessica and Lydia shared a worried glance.

"I mean, it's completely ridiculous, it's Damien. I . . ." Her voice cracked. "He's—I know he's fucking Brie Ellison, and that's not the part that bothers me—I mean, it *bothers* me, but it *is* Damien, so I'm not surprised. It's just . . ." Celeste took a deep breath, cleared her throat, and gathered her thoughts. "I wanted to marry him, I *really* wanted to marry him, and now . . . I don't understand how I could've been so wrong." Celeste exhaled. She felt better just saying it, acknowledging that her marriage was a mistake.

"You don't mean wrong about the person that Damien is, do you?" Lydia asked.

Celeste shook her head.

"You mean so wrong about what you wanted?" Lydia asked.

"Yes," Celeste said softly. She had thought she really wanted the marriage. For two years she convinced herself (and Damien) that their marriage was what she had to have. But it was completely wrong. Celeste wondered how she could be so unaware of her own needs.

"Cici, it's so easy to lose perspective," Lydia said. "They write stories in magazines about what kind of underwear you own. *That* is a little crazy."

"Yeah, maybe. I'm just surprised. I thought I knew myself, knew what I wanted, and when Damien said he was going back to set, it just clicked, you know. That this asshole is not the guy I can spend the next twenty years with," she said, and glanced across the table toward a surprisingly silent Jessica.

"He's a dumbass," Jessica said, wiping her mouth with her napkin. "Brie can't carry the film; I don't care who he puts opposite her in the male lead. She doesn't have an audience to support her."

"She's cheap," Celeste said, referring not to Brie Ellison's tawdry nature but to her acting quote.

"Not that cheap," Jessica said as their waiter took the remains of their meals. "She got first-dollar gross points."

"What?! He told me she got a flat fee of a million."

"Jess, that can't be right. She's not a big enough star for first-dollar gross," Lydia said.

"It's true," Jessica said. "Damien pushed it through the studio, told them he wouldn't make the film with anyone but Brie, and then her agent asked for one million up front and back-end first-dollar gross. I'm sorry, Cici, but I thought you needed to know."

The rage in Celeste's body bubbled. Damien Bruckner was a liar, a cheat . . . and her husband. Gross points! He'd convinced the studio to give his new tart gross points. Brie could make much more than Celeste's $20 million quote with first-dollar gross points. The fucker.

"No, you're right, Jess," Celeste said, tossing her blond mane. "It's much better that I know. Maybe not so good for Damien, but much better for me."

6

Lydia Albright and Her Black Alexandra Neel Calfskin Pumps

LYDIA PULLED HER BLACK RANGE ROVER THROUGH THE GATES OF HOLLYWOOD Forever Cemetery. The Disneyland of death. Here lay the heavy hitters of the past—Rudolph Valentino, Cecil B. DeMille, and Douglas Fairbanks; a Who's Who of Hollywood history fertilized the perfectly manicured grounds. Now it was the final resting place for Weston Birnbaum.

Lydia parked her car behind a long line of Mercedes, Bentleys, and BMWs. She picked up her three-inch black Alexandra Neel pumps from the passenger seat. God, she hoped her feet hadn't swollen on the way over from the studio; she couldn't go bare-foot to a burial. She checked her lipstick in the rearview mirror, then made sure her cell phone was on vibrate. It would be very bad form, even in L.A., to roll calls at a funeral (not that she hadn't seen it happen).

Lydia hated graveside services. Morbid reminders of a finite life. She slid into a chair and scoped out the scene. The service was total L.A. Multidenominational—first a rabbi spoke and then a minister from the Hollywood Church of Science. Betty Birnbaum (Weston's first wife) and Elizabeth Birnbaum (his third and current wife) sat in the front row holding hands and crying. Weston's three sons (two of them film agents and one a painter) sat next in the row, and finally Weston's oldest and favorite child, his daughter, Beverly. A producer and former man-eater turned lesbian, Beverly had given Lydia her first real job in Hollywood (after Lydia's failed attempt at acting) as a script reader at Weston's production company, Birnbaum Productions. It'd been Beverly who told Lydia, "You know more about story structure than you ever will about acting. Stop starving and get smart. Come work for me." Lydia took the job and never looked back. Maybe that was why Weston said yes to *Seven Minutes Past Midnight.* Well, that and the blow job.

Lydia wondered what Bev would think about Lydia blowing Weston in the celebrity suite at the Four Seasons. Maybe she'd be surprised that it had taken this long for Lydia and Weston to rekindle their romance. There had always been a connection between them. In the beginning of Lydia's career with Birnbaum Films, Weston gave Lydia pointers and helped her with story structure. He taught her how to get a studio to say yes to a film and begin writing checks. At the time, Weston was on wife number two and was twenty-five years Lydia's senior. He kept trying to fix Lydia up with any one of his three sons. That never happened.

Lydia and Weston's original affair began just before Lydia left to produce her first solo film, a tiny independent called *My Sad Silly Face.* Lydia had found the script and cobbled together $2 million of financing (with Weston's help, of course). One night Lydia was in Weston's office, and when she leaned over his desk to look at a note he'd made on the script, he turned his face toward her—and kissed her. The magnetism was too intense to repel, and the affair went on for years. No one knew. They met in non-industry places. The affair wasn't something they wanted to be an "open secret" for a number of reasons, not the least of which was Weston's failing marriage to multibillionaire investment banker Oren Highley's daughter.

When the divorce was final, Weston came to Lydia with the biggest diamond she'd ever seen. It had to have been ten carats. He begged. He pleaded. He said she'd be happy forever. And, she thought now, she would have. But something . . .

something—Lydia never really knew what—made her say no. And so they parted. Soon after came wife number three.

It hadn't been until recently, just two months ago, that Lydia and Weston reignited their affair. Neither was surprised that the passion still buzzed between them. The sex, although not as hot as the first time around (Weston was over sixty, after all), was exceptional.

That evening at the Four Seasons, Weston had watched Lydia undress, his lustful eyes roving over her. First she removed her tight-fitting black slit skirt, then her white silk Donna Karan shirt. Weston barely blinked, his eyes never leaving her body. Finally, Lydia stood naked in black Versace stilettos. Weston told her to keep the heels on and get on top. Lydia happily complied. It was her favorite position. Halfway through the sex, he'd flipped her over onto the bed. His vigor surprised her and a small giggle escaped her lips.

"Not bad for an old man," Weston gasped out between pumps, the strain of wanting to come showing on his face.

"Not bad at all," Lydia whispered into Weston's ear just before he climaxed.

But Weston, Lydia knew, loved the ladies. And though his ticker could take Lydia, the gathering today was testimony to his heart's inability to stave off the Asian twins. Lydia pulled a tissue from her Alexandra Neel lace-up bag. Trying to force herself to stop her free-flowing tears, she continued to survey the scene. Behind Weston's two ex-wives and children sat five of the biggest stars in Hollywood. It was a lot of wattage. And in the middle of those five sat Cici. *Funny how celebrities like to travel in flocks,* Lydia thought. It had to be a self-preservation tactic, protection against the agents, who traveled in wolf packs. And there was the pack, seated directly behind the stars. The über-agents. The four founders of ACA, the nine partners of DTA, and the president of CTA—all respectfully distanced from one another, lest a fistfight erupt.

Lydia glanced at Jessica, who pulled down her Dior sunglasses and winked at Lydia, tilting her head to the right. Lydia looked.

There he was, Lydia's leprechaun, Arnold Murphy, sitting in the fourth row next to his minion Josanne Dorfman. *Little fat fuck and his fag hag beside him.* Once a tremendously fat woman, Josanne had become a well-known anorexic-bulimic. It was rumored that she hadn't eaten in three years, and that her stupidity was a direct result of her body feasting on her brain. Hollywood didn't like ugly people (especially in the executive suite), and ugly people knew it, especially the ugly women. Josanne had stabbed and clawed to get as close to the top as she could; a former assistant of Arnold's, she'd attached herself to this angry little man, riding in the sidecar of his success.

"In God we trust in all things," the minister droned on. Weston was a dedicated Jew, so Lydia wasn't sure why a Catholic priest was speaking at the funeral. So L.A. Maybe next they'd read from the kabbalah.

Trying to comfort herself, Lydia shut her eyes and visualized the first day of production on *Seven Minutes Past Midnight*. The director, the actors, the set. She was deep into her meditation when she realized that the seat beside her was no longer empty.

"I hate these things," a gruff voice whispered in Lydia's ear.

Lydia opened her eyes. To her right sat a sandy-blond outdoorsy guy who looked as if he should be hiking in Big Sur instead of attending a funeral in L.A. *Did she know this guy?*

"Jeff Blume. We met years ago, when Weston had his production company and you were still working for him."

Okay. There were so many people she'd met since beginning her career in the film industry.

"I was Arnold Murphy's assistant," Jeff continued. "I was there while you were *both* working for Weston."

"Oh, Jeff. I remember now," Lydia whispered. "Were you there when . . ."

"When the shit hit the fan? Oh, yeah . . . I was on the call."

Lydia muffled a giggle. It was all a little funny. Arnold here, celebrating Weston's death and taking Weston's job as president of Worldwide. Lydia making a movie that Arnold hated and Weston loved. And now this, sitting at Weston's funeral next to Arnold's former assistant who had been privy to the whole event that triggered Lydia and Arnold's infamous feud.

"You know he's never forgiven me," Lydia whispered.

"Forgiven *you*?" Jeff whispered in Lydia's ear. "You're kidding, right?"

Everyone around them stood. The service was finally finished. Lydia turned to Jeff. "What do you do now? You obviously aren't an assistant any longer."

"Acquisitions and distribution for Galaxy."

"I never realized that you were the same guy who was once Arnold's assistant."

"Yeah, well, I try not to advertise. I hear you're going into production. I love the final draft of that script, by the way. Great writer."

"We got lucky. Found her writing sample in the slush pile. Can you believe it? Never happens. You should come by set. We're at Worldwide, stage thirty-six. Let me know, I'll get you a drive-on."

"Love to. Good seeing you again," Jeff said.

"You as well." Lydia edged toward the Birnbaum family, where Celeste and Jessica stood waiting to speak with Beverly.

"Who's that hottie? He looks like Redford when Redford was young," Celeste said, tilting her Versace sunglasses and checking out Jeff.

"Jeff Blume," Lydia said.

"Acquisitions and distribution at Galaxy," Jessica said immediately, while typing an e-mail on her BlackBerry. It was part of her job as an agent to know every "player" in town and where they were currently employed.

"Yes, and Arnold Murphy's former assistant," Lydia said.

"Oh! Not *that* Jeff Blume," Celeste said.

"The one and only," Lydia said.

"No wonder the little leprechaun can't take his eyes off you, Lydia," Jessica said, nodding in the direction of Arnold Murphy and Josanne. "I'm sure he thinks you're plotting something. He's such a paranoid freak."

"I'm going to need a drink after this," Celeste said. "I hate funerals."

"I'm up for it." Lydia pulled a tissue from her purse and again dabbed under her eyes. *Why did she keep crying?* Celeste wrapped a protective arm around Lydia and squeezed.

"Fine," Jessica said, scrolling through her e-mails on her Black-Berry. "Where?" She started tapping away.

"Let's do Spago for Weston," Celeste said.

They watched as the knot of people speaking to Beverly Birnbaum untangled. Six feet tall with closely cropped black hair, Beverly was a commanding presence. She'd inherited her father's amazing taste in scripts and movies as well as his deep, infectious laugh. Beverly was also sincere and truthful; both qualities were unfortunately rare finds in the film business. She was one of Lydia's favorite people in the industry.

"Bev, I'm so sorry," Celeste said, moving away from Lydia and throwing her arms around Beverly.

"Thanks, Cici."

"He was so much damn fun! Look, I'm going to cry again," Celeste said, pulling a tissue from her clutch.

Beverly turned her gaze to Jessica, who'd discreetly slipped her BlackBerry into her purse. "Jessica, thanks for coming. I know you two could really go at it sometimes when you were negotiating a deal, but my dad had tremendous respect for you. He said there was never a better agent in this town. He loved how you fought for your clients." She leaned in to give Jessica a hug.

"You know I loved him—we all did," Jessica said.

Beverly looked at Lydia. "I know."

Lydia looked at the ground, her emotions threatening to overwhelm her. *Get a grip,* she thought. Celeste gently took Lydia's hand. "We'll see you there, okay?" She and Jessica drifted away toward their cars.

Lydia nodded. She didn't know if she could speak. "Bev . . ." Her voice cracked. "I don't know—" Lydia couldn't hold back the flood of tears. Her chest heaved with sobs. *It was too much. Everything.*

Beverly put her arm around Lydia's shoulder, whispering into her ear. "He loved you, too. You were the one for him. I knew it the first day you came to the office. I'm just glad you two reconnected before all this."

Beverly *did* know. Maybe she'd always known. "Thanks," Lydia said, wiping her eyes.

"Here comes trouble," Beverly said, patting Lydia's arm and nodding her head toward Arnold and Josanne, who were weaving their way toward them. "That little shit, I can't believe he had the nerve to show. Especially after what happened. Listen, Lyd, you get *Seven Minutes Past Midnight* made no matter what Arnold tries to do. Dad loved that script. And let me know if I can help."

"You got it." Lydia sniffled.

"Call my office and schedule a lunch," Beverly said as Lydia backed away.

"I'll have Toddy do it tomorrow," Lydia said.

Lydia walked to her car, wondering if she'd always feel so alone.

Deafening silence greeted Lydia at the front door of her Mulholland Drive home. She'd long ago (perhaps the day she refused Weston's marriage proposal) surrendered the shimmery thoughts of children, big holidays, a house bursting with chatter, music, and laughter; that life was a casualty to Hollywood combat. Lydia didn't mourn the loss. Her success in film and the life she'd created for herself, although different from that of most women, were what she'd always wanted. But even knowing her choice was correct, every night when she came home the silence roared in her ears.

Lydia climbed the curving staircase. The house was big for one person, but it was a tax write-off (according to her accountant) that she needed. She spent less than half her time here, sleeping five hours on a good night. The majority of her waking hours were spent in her bungalow on the lot, or on set, and set could be anywhere in the world, for months at a time. No, this place wasn't a home, it was a house. A big, cold house full of marble, granite, and stainless steel. She'd never had the time (or the right partner) to turn it into a home.

She slipped her silk shirt off and let her skirt drop to the floor, thus creating the only mess in the entire ten-thousand-square-foot spread—a puddle of clothes at the foot of her bed. When she awoke in the noiseless morning, that testament to the house's habitation would have been whisked away by Vilma as if by magic, wordlessly replaced by the *New York Times,* the *Los Angeles Times,* the *Hollywood Reporter, Daily Variety,* and a carafe of hot coffee. The clothes would reappear in Lydia's closet exactly three days later, freshly cleaned.

Lydia shivered. The temperature in the house was fine, but she was cold. It'd been a long, emotional day. She climbed to the middle of her king-size bed (the trick to sleeping alone—take up the whole damn bed) and slid under her down comforter. She'd already cried . . . her tears were gone. Like Weston. All that remained were too-fresh memories of their rendezvous, both recent and long ago. She reached for the remote and aimed it at the plasma television hanging on the wall, but she didn't want to watch TV. She dropped the remote on the bed. Lydia glanced around her bedroom, a tribute to a child-free lifestyle, all white and silk. Her gaze landed on the pile of scripts on the floor next to her nightstand. She could read. A lesson learned from both her father and Weston: Read, read, read. "Not enough people in this town read, you'd be surprised," Weston had told her. "And the ones that actually read the scripts, well, they quickly rise to the top."

They were both right. It'd been that very pile from which Lydia had pulled Mary Anne's script. Lydia smiled. Mary Anne was a bright spot. Like a hapless puppy floundering around on oversized paws, Mary Anne bounded through the preproduction unable to contain her excitement and enthusiastic grin. Her talent was undeniable. Within three pages of starting to read her script, Lydia had gotten the tingly sensation at the base of her spine brought on by what her sixth sense always told her was exceptional writing.

That tingling sensation (aside from a good orgasm or a hit film) was the moment she lived for. She loved finding the great story. She knew it could pop up anywhere—an article, a book, a script, or a tale told to you in the doctor's office. But the one commonality was the tingling sensation Lydia got when she stumbled onto the narrative that would support a film.

"It's a gift," Weston had told her while she was working at Birnbaum Productions. "Not everyone has it. Most of them are guessing, flying in the dark. Use it, don't overthink it. You know, your dad had it, too."

So her high cheekbones and dark hair weren't the only things that Norton Albright passed down to her. She rolled toward the nightstand and reached for the light, flipping off the switch, then settled back into the bed, pulling the comforter up around her neck.

She listened for a sound, any sound. The house settling, the wind blowing, a board creaking . . . but there was nothing. Silence.

As silent as a tomb.

7

Jessica and Her Fuchsia Balenciaga Heels

JESSICA WALKED DOWN THE RED CARPET AT THE PREMIERE OF *MY WAY OR THE Highway* knowing that she looked amazing (Pilates three times a week and yoga daily could do that for a body). She prayed she wouldn't trip in her fuchsia Balenciaga heels. This was a CTA-packaged film (or rather a Jessica Caulfield–packaged film). One of Jess's actor clients, Maurice Banks, starred; another client, Rowyn Hertz, directed; and finally Steven Fabian, a third client, had written the script.

Flashbulbs popped. Matt Damon walked in front of Jessica. Her eyes were blinded, and all she could see were spots. A television cable snaked just ahead of her on the red carpet. Jessica picked up her left foot to clear the cable but dragged her right. *Damn.* She felt it catch. She could see the picture and the headline tomorrow: ÜBER-AGENT TAKES TUMBLE ON THE RED HIGHWAY. *Fuck!* Suddenly, a strong hand grabbed her arm.

"Gotcha."

"Thank y—" Jessica turned, her eyes focusing. A bolt of adrenaline surged through her body. There he was. *The* man; the one who taught her to play it safe with men. Mike Fox. He was alone, or he seemed to be alone.

Jessica hadn't seen Mike Fox since the day she left I M FOX Productions to become an agent at CTA, which was shortly after their sordid little love affair (which they pretended nobody knew about) ended. Between the private jets, supermodels, and blow, Jessica couldn't compete, Mike couldn't commit, and Jessica couldn't stay. The parting was neither amicable nor angry; their affair just stopped. But the longing—the "what ifs" and "what could have beens"—popped into Jessica's mind every time she read about Mike's successes in *Variety* or *Hollywood Reporter*.

"Jess, smile," Mike whispered into her ear. "They'll never know."

More flashbulbs popped, the lights again exploding in Jessica's eyes. It always felt as if the spotlight was brighter when she was with Mike. He pulled her closer, not letting go of her arm as they strolled down the red carpet.

"You smell good and you look even better," Mike whispered.

Jess giggled. *Giggled!* She hadn't giggled in . . . well, since she'd stopped sleeping with Mike.

"You know, I always loved making you laugh," his deep voice breathed in her ear.

"I always loved it when you did," she whispered.

The red carpet ended as they crossed the threshold into the theater lobby and joined the mass of Hollywood's who's who.

"I'm glad you're here," Mike said. "I wondered how many of your clients I had to hire to get to see you again. You're coming to the after party. Find me there."

Jessica turned to smile, but in an instant, Mike was engulfed by the sea of handshakes and backslaps that were bestowed on a producer at his premiere. For even though Jessica had packaged the project, it was Mike's film. He'd found her writer's script, set it up at Summit Pictures, and quickly hired her actor and director. Mike Fox's ascent to the top of Hollywood, like Jessica's, had been meteoric; he'd moved rapidly from producer to studio head (a position often reserved for balding middle-aged men) to rehab to producer. Meanwhile, she had stayed at CTA and collected hot male stars, fancy directors, and award-winning writers.

Jessica's thoughts were deep in "what ifs" when Lydia Albright walked up behind her.

"You know, I think he still fancies you," Lydia said.

"Mike will always fancy Mike," Jess said, snapping back to reality.

"Maybe. But you know he's cleaned up. No more supermodels or actresses. I hear he's interested in getting into family entertainment." Lydia raised her left eyebrow.

"You forget I have a man."

"Yes. When was the last time Phil was home?"

"That's a little low, Lyd. He's working."

"I'm just *saying*. Phil's great, but he needs to be working less on software and more on getting married. He better get with the program before someone else catches you."

"You saw my graceful entrance?" Jessica asked.

"Nice save. I don't think anyone who knows you saw it."

"Lyd. Everyone here knows me."

Lydia smiled. "Come on. Sit with me. I hear this thing is pretty good. Should make a ton of money at the box office this weekend."

They walked into the theater. People milled around the rows of seats, talking and smiling, laughing the anxious laughs that come before the start of a film at its premiere.

"Move fast, here comes the leprechaun," Lydia said, trying to weave her way past a Corinthian column.

"Arnold is here? But this isn't a Worldwide Pictures film." Jessica whirled around, looking for the telltale red hair.

"Pre–studio head. He's an executive producer on the film."

"Liideeeaaa!"

Lydia shook her head. "Let's pretend we didn't hear him. Keep moving. The ladies' room. He can't follow us in there no matter how feminine he is."

Jessica cut through the crowd, heading to the side staircase leading to the basement ladies' room, but Lydia trailed after her, caught behind a slow-moving executive.

"Liideeeaaa Albright, I *know* you hear me."

Jessica watched as Lydia took a deep breath, turned around, gritted her teeth, and plastered the professional-producer-who-loves-everyone-no-matter-how-much-she-really-hates-them smile across her face.

"Yes, Arnold, I *hear* you. How could I not? But you know, you're so short, it's difficult to *see* you and know which direction your voice is coming from."

Josanne, ever present at Arnold's side, let out an audible gasp. Jessica heard a few snickers to her left.

"Liideeeaaa, you are *not* making your days on this film," Arnold said loud enough for everyone two rows in either direction to hear.

Public humiliation. So that's what he's after, Jessica thought.

Lydia leaned forward and bent slightly as if addressing a toddler. "Arnold, is this really the correct time and place to discuss my film?"

"I am the head of the studio, Liideeeaaa. I will decide the correct time and place," Arnold said. "If you'd return my calls, then we wouldn't have to discuss this now."

"You know, Lydia," Josanne said, "you've been very negligent in returning Mr. Murphy's calls. We've left word for you three times today."

"Really? I must scold my assistant; she had down that you called *four* times."

"I will not allow you to waste the studio's money," Arnold snarled.

"No, Arnold, I don't expect that you would. But we aren't wasting anything."

"You are. I haven't seen any dailies and you're now six days into your shooting schedule."

"No, Arnold, we're still in preproduction. Our start date got pushed back three weeks."

Another audible gasp from Josanne. Jessica watched Arnold's face turn red. The crimson wave began at his neck, just above his collar, and rolled upward, emphasizing the vein in his right temple, which bulged and began to throb. He looked as if he might stroke out.

"Liideeeaaa Albright, who the *fuck* at my studio gave you permission to push your start date?" Arnold screeched.

Bad behavior was common in Hollywood. Name calling, screaming, hurtling phones across the room, all were considered very acceptable forms of stress release. And the whole town talked about the fights afterward. But almost always, disagreements took place behind closed doors, so this display of anger and animosity in such a public setting hushed conversations for ten rows all around them. Jessica saw people in the balcony shushing one another. Suddenly, Arnold Murphy and Lydia Albright (and their ongoing feud) were more important than the film that was meant to unspool. *They* were the entertainment. Jessica knew that Lydia knew that at this moment, she and Arnold were the center of the Hollywood Entertainment Universe, and how Lydia played her next card would determine her viability as a producer and the viability of her film. *God, I hope she's holding aces,* Jessica thought.

Lydia smiled. She again tilted her head toward Arnold as if addressing a petulant child who'd thrown himself to the floor in the checkout line at the grocery store when denied a chocolate bar.

Very clearly and very loudly, Lydia said, "Arnold, it was Ted Robinoff, the chairman of your studio, and I do believe your boss, who approved the delay of my start date. Perhaps you should call me less and Ted more?"

Royal flush, Jessica thought. *Good for Lydia.* The vein in Arnold's head throbbed as the snickers around them grew louder.

"You bitch," Arnold muttered under his breath. "This doesn't end here."

"No, Arnold," she whispered. "I doubt that it does. But this moment must be very embarrassing for you."

The glitteratti was out in full force. Everyone in Hollywood wanted to work with, sleep with, or just be near Mike Fox, and after watching his latest film, Jessica understood why. Stars and studio executives hoped he'd sprinkle them with his gold dust—the license to print money that Mike Fox seemed to have. *My Way or the Highway* was going to be another hit.

Mike Fox sure could throw a party, especially on the studio's dime. He'd rented out Havana Vin Vin. Jessica and the movie's star, her client Maurice Banks, followed William White (the megastar) and Julie Jensen, megastar in her own right and William's wife in name only (they both had same-sex partners on the side), into the club. The room was draped in bloodred swaths of velvet. The lights glowed red. Even the Cristal and Absolut had a touch of red food coloring.

"We were going for an Asian/James Bond feel," Jessica overheard the party planner say to an interviewer for *Entertainment Express*. Sushi and proscuitto, Camembert and Thai dumplings—California fusion cuisine.

"This thing is crazy. I've never been to a premiere party like this," Maurice said as Taryn Reed, the film's female lead, grabbed Maurice by the other arm and steered him toward the bar. Most premiere parties took place at the same tired restaurants where tepid egg rolls and over-iced drinks were served.

Go-go dancers stood on tables, performing what looked like a cross between lesbian porno and a striptease from Girls, Girls, Girls Gentleman's Club. But the trendiest bit (and the nearest to an X rating) was the sushi display. Six *Maxim* models wearing two tiny red strips of cloth lay in erotic poses on a buffet table. The sushi sat on their skin. Guests circled the table with chopsticks, lifting pieces of salmon sushi, albacore sushi, and California rolls from patches of bare skin. The wasabi and soy sauce sat (thankfully) off to the side.

Jessica smirked. *Nothing like presentation . . . or flouting one's conquests.* She suspected that Mike must have slept with at least five of the six models.

"Jess, Maurice was phenomenal," Paul Peterson, the head of Summit Pictures and the guy financing the film, the food, and Maurice's $17 million fee, shouted over the music. "This thing is going to make barrels of money. We really want to do Maurice's next film," he said, pointing his chopsticks at Jessica. "I have the perfect script for him. I'll send it over to your office tomorrow."

"Sounds good. But you know Maurice's next two slots are filled. He's booked for a year."

"Jess, I promise when you read this script you'll push the other two films. This is a fantastic script. *You* are going to want Maurice to do this film."

"Who's producing?" Jessica asked.

"You put Maurice in it, and we'll get whomever he wants," Paul said.

"What about Lydia Albright?" Jessica asked.

"After what I saw tonight, anything you, Maurice, or Lydia want. Did you see her dress down that little prick Arnold? She was fantastic!"

Jessica sipped her Diet Coke. "I was standing right there."

"I wish he'd get that bug out of his ass. That feud he thinks he's got going with Lydia is old news. Arnold isn't going to hold Lydia back—she's too good, always has been."

"I agree," Jessica said.

"If Arnold isn't careful, some other studio may offer her a deal on their lot that she can't refuse."

"I doubt that Lydia would be opposed to that," Jessica replied coyly. "Her overall deal at Worldwide is up after the first of the year." Jessica glanced across the room. Lydia was talking to Douglas Thomas, the A-list star whose last movie had tanked. Lydia was brilliant. She got them while they were vulnerable. *Lydia's so good and she doesn't even realize it,* Jess thought.

"I can't believe Robinoff gave Arnold that job. What was he thinking? Well, bad news for Worldwide is good news for Summit." Paul bit into his albacore tuna sushi. "Hey, isn't that Holden Humphrey over there with Josh Dragatsis? Holden's your client, right?"

Jessica smiled. "Yes. Looks like I better shoo away a pesky little bug. Send me the script."

Jessica watched Josh Dragatsis lean in and whisper to Holden. She was pissed. Where were CTA's junior agents who had been assigned to cover Holden at this event? Every A-list star was supposed to have a minimum of two agents surrounding him or her at premieres so just this sort of thing *never* happened. *Where the fuck were they?* She hadn't spent the better part of her reproductive years working her ass off just to stand back and watch while a pissant baby agent from a B-level shop hit on one of her highest-paid stars.

"Holden, my love," Jessica purred, strolling up and putting her arm around Holden and kissing his cheek. "Josh, trying to convince my star that he should work for free on your little independent film?"

"Nah. Just talking football. Well, that and strip clubs. You a fan, Jess?" Josh asked, his eyes sparkling with mischief.

Every female agent's Achilles' heel: football and strip clubs. You could get the star, put the star to work, hone his career, build his résumé, increase his quote . . . but *never*, as a female agent, would talking about football and strip clubs with one of your male stars (and male stars were the ones with the longest shelf life and the highest quote) ever sound legitimate.

"Not I. Me, I just like to shop for expensive shoes. But Tyler and Zane, now, they are agents at CTA who I think indulge." Jessica waved her hand, and as if by magic two of the most beautiful (noncelebrity) men appeared. Holden's CTA covering agents for the evening. Jessica smiled at them both, but her eyes were cold steel. Tyler and Zane would be in her office by eight A.M. so that she could scream at them for letting Josh Dragatsis get so close to a CTA star. Then she'd have them detail her car as punishment.

"Tyler, man, where'd you go?" Holden asked, smiling. "I lost you at the bar."

Tyler sniffed and wiped under his nose. "Bathroom."

"Josh, do you know Mike Fox?" Jessica asked.

"Uh . . . well, we've spoken but—"

"Really? That's *too* bad. Holden, why don't you come with me? I *know* Mike would love to meet you and he's having a private party in back." She gave Josh the stay-the-fuck-away-from-my-star smile. *Take that, you little shit,* she thought.

Jessica walked toward the back of the club with her hand wrapped around Holden's arm. If she knew Mike (and she did—intimately), she knew that behind the giant red velvet drapes at the end of the room (where two bodyguards stood) he was ensconced with his stars and models. No agents allowed. She took a deep breath—she hoped Mike didn't consider her one of the "no agents allowed." In between the two goons, Jessica spotted a velvet rope. She was used to always being on the exclusive side of the rope and it irritated her that at this moment she wasn't. As she approached, she noticed that each guard wore an earpiece and a microphone—very high-tech and a little extreme, even for Mike.

"Miss Caulfield." The bouncer on the right side unhooked the rope and pulled back the velvet curtain. "Mr. Fox is waiting for you and Mr. Humphrey."

And with that, Jess was in.

8

Mary Anne's First Pair
of Ferragamos

MARY ANNE SAT IN A TUB FULL OF AMAZONIAN-RIVER-MUD-INFUSED-WITH-
Peruvian-volcanic soil. It was the exact temperature of her body
(the relaxation therapist, to Mary Anne's surprise, had taken a
rectal temperature reading during her prebath rubdown). She had
a citrus-mint-cucumber slice over each eye. Everything at the spa
was a multi-hyphenate. It wasn't just salt, it was Dead-Sea-salt-
infused-with-Mesopotamian-river water. It wasn't just a facial, it
was a rosewater-herbal skin infusion followed by South-Pacific-
kiwi-apricot exfoliation. Even for a writer, it was a lot to handle,
and it was Mary Anne's first time.

Mary Anne wiggled the mud between her toes. It was squishy
and thick, and it triggered a childhood memory of stomping barefoot through summer mud puddles in Minnesota. Cici lounged in
the tub next to her. (Yes, Mary Anne was finally calling Celeste
Solange Cici.) After the last read-through two days before, Cici
had insisted they come to Rancho des Celibre for the day. Cici's
car and driver picked up Mary Anne at six A.M. They were each
assigned two relaxation guides in addition to their various
teachers and technicians. They began at seven A.M. with lemon-
cayenne detox. Then they practiced canyon-side yoga followed
by rooftop meditation. Mary Anne hadn't actually seen many

people, except the staff, and she wondered if Cici had rented out the entire spa for the day.

The food was as exotic as the technicians. They breakfasted on blueberry-flaxseed pancakes soaked in virgin-bee honey (how anyone could tell if a bee was a virgin, Mary Anne had no idea) with mango-kiwi-passion-fruit salad. Once their tummies were full, their relaxation guides led them to a "dim" room, where they were undressed. Then it was time for side-by-side hot rock massages. Cici and Mary Anne lay on massage tables, getting their pre-mud-tub rubdowns.

"Darling, I always say get the wax first, then the mani-pedi, and then the massage," Celeste said. "You want to relax after someone pulls out your crotch hair. You know?"

"Oh."

"And you *have* to wax before the mani-pedi because you don't want some stray pube flying into your nail polish. *Very* unattractive. Believe me, I know. The last Oscars—oh my God! Scrambling to find Chanel red backstage before I went on. This little hair . . ."

Mary Anne had tried to listen to Cici as Ferdinand pushed his thumb deep into the muscle around Mary Anne's left shoulder blade, but Cici's voice faded in and out as Mary Anne relaxed.

". . . but we just couldn't get in to Olivia until three P.M. I mean, she would have taken me, of course, but she couldn't rearrange her schedule for both of us. You get what I'm saying?"

"Hmm . . . ," Mary Anne mumbled.

"So we'll just go to Ferragamo to relax after the wax job. Olivia does the best Argentinean."

"Argentinean? I've heard of a Brazilian, but—"

"Next step, sweetie," Celeste said.

Mary Anne flinched. She'd never even been waxed. They shaved in Minnesota. And since she'd lived in Los Angeles, she'd never had enough money (until now) for this type of maintenance.

"You know it's impossible to get on Olivia's client list. But now that you're going with me, you'll definitely be able to get into a two-week rotation. It's *so* worth it."

Mary Anne couldn't imagine what "so worth it" meant to Cici, who was normally paid $20 million per film. This spa day was Cici's treat, but Mary Anne had been speculating on price and doing the math in her head. She guessed that Cici had easily dropped eighteen grand. Mary Anne couldn't stop counting pennies just because she had more pennies to count. Once poor, always poor. She was terrified that an accountant from the studio would knock on her door, tell her it was all a big mistake, and demand that she return all the money she'd been paid.

Cici sat up from her massage. "Mud bath next. Then we exfoliate." Cici marched naked across the heated marble floor to the mud tub. Mary Anne watched her slip into the mud. She couldn't stop herself from staring. *Was it possible to be that physically perfect?* It must be, because Cici's body was. Not an ounce of fat. No stretch marks. No sags. Not even a tan line. *Jeez. That was perfection.* Feeling self-conscious (who wouldn't next to a blond goddess), Mary Anne wrapped her towel around her body and padded over to the mud tub. Tatiana (one of Cici's relaxation therapists) was placing cucumber slices onto Cici's eyelids as Mary Anne slid into her tub. Perfect temperature. It was heaven.

"Do you think Bradford Madison would be a good fuck?" Cici asked a few minutes later.

The question snapped Mary Anne out of her reverie and she choked on the mango-lemon-infused water she was sipping. She cleared her throat. "He's definitely good-looking."

"Yes, but good-looking doesn't mean he's a good fuck. In fact, I've found it's usually the opposite," Cici said, turning her head and cucumber-covered eyes toward Mary Anne. "Good-looking men are usually so self-absorbed, they think *you* should feel grateful to fuck them. Now, the not-so-good-looking-guys, the ones that are a six or a seven on the scale, *they* are the phenomenal fucks. At least the best ones I've had. I guess it's because they're grateful to be fucking you. Right? I mean, they realize they're going to come either way, and they don't know for sure when the next time is they'll be with a beautiful woman, so they make it all about *your* pleasure. Plus, they *really* enjoy it. And they make sure that you enjoy it, too. It's usually the swarthy Jewish guys. They fuck like it's a five-star meal or a bottle of Château de Beaucastel. So based on that, I don't know about Bradford. What do you think?"

Mary Anne didn't know what to think. Or what to say. She was so out of her league, in over her head . . . every cliché applied. Sure, she'd been in Los Angeles for nine years, but it wasn't like she'd been speeding down the fast lane. She was from *Minnesota*. They didn't talk about fucking celebrities or little swarthy Jewish men there—in fact, they didn't have either in her hometown. She'd only slept with three men in her entire life. One was her high-school boyfriend, Tod, who dumped her six months after she moved to L.A. He was now married with a fat wife and three kids, running his dad's car dealership in St. Paul. Until recently, Mary Anne's mother, Mitsy, liked to point out that if Mary Anne hadn't moved to L.A. she could be the one living in a five-bedroom brick Tudor with three kids and a membership to the St. Paul Country Club.

The second guy, Lewis, was an artist/waiter Mary Anne had met the first year she was in L.A. It was a quick love affair; seven weeks. It ended one day when Mary Anne came home to her apartment after work to find her stereo and television gone and a note letting her know that Lewis owed money and needed to get out of town fast. His note said he'd replace everything soon (he never did).

The third, the one she didn't want to think about, was the main reason she'd thought the dream was dead, the final humiliation in a long list of Los Angeles's insults. Mary Anne had met Steve at a screenplay writers' conference; he was the computer guy. He gave a stilted and somewhat boring forty-five-minute presentation on how to make your laptop your best friend. But he was tall, gangly, quiet, and cute. Steve was also the reason Mary Anne ended up broke and homeless on Sylvia's couch. Well, Steve and the red-headed actress, Viève, who lived next door. Mary Anne walked right in on them. What a scene. She couldn't even talk about it yet.

"Well? What do you think?"

"I don't know. I've never slept with a celebrity or a Jew."

Mary Anne heard Cici giggle, then snort, and one guffaw turned into a belly-rolling laugh until Cici was hooting, barely able to catch her breath.

"Oh *my God!* Mary Anne, no wonder you are such a fantastic fucking writer! Where do you come up with this stuff?"

Mary Anne smiled and sank down into the mud tub. "They say write what you know. Just my life, I guess."

"What a life," Cici said, snickering and relaxing deeper into the mud.

Mary Anne could hear the smile in Cici's voice. *Yeah, what a life,* Mary Anne thought.

Mary Anne watched the shops and restaurants on Hollywood Boulevard fly by from the backseat of the chauffeur-driven Town Car, the sixth (or was it the seventh?) time today she'd had a driver. She leaned back into the leather seat, trying not to disturb her freshly cut, colored, and curled coif.

"That dress looks fabulous with your skin color and eyes," Cici whispered into Mary Anne's ear.

Mary Anne was nervous. Cici had invited her to this "event" only four hours before, while Mary Anne sat in Ferragamo watching Cici try on shoes. Shoes, Mary Anne realized, that cost more than Mary Anne's monthly rent in her first Hollywood apartment.

"It's a charity event. *Everyone* will be there," Cici had said, admiring a pair of strappy leather sandals with a silver heel. "I'd love it if you'd come with me. Kiki Dee is organizing it and she'll die if I don't show."

"Kiki?"

"Dee," Celeste said, turning around to face Mary Anne. "My publicist."

"Oh," Mary Anne said. *An event?* Prior to moving to Los Angeles, an event for Mary Anne was a graduation, a wedding, or a funeral, the first involving a barbecue grill and shorts, the other two nude-colored panty hose, and all three, extended family. But a Hollywood event? What would she wear? What did she own that she *could* wear? Where would she shop? How long did she have to prepare?

"It's tonight, around eight," Cici said.

Mary Anne swallowed hard. *Tonight?* There was no way she could be ready. She could barely comprehend getting ready in seven days, much less four hours.

"Celeste—I mean, Cici," Mary Anne corrected herself, "I'd love to, but, well . . ." Mary Anne let her sentence drift and stared down at the sixth pair of Ferragamo shoes adorning Cici's feet. Even after this delicious day of self-indulgence—mani-pedi, wax (her crotch still burned), massage, mud bath, exfoliation—there was no way Mary Anne could shop, get her hair and makeup done, and be presentable in four hours.

"Darling," Cici said, sitting down on the leather seat next to Mary Anne, "it's all taken care of. You're coming with me. I've already called Emily, my stylist, and she's bringing some outfits for you to try. Jonathan and Que are bringing extra people, so you don't have to worry about makeup or hair."

"I don't?"

"No, darling. They're professionals; it's what they do." Cici leaned closer to Mary Anne and whispered, "You don't think little ole me can get myself to look this good all by myself, now, do you?"

Mary Anne smiled and exhaled.

"That's better," Cici said, nodding toward the salesclerk and gesturing at the five pairs of shoes that lay at Cici's feet. "And these, too," Cici said, handing the clerk the shoe she'd just slipped off her foot. "What size, Mary Anne?"

"Hmm?" Mary Anne pulled her gaze away from the crowd beginning to gather outside the locked glass front door to the Ferragamo store.

"Madame, what size? Your foot? I'm guessing a six and a half," said the store manager. *Was that a Ferragamo suit he was wearing?*

"Yes," Mary Anne said, still a little confused. *Had Celeste Solange just picked out her shoes?* The flashbulbs began popping outside the store's front windows.

"Okay, let's go," Cici said, glancing toward the front door, a tired look crossing her face. "Is my car out back?" she asked.

"Yes, Ms. Solange," said the manager.

"And it's running, ready to go the moment we get in?"

"Yes, ma'am," said the clerk, carrying the Ferragamo bags.

"Come on, then," Celeste said, clipping across the marble to the back door.

Mary Anne watched the swarm of people pressed against the glass jump in unison as soon as they saw Celeste walking toward the back of the store.

"Madame, I think they're coming."

"Yeah, quick, then."

Just as the manager pushed open the back door, the cameras started snapping, the flashes bursting in Mary Anne's eyes.

"Put on your sunglasses," Cici hissed. "The bulbs still blind you, but it helps."

Mary Anne fumbled with her Ray-Bans, forcing them onto her face. It was like a swarm of bees, but instead of stingers they had flashbulbs. They pushed and screamed trying to get to Celeste.

"Celeste, over here!"

"Celeste, where's Damien?"

"Are you getting divorced?"

"We hear your tits are too saggy for him?"

"Celeste, give us a smile?"

Celeste and then Mary Anne ducked into the car as Celeste's driver pushed the paparazzi away and slammed shut the door. But that didn't stop the photogs. They pressed against the back and side windows with such force, they began rocking the car. Even as the driver pulled forward they refused to move. The car crawled ahead an inch at a time until finally they reached the street and the driver gunned it.

"That was—"

"Something, right?" Celeste said, reaching for her purse and rummaging around.

"Awful. How can they say those things to you?"

"They want *the* picture. The one that's worth a boatload of cash, the one that could destroy a career. The one where I'm completely pissed off and slugging a photographer. That is the photo they're after." Celeste pulled a tiny diamond-encrusted vial from her purse and popped open the lid. "Want a lift?" she asked, sticking her newly manicured pinky nail into the white powder.

"No, thanks, I'll pass."

Mary Anne watched as Cici took two quick snorts and wiped under her nose.

"So much better than caffeine." Cici popped the lid back on and dropped the vial into her purse. "So tonight, nothing to worry about, just a quick charity event. We get in, stay for an hour, two if the party's hot, then home. Get some good shots and we're done."

"Shots?"

"Photos. It'll be good for the film, you and I together. Be very good for you. This will be your first press, right?"

"Um, yes. I haven't been to anything like this before."

"It'll be fun," Cici said as they pulled up to the locked gate in front of her home. "Don't worry, everything is taken care of."

And everything was. The makeup, the hair, the clothes. When Mary Anne looked into the full-length mirror three hours later, she didn't recognize the woman looking back at her. Gone were her mousy locks, with little wisps of curl sticking out at odd angles, replaced by a do that looked straight out of 1940s Hollywood. Her lips were colored a deep red, and her eyes were now "smoky" according to Que, Cici's makeup artist. *Glamorous* was the word that sprang to mind. *They are professionals!* Mary Anne had thought, turning from side to side.

The Town Car pulled up to the red carpet in front of the Roosevelt Hotel.

"Stay close to me," Cici said, preparing to hop out of the car. "Kiki will be right outside the car. We have to work the line a little."

The minute the car door opened, she was swallowed by the swarm. But this time the swarm was contained. No rude comments, no obscene remarks. The photographers, although still yelling for Cici to twist this way and that, stayed politely behind the metal rail on the far side of the red carpet. Mary Anne thought the press passes around their necks acted like electric shock collars on unruly Rottweilers.

Kiki Dee rushed toward Celeste and Mary Anne, guiding them to the center of the red carpet.

"Smile, my darlings," Kiki whispered before stepping back and off to the side.

"Celeste, over here!"

"Give us the look, Celeste. Cock your eyebrow for us!"

"Celeste, give us a side shot."

Mary Anne stood beside Cici, smiling and trying not to look like a deer caught in the lights of an oncoming semi-truck.

"Who's your friend? She's awful pretty!"

"Mary Anne Meyers. She's the most brilliant screenplay writer I've ever met," Cici called out. "We're working together on Lydia Albright's movie *Seven Minutes Past Midnight*."

"That was perfect." Kiki appeared beside Mary Anne. "You're a natural. What a beauty," she gushed, grabbing Mary Anne's elbow and steering her away from the photographers. "We need to move."

"But where is Cici?" Mary Anne asked.

"She'll do a quick two-minute bit for *Entertainment Express* and then she'll be in," Kiki said before flitting away back toward the swarm.

Mary Anne stood just inside the door watching Cici talk. Suddenly the flashbulbs began to explode again.

"It's Brie!" a paparazzi screamed.

"Brie, is Damien with you?"

"Brie, Celeste is here. Want to say hello?"

Mary Anne watched Celeste's face. She was on camera and could hear everything the paparazzi said, but she didn't flinch. If Mary Anne hadn't been standing right there, she'd never have believed that Brie had been there at all. When the interview was over, Cici glided through the doorway and almost walked right by Mary Anne.

"Cici." Mary Anne reached for the star.

"Fuck!" Cici hissed. "How could Kiki let this happen? That bitch is here, too?"

"You okay?" Mary Anne said, concern lacing her voice. It had to be embarrassing for Cici. In the last few days the tabloids had published dozens of pictures of Damien and Brie soaking up the sun together in New Zealand, holding hands and groping each other on the beach.

"At least I got here first." Celeste looked around the lobby. "Come on, there's got to be a back way out of this place."

And with that, Mary Anne's night was finished.

9

Celeste and Her Gold Bruno Frisoni Sandals

THE PENINSULA HOTEL WAS QUIET. THE MONDRIAN HAD BETTER BEDS. BUT THE underground entrance and private elevator to the penthouse suite at the Four Seasons won for discretion. And there wasn't *that* much difference in the beds; Celeste had fucked on all three.

This fuck, though, had been a very good one indeed. Celeste leaned back in the penthouse suite marble tub for a postcoital soak, the suds rising around her. She glanced through the bathroom door and saw her gold Bruno Frisoni sandals poking out from under the clothes she'd flung on the floor a few hours earlier. The afternoon had been unexpected—in fact, a complete surprise. But you never knew whom you'd run into on a studio lot. *Hmm. Surprising yet fun.* Celeste hadn't felt this free in years. No hang-ups, no problems, just great sex. No mind games or feelings of guilt (her husband was banging an adolescent, after all).

Before today, their relationship had been purely business, and Celeste thought that was what *he* always wanted. There had never been a hint or innuendo. Most men salivated over her breasts—some actually dropping spittle into her cleavage—but this guy was a class act. He'd gotten into movies simply for fun, had been doing it for twelve years, and despite his success, he really seemed quite bored by it all. The pace, the games, the bullshit. Everyone thought he was "inaccessible." Celeste had always been able to get him on the phone, but they'd only actually met two times before. This was their third. *And what a third.*

They'd been at it for hours. It had to be nearly seven, Celeste guessed as she slid lower in the bubbles. How had it happened? So smoothly.

"I have the penthouse at the Four Seasons while I'm in town. Would you like to come over?" he'd asked over a lunch of grilled snapper.

"Now?"

"I would love that," he'd said, and placed his hand on top of hers.

The penthouse suite was the same as Celeste remembered. Plush Oriental rugs, expensive furniture, and scattered, tasteful art. The sitting room overflowed with bright bouquets of roses, hydrangea, and cymbidium orchids. She knew he was watching as she tossed her Jacqueline Jarrot clutch onto the couch. Celeste teasingly walked toward the bed, twirling a lock of her hair in her right hand.

He walked up behind her and placed his hand on the small of her back. She tingled with anticipation. He gently lifted her golden hair and kissed her neck. She unbuttoned her Christian Lacroix shirt and let it drop beneath her shoulders. His right hand stroked the skin underneath the silk strap of her Agent Provocateur black bra. In one deft motion he unsnapped it, letting it and her shirt drop to the floor. Celeste, knowing the power of the moment, stopped, turned, and looked into his eyes. He knelt in front of her, meeting her gaze. Then he untied and unlaced her low-riding Lucky jeans and slid them over her tiny hips, letting his fingers glide ever so smoothly over her skin. He pulled her pants over her thighs, gently lifting first her right leg, then her left, out of the denim. Her Bruno Frisoni sandals remained. He kept his eyes on her as he knelt at her feet and worked his way back up her legs with his lips and tongue.

She was hot, and she was wet when finally he gently pushed her backward onto the bed. His tongue ran along the inside of her right thigh until he parted her, finally stroking her in that one tiny spot, the spot that already tingled and longed for his tongue. And there he stayed for their first orgasm together.

Most men wanted to dominate her during sex. They'd throw her legs up over her ears and thrust as if they were a battering ram and she a castle they were storming. Some tried to flip her over onto all fours and ass-fuck her. Others stuck their cocks in her mouth before coming on her breasts. All of which she'd engaged in, at times enjoyed, but recently been reviled by. But this sex, this sex was smooth and soft, with just the perfect hint of aggression and domination, each of them taking a turn at the controls.

The sex, the afternoon, felt good; it felt right. Nothing slimy or lascivious. Just a lovely older, widowed man asking for company. And why not, really? He made her feel good. Made her laugh. He was the first man in a long time who didn't have an agenda, who didn't need or want something from her. This time it was lust and the satisfaction of that lust. Nothing more, nothing less. No angle. And she liked him. She realized she hadn't really liked Damien in years. Amazing. She'd wanted to marry Damien and still, Celeste now realized, she really didn't like him. Had she ever? It seemed so silly now.

Celeste reached for her glass of red wine. She ought to get up, dry off, and go home. But why? The house was empty. Mathilde was gone. Damien was in New Zealand.

Before he left for his meeting, he asked if she'd stay.

"Please stay the night. I have a meeting, but I'll be back by eight. We'll have dinner. I can send someone to pick up your clothes."

"You're lovely," Celeste said, turning her back to him and rolling toward the edge of the bed. "But really, this is what it is. I'll take a soak and then head home."

"Celeste." He placed his hand on the small of her back. "It's not like that for me. I don't . . . I haven't . . . Well, this just isn't my thing. I know it could seem that way. But really it's not."

She rolled back over and looked into his blue eyes. He was telling the truth. It wasn't a line. She could feel it in her gut.

"I care for you. I know it sounds hokey, but you are an amazing woman. I'd love it if you'd stay."

Celeste smiled her oh-please-you-are-sweet-but-don't-be-so-silly smile and ran her fingers through his hair. "*You* are a lovely man. And I enjoyed every moment of the last four hours. But you have a meeting, and I have a dinner engagement. Some other time?"

He smiled. His lips turned upward, but his eyes looked so sad. "Of course, another time. Any time. Please, know that," he said, and kissed her fingertips as she slid away from him.

So she could stay. Surprise him. But what man *really* liked surprises? How embarrassing if he showed up with woman number two of the day and woman number one was still lounging around in a Four Seasons robe? Not a good scene. She could call. He'd left his cell phone number. Besides, his meeting was at CTA. She had *that* number. There were a million ways to get in touch with him. *Hmm* . . . She sipped her cabernet (nice year). It was enticing. The sex. The man. Dinner . . . companionship.

The whole idea of someone who cared whether you stayed or left appealed to her. Someone who checked in throughout the day. Someone to miss. She hadn't really had companionship in years. The irony astounded her. Married, biggest star in the world, and no one to make her feel missed? *Jeez,* Celeste thought, *I'm getting sappy. It's a bad romantic comedy for sure.* She was going home.

10

Lydia Albright and Her Christian Louboutin Peekaboo Pumps

LYDIA WAS GLAD SHE'D TRADED IN HER CHRISTIAN LOUBOUTIN PEEKABOO pumps for Pumas before disembarking Worldwide Pictures' private jet, because she wasn't sure what was in the brown sludge she'd just walked through to get to this Balinese hellhole, but the muck was near her ankles and sticking to her shoes (it would have demolished her nine-hundred-dollar heels). Lydia gazed at the dilapidated building before her. She'd read somewhere that Balinese women were the most beautiful in the world, but that little tidbit of information didn't apply to the ninety-year-old toothless crone squatting in front of the hotel. If nothing else, this woman's existence proved that Balinese women didn't age well.

At least it was meant to be a quick trip (if you disregarded the eighteen-hour flight each way). Lydia hoped to spend less time on the ground than the round-trip took in the air. She only had the Worldwide jet for another twenty-six hours (it was the longest she could keep it out without Arnold knowing). Shit. She had to find Zymar.

She'd started south of Kuta, on the coast, where Zymar was famous for hibernating between films. But his home, a hut with a porcelain pot in which to pee and no running water, was empty. His neighbor, a tiny stick of a man, told Lydia's interpreter (Thuan, a local she'd snagged at the airport and offered a hundred U.S. dollars to if he'd translate for her for the day) that Zymar had left the day before to visit Denpasar. So she and Thuan loaded into Thuan's Volkswagen Bug (he demanded that he drive his car as part of his services) and headed inland. Three hours later, Lydia's legs were cramped and she was slogging through brown sludge, watching her interpreter try to communicate with the toothless old woman.

"She say go on up. But leave her five first."

"Five?" Lydia asked. Then she thought, *Of course, the universal translator—cash.* Lydia smiled at the woman and handed her a five-dollar bill. The old woman cackled and said something to Thuan.

"She say room six and thank you. She also say if you are wife to knock first."

"Tell her not to worry—not his wife. Not anybody's wife," Lydia said, and moved toward the front entrance of the hotel. There, between Lydia and the door, sat a giant baboon defecating on the step. The baboon finished and scampered up a palm tree beside the hotel. Lydia stepped over the steaming pile of shit, realizing what, in part, made up the brown sludge she'd waded through.

The lobby was filled with orange vinyl chairs that looked as if they came straight from a Denny's in Sherman Oaks. Once past the lobby, there were, of course, no lights to illuminate the creaky wooden staircase. Room six was on the top floor. She felt as if she was in a scene from *Apocalypse Now* as they ascended. She might as well get a gunboat and go upriver. She hoped Zymar didn't have a machete. Lydia reached for the doorknob and Thuan cleared his throat.

"Lady, maybe I go first. You might get surprise."

"I promise it's nothing I haven't seen. I'm from L.A."

And it wasn't. Weston may have liked Asian twins, but Zymar preferred Balinese triplets. Lucky for Lydia, all four were taking a breather. One was in the bathroom and two were passed out on the bed, where Zymar lay smoking a Thai stick with his eyelids half closed.

"Bollocks, this must be good stuff," Zymar said as he exhaled. "I see Lydia Albright."

She'd never determined exactly where Zymar's accent was from. It sounded to her like British-Australian with a hint of New Zealand thrown in. Pacific Eurotrash, she guessed. Damn, she'd always been a sucker for accents. Weston's was New York Jew. It didn't matter the type of accent, she just loved how it sounded on a man.

"Not such good stuff, Zymar. It's actually me," Lydia said.

"Eh. She even talks. Sounds like Lydia Albright, too." Zymar smiled and took another toke on his Thai stick.

Lydia looked around the room. She needed Zymar's clothes and—she hoped for his sake—his shoes. She couldn't imagine what kind of parasite you could pick up slogging barefoot through baboon shit.

"Girls. Looky here. It's Lydia Albright from 'Ollywood." Zymar laughed and nudged one of the sleeping triplets. The third one emerged nude from the bathroom and curled up on a divan in the corner.

Lydia grabbed Zymar's jeans and Paul Frank T-shirt off the floor and dumped them on the bed next to her director.

"Work with me here, big guy. I've only got the plane for twenty-six more hours. We need to get going."

"Goin'. Lyd, look around you. You think a man like me would leave this lot?"

Lydia spotted Zymar's flip-flop sandals (covered in brown goo) in the corner. Careful not to touch the soles, she walked them to the edge of the bed.

"No, but I do think you have a pay-or-play contract to do my film, which means that either you come back with me to do my movie, or forget about your ten-million-dollar fee and pay the studio back the two million they already paid you. Plus go to movie jail for the next five to ten years because I will make it my *personal* mission in life to make sure you don't work in film— *any* kind of film—for at least that long."

Zymar smiled. "Lyd, if you'd get rid of them tits and grow a wank, you'd be me best mate for sure."

"Say good-bye to your friends. You can come back to visit as soon as you're finished shooting my film."

Zymar lifted the sheet and Lydia caught herself looking. So did Zymar.

"It's a big one, ain't it, Lyd?" he asked, mischief dancing in his eyes.

Lydia blushed like a fourteen-year-old girl. "Uh, we'll be in the hall." She and Thuan walked out the door. Lydia felt her heart racing in her chest. Zymar was correct—it indeed was a big one.

M s. Albright and Mr. Zymar, please fasten your seat belts for the descent into Los Angeles," the pilot said over the intercom.

For fifteen hours, Zymar had slept while Lydia read scripts, rolled phone calls, pestered her assistants, and paced the cabin of the Gulfstream 5500. Zymar finally woke two hours outside of L.A., hungover, dehydrated, and disoriented. First she had pumped him full of Fiji water (he had pissed eight times in the last ninety minutes), then she fed him vitamin C tablets and multivitamins. Lydia needed him ready to roll the minute they touched down. And finally they talked about the script.

"We had one read-through, last week. It was okay. But just okay. Mary Anne is working on a couple more notes."

"Your writer's a cute one," Zymar said, slurping more coffee.

"You cannot fuck my writer," Lydia commanded. "Do you understand? This is her first film, and that will be overwhelming enough. She doesn't need you mucking up her head."

"Yes, ma'am. See we've got a bit of a mother 'en in us, 'eh, Lydia? 'Oo would have thought it? You with that set of brass balls and all."

"Celeste Solange is playing Raphaella."

"Don't know 'ow you pulled that off."

"Magic."

"I'd say so. Speakin' of magic, that little short redheaded fart who reminds me of a leprechaun, the one 'at got the World-wide job?"

"Arnold Murphy. Yes."

"You know, Lydia, when I 'eard that was when I 'eaded inland. I wasn't meaning to be dodgy or nothin'. I just figured with you two's feud, wouldn't be a movie to make."

"You and me both. I got lucky."

"You know the saying 'bout luck? When chance meets a pre-pared mind. What saved it, then, Lyd?"

"Cici. Cici and Jess."

"Yeah, well, I always did like them in threes." Zymar's lascivi-ous grin would have been offensive if Lydia didn't think he was so damn good-looking.

"And Bradford, then. 'E's out of rehab? Cleaned up?"

"He seemed clean at the read-through. I hope it holds."

" 'E's unstoppable in front of a camera, Lyd, if you can keep him off the blow for the shoot. But it's impossible when 'e's on it."

"You take care of him on set. I'll take care of him at the end of the day."

"So what are we lookin' at for a start date? Ten days from now?"

"Three. Arnold is already ripping me apart for dailies," Lydia said.

"That fric frac. 'E wouldn't know a good film if it spanked him on the ass."

Lydia laughed.

" 'E worked on my second film years ago. Right after that little thing with you. Didn't know which side of a camera the lens was on. 'E's a wanker or the waste of one."

They both bounced as the wheels touched down on the tarmac.

"He may be a wanker, Zymar," Lydia said, looking at her watch, "but he's our wanker for the next eight weeks."

11

Jessica and Her Louis Vuitton Marble Leather Pumps

JESSICA LOOKED AROUND THE CTA BOARDROOM AT THE FIFTY-FOUR MOTION picture agents in attendance. This small group of individuals, with Jessica as their leader, dominated the entertainment universe. Clustered in the room were a whole lot of ties and dark suits and not many skirts and high heels. But the heels that were in the boardroom were remarkable: Louboutin, Choo, Blahnik.

Seven female agents, including Jessica. Not even twenty percent of the motion picture department's agents (who represented eighty percent of the world's top stars) were women. Talent representation was a male business; it was sales. Agents sold actors, directors, writers and their ideas. This sales job was intense and competitive. Seven days a week, twenty-four hours a day. You lived for your clients and their needs.

CTA had lost two female agents in the last eighteen months; one to a management company and the other to motherhood. Jessica was among the third generation of women in Hollywood even allowed to be agents. None of the first generation had children (few had husbands) and just a handful in the second did. Even today many female agents never married, and the majority of those who did eventually divorced. What man wanted to compete with this life?

Jess glanced at her ten-thousand-dollar diamond-encrusted Rolex (a gift from a client who had won an Emmy). Nine fifty-eight A.M. Two more minutes before the Wednesday-morning meeting was finished. A weekly ritual, this staff gathering required every junior agent who was responsible for "covering" a studio to report on all the jobs that were available as well as the gossip. Tyler Bruger, the twenty-five-year-old junior agent who covered Summit Studios (and who had failed miserably at covering Holden Humphrey), was yammering on about a script Summit paid seven figures for. He floundered, his comments going nowhere.

"What director do they want?" Jess interrupted.

"Excuse me?" Tyler stopped and swallowed. Every junior agent feared being put on the spot at the Wednesday-morning meeting. It'd been less than a decade since Jessica had sat in Tyler's spot, her unease creating pit stains on her silk shirt.

"What director? You've talked about our clients, but which one does the producer want?"

"Mike Fox is the producer, and he didn't say who—"

"Didn't say? When did you speak to Mike?"

"At the premiere."

"Really?"

"He mentioned—"

"You're telling me that you spoke to Mike Fox at his premiere party?" Tyler was lying. He knew it, and Jessica knew it. She could eat him alive right now. If she wanted.

"Yes, and he mentioned Van der Veen and Tuttle as our two directors he'd be most interested in for this project."

Nice save. At least Tyler didn't crack under the pressure. Jessica looked around the room. "Is that all?" she asked. No one else had anything. She stood, signaling the end of the meeting. And she was sure she heard Tyler breathe a sigh of relief.

For the past three years (as long as she'd been president of the company), immediately after the meeting Jessica talked with Jeremy Sullivan, the CEO of CTA. An Americanized Brit, Jeremy had purchased his way into the entertainment business with his wife's money (she being the favorite daughter of an obscenely wealthy oil magnate). Three years before, Jeremy had managed a semi-friendly buyout of CTA with enormous help from Jessica. He had first approached her on a movie set, where she was visiting one of her director clients. Jeremy was executive-producing the film (another investment by his father-in-law). Forever interested in cinema, Jeremy believed the fastest way to get movies made was to have access to the talent. And what better access, Jeremy believed, than to own an agency.

Still a junior agent, Jessica recognized an opportunity for rapid advancement when she saw one. She courted Jeremy, tantalizing him with CTA client lists and scripts that the agency represented and controlled. Her savvy expertise in the film industry combined with Jeremy's money and desire to learn created a relationship primed for power.

Jeremy's first offer to the seventy-year-old owner of CTA, Ezekiel Cohen, was summarily refused. But then Jessica truly proved her agenting skills. Ezekiel had hired Jessica. As old and hard-bitten as Ezekiel was, and still believing, as most men from his generation did, that a woman's place was in the home, he'd nevertheless recognized Jessica's innate talent for handling stars. Jessica leveraged his feelings for her and began to push Ezekiel from the inside of not only the agency, but also his home.

As one of the few female agents at CTA, Jessica was granted the privilege of monthly lunches with Mrs. Cohen. It was, in Sylvia Cohen's good-hearted way, an attempt to make the shark-infested waters of CTA feel like a family-owned business. Jessica was aware that after forty years of sharing her husband with the film industry (and it wasn't a fifty-fifty split, more like twenty-eighty), Mrs. Ezekiel Cohen was ready for her husband to retire. It was at one of their monthly lunches that Jessica let drop the "rumor" she'd heard that Jeremy Sullivan was interested in buying the firm. Between Mrs. Cohen's prodding and Jessica's persistence, Ezekiel grudgingly accepted a meeting with Jeremy Sullivan. And Jeremy Sullivan, in person, was persuasive.

It'd taken only two weeks to complete the buyout once Ezekiel met with Jeremy. Jeremy got his agency, Mrs. Cohen welcomed her husband back, and Jessica jumped from junior agent to president of CTA.

Jessica and Jeremy formed an impressive team and an ideal working relationship: Each had complete trust in the skills and loyalty of the other. Jeremy, an erudite Brit, preferred to hobnob with celebrity clients while on set in exotic locales such as Greece or Spain, having little patience for the day-to-day affairs of CTA. He gave Jessica full authority to oversee the operations of what was now, thanks to her tireless efforts, the biggest agency in the world.

Jessica walked into Jeremy's corner office without bothering to have any of his three assistants announce her. She visited his office daily (when he wasn't sailing on his yacht or jetting to Spain), but she didn't often see a man sitting in front of Jeremy's desk, as she did today.

"Oh, sorry, Jeremy, I'll come back. I didn't realize you were in a meeting," she said.

"Jess, no, come in. We've been waiting for you. I believe you know Tolliver Jones."

Jessica did, in fact, know Tolliver Jones. He was a senior vice president at DTA, one of CTA's biggest rivals. She had met him years ago at a wrap party for *Gruesome,* a film she'd coproduced while still an executive for Mike Fox. Jessica remembered being unimpressed with both Tolliver's work ethic (he'd represented the director of *Gruesome,* someone Jessica believed to be exceptionally talented and completely underrepresented) and his agenting skills. A complete blowhard, during negotiations Tolliver often resorted to both lying about the amount his clients were paid and screaming at attorneys in studio business affairs.

Tolliver turned his head and rose, extending his hand toward Jessica. "Jessica, it's been too long," he said.

Jessica gazed at Tolliver's well-tanned face and blond hair. He could easily pass for a celebrity. His suit was perfectly tailored and pressed, without a crease, and she was certain his shirt was handmade. All the accoutrements of a successful agent.

Jessica shook Tolliver's hand, and an alarm bell blasted in her head. *This is not going to be good,* she thought as she sat down.

"Seems Tolliver is in the market, shall we say," Jeremy said, smiling at Jessica.

"I was telling Jeremy that my contract at DTA is up in two weeks, and I want to try something new. I've spent my entire career at one shop, and now that my client list is so exceptional, if I'm going to move, now is the time. So I came to you first. After all, why not try to play for the Yankees if you're going to play?"

"Indeed." Jeremy laughed. "Baseball; afraid I know nothing of it. But as far as us being the best in town, you'll have to thank Jessica for that. I had very little to do with it."

Tolliver's obvious disregard for protocol irritated Jessica. Tolliver knew how this town ran; he'd been in the business for at least ten years. If he wanted to move agencies, he should have come to her, as president of the company, before approaching Jeremy.

"I was telling Tolliver how CTA always has room for someone of his caliber. Especially after reviewing his client list." Jeremy held out a piece of paper. Jessica took it and scanned the names. Admittedly, it was impressive, but she knew for a fact that the majority of names on the list were not Tolliver's clients; most were represented by other agents at DTA. But when an agent jumped to a new shop, you never knew for sure which clients would come with him.

"Of course, always, if we can make a deal," Jessica said, handing the list back to Jeremy.

"Always the agent, aren't you, Jess," Tolliver said, his tone snide while he smiled. Jessica realized that he, too, knew you could say anything in Hollywood as long as you smiled. "Well, I need to get back." Tolliver stood. "I still have two weeks, and I want to make sure that my employer gets what they paid for."

Jeremy and Jessica both stood as Tolliver shook their hands in turn.

"Excellent, then. Tolliver, we'll be in touch," Jeremy said as Tolliver strolled out of the office.

Jessica watched as Jeremy read over Tolliver's supposed client list yet again, enthusiasm building on his face. "Exceptional, isn't it, Jess." Jeremy grinned as if he'd found a nugget of gold in a piece of dirt. "I think he'd be a tremendous addition to the team, especially with all these fellows."

"If the price is right. How much is the ask?"

"One-point-two."

Jessica was surprised; she thought that was actually reasonable. She doubted that Tolliver made much less money at DTA. "Really? That seems a bit low." Maybe it was a good deal.

"And copresident," Jeremy said, looking into Jessica's eyes.

"What?" Her stomach lurched. So Tolliver was after the direct access to Jeremy, and the power that being copresident of CTA provided. "Jeremy, I hardly think—"

"Come on, Jess, we discussed this, you and I, that if the right person came along, you'd be willing to share the crown, so to speak."

"Yes, if the *right* person came around. But I hardly think that Tolliver is that person. His reputation around town isn't pristine."

"Whose is? Jess, this is big, I can feel it. With this list, we'd have everyone that we wanted."

Jessica wasn't convinced, and it wasn't her ego. She truly believed that Tolliver wasn't the right fit, that he would topple the precarious balance she and Jeremy had struck. Not having come up through the trenches, Jeremy wasn't aware of how cutthroat the film business was. It was unusual to find a trustworthy counterpart within the viper's nest, and when you did, you didn't fuck around with it.

"I want this, Jess. I think it's a good move." Jeremy's enthusiasm didn't dampen even with Jessica's hesitancy. "Besides, we both know he'll be copresident in name only. You, my dear, have done too much to ever not be the one truly leading this agency."

"Jeremy, I don't know. I've always trusted your instincts, but this time it doesn't feel right to me."

Jeremy gave her his euphoric grin. "Come on, Jess, have I ever been wrong?"

Jessica brushed by the three assistants sitting outside her office. She didn't own any part of CTA, so she knew hiring Tolliver was entirely Jeremy's decision. And it appeared that the decision was already made. Jeremy had called CTA's Business Affairs attorney while she was still in his office. She'd never seen Jeremy so enthusiastic and willing to move on something so quickly. He was decisive by nature, but this bordered on impulsive. Jeramy told CTA's attorney to make a preliminary offer, with a substantial increase in the money Tolliver asked for but with a different title than copresident. Jessica knew that Tolliver would refuse. He wanted the title.

Jessica entered her office and stopped.

"What the fuck?" A sea of red flooded the room. Jessica's number one assistant, Kim, appeared beside her.

"The florist said there are exactly one thousand eight hundred and ninety-three red roses in there."

Jessica looked at Kim. "One thousand eight hundred and ninety-three? Is that number supposed to be significant to me? Did he say why?"

"Nope."

"Is there a card?" Jessica asked.

"Yep." Kim handed her a red silk envelope. "And it's sealed with wax, so you can tell if it's been opened."

"It's been opened."

"I open all your mail," Kim said. "I didn't read it."

The scent engulfed Jessica as she walked farther into the room. Every table, console, and bookcase held a bouquet. There were vases overflowing with roses packed on the floor. Jessica squeezed past them to her desk, put her finger under the silk flap, and pulled out the ecru card. The writing was in black fountain pen.

Jess:

One rose for every day I've spent without you.
Please, don't make me buy any more.

All my love,
M. Fox

Jessica's head felt like it was spinning. This had to be a joke.
She'd seen Mike at the premiere, but they hadn't slept together.
They'd barely talked. *What the hell was this?*

"Mike Fox on line one," Kim called out.

Jessica put on her wireless headset and took a deep breath.
"Are you crazy?" Jessica asked.

"Good morning to you, too," Mike said.

"I already told you that you can't have Holden for less than his
fifteen-million-dollar quote—"

"Jess—"

"He's worth every penny, and if you think some roses—"

"Jess—"

"—are going to make me change my mind . . . His last film
made—"

"JESS! This isn't about Holden."

She paused and inhaled. The sweet scent of 1,893 roses filled
her nose. *No, no, no!* This was typical Mike Fox, all show and no
substance. He'd come on like gangbusters, and then as soon as he
got bored or there was a new hottie on the cover of *Maxim* or
FHM, he'd be gone. Just like last time, no big blowout, just no
more Mike and only the photos in *People* of him canoodling in
Paris with a supermodel to keep Jessica company.

"Then what is it?"

"You got my card?"

Jess fingered the red silk envelope. "Yes."

"I'm very serious. I'm ready to settle down, be a father, a husband, a committed stand-up guy."

Jess heard a collective gasp from her three assistants sitting
outside her office. She'd forgotten they were on the line.

"There is no one else I know who would make a better wife or mother."

Jess felt tears start to form in her eyes. *A better wife or mother? Prick. Nothing about love? Not a word. And five years too late.*

Jessica stood up from her chair. "Have you fucking lost your mind? Wife and mother? For whom? You? I've spent the last five years rebuilding my life. I built the best client list in town. I've created the most respected motion picture department in the entire industry. Then you waltz in here and do this. Five years! Five *years*, Mike. Not days, not weeks, not months but *years* since we dated, and you tell me I'll make a great wife and mother? What? You think you're some great knight and I need to be rescued?

Mike laughed. "You haven't changed a bit."

"You laugh?! Did you just laugh?"

"Yes, Jess, I laughed. Don't you remember I always laugh? It's funny. You're funny. God, I still love you."

"Who do you think you are?"

"Jess."

"No, really. I want all these roses gone by lunch."

"Jess, come on—"

"I mean it. Or you will never hire another CTA client again, for any of your films."

"Jess—"

"I'm done." Jessica pushed the Release button and hung up. *What the fuck was he thinking?* She looked at the red surrounding her. She was engaged. She was planning a wedding. Living with Phil. Mike knew all that. Mike Fox might be used to getting everything he wanted, but he was not getting her. He did not get to tromp on her heart and then show up five years later and expect her to get married. He had to be back on the blow.

"Kim!" Jessica yelled. "Get in here!"

Kim appeared in Jessica's office door with a sheepish look on her face.

"Not a word. You tell the other two if I hear a peep about this from anyone, and I mean anyone, you're all fired. Got it?"

"Got it."

"Can you believe this?" Jessica said, deflated.

"He's pretty cool, isn't he?" Kim said.

Jess glanced at her. "Don't believe all the hype. Get on the phone and start calling retirement homes. I want all of these gone by the time I'm back from the screening. Have the trainees in the mailroom deliver them."

"Okay."

Jess picked up her Prada bag. She had ten minutes to get to Summit to watch a screening of *Never So Faithful.*

"Jess, Lydia called while you were on with Mike. She found Zymar."

"Really? What else?"

"Their start date is Monday. She's having a dinner at Koi on Friday night. Wanted you to come by."

"Call her and tell her yes. Book it into my schedule." Jess glanced over her shoulder and into her office as she stood at the private elevator next to her third assistant's desk.

"I'm not kidding," she said. "Get rid of those fucking flowers."

12

Mary Anne and Her Chloe Leather Sandals

MARY ANNE PULLED HER WHITE 500 SL MERCEDES CONVERTIBLE UP TO THE valet at Koi (the trendiest sushi restaurant in L.A.). She was third in line, behind two black Range Rovers. And there was a Jaguar behind her. Busy night, but it was eight-thirty P.M. on a Friday. Lydia had rented out the entire back room. A good-luck sushi celebration, she called it, for the cast, the director, and the writer. About fifteen people were coming.

Beeeep. Mary Anne looked in her rearview mirror. Some asshole in a 1972 T-Top Trans Am (she only knew because she'd seen *Smokey and the Bandit* four times when she was a kid) pulled in two cars behind Mary Anne and was honking his horn. Mary Anne watched as the driver popped his head out of the T-Top and yelled.

"You people know who I am? Come on already! I'm hungry."

What a jerk. The valet pulled open Mary Anne's door. Sweat dripped down the side of his cheek.

"Busy night?"

He smiled. "Welcome to Koi."

"Hey, what the fuck? This isn't social hour! Take her car. Go! Go! Go!" yelled the asshole.

Mary Anne gave the valet an I'm-so-sorry-people-are-assholes look as she handed over her keys.

"God, honey. No wonder you're alone, if you're that slow!"

That was enough abuse for Mary Anne. She stepped out onto the street and squinted toward the low-hanging headlights of the Trans Am. Standing there, she glared, giving the driver what she believed to be her dirtiest look. Suddenly she heard the screech of tires and the roar of an engine.

The light blinded her as the Trans Am barreled toward her. *Oh my God!* she thought as she fell to the pavement.

Ma'am! Ma'am, are you all right?"

Mary Anne lay facedown on the asphalt. She could see dozens of shoes in front of her.

"Can you move? Can you hear me?"

"Should we call an ambulance?"

"Oh my God. Oh my God."

"Did you see that idiot?"

"Did anyone get a license plate?"

The valet knelt beside her and tilted his head. "Ma'am. Are you okay? Can you move?"

Mary Anne rolled to her right side. Her head hurt. And the palms of her hands stung. "Yeah. Um. I can move." She sat up. Three guys lifted her from the pavement.

Mary Anne glanced at the crowd. She was embarrassed to get so much attention. She looked down at her feet. She was missing a shoe. An older man handed her the Chloe leather sandal (a gift from Cici), which he'd retrieved from the center of La Brea.

"Thank you," Mary Anne whispered, unable to meet his gaze.

"Come inside. Do you want an ambulance?" the valet asked gently.

"No. Inside please?"

A woman handed Mary Anne her Stella McCartney bag.

"Thank you," Mary Anne said as she clutched her purse and hopped along in one shoe.

* * *

Mary Anne sat in the general manager's office holding a tepid glass of water between her knees, gauze wrapped around the scrapes on her palms. Her head ached. The manager wanted to call an ambulance, but all Mary Anne wanted was for somebody to find Lydia. Mary Anne glanced at the mirror across the room. Her hair was a mess, and there were black streaks from her eyes to her chin, not from asphalt or dirt but from crying. She couldn't stop the tears, even when she talked to the cops. She was alive. No permanent damage, no stitches, nothing serious. Mary Anne didn't remember diving out of the Trans Am's path, but it happened so fast, and she felt as if she'd come so close to something truly terrible. The irony wasn't lost on Mary Anne: How cruel to get everything you've ever wanted and then get killed outside the hippest restaurant in L.A.?

Mary Anne heard the clipping of stiletto heels on tile.

"Where is she?" Lydia asked.

But Lydia wasn't alone; it sounded like a herd right outside the office door. God, she didn't want an audience. Mary Anne just wanted to tell Lydia and leave.

"Has anyone called the police?" Jessica demanded.

"Yes, ma'am, she's already spoken with the police. They're interviewing people out front now."

"What about an ambulance?" Lydia asked.

"Ms. Albright, she refused. We offered."

Mary Anne sat motionless, listening to them discuss her. It was just like being a seven-year-old again, vulnerable and wounded. The door opened.

"Oh my God. Baby, are you all right?!" Cici rushed to Mary Anne and grabbed her out of the chair.

"Yes," Mary Anne whispered. She pulled away from Cici and sat back down.

Lydia sat in the chair next to Mary Anne. "Sweetie, I think you should go to Cedars just to get checked out. We'll take you to the celebrity suite. You'll be in and out in forty-five minutes. I promise. Just to be on the safe side."

Jessica stood at the door talking on her cell phone. "Get me Mayor Rosenman. Yes. Tell him that it's Jessica Caulfield. I need him to get the chief of police on the phone. I don't care who the fuck he's with. We've got some crazy guy trying to run over people in Beverly Hills. Uh-huh. Well, you tell him when he's finished with his *massage* to give me a call. Yeah, he's got my number."

Cici rifled through her Prada bag and pulled out a brush and a tiny makeup clutch. "Here. I can fix you up in two minutes. I know I never feel good when I don't look good." Cici unclipped Mary Anne's hair and started to brush it back into an up-do.

Lydia leaned forward. "So, Cedars?" she asked in a soft voice.

"Really, I think I'll go home. I just wanted to see you before I left."

"Home? No way. You're coming and staying at my place," Cici said, putting a turquoise rhinestone clip into Mary Anne's hair. "What if you've got some brain thing or something? If you won't go to the hospital, you have to at least come and stay at my house."

"I really just want to go home and go to bed—"

"Cici might be right," Lydia said. "Besides, you guys only live a half mile from each other."

"It will make us all feel better," Cici said.

"I cannot believe this shit," Jessica said, pacing in the doorway.

Cici leaned forward and whispered in Mary Anne's ear, "Don't mind her. Jessica likes control. It's tough for her when she can't fix everything."

Lydia handed Mary Anne a tissue. "Don't worry. I got shot once. You'll stop crying in a couple of days. The near-death thing is really a wallop."

"Shot?" Mary Anne asked.

"Story for another time. Promise." Lydia glanced over Mary Anne's head and gave Cici a half smile.

"Okay, so the hair and makeup are good. Come on, let's get you a drink," Cici said.

"I want to go home."

"The manager is calling my driver, but it's going to be twenty minutes at least. He's playing poker with some buddies in West Hollywood. I told him I'd be here all night. So until he gets here, let's go back to our room and have a drink."

"But I look so—" Mary Anne glanced across the room into the mirror and stopped speaking. Actually, she looked . . . *amazing*.

Cici leaned in and placed her hand on Mary Anne's shoulder. "Had to do my own makeup and hair on some of my early movies. I know a couple of tricks. Let's get that drink."

There she is. Our little survivor!" Zymar said, and hugged Mary Anne. "You going to make it, then?"

Mary Anne smiled. She'd met Zymar in person only twice before, but had been speaking on the phone with him about character and script notes five times a day since his return from Bali. Next week, on set, they'd see each other every day. She liked him. He was quick and fun and full of mischief. Mary Anne suspected that Zymar had eyes for Lydia, but she didn't think Lydia had figured that out yet.

"Vodka tonic for this one, light on the tonic," Zymar told one of their waiters. "You know, I was once run over by a truck."

"And you're still alive?" Mary Anne said, feeling tears sting the back of her eyes.

"Story for another time." He squeezed Mary Anne's arm. "So the lot is here. At least all the important ones." Zymar and Mary Anne turned and surveyed the guests.

Across the room stood Bradford Madison. Mary Anne tried not to stare. The son of a superstar father and an exotic European model, Bradford was entertainment royalty, the third generation of Madisons to be Hollywood leading men. Zymar caught and followed Mary Anne's gaze.

"There's Bradford," Zymar said, grinning. " 'Ave you met him, then?"

"No, not really," Mary Anne mumbled, mesmerized by the

star. She'd seen him at the most recent read-through, but they'd never spoken.

"Eh, Lyd. Don't monopolize the boy," Zymar called. "'E's never met the writer. Bring 'im over."

Bradford sauntered toward Mary Anne, Lydia trailing behind. *God, he was beautiful*. Perfect teeth. Perfect smile. Perfect dark hair and chocolate-colored eyes. Mary Anne felt her legs start to tremble. She hadn't been this starstruck since she met Cici.

"Bradford Madison, meet the woman who's been putting words in your mouth. Mary Anne Meyers," Zymar said, grinning.

"Mary Anne. Beautiful name. My first crush in grade school was named Mary Anne."

Mary Anne couldn't speak. She knew the silence was painful, but she couldn't think of anything to say and doubted that even if she did have something clever to talk about, she would be able to form the words. Mary Anne stared at Bradford, the uncomfortable silence growing.

"Well, so what 'ave you two been talking about?" Zymar asked, trying to cover for Mary Anne.

"Seems Bradford just bought himself a new toy," Lydia said, smiling.

"Yeah, you know I've always wanted one, and when I saw this beauty in perfect condition, I just had to have her. And the price was right. Man, she can really fly."

"Fly?" Zymar said. "I didn't know you flew. That used to be me 'obby, too—well, until the crash I 'ad in '97. Since then I just let the professionals keep'm in the air."

"No, man, no. I'm talking about my sweet new ride," said Bradford, a grin lighting up his face. "You a *Smokey and the Bandit* fan?" Bradford looked at Mary Anne. "Figure as good as you write, you must have seen that one. The Trans Am, man. The hot ride. I just bought an exact replica. Set me back—"

Mary Anne couldn't hear any words. There was a roaring in her ears. The room became dark and started to spin. She felt cold; she was slipping, slipping. . . .

"Mary Anne!" she heard Cici scream.

* * *

Mary Anne's head throbbed. Her tongue felt swollen and stuck to the roof of her mouth. *Did I drink that much?* She shifted her weight and felt a tug on her right side. As she opened her eyes, she glanced toward where the clock normally rested on her night-stand. But there was no clock. This definitely wasn't her room. The sensation was one of being in a different life. *Where was she?* She glanced at the navy blue velvet drapes on the window and soft pink marble tile. *How did she get into a hotel?* She looked around the room. *Why did a hotel have a heart monitor and an IV bag? And why was she connected to both?* Her eyes finally focused on the darkened far corner of her room, and there, slumping side by side on a plush couch, were Zymar and Lydia. Mary Anne blinked, her eyes seeing into the darkness. Zymar's head was thrown back over the couch, gurgling snores emanating from his open mouth. Lydia's dark hair spilled over Zymar's chest as her head rested on his shoulder.

Why are they in my hotel room? Mary Anne's groggy mind worked it over as the door to her room opened.

"She's awake," she heard someone whisper, and then she heard a soft beeping noise. "Hello there," Jessica said, walking toward the bed and slipping her BlackBerry into her purse.

"Where—" Mary Anne tried again to sit up in bed.

"Hey, no, don't. You're okay. You're at Cedars," Jessica said, placing her hand on Mary Anne's arm.

Cedars? "The hospital?" Mary Anne warbled. Her thick tongue wouldn't move properly.

"You passed out at Koi."

Mary Anne closed her eyes. Memories of the night began to crawl through her mind.

"What time?" she managed to get out.

"It's around midnight." Jessica perched gently on the bed. "The doctor said you should be fine. Slight concussion from the first fall, but the second, well, he caught you," she said, nodding toward the snoozing Zymar.

"How are you feeling?" she asked, and reached out to brush a stray strand of hair off Mary Anne's face.

"Woozy," Mary Anne whispered through her parched lips, "and thirsty."

Jessica stood and poured water into a glass from a crystal pitcher on the nightstand. She lifted it to Mary Anne's mouth.

"Little sips," she said, still holding the glass.

The water was cool, the dryness in Mary Anne's mouth washing away.

"Thank you," she whispered.

"You gave us quite a scare," Jessica said.

"Bradford, he was the one driving the car," Mary Anne murmured. She sank back into her pillow.

"Yeah." Jessica glanced at her hands. "So what do you want to do about that?"

What did she want to do? Didn't people who commit a hit-and-run (or a near-miss-and-run) go to jail?

"I can call the police," Jessica said, then paused, "but if I do"—she looked up and into Mary Anne's eyes—"there won't be a movie."

No movie? How could there be no movie? "Can't they get someone else?"

Jessica shook her head. "The new president of Worldwide, Arnold Murphy, doesn't really want to make *Seven Minutes Past Midnight,* but the studio is already in pretty deep, at least financially, so he doesn't have much of a choice. But if Bradford gets bumped for violating his probation"—Jessica crossed her arms over her chest—"it'll push our start date, everything gets rescheduled. Cici has another gig in three months, so we may lose her. Zymar is supposed to do another film later this year, so then he's gone. If the film doesn't start on Monday, well, then there might not be a film. It gives Arnold a lot of ammunition to shelve the whole project."

"And Lydia?" Mary Anne looked toward Zymar and Lydia asleep on the couch.

Jessica sighed. "She'll be a lame duck, at least at Worldwide. She probably won't get another film into production there until Arnold leaves. Her overall deal is up after the first of the year, so she'll move studios, but *Seven Minutes Past Midnight* is the film that's meant to put her back on top."

Mary Anne closed her eyes. The pain beat a rhythm inside her forehead above her right eye.

"Also, you won't get your fee," Jessica said, shifting her weight on the bed. "You keep the money you've gotten so far, and we'll probably be able to get you paid for a couple weeks of production work because of the late notice, but you won't get the five-hundred-thousand-dollar production bonus, or the seventy-five-thousand weekly fee for production writing, and . . ."

"And?"

"Well, two things. First, to have written a screenplay that's actually become a film is a huge thing, as far as your career as a screenwriter is concerned. Both in terms of the work you'll be offered and the money you'll make."

Money? It somehow seemed silly to talk about money while Mary Anne lay in a hospital bed strapped to an IV.

"And the second?" Mary Anne whispered.

"Well, it's a small town, and it's never a good thing for your career to be the reason why a big star goes to jail and a movie falls apart." Jessica pursed her lips and raised both her eyebrows. "It's a lot like high school; nobody wants to hang around with a tattletale."

"A tattletale?" She could feel tears again. *Bradford Madison came a half-inch away from hitting her with his "sweet new ride" and she was the tattletale?*

Jessica leaned forward. "Oh, sweetie, I'm not saying that's what you are, I'm just saying that's how it might be perceived."

Mary Anne fought to keep her composure. So these were her choices: ignore her near-death experience, go to work on set with Bradford Madison every day, and pretend nothing happened, or never work in Hollywood again. Mary Anne exhaled.

She glanced across the room at Zymar and Lydia. "Don't call," Mary Anne whispered.

"Okay," Jessica said. "Good choice."

Mary Anne heard a snort and a cough from the direction of the couch.

"She's awake." Zymar nudged a sleeping Lydia.

"Wha—" Lydia's head bobbed up and she rubbed her right eye. "Oh, Mary Anne."

Mary Anne watched as a sleepy smile crossed Lydia's lips. Both she and Zymar stretched and stood.

"I see you'll pull through, then." Zymar walked toward the bed.

"Celeste told me she was tough," Jessica said.

"She'd know it. Cici could eat nails if she wanted to," Zymar said.

Mary Anne lifted her hand to her forehead. There was a gauze above her right eye.

"Now, don't blame me for that," Zymar said. "I caught you at Koi, but seems you got in a bit of a fisticuffs with a nurse in the emergency room. Don't like redheads much, do you?"

"Two stitches." Lydia stood next to Zymar.

"Probably why you're so groggy."

"Good drugs." Zymar grinned. "The real stuff in the 'ospital."

Jessica stifled a small laugh.

"She's awake?"

Mary Anne glanced to her right, where a tall blond woman wearing scrubs was walking toward her. "Hello, Mary Anne, I'm Dr. Raker." She pulled out a small flashlight and peered into Mary Anne's eyes. "You seem pretty good. How do you feel?"

"My head hurts."

"You conked it twice," Dr. Raker said, checking Mary Anne's pulse. "You're quite a little fighter."

Mary Anne felt a flush creeping into her face. She was embarrassed; she couldn't remember anything she'd said or done after meeting Bradford Madison at Koi, and that included her fistfight in the emergency room.

"Sorry," Mary Anne said meekly.

"Don't worry about it. But look out, whoever the redhead is that made you mad." She smiled.

"Please tell the nurse I am so sorry."

"I will." Dr. Raker looked across the bed at Jessica, Lydia, and Zymar. "So she's good, but she needs her rest."

"When will she be released?" Jessica asked.

"I'll check in again tomorrow morning. If everything looks okay, we'll discharge her around eleven. Go home, get some rest, let Mary Anne sleep, come back in the morning."

"I'll be here at nine," Jessica announced.

"And I'll meet you at your house," Lydia said, following Jessica to the door.

"And I'll see you on Monday," Zymar said. He tapped Mary Anne lightly on the arm, leaned in and whispered, "You know, this means we'll make a fantastic fucking film! Always good when we get a bit of drama before we start shooting." He gave her a wink and turned toward the door.

A melancholy swept through Mary Anne as they filed out of her room. So this was her Hollywood life. A new language, new friends . . . a new set of rules. Cici's words on the ride home from Ferragamo chimed in Mary Anne's head.

"It's a compromise," Cici had said. "With the paparazzi, with the press, with the studios, with the producers, with myself. They need me, and I need them. You'd be surprised what you can learn to accept."

Mary Anne closed her eyes. Her head hurt.

13

Celeste Solange and the
Cowboy Boots on Egyptian Cotton

CELESTE MARCHED INTO HER TRAILER AND SLAMMED THE DOOR SHUT BEHIND her. Bradford Madison was a dumbass. First he almost killed their writer (thank God Mary Anne hadn't pressed charges), then he consistently arrived two hours late for his seven A.M. call time (while the rest of the cast and crew, including Celeste, waited around for him to show up), and now he didn't know his lines. Celeste didn't care if he was third-generation Hollywood royalty. It was bullshit. She knew it, Lydia knew it, Zymar knew it, and Celeste was going to make sure that Bradford knew it, too.

Seven Minutes Past Midnight was only seven days into production and already three days behind in the shooting schedule. If Bradford didn't pull his head out of his ass and get it together, this film was going in the shitter.

Celeste sat in front of her makeup mirror and pulled off her wig. If it wasn't Lydia's film, she would walk off the set right now. She'd have Jessica call Arnold Murphy and tell him to go fuck himself. But that would ruin Lydia's career and make Arnold Murphy cackle with glee. Celeste heard a knock on her trailer door.

"Cici, it's me," Lydia called.

"Enter at your own risk."

Lydia held a cell phone in one hand and a bottle of bourbon in the other.

"Thought you could use one of these," Lydia said, offering up the bottle.

There was a reason Lydia was Celeste's good friend. Just when she wanted to cuss out the producer on this fucking film (which could ruin all their careers), Lydia showed up with Celeste's favorite bourbon.

"He's killing your movie. And your star," Celeste said. She started removing the thick makeup that had been spackled on hours before.

"I know. I know. It's been a rough couple of days."

"Rough?! Lyd, this is not rough. This is fucked up. This is taking it up the ass because some pissant cock can't keep his shit together. He's doing a better job of fucking up your film than Arnold ever could."

Lydia poured bourbon into two crystal glasses, walked over to Celeste, and set the tumbler down on the vanity in front of Celeste's makeup mirror.

"I don't care who his father was, Lyd, he needs to pull his head out of his ass and act professional."

"He's got the goods, Cici."

"Only when he knows his fucking lines. He hasn't been doing it long enough to fake it. If he doesn't know his lines, he can't do shit." Celeste threw a tissue on the vanity and took a swig of bourbon.

"You're right."

"Look, I get paid either way. And my performance is solid. But you? Lyd, Arnold will jump all over you if this tanks or you go over budget. And Zymar? Come on. After his last film? If this one doesn't hit, he's done."

Lydia sighed and sat down on the chaise behind Celeste.

"Is he on the blow again?" Celeste asked.

"Zymar watches him every day. I'm around him some evenings. Plus—and I'll deny that I ever told you this—his probation requires he take tox screens, and so far they've all come back clean."

"If he's using his own piss."

Lydia sipped her bourbon. "I guess we could get him a sitter."

"That cock? He'll never agree to it."

"It's in his contract. The only way we could get the film insured was if Bradford agreed to a sitter clause."

Celeste stopped scrubbing her face and looked at Lydia in the makeup mirror. "So what are you waiting for? Call Jess and get her to call his agent and tell him that you're getting Bradford a babysitter."

"Arnold."

"What?"

"The minute I do that, Arnold will know we're in trouble. He'll smell blood and be all over us."

"Like a set visit two times a day by Jojo the Monkey-Faced Girl isn't all over us already?" Celeste asked.

"I know, but there are all kinds of things he could do. Require us to find a new star. Reshoots. New start date. The whole film gets pushed. If he really thinks Bradford is impaired, he could shut us down."

"Fine! Fine, fine. I'll do it."

"Do what?" Lydia asked.

"I'll do it. I'll watch him."

"Cici, I wasn't suggesting that at all. I was just—"

"Look, I'm a producer on this film, too, and I want to pull my weight. And I know actors. Tell the little fuck he has to stay at my house."

"What about Damien? He'll flip, you know—"

"Lyd." Celeste paused and looked into the makeup mirror. "Damien moved out."

"What? Oh, Cici, why didn't you tell me?"

"The day we started shooting. I came home from set and all his clothes were gone. He left me a note, though. Good guy, huh."

"I'm so sorry. I didn't know."

"Save it. It's better this way. He's a bad man. Besides, I'm taking all his money, and right now he's miserable. He's staying in Silver Lake at Brie's house, and she's got six cats."

"Isn't he allergic?"

"Deathly. I hope he dies. Especially before he changes his will."

"How you doing?"

"Okay. The house is big, old, and lonely. Poor Mary Anne, she ends up staying with me four nights a week. I'm always enticing her with something. That's another thing." Celeste turned away from her makeup mirror and faced Lydia. "Do you think that little peckerhead even realizes how close he came to killing someone? Or at the very least going to jail for the third time?"

"She's a saint."

"Yes, she is. Because if I were writing his lines, after all that shit he'd be down to monosyllabic ape sounds."

Lydia arched her eyebrow and looked at Celeste in the mirror.

"Oh, I forgot—we are down to monosyllabic ape sounds. But he *has* lines. So tell him. It's my house every night but Saturday."

"Starting when?"

"Starting now. We're going to be running his lines tonight. Until he gets them. Plus, I'm drafting a set of house rules for him."

"He's not going to like this."

"Too fucking bad. You tell him I know his grandfather, and if he doesn't comply, that's my first call," Celeste said.

Lydia smiled.

"It'll scare the shit out of him. That old man can still kick some ass. Who do you think confiscated his Trans Am?"

"Got it."

"He can meet me at the car in twenty minutes."

Lydia stood at the trailer's door. "Thanks, Cici."

"Yeah. Wait till tomorrow. If Bradford comes to work, then thank me."

Celeste opened the door to the guest suite in the east wing of her Hollywood Hills home.

"This is your room. The bathroom is connected. It should be stocked with everything you need. Towels, toothpaste, soap. If it's missing anything, just let me or Mathilde know."

She watched Bradford throw his Louis Vuitton duffel on the floor and check out the room. He stopped at the plasma television on the wall.

"The cable is the full package. It's all wired to our digital-media library. We've got two thousand films stored. You can watch them whenever you want. The computer has Internet; feel free to hook up your own laptop." Celeste turned toward the walk-in closet and slid open the cherrywood-and-glass-panel door. "Now, this is nice. It's lined with cedar and has silk hangers," she called. Bradford didn't respond. *Maybe he's using the toilet,* Celeste thought. *Or he's tried to run away.* She walked toward the door.

"I thought we'd run our lines—" She stopped and looked at Bradford.

He stood in the center of the king-size bed, naked (except for black snakeskin cowboy boots). His dick was erect and he stroked it with his right hand.

"Well, come on, then. I know this story about lines and acting is bullshit. This is why I'm captive in your house, isn't it?" Bradford said, with a bored look on his face.

Celeste fumed. *Who did this infant think he was?* First of all, she'd seen bigger cocks on midgets. Second, everything about Bradford was the biggest turnoff in the world. His self-obsessed nihilistic bravado overwhelmed even his impressive good looks. *For fuck sake. Once you started sleeping with a real man, a true adult, children like Bradford were just impossible.*

"You've got to want it. Brie told me Damien's been at her house for the last week," Bradford said, and flopped down on the bed, landing his ass on the mattress.

No wonder. Bradford was traveling in the Brie Ellison circle. Young Hollywood: obnoxious, oversexed, overpaid, under-achieving postadolescent children. Actually, though—Bradford could come in handy. With the divorce just around the corner, Celeste could use a spy. *A little inside information.* Better not piss Bradford off by telling him about his tiny penis size.

"Bradford," Celeste said, fluttering her eyelids, playing the starstruck star. "It really is very tempting. But, growing up in this town, surely you know I never, ever sleep with my costar."

"I thought that was bullshit."

"Sometimes after, but never during." Celeste sat on the edge of the bed and leaned toward Bradford. "Although with you it is very, very hard to resist." With his ego, he was such an easy mark.

"I know," Bradford said, and flexed his bicep. "I don't think you'll make it through the whole shoot, especially with me staying here."

"Well, at least let me make it through one night," Celeste said. "Why don't you put on some clothes and come downstairs."

"I'm hungry. You cooking?"

"Mathilde will serve dinner in about an hour. Bring down your script pages for tomorrow and we'll run lines and have a drink."

"I know my lines," he said, reaching for the TV remote.

"Of course you do, lover, but what about me? Didn't you see how I struggled today? You don't want me to have a horrible day tomorrow, too," Celeste said. She should win an Oscar for this performance.

Bradford smiled. "Babe, for you, of course." He rolled off the bed and reached for his Armani jeans.

"Thanks," Celeste said, and walked toward the bedroom door. "Oh, and Bradford?"

He looked up from pulling his jeans on over his boots. "Yeah?"

"From now on, leave your cowboy boots at the front door."

Lydia and the Stella McCartney Pumps

LYDIA LOUNGED ON A SUEDE RECLINER (ONE OF TWELVE) IN HER HOME
screening room, waiting for the lights to come up. So far, after
four weeks of shooting, the dailies had been brilliant. The color,
the performances, the camera angles, all exceptional. Zymar
made a great director . . . as well as a great lover. A wicked smile
curled across Lydia's lips. She knew that the first rule of producing was to never fuck your star, so she hadn't. Besides, who really
wanted to have sex with Bradford Madison other than Bradford
Madison? With his ego, there wouldn't be room for anyone else
in the bed. Instead, Lydia slept with the director.

It'd been a month since Lydia woke up alone. Thirty glorious
nights. Ever since Bradford almost killed Mary Anne at Koi.
Lydia and Zymar had spent some tense moments in the back of
the ambulance with Mary Anne in and out of consciousness.

"She looks so pale," Lydia had whispered.

"Gray," Zymar said. "Sickly gray."

He was right. Mary Anne's eyes fluttered open.

"Steve? Where's Steve?" Mary Anne asked.

Lydia leaned forward and reached for Mary Anne's hand.
"Honey, you're okay. We're in an ambulance—"

"But where's Steve?" Mary Anne asked, with wild-eyed terror.

" 'Oo is Steve?" Zymar asked.

"Honey, is Steve someone you want me to call?" Lydia asked.

"He's fucking Viève," Mary Anne whimpered, then closed her eyes.

" 'Oo's Viève?" Zymar whispered into Lydia's ear.

"You've got as much information as I do," Lydia whispered back.

By the time Lydia and Zymar left Cedars Sinai, Lydia was exhausted. It was a shorter distance to Zymar's hotel than to her home (at least that's what Lydia told herself), and so much less lonely.

Once in Zymar's room, Lydia went to the bathroom to take out her contacts (years on a movie set taught her to always carry an extra case—you never knew for sure where you might end up sleeping).

"Lydia, you take the bed," Zymar called.

"The couch is fine," she said, walking out of the bathroom as Zymar pulled off his shirt.

Lydia stood and stared. For a director, he had a hell of a body. His torso was lean and well muscled, like that of a rock climber or swimmer, his chest hair beginning to turn silver. She glanced at the couch that Zymar had already made up for one of them. Did she really believe either of them would be sleeping there?

"Lyd, found a T-shirt for you." He handed her the shirt, his own chest bare. He stood so close to her, too close. She wondered if he could feel the heat he was causing inside of her.

Zymar looked down at her. "You look tired," he said, running his fingers through her chestnut-colored hair.

She tilted her head. Zymar moved closer, his cock pressing against her. He put his hand behind her head, firmly tilted her face toward him, and pressed his lips to hers. His kiss wasn't soft; in fact, it was a little rough, but Lydia liked it that way.

He slid his hand down the back of her pants, cupping her ass and pressing her body against him. Lydia unbuttoned his jeans and slipped her hand into his pants and grasped his cock. A low moan escaped Zymar's lips and Lydia grew wetter.

Zymar lifted her and Lydia straddled him, grasping him around the neck as they moved toward the bed. He flipped Lydia onto all fours as he dropped her onto the comforter. He unsnapped her pants, pulled them over her ass, and then reached around and with two fingers gently massaged her clit.

Zymar leaned forward over Lydia's back. "I want to fuck you," his husky voice rasped in Lydia's ear.

"Then fuck me," she hissed, taking a deep breath.

He spread her legs with his knee and gave her a sharp slap on the ass just as he thrust his cock into her. Lydia moaned. She was going to come fast; she loved it rough.

Four weeks later, the thought of that night still made Lydia wet. She tried to get Zymar out of her thoughts, but it was impossible. He was loud, obnoxious, oversexed Eurotrash, but God, he was fun. That damn accent. *That accent and his blue eyes.* This, their ongoing fling, was good, bordering on fantastic. She hadn't experienced such good sex with such an interesting and entertaining man in almost ten years. Weston was Lydia's last phenomenal affair, but that was the first time around.

She heard her BlackBerry give a soft beep. She picked it up and clicked on the phone. "Hello, Lydia Albright."

"Ms. Albright, this is Madeline Darmides."

"Uh-huh, yes." *Who?* "How can I help you?"

"I'm trying to contact Zymar."

"Oh, yes, Zymar. He's directing my film. He should be here soon, in about an hour."

"Okay. Well, this is his wife, and I just wanted to tell him that his daughter, Christina, is on her way to L.A."

Lydia closed her eyes and inhaled. *Relax.* "Really?" she said. "I didn't know he had a daughter."

She's my *ex*-wife," Zymar said, leaning against Lydia's kitchen sink. "E-X, ex. She's Greek Orthodox, it's hard for her to say the word. In her mind we'll always be married. But we *are* divorced."

"In what country?" Lydia sat at the table in her lavish, never-once-used kitchen. She didn't see the humor. Sure, she and Zymar weren't engaged, or even really living together, and it had only been four weeks. But still. You'd think if a man was truly interested, he might have mentioned an ex-wife and a kid.

"How old is Christina?"

"Twenty-one."

"What were you, twelve when you had her?"

"That was part of the reason for the marriage. 'Er mother was sixteen."

"And you?"

"Eighteen."

"That's legal in Greece?"

"Marriage seemed like a much better option at the time than jail."

Lydia glanced over her cup of ginseng tea. Finally, some of the much-delayed details.

"I was traveling abroad. Me grandfather on me mum's side lived in Greece. I spent the summer there. And like a lot of eighteen-year-olds, I met a girl. And well, there you 'ave it."

"How long were you married?"

"Four years. Neither of us was very 'appy."

"And Christina?"

"She always lived with her mum in Greece. Smart girl. She's at Oxford. Studying business or some such thing. She'll graduate next spring."

"Did you see her much while she was growing up?"

"As much as I could. Her mum remarried twice and I did—"

"And she still tells people that she's your wife?"

"Well, she's widowed now. Suppose it's back to me now that both of them are dead, and I'm the only one alive."

"Got it."

"So I saw Christina some. 'Olidays. In between films and commercials. She came to a lot of my sets. Seemed to have fun."

Lydia nodded.

"Did you get the info for when she gets in, then?"

"Uh-huh. Wrote it all down. It's on the refrigerator."

"Thanks, Lyd. What time?"

"Couple of hours."

"I better snap to if I'm going to make it to LAX."

Lydia blew on her tea. "I sent a car and a driver."

"What?"

"I thought it'd be helpful. I can call them back, I just . . . I didn't know for sure and . . ."

"Lyd, it's fine. She'll probably love it. Think it's very L.A. or something."

"You need to call them and tell them where to drop her off," Lydia said, eyeing Zymar.

"I see."

"Well, I didn't know. I didn't know for sure that you weren't still married to Christina's mother until just five minutes ago."

"Right. We'll just stay at the 'otel, then."

"Oh."

"Unless you want us to stay 'ere?"

"I'd love that."

"Really? Lyd, I don't know 'ow long Christina will be 'ere. It could be till the end of the shoot."

"I don't mind."

"You sure?"

"I'm sure. If you don't mind."

"Good by me," Zymar said, making his way across the kitchen and wrapping his arms around Lydia.

"What about Christina?" Lydia asked.

"Hmm. Now, that's a fair question. I 'aven't really brought 'ome anyone to the daughter before." Zymar nuzzled his lips against Lydia's neck. "Nothing quite so serious in a long time."

"Really? Serious, huh." Lydia whispered, letting her hand run down the bulge in Zymar's pants.

"Pretty serious."

"Well, I guess she ought to know, then."

"Well, I guess so," Zymar said, and leaned in and kissed Lydia. Yeah. It was phenomenal.

* * *

The woman standing in Lydia's living room was breathtaking: black hair, dark brown eyes, and olive skin. Wearing Stella McCartney pumps and a matching bag. You'd never know that Christina Darmides had spent the last nine hours on a plane. Lydia noticed a faint resemblance to Zymar around her eyes. She couldn't help but wonder how beautiful Christina's mother must be.

"You're Lydia," Christina said, giving Lydia a disarming smile. "Dad's disappeared with my bags."

"So nice to meet you," Lydia said. "Can I get you anything? How was your flight?"

"Good. A little bumpy on the landing, though. Thank you for the car—Dad mentioned you sent it."

"My pleasure."

"Dad says that the film is going quite well. You know, I read the script on the flight over. I'm not familiar with the writer, but it's quite good. And Bradford Madison is starring?"

"Yes." Lydia motioned for Christina to sit and then sat in one of the chairs opposite the couch. Christina's knowledge about the details of *Seven Minutes Past Midnight* surprised her. "Do you read a lot of scripts?"

"Actually, I do. I'm quite keen on USC's Stark School for producers once I'm finished with Oxford. I'm meeting with the director while I'm here. I try to read everything."

"That's a great start," Lydia said, knowing that the best producers, agents, and executives were the ones who read every script in town. "Stark is a great program." The program was fantastic, but it didn't accelerate the path for producers or studio execs. They were still destined to be overeducated assistants for a minimum of two years, perhaps longer, upon graduation. Unless, of course, they found a great script, got some independent financing, and made a film that got a good buzz around town. The holy trinity.

"I'm hoping to spend most of my time in L.A. on set with Dad—that is, if it's okay with the producer." Christina gave Lydia a grin.

"I think that would be great," Lydia said. "We need all the help we can get."

"You've met, then," Zymar said, entering the living room.

Lydia watched Christina look at her father with admiration. Despite the distance and odd work schedule, Christina seemed to adore him.

"I think I'm off to bed." Lydia rose to leave. She wanted to give Christina and Zymar some time alone together. She'd have time to get to know the girl.

"Well, then." Zymar leaned forward and gave Lydia an awkward peck on the cheek.

Lydia smiled. Zymar seemed flummoxed by having both Lydia and Christina in the same room. It was adorable.

"Good night, Lydia," Christina called as Lydia made her way up the stairs. "And thank you."

With or without the Stark program, just by virtue of being Zymar's daughter Christina could easily become a producer. In fact, Lydia thought the graduate program might be a waste of Christina's time. If she asked, Lydia would tell her to skip it and start looking for the perfect script. Lydia was sure that if Christina truly wanted to produce, between Jessica, Zymar, Cici, and herself, they could get her started. *I am a control freak*, Lydia thought.

As she slipped into bed, Lydia listened to the sounds of animated chatter and Zymar's infectious chuckle drifting up from downstairs. She loved the noise.

15

Jessica and Her
Dior Mary Janes

THE WIND WHIPPED THROUGH JESSICA'S HAIR. SHE DIDN'T LIKE RIDING IN convertibles. Take that back—she didn't like riding in Phil's convertible when Phil drove. He was a shitty driver. Accelerate and brake, accelerate and brake (very similar to when they fucked). Her stomach felt as if the seared ahi tuna she'd eaten for lunch in Carmel might reappear.

This weekend was meant to be a combo getaway-slash-work weekend for Phil. He was working on new GPS software, and he'd brought his laptop so he could plot their trip-progress data and cross-reference their position with the software. It was the only way Phil could expense part of the trip to the company and write the other part off on his taxes. It wasn't as if they couldn't afford the trip or that he couldn't take the time off; it was that Phil was as disciplined (cheap) with cash and tax deductions as he was organized.

Usually their weekends were spent at Jess's house in L.A. Except for Saturday night. Saturday night they always went to Morton's (thousands of restaurants in L.A., but the only one Phil would go to). But this weekend was their Pacific Coast Highway weekend. So at exactly 6:05 A.M. Saturday morning (per Phil's itinerary), they climbed into Phil's Z4 and headed up the coast, making their scheduled stops.

They had planned this little coastal getaway for the last two months. Or at least Phil had planned it, down to every detail. Every minute. Every break. God forbid spontaneity. Phil loathed it (which spoke volumes about their sex life). Phil had even provided Jessica with a laminated itinerary, in a waterproof travel folder (according to Phil, you never knew when there might be spills in the car). He had also e-mailed a copy of their schedule to Jessica's three assistants so they could put it in her BlackBerry.

They had stayed in a bed-and-breakfast last night. But of course, as it was the second Saturday of the month and not their "sex Saturday," as Phil liked to call it, he slumbered peacefully, while Jessica quietly masturbated facedown in her pillow. They weren't even married and already she felt like a desperate housewife, frustrated by her soon-to-be husband's lack of desire.

She needed a man to fuck her. Really fuck her. Grab her, bend her over a table, and make her *feel*. But the men Jessica knew acted as if she had taken a bowie knife and sliced off their balls. She spent all day, every day, walking around a fraternity (that's all a talent agency was), and every person with a penis inside CTA was terrified of her, she could tell. Jessica beat the men at everything at every turn, and she did it in Ferragamo heels. And her fiancé didn't want her (except for a dutiful fuck the first and third Saturday of every month).

"Most women don't even like sex," Phil said when she'd pushed him on it.

"Most women don't work eighty hours a week and pull down three million a year."

"Jess, that's so crass."

"Fine. It relaxes me."

"Do more yoga," Phil said.

"You're actually trying to get out of sex two times a month? Some men would die for a woman with my sex drive," Jessica said.

"Our drives have always been different."

"I've emasculated you."

"How? I make more money than you do," Phil said.

"Then you just don't want me."

"That's not it."

No therapy, no counseling. Just sex twice a month, her vibrator and her right hand. She could take a lover, but when? Who had time? Jessica tried to remember the last time she'd been fucked. Really, really fucked, the kind that when you thought about the sex days later, the memory made your toes curl. Of course—it was Mike Fox. With so much practice (he'd put his dick in every pussy in New York and Los Angeles), no wonder he was her best lay.

Eight months after Mike and Jessica's torrid affair ended, Jess had met Phil. They were at Rage in West Hollywood; Jessica's very gay hairdresser and his lover were trying to pull her out of her funk. Jessica wasn't sure how a gay club would make her feel better or improve her chances of meeting a man, but she'd agreed to go. Phil had been there celebrating his roommate Len's decision to get married to his longtime lover.

That was one of the things that Jess had always been impressed by—what great friends Phil and Len were; best buddies since junior high. Phil was pretty much Len's only straight friend. They both grew up in Orange County (the most conservative place in all of California) and then attended Stanford. They'd shared a dorm room there, and even after Stanford, Phil and Len had continued to live as roommates. As uptight and prudish as Phil was, Len's being gay never seemed to bother him.

Currently, Len lived with his "husband" (aka domestic partner Brian) in San Francisco, where Phil and Jess were headed today. They'd spend the night and Jess would fly back to L.A. Monday morning while Phil stayed in San Francisco until the following weekend (as always).

"Time to stop!" Phil yelled out over the wind. Angry gray clouds rolled in from the ocean. "I need to put up the top and do a GPS input. And I bet after all that coffee you need to potty." He pulled the Z4 into a gas station. "I'm filling the car here. That way I won't need to do it in the city and we can go straight to Len's."

Jess hopped out and headed for the bathroom.

"Jess," Phil called from the gas pump, "those new Diors make your legs look sexy. They're adorable on you."

Jessica looked down. The crocodile-and-leather Dior Mary Janes were a fabulous find; she knew they made her calves look good. Jess smiled. At least her man liked her shoes.

Jessica's migraine began the minute they pulled into Len's drive. Eight hours later, the pain started to subside. She glanced at her digital travel clock; it was two A.M., she was wide awake and alone. Phil had offered to sleep in Len's den on the fold-out couch, since any light or noise made Jess vomit during her migraines. Her last migraine had been only two weeks ago. They usually came months apart, but for the last six months they'd been more frequent. Sometimes twice a week since Tolliver had entered her life. Better have Kim schedule another appointment with the neurologist.

Only three more hours until her alarm would sound—her flight to L.A. took off at seven. But the room and the bed were so big and lonely. She wanted Phil. Jessica slid out from under the goose-down comforter and slipped her feet onto the hardwood floor. She shivered; it was so much colder in San Francisco.

Jessica thought she could find her way to the den, although she'd only visited Len and Brian's once before. Last March, she flew in to surprise Phil, but it was she who got the big surprise. His residential hotel room was empty. You'd think he would've told her the hotel was being remodeled. Brian was gone on business that week, too, but he seemed nice enough the few times she spoke to him over the phone. Jessica walked down the hall toward the stairs.

"Oh yeah," she heard Len moan. "God, I missed you." Jessica stopped. *Brian must be home.* She knew she shouldn't listen, but it was like a car wreck—you couldn't help it. *Guess Brian will finally introduce himself over pancakes tomorrow.*

"Ooooh. Yes, baby. Please spank it."

Jessica heard a hard smack against what sounded like a very tight ass. She covered her mouth, trying to stifle a giggle. She should turn around and go straight back to bed. But she wanted to cuddle with Phil. *Shit.* That meant she had to walk by Len and Brian's room. And the door was only half closed. But she was a grown-up. She would stare at the ground and get by the bedroom door.

"Yes, baby. Please, oh, yes," Len moaned.

Fast. She needed to get past that door and to the stairs. Jessica rushed toward the end of the hall, as the noise from Brian and Len's room escalated in speed and intensity.

"Uh-huh, uh-huh, uh-huh. Baby, yes, say my name, yes."

Only three more steps. God, this hall is long, Jessica thought as she neared the door.

"Len, oh God. Len, oh God."

Who?! Jessica gently pushed the half-open door away from her. "Phil?"

"Jess?" Phil said. A look of horror flashed on his face as he lay slumped over the back of his best friend.

Jessica shook her head.

No wonder he always liked her shoes.

Jess drank her coffee while Len poured blueberry pancake batter onto a griddle, a Tiffany-blue apron tied neatly around his waist. So far no Phil.

"He's horrified," Len said.

"He should be. I'll give him five more minutes and then I've got to go. I can't believe I didn't figure this out."

"You really are taking this well." Len set a plate of pancakes in front of her.

"Look, if you were a woman, I might be in handcuffs downtown, but you're a man. I don't have the same equipment and never will. I can't believe he didn't tell me."

"He wanted to. I swear to you, Jess, it didn't start until after Brian moved out this year. Never once growing up or in college.

I think Phil and I both thought that he was straight. I always had a crush on him and even told him once at Stanford, but he said no way. He just wasn't interested."

"Talk about latent homosexuality."

"I know he loves you. He just didn't know how to tell you."

"How about 'Hi, Jess. By the way, I'm sleeping with Len'?"

"I know it sounds simple."

Jessica glanced out the kitchen window. "My cab's out front. I've got to go or I'll miss my flight. Tell him I'll ship his stuff here. He really doesn't have much left at my place." She stood and grabbed her Vuitton overnight bag. "Send pictures. An invite to the wedding. I'll send a gift."

"I know he'll want to talk to you. When everything is a little calmer."

"I'm pretty calm." Jessica walked toward the front door. "Len." She turned to face her gay ex-fiancé's lover. "Tell Phil this one thing. Tell him thank you. He always used a condom with me. I used to bitch and bitch about it, but he always did. For that, tell him I say thank you."

"You got it, Jess. Take care of yourself." Len reached out and hugged her.

"You two are going to be very happy. I know it." Jessica turned away and walked outside. She waved toward the driver, who bounded up the brownstone steps and grabbed the overnight case. Then she heard the front door open behind her.

"Jess, wait," Phil said, stepping out onto the small porch.

She wanted to be angry—she really did—but she wasn't. She wasn't even disappointed. In fact, surprisingly, the emotion she felt was something akin to relief.

"Phil." Jessica sighed, "I don't have much to say. . . ."

"This was not how I wanted you to find out. I wanted to tell you, planned on telling you, but I just couldn't find—I'm sorry."

"I'm sorry, too. I mean, I should have known, guessed, I don't know, something. I hadn't realized how completely disconnected we've become."

"It's your work," Phil said.

"What?" Jessica bristled.

"No, not what caused it, but maybe why you didn't notice. I mean, Jess, you're completely consumed."

"Obviously, I don't have much else to care about." Yes, work was important to her, but wasn't work important to *all* successful people? You couldn't win without sacrificing something.

"Jess, please, I'm not judging, I am the last person who should judge. You are brilliant at what you do and I know you love it. I just . . . it's my fault and I'm sorry. Please know that; please accept my apology."

Jessica's face softened. She didn't hate Phil. She now realized he'd been an easy fit into her complex lifestyle.

"Yes, I accept it," Jessica said as the cabbie honked the horn. "Listen, I need to go. I told Len I'll ship your things." She didn't know whether she should hug Phil or shake his hand.

Phil grabbed her and pulled her into a bear hug. "Thank you, Jess, for being so understanding. I feel so guilty about what I've done."

"Don't." The cab beeped again. Jessica bolted down the steps. "You'll be very happy, I know it," Jessica yelled to Phil.

She climbed into the backseat and looked back at the house. She'd be fine without Phil. Losing him didn't make her sad. No, what saddened Jessica—perhaps even terrified her—was the thought that Phil had been the easy solution to a difficult personal problem. She was drugging herself with her work, using her constant pursuit of success to mask any personal pain. *That problem,* Jessica thought, *is a much more difficult one to solve.*

16

Mary Anne and the Minnesota Stride Rites

MARY ANNE'S MOTHER HAD TO FLY BACK TO MINNESOTA IMMEDIATELY OR
Mary Anne would kill her. For six weeks Mitsy Meyers had stayed
with Mary Anne, and already Mitsy had managed to repaint two
rooms, wallpaper a bathroom, clean out Mary Anne's closet,
reseed the front lawn, and make plaid curtains (not Burberry plaid
but a garish red-and-yellow Scottish plaid) for the guest room.

After the Koi incident, Lydia had called Mitsy to let her know
that Mary Anne was in the hospital. Had Mary Anne been lucid,
she would have begged Lydia to hold off ever calling Mitsy
about anything other than funeral preparations or an organ
transplant.

But Mitsy, being the ever-dutiful Minnesota mommy, had purchased a plane ticket within minutes and landed in L.A. the next
day. And upon her arrival, Mitsy, the Methodist and PTA home-
room mother for her children's second-, fourth-, sixth-, and
eighth-grade classrooms, methodically began making Mary
Anne's new Hollywood home into a Minnesota microcosm.

Mary Anne looked around her writing room, as yet untouched
by her maniacal mother (but Mary Anne didn't know for how
long she could keep Mitsy at bay). Already Mitsy had moved
in on Mary Anne's bedroom, organizing her walk-in closet
and hanging silver-framed pictures of Mary Anne's niece and

two nephews. It wasn't that Mary Anne wasn't grateful; she was. But her hand had healed, she didn't have a concussion, and her mother had worn out her welcome.

Mary Anne wasn't sure why Mitsy was driving her nuts. They hardly saw each other. Mary Anne left for set most days at seven A.M. (except Sunday and the occasional day she wrote at home), staying sometimes until nine P.M. Mitsy retired early and was always in bed when Mary Anne returned home (having, of course, fixed dinner and left Mary Anne a plate in the microwave). And when they did see each other in the morning, Mitsy always offered to fix Mary Anne breakfast. Maybe it was the Post-it notes Mitsy left on Mary Anne's bathroom mirror (letting Mary Anne know who called or simply writing *I love you*, punctuated with a smiley face). Maybe it was Misty alphabetizing her canned goods or sorting Mary Anne's shirts by color and type in her closet (not that Mary Anne didn't wish that she was more organized). Or maybe, just maybe, it was the guilt that Mary Anne felt required to carry for all these "great" things Mitsy did without being asked.

Mary Anne stood up from her desk. She'd avoided it for days, but it was time to have "the conversation" with her mom. Mary Anne knew where Mitsy was—where she always was, when she wasn't organizing closets or sewing hems; Mitsy was in the kitchen.

Mom?" Mary Anne walked into her Spanish-tiled open-air kitchen.

"Down here."

A pair of soft-soled Stride Rites stuck out from the lower cabinet (which seemed to have swallowed Mitsy's body whole) next to the stove. Mitsy crawled backward out of the cabinet and sat on her sensible shoes.

"I wanted to clean these out before I painted them and put in new contact paper."

"Mom, you don't have to do that. Flora cleans once a week."

"I know, dear, but that is surface cleaning. This, what I'm doing, is *deep* cleaning. I mean, look at what I found in there." Mitsy turned the paper towel she was holding so that Mary Anne could have a look. "Mouse turds. Disgusting. After lunch I'm getting some traps. You know, you might want to think about getting yourself a cat. We never had mice because of Mr. Fur."

"Mom—"

"And I think the hardware store has mouse traps that—"

"Mom."

"—will fit. Maybe you should go buy one of those Pet Rescue cats. Tabbies are best because—"

"Mother!"

"What, dear? I'm standing right here. There is really no need to raise your voice."

Mary Anne inhaled. "I'm sorry. Mom, will you sit? I need to talk to you."

"You know, honey, there really is quite a bit left for me to get done."

"I know. But it'll just take a minute."

Mitsy moved toward the kitchen table. "I'm just doing this for you. Trying to help. I want to turn this big house into a home for you. I mean, God knows you'll have to sell it eventually, because what man is going to want to live in his wife's house? I mean, really, when you think about it, maybe you should have waited to buy. I know your accountant said you needed it for your taxes, but still, if you'd waited until you were married or at least engaged, then your hus—"

"Mom, I'm not even seeing anyone."

"Well, there is always Steve. I liked Steve," Mitsy said, and sat.

Mary Anne looked at her mother. "I know, Mother, that you liked Steve. You've mentioned that a number of times. Unfortunately, Steve liked a lot of people. Do you want some tea?"

"I can get it, dear." Mitsy started to stand.

"Stop. Sit. I will get it."

"Okay, but plain for me. None of the green or ginseng tea. They give me a headache."

"Sure." Mary Anne grabbed the kettle off the stove and walked toward the sink.

"Oh, don't use the tap water, dear. You never know about that. There's water in the pantry. I signed you up for a delivery service."

"What?"

"Two years. The third year's free."

"Really, Mom, I wish you would've checked with me first."

"Just thinking of your health. Important during your reproductive years. And since you seem to be stretching those as far as they'll go, very important you look out for environmental toxins. You know, you're born with all your eggs. They get old, too."

Count to ten. Mary Anne walked to the pantry and filled the kettle from her new toxin-free water supply. She'd wanted a water service for months, just hadn't found the time to call. But that wasn't the point! The point was it was Mary Anne's house, her pantry, her kitchen, and her water service to call or not call. She walked back toward the stove. Mary Anne cared little if a ticket to Minnesota cost ten grand; she'd pay it. Mitsy had to go home.

"I seem to remember when you brought Steve home that one time, he said he wanted children. A large family, I think," Mitsy remarked.

"Yeah, how many wives did he want? Did he mention that, too?"

"Mary Anne, I don't see why you're so upset. It's not like you were married to him. Forgive and forget. Get on with it."

Mary Anne couldn't take it anymore. "You're kidding, right? We were living together. I came home from work early and he was fucking our neighbor."

"There is no reason to use coarse language," Mitsy sniffed.

Mary Anne set the kettle on the stove. How did Mitsy do this to her every time? No matter how old she got, how much therapy she sat through, her mother drove her bonkers.

Mary Anne exhaled and walked to the table. Mitsy was rummaging through her purse. "Mom, I wanted to talk to you about Minnesota."

"Here it is," Mitsy said, pulling out a paper, then putting on her glasses. "Now, what is your day like tomorrow?"

"Tomorrow? Saturday? Well, I'm meant to go to set, but not until five. We have night shoots for the next seven days."

"Well, that is ideal. My flight leaves at twelve-ten P.M. Can you drop me off, or do I need to call for a car?"

"Your flight?"

"Dear, you didn't think I was going to stay forever, did you? I do have a life in St. Paul. It might not be as fast and glamorous as movies and celebrities' but it is mine, and I do like it."

"Right. Tomorrow. Of course I can take you to the airport."

"Now, tonight I made dinner reservations for us."

"Reservations?"

"Yes, I was in your office. I was measuring for carpet—that hardwood in there feels so cold to me—and I got on your computer and found a restaurant I wanted to try. It's called Ivy at the Shore. Have you heard of it?"

"You? You wanted to try Ivy at the Shore?"

"Well, yes, dear. I've been cooped up in this house for almost six weeks now. I would like to go to dinner at least once. And Lydia said—"

"Lydia?"

"Your producer friend. She said Ivy at the Shore was the best place to see movie stars on the weekend. Now, I called, and they were very rude to me when I tried to get a reservation."

"At the Ivy on a Friday night?"

"Yes. So then I spoke to Kim in Jessica's office."

"Kim?"

"Your agent's assistant. Very nice girl and smart. Did you know she has a joint MBA and law degree from UCLA? Anyway, Kim called the Ivy and got us a reservation for eight P.M. tonight. The car will pick us up at seven."

"The car?"

"Well, we can't drive, can we? I mean, you'll drink and I'll drink, so who will drive? The car will take us home. I don't want you ending up on the cover of some tabloid. That's just what

I need, one of the ladies from my canasta group seeing a picture of you in some trashy magazine in the checkout line. So that's okay, then. You'll be ready by seven?"

"Sure," Mary Anne said, a bit dazed.

"Dear, the kettle is whistling. Really, Mary Anne, I worry about you. Sometimes I don't know where your head is."

Mary Anne glanced at the table to her right. There sat Reese and Ryan. Across the room Michael and Catherine dined with their agents. Although growing accustomed to being around "stars" (she even had a couple she might call friends), Mary Anne still fought the urge to stare at the celestial bodies descended from the heavens. She sucked on the straw of her third Grey Goose and tonic. The liquor tasted smooth, the alcohol going down easy, dulling the sharp sound of Mitsy's voice. Mary Anne wanted cabernet next. *Need to keep drinking—less than twenty-four hours to go,* she thought.

"Well. You must have a wooden leg," Mitsy said, nursing her first strawberry daiquiri. "You know, dear, a drunk woman isn't a very attractive woman—at least not to the type of man that wants to have children. You should keep that in mind while you're out here."

Where did Mitsy find these rules? Mary Anne wondered. *Were they in some book handed out to mothers with their firstborn? Did she find them at a store? And why, no matter how old or successful Mary Anne became, did Mitsy insist on sharing the rules?*

"Mother, I don't think I want to get married."

"Don't be silly. I still think Steve is the right one for you."

"Yeah, if I want an open marriage. I'm surprised at you, Mom. I'd think you of all people would believe that monogamy was one of the most important parts of marriage," Mary Anne said, and dug her finger into the ice in her glass, looking for the lime.

"It's important. But not everything. Besides, since women don't really enjoy sex and men do, once you've had the children, what's wrong with a man satisfying his needs?"

Mary Anne pulled her eyes away from the lime and stared at Mitsy. "Mom, did you just say that women don't enjoy sex?"

"Mary Anne, *everyone* knows that. They may pretend but they don't enjoy it. And an orgasm? What is that? I don't believe it. I've never had one. Your father has, but I haven't, and look, we have the ideal marriage."

"You know, I think I need to go to the bathroom." Mary Anne reached for her purse, then paused. "Wait. Ideal? Are you saying that Dad . . ."

"What?"

"If your marriage is ideal and you don't like sex and Dad still has needs, then he . . ."

"Sleeps with other women? Well, of course he does. I'm surprised it took you this long to figure it out."

Mary Anne felt as if she'd been kicked in the chest. "What?"

"Nancy MacIntosh. His secretary. They've been at it for years. I think since I was pregnant with you, after the twins. I'm not sure of the exact date. I usually track their anniversary by when he goes out of town for his Caribbean conference. That's when he takes Nancy on their yearly trip."

"Wait. This has been going on for over thirty years? And you're still married?"

"Why would I leave? It's perfect. I have three great children, a house I love, enough money and credit cards to take care of my needs, and I don't have to do any of the nasty stuff."

"Okay. This is way too much for me. Do Michael and Michelle know?"

"Michelle does. I don't think your brother cares. And neither do I."

Mary Anne looked up as their waitress passed by the table. "May I have another vodka and tonic, please?"

"If I were you, I'd marry that Steve boy. At least he was trying to be helpful. I mean, who wants the mess? The inconvenience? And the smell—"

"Okay, Mom. You *have* to stop. Most women like sex. I love sex. I can't be with a man who wants to have sex with other women."

"Well, they *all* want to have sex with other women."

"That is probably true. But I can't be with a man who *does* have sex with other women."

"Suit yourself. But I think it's ideal. I have to use the ladies' room. Do you still need to go?"

"No."

Mary Anne watched her walk away, the Stride Rites beating a steady path to the ladies' room. She could not believe this conversation. *Thirty years? Her father had had a mistress for thirty years?* Mary Anne thought her parents' marriage was perfect . . . and so, apparently, did Mitsy. This couldn't be happening. Wasn't happening. Their waitress stopped back with the appetizer they'd ordered.

"Your drink is on its way," she said. "May I get you anything else?"

"A red-eye ticket to Minnesota?"

The waitress gave Mary Anne a befuddled look. "Can't help you there, but I have crab cakes." She set the platter in the center of the table.

Mary Anne's tongue felt swollen. Her ability to articulate her words was always the first to go when she was drunk. Not her ability to think up words or put them together to make a story— those abilities never left. Just her ability to *say* words. Well, and her vision. Mary Anne couldn't determine if there were three or five crab cakes on the plate. Good thing Mitsy had insisted on the car. Mary Anne glanced at her watch; just fifteen hours until Mitsy was safely winging her way back to Minnesota. But why did she want to go back to that marriage? And what else didn't Mary Anne know?

"Mary Anne, guess who I found!" Mitsy called.

Mary Anne spit the ice cube back into her drink and glanced up at her mother. Suddenly her fingers felt numb. Not only did she see extra crab cakes, she also saw—

"Steve! You remember Steve," Mitsy said, as though she'd just found Mary Anne's long-lost second-grade teacher from St. Paul. "He just happened to be here, and I asked him to join us."

"Steve," Mary Anne whispered, as waves of fear and nausea swept through her body.

"You don't mind, do you? I told him you wouldn't."

And there he was. Steve. Stepping behind Mitsy to pull out her chair at the table, smiling that sheepish grin. The grin that had convinced Mary Anne to let him move into her apartment, the grin that had made her fall in love with him, that grin that broke her heart.

"Hi, Mary Anne."

"You just happened to see Steve. Mother, where did you *just happen* to see Steve? How did you find him? What is he—" Mary Anne looked up at her ex-lover. "What are you *doing* here?" She must have yelled the last part, because the diners to her left glanced over at her.

"Mary Anne," Mitsy hissed. "Lower your voice."

"Maybe I should go." The grin was gone and Steve stood looking uncomfortable.

"No! Sit, sit," Mitsy said, pulling Steve down into the chair next to her. "Mary Anne, I found him over by the restrooms. I told him that we were just two single gals out for a good time and that he should join us." Mitsy smiled brightly.

"You found him?"

"Mrs. Meyers, maybe this isn't such a good idea."

"Nonsense, you stay right there. Order a drink and have a crab cake." Mitsy placed her napkin in her lap as if to emphasize that the decision had been made. "You two must have a lot of catching up to do. When was the last time you saw each other?"

Mary Anne looked across the table at her philandering ex-boyfriend. He had his head bowed, staring at his fork.

"Well?" Mitsy interrupted the awkward silence that only Mitsy didn't realize was awkward.

"The last time, Mother? Well, I believe the last time I saw Steve was when his bare ass was pumping up and down while he fucked our redheaded neighbor, Viève. That was the last time I saw you, wasn't it, Steve?"

"Mrs. Meyers, I can't, I knew when you called—"

"You called?!" Mary Anne screeched.

"Now, Mary Anne, please lower your voice. Yes, I called. But only after Steve wrote me all those letters."

"You sent my mother letters?" Mary Anne hissed.

"You wouldn't answer my calls."

"To Minnesota? You sent my mother letters in Minnesota?"

"And he called several times, too. Right, Steve?" Mitsy said, smiling. "Mary Anne, this breakup was all silliness on your part. Steve was just feeling a bit trapped, now, weren't you, Steve?"

Mary Anne couldn't believe this. Perhaps she'd had one Grey Goose too many. Maybe she'd passed out. "Is the bed spinning?" she muttered.

"Bed?" Mitsy asked.

"Yes, trapped. You were always pressuring me for a ring and a baby and a house," Steve said.

"So you had sex with our neighbor?"

"Viève was very understanding."

"Understanding of what? Your cock?"

"Mary Anne, please do not use that type of language," Mitsy scolded. "Steve is here to reconcile, reconnect, and restart your relationship."

What kind of sick reality show was this? Betrayed first by the man she loved and then a second time by the woman who bore her.

"I'm out," Mary Anne said, standing and reaching for her purse. "You," she said, pointing at Steve, "are a gelatinous pile of dog shit some wretched mutt crapped out. And you," she said, looking at Mitsy, her tone softening to almost a whisper, "have just broken my heart. Because you, Mom, are supposed to be on my team. You are supposed to want what is best for me, not easy for you. And if you think that a two-timing techno geek is all I can get, then I can't imagine what you must really think of me."

Mary Anne threw her credit card on the table and jammed her clutch under her arm. "Enjoy dinner; it's on me. You two can catch up in person. Mom, I'll send the car back for you." Mary Anne turned and walked to the front door, looking at the floor so no one at Ivy at the Shore would see her cry.

17

Celeste Solange and Her
Chloe Python Leather Bag

CELESTE WANTED EVERY PENNY OF DAMIEN BRUCKNER'S MONEY. SHE DIDN'T need it, and the prenup didn't allow it. But she wanted it. All of it. (And why shouldn't she, after the way Damien was humiliating her in front of the world? Parading around town with an eighteen-year-old.)

"Cici, the prenup is very clear on this, and I'm afraid iron-clad," insisted Howard Abromawitz, her attorney.

"Howie, I know you handled the Preston-Sturgess divorce. Jen told me that prenup was solid, too."

"That one had a loophole if Jen caught him fucking around."

"But Damien is fucking around. Haven't you seen *People, Us,* and *Star*?"

Howard smiled. "Read them every day. Best client-referral service in the world. But Cici, with the Preston-Sturgess divorce there was a tape. That part of the settlement was off the record. Nathan paid Jen to buy the tape—it would have destroyed his career. It wasn't like he was sleeping with women."

Celeste hated spending her only day off from filming at her attorney's office. She looked around the room. Pictures of Howard with U.S. presidents (Bush and Clinton), A-list stars (Tom, Leo, and Arnold), and sports heroes (Michael, Tiger, and Jeff) lined the wall.

"Look, Cici, Damien is a serial wedder. He likes them young, and he likes to find them before he gets divorced from the current wife. You know I handled Amanda and Damien's divorce, too."

"What if I had film?"

"Do you? Wait, don't answer that. We could be getting into a dicey area." Howard leaned back behind his mahogany desk.

Celeste stood and walked to the wall of windows. All of Beverly Hills lay at her feet.

"What about Amanda's prenup? I know what Damien paid her. How'd you get around that?"

Howard swiveled his leather chair and leaned forward. "Off the record. Because I'll deny I ever told you this. You remember the house in Belize?"

"We used to go there all the time. Damien sold it right after his divorce from Amanda was final."

"Cameras."

"What?" Celeste turned toward Howard.

"Security cameras, in every room, including the stables." Howard paused. Celeste felt a flush creeping up her neck. She didn't normally get embarrassed, but at this moment with Howard . . .

"There *is* tape? Videotape of me and Damien . . ."

"Was."

"He never told me there was tape or cameras. Fucker."

"He bought her off. He knew it would destroy your career. And, well, probably your relationship with him."

"But how could it destroy—"

"There are a lot of women in Belize."

Celeste felt her chest tighten. Humiliation again and again. So this is what it felt like to be the cheated-on wife. Not the wife who knew her husband was fucking around and who accepted it as a respite from a tired sex life, but the wife who suddenly realized that the life she'd built rested on the foundation of her husband's lies.

"You know they were destroyed?"

"It's been five years. If there were copies, which there aren't, they'd have surfaced. You're a big star, Cici. If someone had them, they could've made a fortune by now."

"I could kill him."

"Okay, well, I never heard that. And don't ever repeat it to anyone. That's advice from legal counsel."

Celeste sat on the cashmere couch in front of Howard's desk. "What now?"

"Well, unless you catch him having sex with animals or children, your prenup is solid. That is the only loophole: lewd, lascivious, and/or illegal sexual behavior. But as you can see by my story, people have been inclined to disregard their prenups if there are persuasive circumstances."

Celeste stood and grabbed her Chloe python leather bag. "I've been told I can be persuasive."

Howard stood and walked Celeste to the private "celebrity elevator" at the back of his office. He air-kissed her on both cheeks. "I'll call you when I have paperwork." He held both her hands and looked into her eyes. "Cici, call me if you need anything, day or night. I'm here for you." The elevator door opened and Celeste stepped inside. "Or if you come across anything you think I should have."

"Thanks, Howard," Celeste said. She was ready to break a nail or two. It was time to dig into Damien's dirt.

Celeste sat on the floor of Damien's former home office in her velvet Versace sweat suit (Donatella had been wonderful enough to design a one-of-a-kind turquoise one "to match your eyes, darling"). The computers were gone, but most of the files still remained. Damien had been anal retentive about keeping three copies of every document, one at his studio office at Summit Pictures, one at his attorney's, and one at home. But Damien was so busy fucking Brie Ellison, he must have forgotten about his home files. He hadn't returned to the house since he'd moved out (Celeste had the locks and security code changed the day he left), and she instructed Mathilde to call her immediately if she saw Mr. Bruckner snooping around. Eight weeks and no Damien.

Celeste worked her way through the credenza behind Damien's desk. All she could find were old bank statements and movie deal memos. She'd give those to Howard in case his assets-detection specialist could find anything she missed. But there was nothing dirty or sordid. She'd known it was unlikely anyway; she doubted Damien would keep dirty stuff so accessible. He'd hide it, keep it out of sight. But where?

Celeste stood up from the floor. *God, she hated paperwork. She was an actress, not a secretary.*

"Cici, where are you?" Bradford called.

"In here."

It was Sunday evening. Bradford's diligent return to Celeste's house every Sunday evening to run lines and prepare for the workweek had surprised her and Lydia. They were impressed, especially since he was spending every free moment both on set and off with Zymar's daughter. But even with his new girlfriend, it seemed Bradford craved the structure and the rules Celeste provided. His acting had rocketed to the next level with the discipline. His performances in the dailies, Lydia had said, were incredible. And he really wasn't as big of an asshole as Celeste had originally surmised. Like most celebrities his age, he was just young and out of control; inebriated with his money and success. Staying with Celeste (and, it appeared, dating Christina) seemed to have grounded him.

"Cleaning house?" Bradford stood in the doorway and surveyed Damien's study.

"You could say that. Trying to organize and find a few things."

"I've never been in this room."

"Ugly, isn't it? It's Damien's study. Or it was Damien's study. Guess I'll have it remodeled and redecorated. I don't know, maybe I should have a home office."

"So you get the house?"

"Yeah. That's what the prenup says," Celeste said, bending over to put files stacked on the floor back into the credenza.

"Guess Damien will make Brie sign one of those, too."

Celeste stopped. She looked over her shoulder at Bradford. "Married? They're getting married?"

"That's what Brie says."

"Of course they are." She wondered if Brie Ellison knew what she was getting with Damien. But she guessed that, much like herself years before, Brie didn't know and didn't care.

"Well, once her mom and dad sign off on it."

"Close family?"

"Nah. Not exactly. She's only seventeen."

Celeste felt a tingle in her spine. *Did he say seventeen?*

"What?"

"Yeah, her birthday isn't for another four months. Hey, thought I'd take a quick swim before we run lines for tomorrow," Bradford said.

"Sure. Go on. In about an hour?"

"Great."

Celeste stood and looked at Bradford. He had unknowingly provided her with a piece of information that was worth several million dollars. "Bradford, I can't tell you how happy I am that you're here."

"Well, thanks, Cici. See ya in an hour."

God, it was almost too good to be true. Fucking a minor might not classify as lewd and lascivious in L.A., but it was still illegal.

This is Howard."

"Howie, it's Cici," Celeste said into her flip phone.

"Cici, my love. How are you? Do you need me to come over? Are you okay?"

"Fine. I found it."

"What?"

"I found a way to nail Damien's ass to the wall. Brie Ellison. She's a minor."

There was a pause; Celeste could practically hear the legal gears in Howie's mind beginning to spin. "Are you sure?"

"Well, I've been told. I mean, all we need to prove it is a birth certificate. How hard is that? He's fucking a minor. That's still illegal in California, right?"

"It's not enough."

"What? She's seventeen."

"Cici, do you have proof they've consummated their relationship?"

"It's all over *People* and *Us*. On *Entertainment Express* Friday night he had his hand down her pants."

"Then you've got him for heavy petting, but it's not enough. Look, statutory rape is a criminal offense, and for the district attorney to file charges against Damien Bruckner for his relationship with Brie Ellison, you need more than Damien cupping some ass at a premiere. Or you need—and I'll deny that I ever said this—at least enough proof to make Damien believe that the district attorney could file charges. The kind of proof that might have monetary value to someone like Damien. Not that I would ever advise you to extort money or subvert evidence of a crime, but hypothetically speaking, that type of evidence could have great value. Might even break open an unbreakable prenup."

"So we need to see them fucking," Celeste said, pacing.

"Well, in a manner of speaking, yes. And it needs to be before she turns eighteen or gets married."

"She's not marrying him until I get divorced."

"That's correct."

"Stills or film?"

"What?"

"Still photography or film—which is better?"

"Well, in these scenarios, film is more effective."

"Yeah, film always is."

18

Lydia Albright and the Lifts

LYDIA PACED OUTSIDE ARNOLD MURPHY'S EXECUTIVE SUITE. SHE'D BEEN summoned. A summons Lydia had tried to avoid. Lydia had waited for Arnold for twenty-five minutes. Fifteen minutes was acceptable in Hollywood, twenty minutes was making a statement, and thirty minutes was an insult. According to Lydia's watch, Arnold now had three minutes and twenty-seven seconds before she walked out the door. *The little prick. Making her wait.* He'd received their shooting schedule. He knew that for the next three days Zymar was filming the biggest action and pyrotechnic sequence in the movie. Together, the next seventy-two hours would make or break Lydia's film. Today was the money shot. And here Lydia waited flipping through three-day-old *Variety*s and watching Arnold's assistant roll calls. *Unbelievable*. The second hand on her watch clicked onto the six. *That was it*. Her time was too valuable to throw away. She had an explosion in an hour and forty-five minutes. Lydia stood up to leave and turned toward Arnold's prim male assistant.

"Please tell Ar—"

"Mr. Murphy will see you now," he interrupted her, and stood. "Right this way."

Lydia walked through the door to Arnold Murphy's office and immediately bit down hard on her tongue so as not to laugh.

Arnold's chair sat on lifts. Seated behind a giant wood desk in an oversized chair on stilts, he looked like an eight-year-old redhead playing make-believe at his father's desk. *Only in Hollywood do we pretend not to notice this,* Lydia thought.

"Liideeeaaa, sit down," Arnold said.

Josanne Dorfman sat in the chair next to Lydia's, facing Arnold's desk.

"Arnold, good morning. My assistant must have made a scheduling error. I thought our meeting was at nine A.M."

"No, your assistant made no error. I had some important calls to make. And now I am finished and ready to meet with you. Josanne will be joining our meeting."

"Of course. What can I do for you, Arnold? You know today is a big day for us. The beginning of our largest action sequence."

"Yes, so I hear. Let's see." Arnold glanced down at a black binder on his desk. "It looks to me that you are on time and on budget. Is that correct?"

Arnold's even tones stunned Lydia. She expected to be ripped apart for some trumped-up charge. Perhaps crafts services cost too much or she'd overspent on crew overtime. But civility? That was baffling.

"Yes, everything has been smooth."

"Josanne saw the dailies and she tells me they're quite good."

"Really excellent, Lydia," Josanne chimed in. "Perhaps some of Zymar's best work."

"Okay . . ." Lydia glanced at Josanne and then Arnold, warily.

"So you have every reason to believe you'll come in on time and on budget?"

"Yes. The next three days we shoot our primary action sequence. After that we wrap principal production in five days. Then we're ready for postproduction."

"Okay, then," Arnold said, shutting his black binder. "Thank you for coming up, and we'll talk when you wrap."

" 'Okay, then?' " Lydia paused, looking at the little big man behind his desk. "Arnold, I got five messages at seven A.M. this morning telling me to be here by nine or I couldn't shoot my action sequence today. I bust my ass to get here and then wait thirty minutes in the reception area while you make calls. Now you tell me I'm doing a superior job, ask me two questions, and tell me to leave? Arnold, excuse my language, but what the fuck is going on?"

Arnold sat back in his chair and shook his head. "Lydia, it is just this kind of behavior that makes me dislike you so. Your inability to trust. Although I am under no obligation to share any of this information with you, in the spirit of working together and being colleagues I will." He picked up the binder lying on his desk and handed it to Josanne. "Today I am meeting with Ted Robinoff and he's requested that I prepare a status report on every film Worldwide has in production. I've taken this request quite seriously, much more seriously than my predecessor, Weston, and I've had a face-to-face conversation with every producer who's in production on the lot. You, Lydia, because you refuse to return my calls, are the last."

"I return your calls."

"Two A.M. doesn't count, Lydia, unless you are in New Zealand," Murphy said, his neck beginning to flush. "Now, if you are satisfied, Josanne and I have some final numbers to compile, so please." Murphy lifted both hands, and as if shooing an offending bug, waved Lydia toward the door.

Lydia eyed them both as she walked out of Arnold's office. It just didn't feel right. None of it.

Lydia stepped into the empty elevator outside Arnold's office. She put her earpiece in and clicked on her BlackBerry cell phone.

"Toddy, it's Lyd. Get on the phone to the other producers on the lot and find out from their assistants if they've had sit-downs with Arnold in the last five days." Shit, maybe she was just being paranoid. But why not? Arnold had tried everything possible to shut down her film since Weston died. He'd even reassigned her to the oldest soundstage on the lot, number forty-four. The ancient wiring kept blowing fuses, costing them time. Thankfully, her crew was a bunch of pros, so they'd been okay, but it was inconvenient, and who knew what would happen when it came down to crunch time.

Lydia stepped off the elevator and walked through Worldwide's front doors. She glanced at her watch and climbed into her golf cart. One hour and twelve minutes until explosion. She needed to get to set.

Lydia stood in her trailer reviewing the shot list one final time. In fifteen minutes, $5 million of the studio's money would go up in smoke. The pyrotechnics had to go off without a hitch; once the explosions started, Zymar would get one take. Today was easily the most expensive set day of Lydia's career. By the end of the week, they'd have the completed centerpiece for Lydia's $200 million movie.

"Lydia," Zymar called, yanking open the door to her trailer, "we got a problem."

"What is it?" She called over her shoulder.

"Fire marshal is 'ere."

"Zymar, this is no time for jokes." He was notorious for pulling pranks on set, and if she didn't love him, she'd be furious at him for this one. She turned toward her trailer door and saw standing behind her director a guy in a fire helmet and fire jacket. "You even put him in costume. Cute."

"Ma'am."

"Okay, well, we've got ten minutes and this is all very funny, but Zymar, this is a big shot."

"Ms. Albright, Captain Miller. Sorry about this, but the shoot today is going to be a problem."

"Uh-huh," Lydia said, smiling. She looked at Zymar, willing him to cut the joke short.

Zymar leaned forward. "Lydia, this is not a setup. This guy is for real."

Lydia looked Zymar in the eye. *Oh God!* He wasn't joking. The firefighter standing in front of her was the real deal. "Problem?

Captain, we've taken every precaution, gotten all our permits, run everything through Legal, and it's all been approved."

"Yes, ma'am, it has been approved. Or was approved."

"Was?"

"Well, ma'am, you changed places."

"No," Lydia said, holding up her shot list. "The shots are the same, the pyrotechnics, nothing, not one thing has changed since your approval."

"Ms. Albright, please, all those permits and approval were for soundstage thirty-six. And, well, today you are shooting on stage forty-four. And well, ma'am, I hate to tell you, but forty-four isn't zoned for these kind of pyrotechnics. It's a much older sound-stage and it just doesn't have the capability for the event you have planned for today."

Lydia felt the trailer move, or thought she did. She leaned forward.

"Usually when a production is reassigned the studio notifies us and we let them know if their permits are still in order. But Ms. Albright, we didn't get notified of your reassignment until late last night. It came over the fax from Mr. Murphy's office."

"Did it?"

"They also requested that all the stats on soundstage forty-four be pulled, too. I'm surprised the studio put you on this stage. It's usually reserved for dramas. Both those things together alerted us to the fact that you can't shoot this scene on this soundstage, at least not today."

"What?! Do you know 'ow much time and money went into this setup?" Zymar shouted.

"Sir, please refrain from yelling."

"We're talking millions of dollars!"

Lydia's BlackBerry started to beep. "Excuse me," she said to the fire marshal as she put her earpiece in. "What's up?"

"No other producers had a meeting with Arnold."

"What? Toddy, are you sure? Not one?"

"Yeah, I checked with everyone in Production, and no one else had a sit-down. Shit, most of them won't even return his calls.

And, not sure if you know this, but the fire department called. They said they needed to speak with you." Lydia glanced over at Zymar and Captain Miller arguing.

"Yeah, they found me. Okay, I need you to get me Jessica Caulfield. Tell Kim it's important and to have Jess call me ASAP."

"Yes, sir, but you cannot shoot this today," Captain Miller was saying to Zymar. "Ms. Albright, if you'll let my men go through and check it out, we may be able to get you a special-use permit so that you can get the shot. But I can't guarantee it."

"How soon?" Lydia asked.

"Possibly tomorrow."

"Do it," Lydia said, her disappointment buried by rage. Arnold. A very smooth play on his part.

"Lydia, what will we do?" Zymar asked. "We don't have the budget for an extra day."

"We will get the shot. One way or another we'll get it."

W hat do I do?" Lydia whispered into the phone. She watched as the fire marshal and his crew crawled around her set like ants over spilled soda.

"Keep shooting," Jessica said, her voice calm.

"How? I'll be at least twenty million over, based on the extra days, and who knows how many there will be. Plus the fire department will bill us."

"Doesn't matter. Keep shooting. You and I both know the studio's accounting department won't catch it until you're into postproduction."

"Can you believe that little cock set me up?"

"Pretty slick for Arnold," Jessica said. "He's usually not that clever."

"Yeah, but he still didn't cover his tracks very well; we know what he did." Lydia's heart was finally resuming a normal speed. "I am so pissed."

"As pissed as the first time?" Jessica asked, referring to the incident that ignited the Albright-Murphy feud.

"Different. This time I don't feel nearly as used or alone," Lydia said. "This time at least I know I have some friends to cover me."

"Consider yourself covered. Just keep shooting. I know how these things go. By the time he sees the overages, he'll realize how much money Worldwide stands to make. He may give you some lashings, but even Arnold isn't going to turn down a box-office hit. He's not that crazy."

"Hope you're right," Lydia said. She saw the fire marshal bend over an explosive and shake his head. "I better go if I want to get the fire department out of here by today."

"Keep shooting," Jessica commanded one last time.

Lydia looked over at Zymar, who was gesturing to the fire marshal. She watched as finally the fire marshal smiled and nodded his head. Zymar was a pro. With him working all the angles they might lose just one day. Lydia sighed. It was explosions now and explosions later, but dammit, she knew she'd get this film made.

19

Brie Ellison and Her Christian Louboutin Black Velvet Platform Sandals

BRIE ELLISON WAS BORED. SHE SUCKED ON A CHERRY LOLLIPOP AS SHE LAY lolling in the sun at Zuma Beach. Ten feet away, Bradford Madison picked up a volleyball and prepared to serve. *His body is perfection,* Brie thought as she stared at his six-pack abs through her Dolce & Gabbana sunglasses.

"He loves volleyball, doesn't he?" Christina Darmides said. She plopped down on her beach towel, which was spread out next to Brie's.

Brie pulled the lollipop from her mouth and cocked her head to the side. "You'd know better than me, with all the time you two have been spending together."

She watched as Christina blushed. Brie liked Christina, as much as Brie liked any woman. Christina was cute. But Brie knew that cute fades, and although Christina might be fucking Bradford for now, soon enough she would be on her way back to Oxford and Brie would have her turn.

"We're just friends." Christina rubbed sunblock onto her arms.

"If fuck buddies means being friends, then okay," Brie said, flipping onto her back. For a European, Christina was way too uptight.

"He did a great job on *Seven Minutes Past Midnight.* Dad showed us a rough cut of the film last night. You should come by and see it."

"No, thanks. I hear enough about Celeste Solange from Damien. I don't need to see her act, too."

It was all Damien did: visit his divorce attorney and bitch about Celeste. Brie was ecstatic that at this very moment Damien was on his way to Prague to scout locations for *Borderland Blue*. She was so tired of his whining. He complained about the money. He complained about Celeste's film. He complained about his former home. And he complained about Brie's cats. They barely fucked anymore. Not like on set in New Zealand—those had been wild times. Damien was a good lay, for an old guy. Plus, he helped her career. One more million in the bank, her first starring role, and the biggest perk of all, gross profit participation—*that* would make her rich!

Brie glanced across the beach to the volleyball players. Bradford Madison was just the boy toy she needed to liven things up. And Kiki Dee (her five-thousand-dollar-a-week publicist) would cream herself if Brie started showing up at clubs around L.A. with Bradford. The press for a Bradford-Brie tryst would be phenomenal, and just when the spotlight from breaking up Celeste and Damien was beginning to wane.

"So how are things with Damien?" Christina asked.

"Old. In every way," Brie said. "Have you ever fucked an old guy?"

"Um . . . No, not really," Christina said.

"Well, it's okay in the beginning, but they don't have much staying power. You have to get off pretty quick or not get off at all." Brie sighed. "I'm actually just about over it."

"But I thought you two were talking about marriage?"

Brie laughed. "Damien is. I'm not. Do the math; there is no way I'm spending my twenties taking care of a geriatric. Besides, it's about time for me to find my next thing," Brie said, letting her eyes drift back toward Bradford.

Christina propped herself up on her elbows and waved to Bradford. He trotted over and collapsed onto the beach towel next to Christina.

"Babe, I'm getting killed over there. Save me with a kiss," Bradford said.

Christina giggled as Bradford leaned in and planted a long kiss on her lips. Brie watched as his hand wandered down Christina's stomach and across her thigh. A wave of envy swept through Brie. She'd had her chances with Bradford. He'd begged her to sleep with him at least a dozen times. But that was before, when he seemed so childish. *I want him now,* Brie thought. *I am the star. I was a model. She's just a cute little Greek girl with a bad haircut.*

Bradford slowly pulled his lips away from Christina's. "Perfect," he whispered. Brie watched as he stared into Christina's eyes.

"Bradford, I was talking to Damien last night," Brie said, "and he wants you for the supporting role in *Borderland Blue.*"

Bradford tore his gaze away from Christina. "That's great, Brie. When does it start?"

"In about a month."

"Perfect timing, too."

"Damien was wondering if you'd come by our place tonight. Maybe talk about the script."

"Sure. What time should we be there?" Bradford asked while he ran his hand through Christina's thick black hair.

"Well, please don't take this the wrong way," Brie said, looking at Christina, "but Damien wanted to speak to you alone. Man to man, or some shit like that. I mean, *I'm* not even included."

"Brie, don't worry about it," Christina said. "I totally get it. It's business." She smiled and leaned against Bradford. "You go on. You can come by after. Daddy wants me to go to dinner with him tonight, anyway."

"You sure?" Bradford asked. "Because you know I'll give it all up for you," he said, grinning. "Every bit of it. The money, the fame . . . the money." He started tickling Christina.

"Stop. Stop. Go. Go. Just come by when you're finished."

"About eight?" Bradford asked Brie.

"Sounds good," Brie said, starting to stand. "We'll see you then."

"You leaving?" Christina asked.

"I've had it with the sun, and I've got a mani-pedi-wax with Olivia in an hour." Brie stuffed her towel in her square Chanel tote. "I'll tell Damien eight, then."

"Awesome. See you, Brie," Bradford called, not even looking away from Christina.

Brie Ellison stood before the full-length mirror in her bedroom. Her body was the ideal collection of curves and long, narrow straightaways. Dr. Melnick was an awesome surgeon. She'd wanted to go bigger (because wasn't bigger always better when it came to boobs?), but Dr. Melnick convinced her to just go up one size. And he was right. Her thighs looked tight and the butt lift gave her the perfect curve between her ass and leg.

Brie gazed at the black lace demi-cup bra and crotchless panties. She decided the garters were too much, but the Christian Louboutin black velvet platform sandals gave off just the right vibe of sexiness. *I almost want to fuck myself,* Brie thought.

Then the panic hit her. The panic always hit her just before she seduced a man. *What if Bradford said no?* But he wouldn't. He couldn't. No man ever had. Since she was thirteen, she'd gotten everything she ever wanted by spreading her legs. *Everything.* And not one of the dozens of men (stepfather and high-school teachers included) had said no. Married? Engaged? Single? As long as they were straight, it was yes, yes, yes, every time. The sex really didn't matter to Brie. It was this moment that turned her on. The surge of panic followed by the adrenaline rush of conquest. And, of course, the baubles, trips, money, and career advancement sweetened it. But she didn't really care that Bradford liked Christina. It didn't even matter that there *was* a Christina. All that mattered was the sexy woman standing in front of the mirror.

Hot always trumped cute. Brie would win tonight. Bradford might think that he loved Christina Darmides, but for men hot sex beat out love every time. Besides, it wasn't as if Bradford was married (not that marital status had ever mattered to Brie, obviously). This afternoon at the beach, even Christina said that she and Bradford were just friends. Bradford was open game.

Brie heard the security buzzer from the front gate. "Sarah," Brie called to her housekeeper, "will you get that? Send Mr. Madison up to my room." Brie leaned forward, perking her breasts up in her demi-cup bra. *Yes.* She smiled into the mirror. *She looked irresistible.*

Jessica Caulfield and Her Curled Toes

JESSICA CAULFIELD STRETCHED HER ARMS ABOVE HER HEAD. SHE WIGGLED her bare toes under the down comforter and smiled. Early Saturday morning light crept in through the white silk curtains on her bedroom windows. It was already a beautiful day. A perfect day.

She rolled slightly to her left. He was still there. Mike Fox. Adorable Mike Fox, in her bed, snoozing away. When they'd been together years ago, Mike never spent the night. It didn't matter what time they got back from dinner or a premiere. As soon as they finished making love, Mike was out the door. Not anymore. Not this time. This Mike Fox spent the night. This Mike Fox sent her flowers, cooked for her, and even told her he loved her.

Jessica was satisfied. Gluttonously, sexually satisfied. She felt as if she'd feasted after a long famine. Tender caresses, long kisses, and fantastic sex replenished her. She felt alive. And happy. The stress, the anger—it had all drained away. Jessica ran her fingers along Mike's cheekbone as he snored. His brown hair was rumpled. Yes, this Mike Fox was the Mike Fox she'd always wanted.

It was almost effortless, the transition to having him around again. Round two began with a casual dinner party at a mutual friend's home three weeks before. She and Mike both arrived sans date (Jess was still wondering if she'd been set up). Dinner led to an after-dinner drink at the Polo Lounge, which led to two more dates, a party, and just like that, Mike had slipped back into her life. Effortless and fulfilling, the way Jessica had always imagined that the right relationship would be.

Although he was the same Mike (he still loved to have a good time), he was different, too. Not nearly as inebriated with the glitz and the glam as a few years ago, Mike, like a number of Hollywood executives (at least the ones who didn't burn out or crack their nut), understood you needed something *real* in your life. The biz would let you down; it couldn't be the only thing in your life (no matter how tempting the siren song of screen success, the A-list parties, yachts, supermodels, and blow). It was all an illusion, a pleasure palace that in the end couldn't sustain your soul.

Jessica had allowed herself to be numbed by the office, and now, for the first time in seven years, she was coming down from her workaholic high. The last person she'd ever have expected to meet her (with his feet planted solidly on the ground) was Mike Fox.

Jessica slipped quietly out of bed. She'd shower, then go downstairs, make coffee, and read scripts. Jessica looked at the clock; she was to meet Celeste, Lydia, Christina, and Mary Anne at the Four Seasons for breakfast in three hours. Christina was returning to Oxford in three days, and Lydia wanted a confab on Christina's future career in the film trade. Lydia had already offered Christina a job at her production company as a reader (a much easier way to break into the film biz than as an assistant), but as Lydia had mentioned, who better for a producer-in-training to sit down with than a writer, a powerful Hollywood agent, and a superstar?

Jessica wanted to get some reading finished so that after breakfast she could spend all day with Mike. They'd talked about driving out to Palm Springs for the night or maybe going to Coronado. If they wanted to be really naughty, Mike could steal Summit's corporate jet for the rest of the weekend and they could go to Cabo or New York. There were no stars to worry about, no bottom lines to meet, no phone calls to return. Every bit of business could wait. She'd put it all on hold (she'd even turned off her BlackBerry!). Jessica pattered down the staircase, toward her coffee and her scripts.

Settling into the oversized white chair and ottoman in her study, Jessica picked up the first script on her pile of ten. Paul Peterson, head of Summit, had sent her this one with a $20 million offer for Maurice Banks and a $20 million offer for Holden. It was a two-hander, a buddy picture. Thank God Holden had finally started to see the acting coach, Gary Moises; at least now he had a chance of actually doing some acting and having a career for the next ten years. Paul wanted Lydia to produce; he was already asking Jessica if Lydia would consider moving her overall deal to Summit from Worldwide after *Seven Minutes Past Midnight* was released.

Jessica thought a move to Summit was the perfect solution to Lydia's problem with Arnold. Summit would pay for Lydia's overhead (staff, operating expenses) and sweeten her producer's quote ($5 million plus ten percent of gross), and in exchange, Lydia would let Summit look at every project she wanted to make first before she discussed the project with any other studio. Paul was fair, and Lydia had worked with him at Birnbaum Productions. (As his first job in the industry, Paul interned for Weston when Lydia was a reader, so they went way back. And Paul knew what a dumbass Arnold was.)

"You left me alone."

Jessica looked up and smiled. Mike stood in the doorway with a sheet wrapped around his waist.

"Hey, sleepyhead," she said.

"I'm still tired," Mike said, walking over to her. "Come back to bed with me."

"Can't. Already drank two cups of coffee."

Mike bent over, his lips grazing Jessica's ear. "Then you've got some energy. I'll make it worth your while."

Jessica felt a tingle in her spine and her toes curled. Mike was so sexy. She could feel herself getting wet just from his whispering. He wasn't even touching her.

"But then again . . . ," he said, sliding his lips down her neck. "Who really needs a bed?"

Jessica waited for the girls at a big table in the Four Seasons restaurant. All of them were late. Jessica had been worried that she'd be the one keeping them waiting, especially after the rendezvous on the floor of her study at home. She'd rushed through a shower, thrown on silk pants and a shirt, and dashed toward the door, leaving Mike standing in the kitchen (still wrapped in a sheet) grinning and sipping his first cup of coffee.

"I'll be here when you get back," he said.

Jessica stopped at the front door and turned around. "You will?"

"Yes, Jess, I will."

That was when it hit her. Really hit her. Mike Fox would be there. He'd be there when she got home, when she got up, and when she got old.

"Jess, I know I made a big mistake when I left five years ago, and I'm not making that mistake again. So yes, I will be here when you get home."

"Okay." Jessica smiled and picked up her keys from the crystal bowl in the foyer.

"Hurry up and get back here so we can do something fun for the rest of our weekend."

"You got it," she said.

"Tell the girls I say hello. And tell Celeste I want her to do my film next, no matter what her agent says about the script."

"I'll tell her, but you know her agent is kind of a ballbuster."

The memory made Jess smile, and it made her impatient. She had the sexiest man alive standing naked in her kitchen and she was waiting at an empty table.

"I see a grin," Lydia called as she and Celeste clipped across the marble-tile floor to the table. "That must have been put there by one Mr. Mike Fox."

"Is it that obvious?"

Celeste bent down and gave her an air kiss. "Well, if the rumors are true, and they usually are, then I have to agree with Lydia. You are indeed getting banged on a regular basis."

Jessica flushed, smiled, and lifted her menu.

"We saw Mary Anne pulling in when we parked," Lydia said. "Christina's on her way. She was going to stop by Brie Ellison's to pick up some shoes Brie borrowed."

"That's another one making some time. Christina spends more nights at my house with Bradford than she does at your place," Celeste remarked to Lydia.

"Yes, well, her father seems to believe that when Christina's out all night, she's with her girlfriends," Lydia said.

"Only if she's a lesbian and Bradford is having a party. The other night they were so loud I thought the house would come down. Ooh, ooh, OOOH. Do you remember what it's like to get fucked like that?" Celeste looked at Lydia and Jessica. Both of them sheepishly peeked over their menus. "Oh, silly me! I forgot you two and your new loves. Of course you do. How is it I'm one of the sexiest people alive, according to *People* magazine, and you two are getting more action then I've had in the last six months? Hmmm." Celeste looked at her menu.

"That's not what I hear," Jessica quietly singsonged.

"What?!" Celeste put down her menu. "What *do* you hear?"

"I hear that a certain celebrity, who will remain nameless, has been rendezvousing upstairs at this very hotel with a certain movie mogul, who will also remain nameless, whenever that movie mogul happens to be in Los Angeles from New York."

Celeste pressed her lips together and picked up the silver coffee carafe from the center of the table. "Lies, rumors, and more lies. You know how this town is."

"What if I had pictures?" Jessica said, and smiled.

"Oh my God!" Celeste yelped, practically jumping from her chair. "I almost forgot."

"What?" Lydia asked.

"I need film of Brie and Damien fucking."

"Sorry I'm late." Mary Anne rushed toward the table, her hair still wet.

"Sit. You haven't missed much, except Cici wants to film her soon-to-be ex-husband having sex with Brie Ellison," Lydia said.

"Isn't that illegal?" Jessica asked.

"Excuse me?" Mary Anne said, plopping down beside Lydia and across from Jessica and Celeste.

"Film or tape. I need it to break my prenup." Celeste sipped her coffee, then leaned in and whispered, "You know Brie Ellison is a minor."

"No fucking way!" Lydia crowed. "Damien's really gotten his dick in the wringer this time."

"It's too good to be true." Jessica giggled.

"Well, it is true. Howard pulled her birth certificate from the tiny town in Missouri where she was born. Minor equals illegal, and illegal equals big bucks for me. So I need film. How do we get it?"

Lydia's cell phone started ringing. She glanced at the number. "Sorry, girls, it's Christina. Just a sec." She clicked and answered.

Jessica watched from across the table as Lydia's face turned from a smile into a frown.

"What? Oh, no. Christina, I'm so sorry."

Celeste put down her menu and glanced at Lydia and then looked at Jessica.

"Sweetie, it's okay. Stop crying. Shhh. No, they'll understand," Lydia said, glancing around the table. "Uh-huh. Okay. I'll be home right after breakfast. I promise it will be okay. Did you tell your father? What did he say?"

Celeste leaned toward Jessica and whispered, "Who do you think died?"

"No, honey. He won't kill him. He's just being protective. Okay. See you soon." Without looking at any of them, Lydia reached for her spoon, picked it up, and started to stir her coffee.

"Lyd, what is it?" Celeste asked.

"Well," Lydia said, exhaling, "it seems that little Miss Brie Ellison is on quite the sexual rampage."

"What?"

"When Christina got to Brie's house, she found Brie in bed." Lydia paused and lifted her coffee cup to her lips.

"So?" Jessica said.

"Well, Brie wasn't alone, and she wasn't with Damien, either."

"Oh, no," Celeste wailed.

"What? What am I missing?" Jessica asked.

Lydia looked Jessica in the eye. "Brie was in bed with Bradford."

"But Bradford is seeing Christina," Mary Anne said, stating the obvious.

"Welcome to Hollywood," Jessica said.

"Cici, you may run into a bit of a mess when you get home. It seems Bradford is now back at your place and has been calling Christina nonstop. When Zymar asked what was going on, well, Christina told him. Zymar's on his way to your house."

"Might be good for Bradford to get his ass kicked," Celeste said.

"I'm glad we're finished with production," Lydia said. "Bruises have a nasty way of showing up on film. They are such a pain for the makeup department to hide."

"That bitch," Celeste muttered. "That girl must be stopped."

"Christina isn't part of this crazy entertainment world," Lydia said. "She's sweet and young. You know, I think she was falling in love with Bradford."

"Never fall in love with an actor," Jessica said, and glanced at Celeste. "No offense, Cici."

"Don't worry, I'd never fall for an actor. Are you kidding? Marrying a producer was bad enough."

"I know how she feels," Mary Anne whispered.

Jessica looked at Mary Anne, as did Lydia and Celeste. Like any good writer, Mary Anne spent most of her time observing whenever they were together. It was a rare occasion when she actually offered information that was personal.

"I walked in on my boyfriend . . . well, you know. I walked in on him at our apartment with our neighbor."

"Was this Steve?" Lydia asked.

"How did you know?" Mary Anne looked at Lydia.

"You mentioned Steve and Viève in the ambulance the night Bradford almost killed you."

"It's just so awful." Mary Anne gazed into the distance.

"I think it's safe to say we've all been there." Lydia glanced around table. "Or almost there. Maybe not quite as graphic as your and Christina's scenes, but pretty close."

Jessica nodded along with Celeste. She sighed. "Twenty million or not, I'm almost glad Bradford Madison isn't my client."

"I agree with Cici. I think it's time Miss Ellison gets a little of what she gives." Lydia's eyes narrowed. "Cici, you said you needed film. Well, I think I know just the person who can help us, and she just so happens to work for you."

"Work for me? Who?" Celeste asked.

"Kiki Dee," Lydia said.

Mary Anne and Her
Anna Molinari Flats

MARY ANNE SAT IN LYDIA'S LIVING ROOM, RELEGATED TO THE ROLE OF TISSUE passer. Mascara trailed from Christina's long lashes to her chin. Heaving sobs shook her thin frame. Lydia had fled the scene to find Zymar, hoping to prevent a jail sentence for him and bodily harm to Bradford, who wasn't in the house but was making his absence felt by lighting up the phones (all six lines, including Christina's cell).

"I feel so silly," Christina said, and blew her blotchy red nose. "I mean it's a fling, really."

Christina glanced at Mary Anne, who interpreted the look as a request for confirmation. She nodded.

"It's not like we were," Christina sniffled, "in," she said, grabbing another tissue, "love," she wailed, her emotions breaking apart again.

Mary Anne kicked off her Anna Molinari flats. She felt sad for Christina and a little mournful for herself. Images of the afternoon she'd walked in on Viève and Steve flitted through her mind.

"I mean, I know actors. I understand. I've been on film sets my entire life. My mother's an actress—she's been married three times. I get it," Christina said, as if trying to convince herself. "It's just that"—she grabbed yet another tissue—"he seemed different, he seemed different when he was with me." Her forlorn face implored Mary Anne to spout words of wisdom.

"Maybe he was," Mary Anne said.

"What?"

"Different when he was with you."

"Yeah, right, more like just a fucking good actor," Christina shot back, rubbing the tissue under her eyes.

"No, really. Maybe with you he was the very best he could be, as a man, but . . ." Mary Anne paused, testing out her next words in her mind.

"But what?" Christina asked and sniffled.

"But that's just it. When you were around, you helped him to be this really great guy, the Bradford Madison he always wanted to be, but when you weren't around—"

"He became the self-absorbed, nihilistic prick he always was?"

Mary Anne allowed herself a small smile. "You can't change someone's behavior. You can't love him into being someone he's not, and you can't blame yourself for his decisions."

Christina bit her lower lip. "I know all that. I get it, but it still just absolutely sucks." She glanced out the window. "What is it with men? Do they ever get any control?"

Mary Anne sighed and shook her head. "So far, I say no." But in the land of sunshine, community property, silicone, and starter husbands, did it even really matter? The longer Mary Anne lived in Los Angeles and worked in Hollywood, the more she was surprised that anyone still married. Everyone, it seemed, traded up every two years. *Why not sign a lease agreement for a relationship instead of entering into a marriage?* she wondered. Commit for a finite period of time, and then move on; maybe if you knew at the beginning of the relationship that you only had so long together (not open-ended, like till death do you part), it'd be easier for men to keep their dicks in their pants. She wondered if the key component to maintaining a relationship wasn't even easier: Just never give your heart away. Never be vulnerable, never fall in love. It seemed to work for Lydia. Or it had before Zymar.

"That's enough of a pity party for me." Christina took a deep breath. "Besides, I'm back to London in three days, and I don't want to waste this last little bit of time crying over that bugger."

Mary Anne admired Christina's strength. Finding Steve in bed (well, on the couch) with Viève had left her rocking and wailing in Sylvia's apartment for at least four days, unable to eat or speak. Mitsy had threatened to come out and have Mary Anne committed if she didn't at least return her calls.

"Okay then, I am going upstairs to destroy every gift Bradford Madison gave me, except the diamond necklace—*that* I'm keeping. Then I'm going shopping."

"Retail therapy?" Mary Anne asked. She hadn't even known the term existed prior to meeting Celeste.

"Exactly," Christina said, smiling tentatively. "And then we are going out tonight."

"We?"

"Yes, Nobu first and then to Tantric."

"The new club in Hollywood?" Mary Anne raised her eyebrows.

"Opened last weekend. Very hot."

"Hmm, not sure," Mary Anne hedged, looking down at the red toenail polish chipping off her toes (she'd failed to maintain her pedicure).

"Mary Anne, you have to," Christina said, her bottom lip beginning to quiver again. "I asked Cici earlier if she'd go and she promised, but that will be a mob scene. I won't have anyone to speak to if you're not there. Besides, what if I run into Bradford, or worse, Brie?"

Mary Anne sighed. "Okay."

"The car will get you at eight."

Mary Anne sat in a semicircular booth in the VIP section of Tantric, watching as Cici gyrated on the dance floor below with a gorgeous man-child who couldn't have been older than twenty. Cici turned and slid her ass against the man-boy's privates, proudly displaying a white Vivienne Westwood shirt with a neckline that plunged to her belly and showed off not only her perky breasts, but her chiseled abs and tiny belly button. *Enough friction to start a forest fire,* Mary Anne thought as she (and the rest of the clubgoers) watched Cici's ass grind.

"Time to make a friend," Christina said, picking up her mojito and gesturing toward the bar. "That's Boom Boom, Cici's publicist's assistant. She'll love this dirt on Brie." Christina gave Mary Anne a wicked grin and walked to the red VIP rope. She nodded at the bouncer, who quickly unfastened the barrier as he watched Christina in her Jean Paul Gaultier boots and Emanuel Ungaro short shorts.

Mary Anne scanned the club. She'd now participated in "the scene" a half dozen times, but she was always surprised to see the same faces flitting about: Vilmer, Zach, Jessica, Nikki and Paris, just to name a few. Always out, always at a new club, and always drinking.

Mary Anne wasn't surprised, however, when she and the girls quickly attracted two gadflies and a hanger-on. They magically appeared everywhere, and tonight, as soon as the waitress started the bottle service (at $750 for Cristal), the three ladies had company. One was a "baby" celebrity with a show on Fox—or was it CW? The girl either had a massive crush on Cici or a tendency for stalking. She'd practically plopped herself on Cici's lap trying to get close. A second hanger-on (or maybe working man) was the dirty dancer now running his hands across Cici's ass and thighs. And finally, next to the actress sat a celebutante with nothing much for talent other than her sparkling blue eyes, her father's name, and her immense bank account. Those attributes, thus far, had been enough to get her four films and two television shows.

Mary Anne glanced toward the table on her left, where one A-lister sat surrounded by his well-paid sycophants, who for a fee would kiss his ass, suck his dick, and spend his money.

"Isn't that Holden Humphrey?" Christina asked, walking back to the table and nodding toward a booth two down from their own.

Mary Anne glanced past the A-lister and his entourage. She remembered watching Holden in *Purple Racer* and thinking that he must have the world's most pleasing ass.

"That's him," said the tiny sitcom actress. "He's with Maurice Banks."

Mary Anne looked at the two action stars and the two girls with them, one a blonde and the other a redhead. *Wait, was that . . . ?* Mary Anne squinted her eyes. The room was dark, but she could just make out the person sitting on Holden's lap like a pet pup. *Viève.*

"Who's the ugly redhead?" Christina asked, sliding into the booth.

"Viève," Mary Anne breathed, unable to tear her eyes away from Holden.

"Do I know her?" Christina asked. "What's she done?"

"My ex-boyfriend," Mary Anne said, sipping her champagne.

"Really?" Christina said. She looked at Mary Anne with new appreciation. "So you know firsthand."

Mary Anne glanced at Christina. "Intimately. This is why I am convinced men have absolutely no dick control. Look at her. No tits, she's odd looking, kind of like a Chihuahua, and still she was not only able to fuck my boyfriend, but now she's being groped by one of the finest-looking men in America. And why?"

"Because it's easy," Christina said.

"Exactly. The only dick control they get is when they're old—"

"Usually fat."

"And bald," the tiny sitcom star chirped.

"And just too lazy to put up a chase," Mary Anne said. "That isn't really dick control, just loss of your game."

Cici strolled up to the table. "What are we staring at?"

"Holden Humphrey," Mary Anne said.

"And Mary Anne's former neighbor who fucked Steve," Christina added.

"That's Viève?" Cici asked, scrunching her nose.

"Yes." Mary Anne glowered.

"Want some payback?" Cici smiled.

Mary Anne considered it. She'd never before participated in the type of female games Cici seemed to have mastered—giggling, hair tossing, collecting men as baubles. But she felt scorned, and the idea of getting even felt empowering.

"Yes." Mary Anne looked from Cici to Christina.

Cici sat next to Mary Anne and waved her hand. A waitress in a red silk bustier approached the table, carrying their fifth bottle of Cristal.

"Will you please ask Mr. Humphrey to come over?" Cici asked, slipping the waitress a hundred-dollar bill.

"Of course, Ms. Solange." She eyed Celeste.

"He can bring Maurice, but not the Chihuahua." Cici handed her another hundred. "Understand?" Cici asked.

"Of course," the waitress said, already moving toward Holden and his table.

Mary Anne watched as the waitress tilted her head and whispered in Holden's ear. First confusion, then a smile crossed Holden's face as he glanced over and gave Cici a small wave. Then he leaned over Viève and whispered to Maurice. Mary Anne felt a burst of vindictive pleasure flood through her as she watched a baffled Viève stare at Holden and Maurice as they got up and walked away. Just as Holden arrived next to Mary Anne (he was a million times better looking than Steve), Viève's eyes focused on her. First amazement, then horror registered on the Chihuahua's face. Mary Anne gave Viève a sweet smile and a quick wave just as Holden Humphrey plopped his gorgeous ass on the seat next to her.

Sure, Holden Humphrey was as dumb as a post, but he was Mary Anne's first one-night stand and an amazing fuck. She glanced at her watch: 3:35 A.M. The golden god slept to her left. She could still feel the heat of his kisses across her chest. Which was still bare. *Where were her clothes?* He'd tossed her bra over his shoulder when he carried her to his bed, but her jeans and thong, she believed, were tangled in the mess of pillows and blankets. She smiled. She knew she should feel slutty, but she couldn't muster up any guilt or remorse. Just victory. She came, she saw, she conquered (not in that order, and she'd come at least three times). She wished she had a camera phone. Nobody would believe this—she barely did. She'd just had sex with *People* magazine's Sexiest Man Alive. And it was hot sex. Hot, upside-down, sideways, spank-him-on-the-ass (she'd never done that before) sex.

She slid out from under the covers and tiptoed around the room, picking her jeans out of the blankets and her bra from a far corner. She quietly shimmied into her thong and reached for her shirt on the chair next to Holden's side of the bed.

"Hey, baby." A groggy Holden reached out his hand and smiled a sleepy smile. "You gotta go?"

"Yeah, I need to get home," she said, sitting on the edge of the bed.

"Okay, I can take you."

"No, stay," Mary Anne insisted. "It's good. I'll call a car."

"Sure?" His lids drifted down over his eyes.

Mary Anne smiled. "I'm sure."

She leaned forward and kissed Holden Humphrey's lips.

"Okay, you got my number?" Holden mumbled.

Mary Anne stuck her hand in her jeans pocket for the wadded-up cocktail napkin. "Sure do," she said. "But, Holden, I don't think I'll call."

"Huh?" Holden opened his bright blue eyes.

"This was fun, but I'm not really looking for a relationship right now," Mary Anne said, glancing around the room for her purse. She had a vague memory of tossing it as Holden dropped her onto the bed.

"Oh." Holden looked befuddled.

"Ah." Mary Anne spotted her bag under the night table and grabbed it. "This was so much fun, and I'm sure we'll see each other out somewhere again, but really, this number, not ready to use it." Mary Anne dropped the cocktail napkin onto the night table.

"Wasn't it"—Holden paused, looking away from Mary Anne—"good for you?"

"What?" Mary Anne smiled. "Are you kidding? It was the absolute best. You are the man. It's not the sex, really. It's just, guys right now for me, I'm not in the right mind-set."

Holden smiled, presumably relieved, Mary Anne thought, that her mental instability was to blame and not his sexual performance.

"Got it. Well, babe, you know where I am," he said, reaching out and rubbing Mary Anne's thigh.

"Yes," Mary Anne said, "yes, I do."

22

Celeste Solange and Her Lara Bohinc Shades

PEOPLE HAD A HARD TIME GUESSING KIKI DEE'S AGE. A BALLET DANCER before answering the call to celebrate stars by ensuring the best coverage in *People, Star,* or *Us Weekly,* Kiki kept her body lithe and firm. She was living proof of Dr. Charles Melnick's skill with the scalpel (his best customer and an A-plus referral service). In return for referring all her clients for lips, micro-derm, Botox, breast enhancement, and any other service the best cosmetic surgeon in Beverly Hills could supply, Kiki received a thirty percent discount. A kickback if you will, and Kiki chose to take the kickbacks out in trade. No, you couldn't guess Kiki's age, but Celeste would bet her quote that Kiki had a recent battle scar to complement her signature Louis Vuitton eyeglasses (which matched her Louis Vuitton shoes) and Bettie Page haircut.

Celeste, having made her request prior to Kiki's taking this call, watched as her publicist spoke to a magazine editor and waved her hands to emphasize why the B-list star of whom she spoke should be on the cover of *Vanity Fair.* On the wall behind her hung a calendar studded with notes on film premieres and press schedules for her busiest clients. Celeste knew that Kiki's client list was tiring. Five years before, when Damien had urged Celeste to sign with Kiki, she was *the* publicist to have, but because of a split within Kiki's firm (three younger yet top-level publicists left, taking their clients, and started their own publicity firm down the street), Kiki's roster had shrunk and so had her income. Now Kiki concentrated on signing young talent. Up-and-comers. Actors with a few good credits but great potential. This way, in five to ten years, as these actors emerged from their film roles with awards and big box office, Kiki would once again be on top of the publicity world.

Celeste also knew that Damien had brought Brie Ellison to Kiki. It was a conflict of interest, of course, with Kiki forced to do damage control for Celeste's image during the divorce while trying to keep Brie's name and photos in all the right magazines for as long as the public's interest held. Celeste hoped to get what she needed by playing upon these two things: Kiki's insatiable desire for young talent and her guilt over the conflict of interest. Celeste smiled sweetly at her publicist as she hung up the phone.

"Celeste, I will not give you the security code to Brie Ellison's house." Kiki peered at Celeste through her glasses.

"But Kiki, I need it."

"No way. Can you imagine? Tomorrow I read of a triple murder-suicide, you, Brie, and Damien, and me never knowing who killed who? No way!"

"Kiki, if you don't give me this—"

"What? What will you do?" Kiki's eyes turned cold and her smile faded. "Cici, I know where *all* the bodies are buried, even the ones you killed. So don't take any kind of tone that even resembles a threat. Got it?"

Celeste turned up the wattage on her charm. "Kiki, my love, you are my publicist. I trust you with every one of my flaws. Everything that makes me human. All those things I want to hide."

"All right, then. Now go do what stars do."

Celeste stood and put on her Lara Bohinc sunglasses. "I don't know why I even bothered. I guess it's only because Bradford Madison's become like a little brother to me."

Kiki's head snapped up. "Bradford Madison?"

Celeste knew that dropping Bradford's name would catch Kiki's interest faster than the paparazzi could say cheese. "Yes, Bradford

Madison. He stayed with me during principal photography for *Seven Minutes Past Midnight.* You know, to keep his nose clean."

"Go on."

"Well, it seems like he and Brie started a little thing."

"Really?" Kiki leaned forward. "I had no idea. Brie didn't mention it. How could I not know this? How could *People, Star,* and *Us* not know this? This is huge news."

"It's very new and very under wraps. Especially since Damien is away on location scouts. I guess Brie does have a heart and wants to tell Damien about Bradford in person. Such a wonderful girl. So much more than Damien deserves."

"You're right there. Go on."

"They had a tiff. Bradford and Brie. And, well, Bradford came to me and begged me to help. Darling, what was I to do? Seems that Bradford is really quite the romantic, and he wants to sneak into the house and do the whole rose-petals-champagne-I'm-so-sorry thing for Brie. I know it's a little cliché. But young love . . ."

"Hmm . . . This Madison-Ellison thing could be big. Very big. It needs to be encouraged. Yes. Okay. I'll do it. Have Bradford call me."

"Kiki, my darling, no need. Bradford is here."

"He's here? Bradford Madison, the one client I've been salivating over for two years, is here? Oh God, Cici, I adore you! Where? Where is he?"

"Right outside. Have your assistant send him in," Celeste said.

"Boom Boom," Kiki yelled, "bring Bradford in."

Celeste could tell by Bradford's slow shuffle that he didn't want to enter this lion's den. Kiki had, in fact, pursued Bradford mercilessly for over two years. *But if this is his penance,* Celeste thought, *so be it.* He'd absolutely broken Christina's heart before she departed for Oxford.

"Bradford, so good to see you again." Kiki rushed around her desk and grabbed him and kissed both his cheeks. She pulled back, eyeing Bradford's face over the top of her glasses. "My goodness, lover, *Seven Minutes Past Midnight* must have been a rough set—look at those bruises! But your skin is so young it will heal. Believe *me,* I know, bruises heal. Now, darling, you've been a very naughty boy," Kiki said, wagging her finger at him. "You haven't returned any of my calls. Sit, sit. Tell me all about this little love affair with my client Brie Ellison."

"Well, it's not exactly—"

"Bradford, don't be shy," Celeste interrupted. "Kiki knows everything about everyone—it's her job."

"So rose petals and champagne." Kiki peered over the top of her glasses again. "Well, red is her favorite color, and I think that Veuve is her favorite champagne. We have some in the fridge out front; take a bottle when you leave. Boom Boom, get me Brie's security code," Kiki yelled. "Now, darling, I am happy to do this little favor for you, but you must promise me that when you and Brie go public with your relationship, I get to announce it, and of course a dinner. You and me. There is so much I can do for your career. I have so many ideas."

A tiny Asian girl with dark glasses rushed in and handed Kiki a card.

"Here it is," Kiki said, passing it to Bradford. "Now, don't you share this with anyone."

"Sure," Bradford said.

"And have Boom Boom schedule our dinner before you leave. Now go, go." Kiki waved both the actors toward her office door. "Both of you go make hits!"

Celeste smiled at Kiki and glanced at Bradford. *Yes, they certainly needed to make a hit.*

Celeste had parked up a hill and around the corner from Brie's Silver Lake home. The spot gave her the best view of both the drive and the front door. She held a wireless receiver in her hand that got both audio and video transmissions from the tiny camera (shaped like an exact replica of the Mont Blanc pens Damien used) that Bradford was positioning on the nightstand next to Brie and Damien's bed. She also wore a wireless earpiece with a microphone, as did Bradford, so the two of them could talk.

Very high tech. Who knew that good divorce attorneys came equipped with spy gadgetry.

"Bradford, that's perfect. Great view of the room and the bed," Celeste said into the microphone. "Now get out of there."

Headlights flashed in Celeste's rearview mirror. She scrunched down in her car. The last thing she needed was someone calling the police because they thought she was a peeper. As the black Hummer cruised by, she saw the license plates. BIGD. *Shit,* she thought. *It's Damien and Brie.*

"Bradford, can you hear me? Bradford!"

"What's up?"

"I've got Damien and Brie pulling into the drive. They must have taken an earlier flight. Get out."

"You're kidding? Cici, there's only one way into this place, and I'm on the second floor."

"Then hide." Celeste peeked around the steering wheel. She watched as Brie hopped out of the Hummer and Damien went around back and pulled out their luggage.

"Bradford, she's opening the front door now. Hide, do you hear me? Hide!"

"Cici, shut up. Okay, I hear you. Just make sure the damn thing is recording."

Celeste looked at the wireless receiver. "We're good. Bradford, where are you?"

"Closet."

"Their closet?"

"Yeah."

"But they've got luggage. Clothes to unpack."

"Cici, I know Brie: There won't be any unpacking tonight."

Celeste watched Damien haul the last bag into the house and shut the door.

"Damien, let's go to bed," Celeste heard Brie call, and then Brie walked into frame. "I need to relax. Can we get one on?"

How romantic, Celeste thought. *She sounds just like a man.*

Damien passed into frame. Celeste was shocked. She hadn't seen Damien in months and he looked haggard and old.

"Brie, really, I'm just too tired. What about in the morning?"

Damien too tired for sex? That's a new one.

"I'll toss and turn all night if we don't just do a quicky."

"Fine," Damien said. "Let me brush my teeth and then we'll get this done."

Damien walked out of frame.

"Get this done?" Brie muttered under her breath. "Old man."

Celeste watched as Brie approached the full-length mirror next to the closet door. She slowly took off her clothes, watching herself undress as though doing a striptease for herself.

Damien came back into frame, wearing his silk boxer shorts. His body showed the effect of forgoing his morning swims; the aging that Damien managed to keep at bay with rigorous physical exercise and an impeccable diet had assaulted his body. He looked every bit of his fifty years plus five more. The best word to describe his appearance, Celeste thought, was *awful.*

Damien reached for the light next to the bed to switch it off (not that it mattered, since the spy camera had night-vision capability).

"Leave it on, baby. I've got lines to read when we're done," Brie said.

Damien gave an exhausted sigh and rolled over to the sexual succubus lying with him in bed.

Celeste watched as Brie mounted Damien like a dog deciding to dry-hump a leg. *This I don't need to see,* Celeste thought. She flipped the screen down and took the earphone out of her ear (keeping the two-way radio piece in, in case Bradford needed her).

Bradford! Poor Bradford, Celeste thought, stifling a giggle. He'd get the full effect of Damien grunting and Brie moaning while he stood in Brie's closet. Celeste knew Damien would conk out after the sex, but she hoped that Brie would work on her lines in another room so Bradford could slip out of the house. The idea of spending hours sitting in her Porsche in Silver Lake waiting for Bradford to find an escape route irritated her and marred her brief good mood.

In fact, the entire evening was preposterous. Spy cameras, two-way walkie-talkies, video receivers and digital displays. And for what? Revenge. The sweet taste of it. Knowing that every time she placed her Black Card down to purchase a pair of Ferragamos or Louboutins, it wouldn't be her money paying for the purchase but Damien's. He'd always been cheap. Celeste blamed it on his Midwestern upbringing. His family had money; they just never spent it. Damien was the same way.

"Cici!" Bradford yelled into Celeste's earphone.

"What?"

"Start the car," Bradford gasped.

"What?"

"Start the car."

He sounded like he was running.

"Bradford, where are you?" Celeste turned the key in the ignition.

"Unlock the door." Celeste turned and saw Bradford rapping on the glass. "Hurry, hurry. Damien's behind me."

As soon as the door lock clicked, Bradford jumped into the Porsche and Celeste gunned the accelerator. As she turned the corner, she saw Damien, barefoot and wearing his boxers, bent over at the waist gasping for air.

"What happened?" Celeste asked, taking the next corner fast and then slowing down.

"The cats."

"What?"

"All six were in the closet with me. One sitting on my head. One curled up on a box right under my nose and another using my leg as a scratching post," Bradford said, pulling up his leg and examining the marks.

"Were they finished?" Celeste asked.

"Weren't you watching?" Bradford asked, incredulous.

"Couldn't."

"Well, it sounded like it from the closet."

Howard?" Cici heard a rustling noise over her phone.

"Cici? It's one a.m."

"I got it." Cici said, unable to contain her excitement.

"Got what?"

"Tape of Damien and Brie."

"How di—? Never mind, don't answer that. Okay, let me think. God it's late. Tomorrow put it in a plain brown envelope and mail it to my office. Do not put a return address on it, do you understand?"

"Sure," Celeste said, pacing in front of her plasma TV, an image of a buck-naked Brie frozen on the screen.

"And don't lick the stamp on the envelope; use water."

"Not a problem."

"Don't use your local post office, either," Howard said, a sigh escaping over the phone.

"Drive over to West Hollywood or the Valley; yeah, the Valley would be best."

"That it?" Cici giggled. She was giddy, her endorphins running high.

"Yeah that's it. Is it good?" Howard asked.

Celeste turned back to the television and clicked Play, the image of Brie straddling Damian coming to life. "It's good," Celeste said, turning up the volume so Howard could hear Brie's moans over the phone. "In fact, I think it's her best performance ever."

Lydia Albright and Her Dior Open Pumps

LYDIA DIDN'T WANT TO SHOW ZYMAR'S ROUGH CUT YET. IT WAS GOOD, BUT IT wasn't ready. Unfortunately, her desire held little weight when compared to Arnold's order to screen the movie for him privately that evening. Arnold's order, plus an explicit threat that he would pull the film's editor for another film and reassign the editing suite if she didn't obey, was at this critical juncture a fate almost worse than shelving the film. *They were too close to the end to lose the film now*. So Lydia had grudgingly acquiesced, and now she and Zymar sat side by side in the third row of one of Worldwide's screening rooms, with Josanne and Arnold several rows behind them.

"Lyd, it's not even color-corrected yet," Zymar whispered across the armrest.

"They know you're only three weeks into postproduction."

"There isn't a score."

"Don't worry about the music. The shots are fantastic. They'll get a feel for it."

"If you say so, Lyd." Zymar slid down in his seat. "But that little pecker is looking for any excuse to pull the plug."

Lydia cringed. Arnold had them boxed into a corner. The film wasn't ready to be screened, and yet they had no choice but to let the president of the studio view the print. She didn't have any room to bargain; they were already over budget. With the additional shooting days and expense (due to Arnold's fire marshal trick), she was at least $20 million over, probably more. She'd been shuffling paperwork, stalling on reporting expenses and signing off on budget reports to the studio in order to keep the production going and the accounting department in the dark.

Any other studio head, when dealing with a producer like Lydia (a producer with over $1 billion in box-office receipts under her belt) and a huge potential moneymaker like *Seven Minutes,* would accept the overage—in fact, on this big of a production they'd expect it. But Lydia could think of no other president of production who would have "set up" a producer in order to play out a personal vendetta.

Even though Lydia hadn't turned in all her receipts, she was sure that Arnold knew she was over budget, probably down to the last penny. But what Lydia wondered was whether Arnold was aware that Lydia knew of his deceit. Arnold never had learned to cover his tracks well. An ego overage. It was a similar scenario that started their feud almost ten years before.

The lights dimmed as Lydia watched her film flicker to life.

As the lights went up, Lydia knew *Seven Minutes Past Midnight* was a hit. It didn't matter that this was a rough cut, that it wasn't color-corrected, or that it lacked music. *Seven Minutes Past Midnight* would pummel box-office records. Lydia felt it in her core.

"You are a brilliant director," she told Zymar, beaming. She thought she saw him blush.

"Thank you, Lyd." He squeezed her hand. "But it was all you that kept this film on track."

They both tilted their heads over their shared armrest toward the back of the screening room where Arnold and Josanne sat.

"Wonder what that little pecker thinks," Zymar said.

"Liideeeaaa," Arnold yelled from the back.

"Guess we're going to find out," Lydia whispered to Zymar as she watched Arnold stand and strut down the screening room stairs with Josanne close behind.

Not even Arnold is so stupid that he couldn't see how fantastic the film is, Lydia thought. Cici's and Bradford's performances were impeccable. The shots were genius. The action sequences well thought out and worth every dollar. Excellence and hard work had trumped Arnold's petty, backstabbing personality. She'd done it again!

Arnold stopped on the stair above Lydia and Zymar (even though he stood four inches above Lydia, in her Dior heels, Lydia was still taller).

"Unbelievable," Arnold said.

"I know. Really something, isn't it," Lydia said, and smiled at Zymar. "He did—"

"I am absolutely disgusted," Arnold continued.

Lydia felt her body recoil as if Arnold had reached over and slapped her.

Arnold pointed his finger at Zymar. "How could you waste the studio's money like this?" He turned and sneered at Lydia. "And how could you let him?"

"Arnold—"

"No. This is a mess. Worthless. Un-releasable."

"Arnold, what are you talking about? This is a rough cut. It's brilliant. With a final edit and a score, *Seven Minutes* will be number one at the box office."

"You mean with another five million dollars." Arnold's piercingly shrill voice was rapidly approaching a level that he saved for outright rage, a tone familiar to Lydia.

"Our postproduction budget is approximately five million."

"You're already twenty over, aren't you?" he snapped. "Josanne ran the numbers today."

Josanne stepped forward with her ever-present black binder and flipped it open. "Yes, Mr. Murphy, with all the overages, and the invoice that we just received from the Burbank fire department, this film is approximately twenty-one million dollars over budget."

"Arnold, Weston and I discussed this when we made the deal, and with a budget of this magnitude, twenty-one million in overages is nothing less than expected—"

"Nothing? Lydia Albright, are you telling me that you wasting twenty-one million dollars of this studio's money is nothing?"

Lydia saw the red creeping up Arnold's neck toward his face.

"Now, wait 'ere, this film—" Zymar started.

"I am not speaking to you!" Arnold interrupted, shoving his finger in Zymar's face.

"Now, there's no need to get pissy," Zymar argued. "This is just a rough cut. We all know that rough cuts are sixty percent at best. And this is already one terrific film, even at that."

"You *would* say that," Arnold said. "It's your film. Your work is atrocious."

Lydia was horrified. Arnold had just broken one of the cardinal rules of Hollywood. No one ever insulted someone's work to their face. A studio executive might phone a writer or director's agent to pass along a message that the studio was "less than pleased" with their work. But no one, under any circumstances, openly called something crap to the creator's face. Was Arnold losing his mind? Lydia could feel the heat rolling off Zymar.

Zymar stepped forward, his fists clenched at his side. "Listen, you little red- 'eaded prick. You've done nothing but try to sabotage this film since you took over the studio. And now that you know it's going to be a 'it and Lydia was right, you can't stand it."

"You hack! You are swearing at the head of a studio."

"Damn straight, and wishing it was more than swearing I was doing."

"Are you threatening me?" Arnold yelped. "Now you are threatening me? Josanne, call security."

"No need; I'm leaving," Zymar yelled, and stomped down the stairs toward the exit.

"Lydia, control your director," Arnold screeched.

"I am not a dog to be put on a leash, Mr. Murphy," Zymar shot back.

"Come back here; this meeting isn't finished!" Arnold screamed toward Zymar's retreating back.

Lydia watched wearily as Zymar opened the screening-room door and then slammed it shut behind him. "Arnold, there isn't anything constructive that's going to come out of this tonight. Not now. Let's reconvene in the morning."

"Lydia, if you don't get your director back in here right now, he's fired! You're both fired!"

They were so close to the finish line. Just six more weeks and the film would be released and the public could decide. Ticket sales would make the ultimate fool out of Arnold Murphy.

"Sorry, Arnold, got to go." Lydia walked toward the exit. "It's past my bedtime."

"That's it!" Arnold yelled gleefully after her. "Insubordination and job abandonment. He's fired and you, Lydia Albright, are fired as well."

Lydia looked at the little man standing on the stairs. "Good night, Arnold," she called.

"I will shelve your film, Lydia. Do you hear me? You won't work again."

Lydia held up her hand and waved over her shoulder. She needed to find Zymar.

Lydia pulled the Stoli bottle from the silver bucket of ice that rested on the nightstand next to her king-size bed. She topped off her shot glass. It was four A.M. and Zymar was gone, bundled hours earlier onto a private flight to New Zealand with his editor, the footage, and the only rough cut of *Seven Minutes Past Midnight.* Lydia was sure she'd committed a felony and violated a slew of international copyright laws. And now, once again, she was alone.

The silence was loud. She hadn't quite realized how integral Zymar had become to her home—his heavy footfalls, loud singing, Eurotrash accent, even his funky Balinese music that blared over her Bang & Olufsen sound system. The house felt alive when he was in it. Lydia felt alive when she was with him. She sipped her vodka. Now Lydia just felt cold and alone. And not nearly drunk enough.

Arnold would ban Lydia from the Worldwide lot. Toddy had promised to go to the bungalow tomorrow and grab as many files as she could without appearing conspicuous. Thad Blumenthal, the producer of Turning Blue Pictures, whose company occupied the bungalow next to Lydia's on the lot, had offered to have his staff sneak into Lydia's bungalow over the next week to retrieve whatever Toddy left behind. They both knew that studio security would look the other way, as long as Lydia wasn't the one clearing out her office.

Lydia set her shot glass on her nightstand, settled into her pillows, and pulled up her down comforter. Her king-size bed felt huge; she hadn't slept by herself in months. God, she missed him. It wasn't just the disappointment with Arnold and the film. It wasn't the humiliation of being scolded like a child. No, it was the pain and anger she knew Zymar felt that made her melancholy. She ached to reach over and snuggle deep into the safe, warm place inside his arms.

Lydia's home phone rang. *Four A.M.?* There were maybe five people in the entire world who would call her this late. She contemplated leaving it to voice mail, but with Zymar on the lam and her new status as an unconvicted felon, she thought she'd better answer.

"Lyd, it's Jess. How are you?"

"Well, I've been fired, my film and the love of my life are fleeing to New Zealand, and I've nearly completed a bottle of Stoli. I've been better." Lydia felt woozy. It occurred to her that she hadn't eaten since lunch the day before.

"Arnold just called. He screamed for at least a half hour. I thought you should know he's leaked the whole thing to the trades. It's going to be front page in *Variety* and the *Hollywood Reporter* in the morning."

"Nothing like making the trades. Is that it?"

"He's having Worldwide Business Affairs file suit tomorrow in federal court. He's claiming the film's been stolen."

Lydia snorted. That was rich. The film, *her* film, had, in fact, been beaten, bruised, and now abducted. But only to save its potential box-office life. "Yeah, well, I'm sure if he tries, he can track it down. There are only a few postproduction facilities in New Zealand."

Jessica didn't laugh. "Lyd, this could get really ugly. How much more time does Zymar need to finish post?"

"Four, maybe six weeks. Why?"

"I spoke to your attorney. He can probably stall for a while. I mean, the legal system is slow. But you realize you will bleed out in the industry while this is happening. You only have so much juice, and this is going to take most of it. All of your projects at Worldwide will be shelved and no other studio will want to take a chance with you until this gets sorted."

Lydia had already contemplated how the next two months would be the longest and most painful of her entire Hollywood career (including when she nearly starved trying to make it as an actress). She didn't have an office. She wouldn't have an income. And no one in town would return her calls. They'd talk *about* her, just not *to* her. It was going to be very, very cold for Lydia Albright in L.A.

"Thanks, Jess. I know this town. I've already thought about it. Guess I'll finally get all that reading finished." Lydia glanced at the three-foot pile of scripts next to her bed. Writer samples, new scripts, potential films to make. Who was she kidding? There were no "potential films to be made" by Lydia Albright until Arnold got his print back. How could she win this battle? Even if Zymar finished the film—which was a complete long shot, since they didn't have $5 million for postproduction or any money to pay the composer. Plus who would release it? Where would it be shown? Worldwide owned the film. And as long as Arnold was in charge, it would never get a release date.

"Lyd, I'm here. You know anything I can do, I will."

"Thanks, Jess. I appreciate it." Lydia sighed. The sun was almost coming up, but who cared? She didn't even have an office to go to today.

"So I found you an office," Jessica said with a hint of a smile in her voice. "You ought to feel pretty comfortable there."

"What? Where?"

"Just after Arnold called, Beverly Birnbaum phoned. Said she'd expect to see you at her bungalow over at Summit around ten. Wanted me to tell you that your old office is still yours."

Lydia smiled. It was always the Birnbaums who bailed her out. Now, if only Weston's ghost could take care of Arnold . . . "Bev is the best."

"Yeah, the whole family is."

"Then I better get to sleep. I'm going to have a helluva headache in the morning."

"Night, Lyd. Talk to you later."

"Night, Jess." Lydia set the cordless phone into its cradle. At least she didn't have to stay holed up in the house licking her wounds. It was all about perception in this town, and starting later today she'd make sure that every producer, agent, and studio perceived that Lydia Albright didn't have an ounce of worry. Even if every cell in her body was screaming with fear.

Arnold Murphy and the Dolce & Gabbana

ARNOLD MURPHY WASN'T STUPID; HE KNEW LYDIA ALBRIGHT'S GAME. HE'D figured that out years before (when he was stuck kissing Weston Birnbaum's huge ass). Arnold knew her type; they were common in L.A. Fuck queens. Fuck the man (any man) in power and get what you want. The only problem for Lydia was that Arnold was unfuckable. At least by her. He waited impatiently in the back of his Lincoln Town Car for his driver to open the back door. If the lard ass would waddle around to Arnold's side, he could enter Charles's home at exactly 8:17 P.M. A perfect time to join a 7:30 P.M. soiree. *Finally*. Arnold glared at his approaching driver. How unfortunate for a life to be squandered shuffling people around in a car and opening doors, but then obviously his driver was barely capable of these mundane tasks. Arnold sighed, and waved his hands toward the waste of a man who chauffeured him to and from events, work, and home. *What* was *his name? Ralph? Raymundo?* Really, who the fuck cared? It was inconsequential.

He inhaled. *Dead fish. God, he hated Malibu.* The ocean was a toilet; every form of waste churned within the sea and people swam in that filth. He walked up the steps and the security guard pulled open the massive fifteen-foot doors. Charles liked things big.

The party was behind the house, even closer to the sea. Arnold wrinkled his nose at the sight of the buffet table. *A buffet? How unlike Charles. Completely tacky and gauche. Who the fuck was doing his catering?*

"Arnold." He heard the host call his name. Dressed all in white except for a bright-pink silk shirt, Charles Killion stood nearby. Charles had to be at least sixty; he'd been running around Hollywood with the crème de la crème since 1972. His hair was still a golden color although wrinkles danced around his mouth and eyes. Charles ran a lucrative import-export business (what was imported and exported no one knew for sure).

"Charles." Arnold leaned forward on his tiptoes and gave his host a peck on each cheek.

"Where've you been? I was starting to wonder if perhaps you'd received a better offer."

"Than you? Impossible. You know I love Malibu." Arnold accepted a glass of champagne from a shirtless waiter wearing black shorts. "I've had the most horrific day!" Arnold continued.

"Do tell," Charles said, grasping Arnold by the elbow and leading him to a white chaise next to the pool.

"Well, darling, what can I say. It is a problem that I inherited. A two-hundred-million-dollar problem."

"Ah, *Seven Minutes Past Midnight*."

"How did you know our budget?"

"Arnold, please. Everyone knows everyone's budget."

"No, but this is uncanny. You see, I just came from a screening, and this is *the* most atrocious piece of crap I have ever seen. I kid you not."

"That bad? Lydia does have some strong movies under her belt, and Zymar isn't a complete hack."

"Ach. Are you kidding me? You know what the problem is? That bitch hasn't had to do a day of work in her life. This is the first time that anyone has held the purse strings who she wasn't either fucking or related to. And that person just happens to be me." A vicious gleam sparkled in Arnold's eye.

"It almost seems that you're enjoying Lydia's failure," Charles said, a wicked smile dancing across his lips.

"Me? Never. I wouldn't gloat over the revelation that Lydia Albright is and always has been a complete fraud."

"Arnold, you are incorrigible." Charles glanced across the pool. "See that beautiful young thing with the black hair and green eyes? Right next to Stanley?"

"Yes. He's new," Arnold said.

"Very. My caterer."

"Ohhh, I see. I was wondering about the buffet. Never seen you do *that* before."

"What can I say: With a package like that, how could I refuse. Rick, come over here," Charles called, waving his hand toward the handsome young man wearing Dolce & Gabbana from head to toe.

"Charles, where have you been?" Rick said, placing his arm around Charles's waist and planting a kiss on his cheek. "I want you to taste the lox canapés before I bring them out."

"I'm sure they're as savory as you." Charles gave Rick a gentle tap on the ass. "I want you to meet one of my dearest friends, Arnold Murphy."

"A pleasure." Rick held out his hand.

"Likewise." Arnold felt a flutter in his chest as he grasped Rick's hand. *Very luscious.* He wondered if this was a serious fling for Charles or just a dalliance. This was a young man for whom Arnold would happily stand in line. "So, Rick, tell me, where did you pick up your catering skills?" Arnold asked.

"It's something I've always loved. But Charles encouraged me to do it." Rick glanced lovingly at the evening's host. "I'm going back to the kitchen. I've got hot things in the oven," he said, giving Charles a sly wink.

"I'm sure you do," Charles said teasingly.

"So how did this little love affair begin?" Arnold asked, watching Rick saunter around the pool.

"He's an actor and he was a barista at Coffee Bean."

"An actor and a barrrrrriiiista!" Arnold said, dragging out the word. "Perhaps I should start drinking more coffee. Is this serious or just a little late-night rumba action?"

"He's been around for about three months, and so far I'm not bored," Charles said. "That's pretty serious for me. Why? Wondering when I might step off the train?"

Arnold felt his neck flush. "Well, Charles, it's obvious you can't have every beautiful man for yourself. I know you like to be the first one to break them in. . . ."

"Not ready to let this one go yet," Charles said. "Besides, I thought you swore off men under thirty."

"Men under thirty, men over thirty. What men? I haven't had a man in my life in, what, almost six years."

"Except the professionals." Charles looked at Arnold.

Arnold was taken aback. *Who the fuck was Charles Killion to talk about his sex life?* "Yes, Charles, on occasion, the professionals. I find them to be convenient and discreet. Much easier than, say, forcing your guests to eat lox canapés." Arnold felt his voice becoming shrill.

"Arnie, please. Calm down. It was a joke."

"A joke? Really. About my sex life. How funny is that?"

"Stop." Charles sipped his drink and turned away from Arnold.

"No! Really, Charles, how fucking funny is my sex life? I'd like to know. Maybe everyone would like to know," Arnold said, waving his arms and turning toward all the guests standing around the pool.

"Arnold, stop making one of your scenes." Charles sighed.

"My scenes?"

"Yes, you little fuck. Stop it," Charles hissed. "This is a party. People came here to have fun, not listen to your histrionics."

"I see." Arnold pulled on the sleeves of his shirt.

"Go get a drink," Charles said, gliding past Arnold toward another guest.

Arnold walked into Charles's gourmet kitchen. The room bustled with shirtless men exchanging empty trays for fresh ones filled with food and champagne. Bent over peering into the oven was Rick.

Arnold checked out Rick's ass as he pulled a baking sheet from the oven and backed away from the stove.

"Arnold." Rick smiled and set the hot sheet onto a trivet. "Hot stuff. These are my hankie-pankies." Rick grabbed a spatula and lifted the meat-and-cheese-encrusted bread from the baking sheet. "Want to try one?"

"They look delicious." Arnold ran his tongue over his bottom lip. "I'd love to."

Rick handed him an appetizer plate with a hot hankie-pankie on top.

"Charles tells me you're an actor." Arnold took a bite of the hors d'oeuvre.

"It's my first love. But so impossible to get going."

"Do you know what I do?" Arnold asked, watching Rick run water over the baking sheet in the sink.

Rick glanced over his shoulder toward Arnold. "Charles never said."

"I run Worldwide Pictures. Have you heard of it?"

"Heard of it? Isn't that like asking if someone's heard of Porsche, or McDonalds'? Of course I've heard of it. So you run it?" Rick said, walking toward Arnold.

"Every last bit of it." Arnold leaned toward Rick. "Here's my card. I put my cell number on the back. I was hoping we could get together, maybe later tonight."

Rick plucked the card from Arnold's hand and glanced around. "Eleven. I'll meet you at the surf shop near Point Dune. Sound good?" Rick's eyes sparkled.

"Very good," Arnold said, letting his gaze rove across Rick's body.

I need to see you," Arnold barked into his cell phone. "Twenty minutes, at the surf shop at Point Dune." He slammed it shut and watched as a black Mercedes convertible pulled into the parking lot. "Flash the lights," he spat at his driver. The Mercedes flashed back. Rick exited the car and jogged across the parking lot toward him. "You know what you're meant to do, right?" Arnold asked. He was putting way too much trust in his driver's ability to follow simple instructions.

"Yes, Mr. Murphy." He looked at Arnold in the rearview mirror.

Arnold heard a knock at the back-door window. "Okay, put the partition up."

"Right on time." Arnold pushed open the door and extended his hand to Rick. "Let's talk about your movie career."

Ray stood outside the Town Car smoking a cigarette. You couldn't see through the partition, but it wasn't soundproof. He didn't need to hear what was going on in the back of the car. The slight swaying was enough evidence of the events in the backseat. This fucking job. If he didn't have two kids in college and need the benefits, he'd walk away and leave the asshole here to find his way home. At least three times a week he had to pick up Mr. Murphy's "friends," wait outside the car, and then drive them home. Ray watched a Bentley pull into the parking lot. *What was the little shit up to now?*

"Hey, you Arnold's driver?" a blond older man called out from behind the wheel.

"Yeah, who are you?"

The car pulled forward and the driver cut the engine. "Charles Killion. Where is the little prick?" Charles asked, smiling. "Think I may have pissed him off tonight." He exited his Bentley and walked toward the Town Car.

"Mr. Killion, right. Mr. Murphy is waiting for you," Ray said, noticing that the car was still rocking. He did as he had been instructed and pulled open the Town Car's back door.

Jessica and Her Givenchy Heels

JESSICA WAS IN THE SHOWER (POST—POWER PILATES) WHEN HER BLACKBERRY started beeping. Six forty-five A.M.? She shut off all five of the shower jets, grabbed her towel and then her phone (sitting conveniently on the commode next to the shower for just such an emergency). Glaring down at the number, she felt her heart sink. It was her office, and Jessica guessed it was about Holden.

"What's up?" She answered briskly, wrapping a towel around her head.

"I'm hearing bad rumors," Kim replied.

Jessica wiped the steam from the mirror. Dark bags sat under her eyes. She'd been exhausted for the last two weeks.

"Like what?" Jessica picked up her eye cream. At five hundred dollars an ounce it should give her entire face a lift.

"Holden is going to Josh Dragatsis at ACA."

Glass splintered onto Jessica's marble bathroom floor. "Fuck!"

"What was that?"

"My fucking eye cream. Five hundred dollars an ounce."

"That's more than I make in a week," Kim muttered.

Jessica looked down at the tiny trickle of blood oozing down her leg; a fleck of glass stuck out below her knee. "Where? From where are you hearing these rumors?" Jessica sat on the closed toilet seat and pulled the shard from her leg. The floor was covered with glittery fragments.

"Holden's attorney's assistant dated my roommate's ex-boyfriend. And also, Maurice told me last night."

Jessica stopped sweeping up glass with her hand. Maurice and Holden were best buddies; one didn't take a piss without the other one holding his hand. And they were two of her biggest clients. Jessica still held an offer from Paul Peterson at Summit for the two of them to work together, $20 million each to do a film. They also got ten percent of first-dollar gross, which meant that Maurice and Holden would each receive ten cents of every single dollar that every man, woman, and child in the world paid to see their film. It didn't sound like much on a small scale, but when the average gross for one of Holden or Maurice's movies was $250 million, that meant $25 million to the star (in addition to their $20 million fee) and $2.5 million plus $2 million to CTA. A grand total of $4.5 million to the agency per star. Money that might have just vanished.

"What do you mean, last night? How did Maurice tell you about this last night?"

Kim sighed. "We all went to Bradford Madison's birthday party. Maurice and I hung out for a while."

Suddenly Jessica felt very old. One of the many perks to being the assistant to one of the most powerful people in Hollywood was the A-list party invites. She remembered her own assistant days; she barely spent a night in her apartment. She should've been at that party. Or at least known about it! She'd spent the last few days dragging her ass around, barely able to crawl into bed at ten P.M., she'd been so tired. That was no way to stay on top. She had to be at every party, know every player, and have contact numbers for the entire A-list if she was going to keep her place at the pinnacle of the entertainment business.

Jessica knew that if Maurice was brazen enough to tell Jessica's own assistant that Holden was thinking of leaving, then the ship was about to sail. She also knew that wherever Holden went, Maurice was sure to follow.

"Did you sleep with him?" Jessica inquired. Her tone belied her anxiousness.

Kim hesitated just a second.

"It's not the first time, is it?" Jessica said.

"Jess, it's not like . . . I mean, he's a great guy—"

"Make them stay," Jessica said, her tone hard edged.

"What? Jess, I can't—"

"Yes you can, and you will. If you fucked Maurice more than once, he's interested. Shit, for an actor under thirty, that's almost like being engaged. We can't lose them, Kim, do you understand? And especially to that little fuck face Josh Dragatsis. Call Maurice and convince him."

"Jessica, I don't think he'll listen to me."

"If he stays, I'll promote you." Jessica knew she'd just said the magic words. Every assistant lived for the day when his or her boss finally said the words that instantaneously morphed them from persona non grata within an agency to a respected colleague.

"What?"

"It's time. You've done two years with me. Make this happen and you'll be the newest CTA talent agent."

"I'll call him. I'll try. But he seemed pretty determined to leave."

"Don't try, Kim. Just do it. Get him into the office. I'll call you from the car."

Jessica looked at herself in the mirror. Nothing like an adrenaline rush to sweep away the tireds.

Jessica pulled up to the stone gate on Mulholland and entered the seven-digit security code. It was seven-thirty A.M. No one at Holden's house would be awake, not even the dog. Jessica gunned her Mercedes through the entrance and zipped up the drive. She grabbed her Lacroix bag and walked to the door. Turning the handle (Holden never locked the door), she let herself into the house and walked straight through the foyer to the kitchen.

Jessica's personal designer had decorated the entire interior. The floor-to-ceiling windows provided a fabulous view.

She pulled open the refrigerator. Holden would starve if she didn't have Gelson's market deliver a standing order to his home twice a week. Anything special he wanted, he called and told Kim. Thanks to Jessica, fresh fruit, beer, vegetables, and toiletries all magically appeared at Holden's door. *See if the little fuck Josh Dragatsis takes care of this.* She could almost picture Holden's confusion once his provisions ran out and he actually had to *find* a grocery store.

Jessica cracked half a dozen eggs into a glass bowl and started to whisk them. *Josh Dragatsis?* What a way for Holden Humphrey to piss away a career. She knew it'd be less than twelve months before Holden would beg for Jessica to take him back. But by then his quote would be $10 million, tops. And Holden could say good-bye to the big gross dollars. He'd lose more than fifty percent of his value in the marketplace. And why? Because Josh Dragatsis would whore Holden out. He'd have him do any crappy teenybopper film that would pay Holden's quote. One, maybe two, of those, both of which would tank and would completely erode Holden's fan base. Any credibility Holden was beginning to earn as an actor would vanish. Never mind career longevity.

Jessica knew the kind of agent Josh Dragatsis was. Agenting for his kind wasn't about building a relationship or creating a career. For agents like Dragatsis, it was wham, bam, thank you, ma'am.

Jessica poured the eggs onto the hot, ironclad omelet pan on the stove. She pulled strips of turkey bacon out of a package and dropped them into the hot fry pan. But Dragatsis, Jessica was sure, could talk sports, go to strip clubs, and even score drugs, things Jessica never did for her stars. No, the only things she did were read scripts, get meetings with A-list directors, and sometimes cook them breakfast. Oh, and she also honed careers. Jessica spent every waking moment thinking about how to make each of their careers better, more solid, more lucrative.

She tried to determine what each of them needed to feel creatively fulfilled and spiritually satisfied. It wasn't how most agents, at least these days, operated, but it was, for her, the only way to do business.

Just as Jessica plated his eggs, bacon, and toast, Holden stumbled into the kitchen, sporting tighty whiteys and bed head. She'd already set the table. The coffee and juice carafes sat next to a bouquet of fresh flowers from the backyard.

"Jess?" Holden stared at her dumb-faced.

"Sit." Her waitress days from law school were proving very handy this morning.

Holden lumbered to the table and flopped into his chair. Jessica pushed the steaming food toward her client and sat down across from him.

"I will not let you fuck up your career like this," Jessica said, her tone hard and her eyes full of steel.

"Jess, I—"

"Holden, please. Just listen for one minute," Jessica said very slowly. "I will *not* let you fuck up your career like this. Do you understand?"

"Jessica, what are you talking about?" Holden shoveled eggs laced with mozzarella into his mouth.

"Josh Dragatsis."

Holden dropped his fork on his plate. "Oh, man. Jess, I didn't want you to hear it from someone else."

Jessica watched Holden's face. It was hard to read actors, as it was their business to make you believe the unreal was actually real. But Holden wasn't such a good actor that Jess couldn't pick up on his subtle tells.

"Tell me what?" Jessica asked, pushing Holden to say it. Admit to it. Then she could have a real conversation with her star.

"He's been hounding me day and night. Really mostly nights. Parties and girls and strip clubs . . ." Holden's voice trailed off.

"And blow?"

Holden gave Jessica a sheepish grin. He was a good boy, but this *was* Los Angeles.

"Not so much." He looked at Jess. "Well, maybe a little. But Jess, it was just guys being friendly. Well, it started out like that."

"Holden, when you make twenty million dollars per film and ten percent of gross, there are no guys just being friendly. You are a commodity. We talked about this. And people who can get close to you will want things."

"I know, Jess, I know. It's just, I mean, Josh and I have so much in common. We're both single. We both love sports. We both come from small towns."

"What small town is Josh Dragatsis from?" Jessica asked.

"I don't know. Someplace in Indiana, I think. Fayetteville. Not far from where my mom grew up."

"Uh-huh." Jessica made a mental note to check on this point. She didn't think there were many Greeks with New York accents from Fayetteville, Indiana, and a lie like that could completely sour Holden on Josh, making him realize that Josh wanted to advance his own career by pretending to guide Holden's.

"Jess, you've been so good to me." Holden looked down at the floor. "But lately I just don't feel like we connect." He seemed honestly hurt and a little scared.

"Holden, I know agents like Josh. He will ruin your career. He's not in it for the long haul. He's going to book you into crappy films so that he can make some big dollars, and you will lose any acting credibility that you've established. For God's sakes, you're up for *Inside the Fire*—Tony Scott is directing that. Every actor in town wants that role. Tom, Brad, Will. You have a real shot at this, but if you go do some crappy film or if Josh doesn't have the same type of relationship with Tony and the studio like I do, then this opportunity will disappear."

"Jess, Josh already got me in to meet with Tony."

Jessica felt her stomach lurch. She was speechless. That meeting, the meeting she'd scheduled for Holden with Tony Scott, was for Thursday. *How had Josh Dragatsis gotten Holden Humphrey in to see Tony Scott before now? And how had Tony's office not called Jessica's office to confirm?* She was going to vomit.

"I can't—"

"Jess, you're the very best agent in town. It's just that right now, where I am, I just think I need a guy agent. I think he understands me better."

"So that's it?" Jessica asked.

"Yeah. I'm sorry," Holden said. He pushed the plate away from him. "The eggs were really good, Jess," he said as though trying to soften the $20 million blow.

"Thanks." Jessica gave him a half smile as she stood. She'd found Holden in obscurity. Gotten him his first head shots and acting gig. Even loaned him money in the lean years so that he could stay in Hollywood and not have to return to Podunk wherever. And now, after five years and some success, Holden was canning her for a young guy with a good connection for blow. It was ludicrous. Insanity, really. Jessica walked over to Holden. He looked a little afraid, as if she might dump the carafe of hot coffee in his lap.

"Stand up," Jessica said.

Holden stood. He wasn't really much taller than her, at least not when she was wearing four-inch Givenchy heels. "Give me a hug." Holden obeyed and wrapped his arms around her. "Now listen, when this little pecker fucks it up, you come back to me. You hear me? Don't ever feel embarrassed or ashamed to make that call. You got it?"

Holden nodded his head in the affirmative. He looked as though he might cry.

"Don't let them fuck up your career, Holden. You are in charge. Got that, too?"

Again he nodded. Jessica pulled back from Holden's embrace and turned her back to walk away. She'd been officially shit-canned. Her noble words in parting were complete. Just a little sucker punch at the end to plant the seed that Holden Humphrey had, in fact, made the biggest mistake of his career.

Jessica stepped off the private elevator next to her office. She still felt queasy; the eggs, the coffee, the being fired. She'd just lost a huge client for the agency, and if Kim didn't come through with Maurice, the bloodbath for the day had only just begun. Jessica walked toward her office, eyeing her number two and number three assistants. She glanced at Kim's desk. Her chair was empty. Jessica stopped.

"Where's Kim?" Her question was met by deafening silence.

"Lauren?" Jessica looked at her number two assistant, who was juggling three phone lines and typing an e-mail.

Lauren hit the Mute button on her phone and glanced up at Jessica. "Gone," she said.

Gone? On a morning like this one, her number one assistant decided to leave her desk? Maybe this battlefield promotion needed to be reconsidered. Jessica started toward her own desk. Or perhaps Kim was, at this very moment, convincing Maurice that he had to stay with CTA.

"When will she be back?" Jessica called out to Lauren.

"Jessica," Lauren answered, sounding irritated, "she's gone."

"What?"

"Not out-of-the-office gone. *Gone* gone."

"What?!" Jessica screamed. The reality of the situation hit her. The Tony Scott meeting. The fucking stars. The parties. The 6:45 A.M. phone call. Kim's absence from her desk.

"Dragatsis," Lauren said. "He got Holden, Maurice, and Kim. Offered her senior agent status, a huge salary, and to be on Holden's and Maurice's agent teams."

"That traitorous bitch!" Jessica inhaled deeply and grabbed her headset. "Who else?"

"No one yet. But we're bleeding here. She took all the numbers. Not just your clients, but also every number of every client with any value in the building, including writers and directors. She's got copies of files, submission logs, deal memos, and e-mails."

Within the heat of rage, Jessica felt the emergence of fear and panic. CTA had just taken a torpedo hit to the hull.

"Jeremy's on his way to your office."

This was war. Jessica started barking orders. "Okay, send an agent-only e-mail announcing an emergency meeting in twenty minutes. In the e-mail, tell all agents to start calling and checking in with all their clients. Tell them to begin with their biggest clients first. Now get me my client lists. *Now!* We are calling everyone this morning."

"Got it."

"Call Human Resources and get a trainee up here."

"They're on the way."

"Lauren, get me Angie first."

"Dialing."

"And Lauren," Jessica called.

"Yeah?" Lauren glanced up from her phone keypad.

"Congratulations on your promotion. You're number one now."

Lauren smiled. "Thanks. I had the computer department turn off her BlackBerry and purge her security codes the minute she got on the elevator. Hope it helps."

"Probably not, but good call."

Okay, love. Just wanted to check that you were well." Jessica smiled and cooed into the ear of one of her biggest stars. "Please give Maddy hugs and kisses from Aunt Jess." Jessica looked up to see Jeremy entering her office. She smiled at her boss and mouthed the word "Angie." Jeremy nodded, understanding the importance of the call, and sat down. "Okay. Great, I'll see you when you're back from Africa, then. Mmm-hmm. Bye-bye." Jessica unwrapped her headset from her ear. She looked at Jeremy. Always the dapper Englishman, he looked cool and well dressed even with the mounting stress.

"Quite a day," Jeremy said.

"Quite. And it's not even ten A.M."

Jeremy leaned forward in his seat and moved the knot of his tie.

"Listen, Jess, I know we're under attack, and I don't doubt you for one second, but we've been thinking—"

Jessica arched her right eyebrow.

"Tolliver and I."

"Tolliver?"

"And I believe that in this situation with a day like today, we need a show of strength," Jeremy said.

"I completely agree. I've got the client lists and we've just closed three huge deals. I think we need to leak the deals to *Variety* and the *Reporter*. They need to be on the front page tomorrow."

"Right. Yes. Jess, that is absolutely brilliant. But Jess, I think also that now is the perfect time to announce Tolliver."

"I see." She was sitting wounded in the water and Jeremy wanted to fire the shot that would kill her in front of the entire town.

"Jess, I am a big believer that two heads are better than one. You and Tolliver have such complementary skill sets. The two of you really will be unbeatable."

"Yes, but Jeremy, today is not the day. It will look to the community as if you are replacing me. That you are concerned with my ability to run the company during a crisis."

"Rubbish. Everyone knows that Tolliver's been here for quite some time."

"Jeremy, most people in this town can't remember the last twenty-four hours. All they're going to see is that I took two very bad hits to my client list and that you decided to bring some man in to help me."

Jeremy visibly bristled. "You said 'my.'"

"Excuse me?" Jessica didn't understand Jeremy's meaning and really didn't have time to play games.

"You said 'my' client list when referring to Holden and Maurice. Don't you mean 'our' or 'CTA's'?"

"Well, of course I do, I only meant that—"

"Jess, I'm sorry, but I've already decided. Today is the day."

"No. Absolutely not. This was not part of the deal with Tolliver coming over here. Jeremy, you specifically told me that I would never, ever look undermined by him. You gave me your word."

Jeremy stood when Jessica completed her tirade. It was a gentlemanly act for Jeremy to even walk over to Jessica's office; since he owned the company, it was Jessica's place to come to him. Jessica had now not only infringed upon Jeremy's courtesy and civility but had also yelled at her very uptight and stuffy British boss.

"I did, Jessica, tell you when Tolliver arrived that he would never be used to undermine your authority. Nor would the perception ever be present in the Hollywood community that Tolliver had more power within the company than you. You are correct. However, Jessica, with respect to you and your abilities, I have made my decision and the story will run tomorrow. As for appearing 'undermined,' Jess, I think that *your* two clients who have chosen to leave and fire you, as well as *your* former assistant, took care of that."

Jessica crossed her arms in front her chest. In less than four hours she'd lost two clients and an assistant, alienated her boss, and gained one backstabbing, career-climbing Tolliver Jones. She gave Jeremy her very best Hollywood smile (maybe she should act; she'd become very adept at faking emotion).

"Jeremy, I apologize. It's been a very emotional morning for me." She played upon her womanhood and gave in to the one thing that Brits truly believed was an American weakness, the display of unpleasant emotions.

"Of course, Jessica. I do understand. And I am so glad that you, too, understand." Jeremy smiled, pleased to have the distasteful interlude behind them.

Jessica smiled, her eyes sad, her mouth tight, and her mind furious.

"Oh, I do understand, Jeremy. I really do."

26

Mary Anne: When the Shoe Drops

MARY ANNE HAD SPENT TWO HOURS AT THE STUDIO LISTENING TO EXECUTIVES (who had never written a script) give her notes on her next project. Then she fought her way through six P.M. Los Angeles traffic back from the Valley. She was exhausted. Drained by the entire experience. And now she juggled three bags of groceries, her purse, her mail, and her keys as she pushed the front door open while her home phone rang. She slammed the door closed with her foot (losing a shoe), dropped everything on the couch, and leapt for the phone.

"Hello," she gasped.

"Mary Anne?"

"Dad?" Mary Anne was surprised to hear her father's voice.

Marvin Meyers never called, except on birthdays and holidays. It was always Mitsy who phoned every Sunday, Tuesday, and Thursday. A wave of guilt crested over Mary Anne. She hadn't spoken with her mother since Mitsy left L.A.; she'd ignored her calls and letters. Mary Anne glanced at the clock; it was almost ten P.M. in Minnesota. Late for anyone, especially Marvin, to call.

"Mary Anne, yes. Um . . . How are you?"

Her stiff Midwestern father sounded even stiffer and more Midwestern than Mary Anne remembered. It'd been almost two years since Mary Anne visited Minnesota for her grandfather's funeral, and about a year since Marvin came to Santa Barbara for an insurance conference. Mary Anne had dutifully driven the seventy miles to have dinner with her father at a very nondescript Santa Barbara restaurant, one that felt as Midwestern as you could find on the coast, with lots of brass, pastels, and booths. They'd eaten early. Mary Anne remembered being surprised that Marvin bypassed his usual uptight Methodist single scotch on the rocks and downed two vodka and tonics.

It was the first time that Mary Anne could ever remember eating a meal alone with her father. Marvin was often away on business, or at work. As a child, Mitsy ate many family meals with her children sans Marvin. But Marvin, well, he rarely spent any time alone with his offspring.

The evening ended with an awkward hug and an abrupt kiss. She recalled her guilt at the relief she felt, finally being finished with the uncomfortable encounter.

"Dad, is everything okay?"

"I know it's late, but well, I was wondering, have you heard from your mother?"

Guilt again. *Was he calling to try to patch things up between her and Mitsy?* "Dad, I know I haven't called her back, but you really didn't need to call. I'll call her. I promise. I was just a little angry, that's all."

"Um . . . No. Mary Anne, really, I don't know about that. But today, or yesterday? Have you heard from your mother?"

He wasn't calling about their argument?

"Heard from Mom? Dad, you *live* with Mom."

"Well, yes. I mean no."

"Isn't she at the house?"

Marvin paused.

"Aren't you at the house? Did you look for her?" Mary Anne wondered if Marvin was suffering from early-onset Alzheimer's. He insisted on drinking soda from a can, and she remembered reading that soda in a can had some connection with Alzheimer's.

"Well, she's not here."

"Dad, Mom has a ton of meetings. Maybe the Methodist Mothers or her book group got together tonight. Did you check the schedule in the kitchen?"

"No, I mean . . . she's not in Minnesota."

"What?"

Marvin sighed. "This wasn't how I wanted to tell you. We were going to tell you."

"Tell me what?" Mary Anne panicked. *Mitsy not in Minnesota? Her father had no idea where Mitsy was?* Her mother was missing and her father was, quite possibly losing his mind. "Have you called the police?"

"No."

"But Dad—"

"Mary Anne, she left a note. I mean a letter. Well, actually, a list. Of all the things I need to do while she's gone."

"But where? Dad, this isn't like Mom. She'd never go anywhere without telling someone."

"Oh, Mary Anne," her father moaned.

Was he crying? Mary Anne heard Marvin gasp.

"Your mother and I, well, we've—" His voice cracked.

"What is it, Dad?"

"We've decided to separate."

Mary Anne felt a pit open in her stomach. A deep chasm that was splitting her, making its way toward her heart. She sank into a chair next to the phone. "Separate . . . you mean as in separate, like, divorced separate?"

"No. I don't know. We've just decided that I should live somewhere else for a while. I've been staying at the St. Paul Inn."

"When? Why? How come no one told me? Do Michael and Michelle know?"

"We had a family meeting last night. Your mother and I decided we'd call you together this evening. I came over after work, and well, she's gone. So are some of her clothes and her navy Tourister overnight bag, so I know she packed. And she left the list."

"It doesn't say where? The list."

"No. Or when she'll be back."

Mary Anne felt tears well up in her eyes. Her mom and dad were divorcing, and Mitsy was somewhere out there in the world alone.

"We've tried all the relatives, your aunt, your grandmother. No one's heard from her."

"Okay; I'm sure she just needed a little space."

"I thought maybe you'd hear from her. You've always been her favorite."

"Yeah, right," Mary Anne scoffed through the tears running down her face. "That spot is saved for the twins."

"You are. Her daughter the writer; the brave one that moved away from Minnesota. Lived out all the dreams your mother had."

Mary Anne wiped her cheek with the back of her hand.

"What are you talking about, Dad?"

"Rambling, I guess. It was a long time ago. Forever ago. You know she used to write."

"What?"

"When I met her. Poetry, short stories. She was talented, won a couple of contests at the university. Was even published. She had a gift. But then I came along, then you and Michelle and Michael. There just wasn't time."

"I didn't know that."

"Remember the Sunshine Stories?"

"The hand-drawn children's series. I loved those books."

"They were hers."

"No!"

"Illustrations and story. She wrote them and then had them printed and bound. She wanted those books to be the first thing you read when you learned to read."

"They were hers?"

"Yes. She never sent them to a publisher."

"But all my friends had them. They loved them."

"Gifts from your mother. Handmade for her friends' children. She was thoughtful like that. Doing things for everyone else, never thinking of herself." Marvin's voice cracked. Mary Anne heard her father's chest-racking sobs. It was disconcerting to hear him speak about Mitsy in the past tense, as though they were preparing for her funeral.

"Dad, I'm sure she's fine."

"I've been such a bad husband."

"Dad, she loves you. I'm sure you just needed time as far as the separation—"

"Oh, Mary Anne, no. You don't understand. I didn't leave your mother, your mother left me."

Mary Anne placed the phone in its cradle. It was the longest conversation she'd ever had with her father and definitely the most emotional. *Where would Mitsy go? Frugal to a fault (some people said cheap), Mitsy wouldn't actually spend the money to stay at a hotel,* Mary Anne thought. She had to be with a friend. But Mary Anne knew Marvin and Michelle had spent the evening scouring Mitsy's address book, which contained more than five hundred names (the Meyers' annual Christmas letter went to each and every one), and Michelle had managed to get through most of the family and Mitsy's closest friends. *Perhaps an old college roommate? Someone she'd recently met?* Mitsy didn't have a cell phone; she didn't own anything that remotely resembled an electronic gadget. Her bifocals were as "high tech" as Mitsy got.

Mary Anne had promised to call Marvin if she heard anything from Mitsy. He seemed convinced that Mary Anne would be the first family member to hear from her, but Mary Anne wasn't so sure. They'd left on very unfriendly terms when Mitsy returned to Minnesota after her last visit, and they hadn't spoken since. Another wave of guilt crested over Mary Anne. If only she'd returned her mother's phone calls, maybe none of this would have happened. She could have talked Mitsy down, or at least convinced her to stay with Marvin. In her head Mary Anne replayed the most recent message that Mitsy had left on Mary

Anne's cell phone voice mail. It was two days old (Mitsy's Tuesday call). Mary Anne couldn't remember a trace of sadness or anger in her mother's voice. No mention of marital strife or disappearing acts.

But today was Thursday. Maybe her dad was right; maybe she would hear first. Mitsy was a complete creature of habit, almost compulsively so. She never missed a Thursday call. Not when she was sick, not when she was busy, not even when she and Marvin went away on vacation. Mary Anne clutched her cell phone to her chest. *Oh please, Mother, be predictable,* Mary Anne thought. But it was already after ten in Minnesota, and Mary Anne usually called at nine-thirty. *Maybe she's out to dinner?*

Mary Anne walked down the hall toward the kitchen, still clutching her phone to her chest. She wasn't hungry, but she desperately wanted a glass of wine. She turned the corner to the kitchen and reflexively looked at the sink. And there, chopping carrots, was Mitsy.

"Hope you're hungry, dear. I'm fixing grilled salmon and rosemary potatoes for dinner."

"Mom?" Mary Anne cautiously walked toward the kitchen island where Mitsy stood slicing and dicing. *Was it an apparition or really her mother?*

"Yes, dear? Were you hoping I'd call?" Mitsy cocked an eyebrow and pointed the serrated knife toward the cell phone pressed against Mary Anne's breasts.

"Dad just—"

"How is your father?" Mitsy asked, resuming her cutting.

"He's—"

"Worried? Upset? A little lost?"

"And emotional."

"*Reeeally.* Welcome to my world. Serves him right." Mitsy thrust the knife through a carrot.

"Maybe you should call him." Mary Anne cautiously held her cell phone out to her mother.

"No."

Mary Anne looked at Mitsy. *Who was this woman? A woman who made a list, packed her bags, hopped a flight to L.A., and left town without so much as a good-bye?*

Mitsy looked over her bifocals. "I'm letting him stew one more night." She slipped the already diced potatoes into the steamer on the stove.

Mary Anne sat on the stool at the kitchen island as Mitsy continued to julienne carrots.

"I thought we'd have gingered carrots, too. You like gingered carrots, if I remember correctly?"

"Uh, yes," Mary Anne said, setting down her cell phone. Mitsy seemed calm. Preparing a meal was always her favorite way to relieve stress. Chopping seemed to be especially therapeutic if Mitsy was angry.

"So you know?" Mitsy asked. "Your father told you." She cracked the knife through a large carrot.

Mary Anne nodded.

"I wanted to tell you in person. It didn't seem fair to me that Michael and Michelle got the benefit of a family meeting while all you got was a phone call."

"When did you get to L.A.?"

"Around three. I had the driver stop at the store on the way from the airport. That Gelson's has everything. A little pricey, though. There's a bottle of cabernet next to the sink. Why don't you open it?"

Cabernet? Since when did Mitsy like cabernet? Zinfandel was the only wine Mary Anne ever saw Mitsy drink.

As if reading Mary Anne's mind, Mitsy said. "Yes, dear, I do drink red wine. Zinfandel is for wimps."

Mary Anne frowned as she picked up the bottle and inserted the corkscrew. *Her whole world was upside down.*

"You know, dear, you can't blame yourself for your father's and my marital problems."

Mary Anne twisted the wine key deeper into the cabernet's cork.

"Why would I blame myself?" Mary Anne asked.

"Because it's in your nature. You, my darling daughter, blame every bad thing on yourself. You've done it your entire life. Calling me back would not have changed this scenario. Nor would it have postponed it. I'm just sorry it took this long."

Mary Anne pulled hard on the cork. It gave way with a large pop. She opened the cabinet and reached for wineglasses.

"No, dear, those are for white wine. You didn't have any red-wine glasses—I noticed the last time I was here—so I picked some up for you. They're behind you, on the counter next to the coffeemaker."

Mary Anne turned, picked up a glass, and poured the cabernet.

"That's enough. Can't have the cook caught up in the sauce." Mitsy giggled. "At least not until I've finished cooking the meal." Mitsy swirled the wine in the glass and tilted it to her lips.

Mary Anne poured a second glass, more full than the first. She needed a large amount of alcohol to make it through the evening. *Can you lace cabernet with vodka?* She wondered.

"Is that stiff enough for you? I'm sure this evening is quite a shock," Mitsy said. "Time to start the salmon." She picked up a platter that held two fillets and headed to the back door. "Are you coming? Surely you aren't going to drink alone?" she asked as she opened the screen door.

Mary Anne lifted her glass and wandered toward her mother. Then she quickly turned back and grabbed the bottle of cabernet.

"Good thinking, dear. There's two more when we're finished with that one."

They dined outside under the stars. The meal, as always when Mitsy cooked, was impeccable. The remains of the food and two empty wine bottles littered the table between them. Mary Anne watched as Mitsy reached into her pockets and pulled out a lighter and a pack of cigarettes.

"Mother, what are those?"

"Cigarettes, dear. You've never seen them before?"

Mary Anne was horrified. She had listened to Mitsy lecture about the ill effects of smoking her entire adolescence.

"It's an old habit of mine. From my college days. I haven't had one in forever. Want one?" Mitsy put a cigarette to her lips and then held out the open pack to Mary Anne.

"Thanks, I'll pass," Mary Anne said, standing. She reached across the table and lifted her mother's plate and then her own. "I'll take these in."

"There's dessert if you want. Strawberry shortcake in the fridge," Mitsy called after Mary Anne. "Dear, will you bring the other bottle of cabernet when you come back outside?"

Mary Anne set both plates in the kitchen sink. She hadn't anticipated going back outside. But then, she hadn't expected her parents to announce their separation, or her mother to show up at her house. Never mind Mitsy's drinking and smoking. Mary Anne peered out the window above the sink toward her mother's silhouette. The reflection of the pool lights and the candle on the table cast a glow around her mother. Their conversation over dinner had been mundane. Mitsy had posed questions about Mary Anne's newest script and the chaos surrounding *Seven Minutes Past Midnight*. Neither of them had summoned the courage to address the white elephant standing to the side of the table.

How had it happened? When had Mitsy decided to leave? And why now, after all these years? Just when Marvin was talking about retiring next year. Mary Anne thought her parents would finally have time alone. Get to know each other again. And surely Marvin would end his affair with Nancy MacIntosh. Mary Anne thought they'd finally travel together, split their time between Minnesota in the summer with the grandkids and someplace warm (preferably not Los Angeles, but perhaps Phoenix) during the winter months.

"Are you coming, dear?" Mitsy called. "I'm out of wine."

Mary Anne walked out of the back door carrying the open bottle of cabernet. She poured some into Mitsy's wineglass and then sat.

"So shall we discuss the obvious?" Mitsy asked, exhaling smoke. "Now, some of this will be uncomfortable for me, and a great deal of it will be uncomfortable for you. But I am here, and now, my dear, is the time to ask me any questions you might have. I am halfway loaded and completely relaxed."

Mary Anne was petrified, as if she'd finally been offered the keys to the kingdom and suddenly didn't know how to work the lock.

"Well, come on, dear. It's getting late and I'm getting plowed. After this next glass, I can't promise anything I say will make much sense."

Mary Anne gave her mother a half smile. She wanted to know this woman. Not the Minnesota Mitsy whom Mary Anne thought was her mother throughout her life. But this Mitsy, the one who smoked and drank and said everything she thought, regardless of the impropriety.

"Okay, then," Mary Anne said. "Let's start with your writing."

27

Celeste Solange and Her Givenchy Spikes

CELESTE LOOKED STUNNING. HER EXPERTLY COIFFED GOLDEN MANE SPREAD across her bare shoulders (she'd had a priority sitting with Jonathan, who'd come to the house for a color and cut, per Celeste's request). Her personal makeup artist, Que, had completed her face immediately after Jonathan had finished styling her hair. She wore a low-cut Dior shirt that emphasized her perfect C cup breasts and tiny waist. Low-slung Armani pants that gave a tiny peek at her tummy and Givenchy spiked heels completed the look. Celeste was dewy, megastar perfection. She drove straight from home to Howard Abromawitz's office.

Damien would be jealous. He'd be furious with himself for throwing their marriage away on that tramp Brie Ellison. Celeste would make sure of it. None of her preparation would be lost on him. A self-declared addict of female eye candy, Damien wouldn't be able to take his eyes off of her. She'd even made sure to wear his favorite color, turquoise. He always said it accented the blue in her eyes.

Celeste enjoyed the attention as every head (both male and female) turned as she walked the short distance from the celebrity elevator in Howard's office to the fishbowl conference room in the center of the suite. Howard's paralegal escorted Celeste into the conference room and immediately started twisting the blinds, shutting out the rest of the office so everyone would stop staring. She didn't realize that Celeste needed the attention, wanted that energy that strangers propelled toward her. Celeste fed off it, storing it, gearing up, preparing to do battle.

"Ms. Solange, Mr. Abromawitz will be right here," the mousy-haired, middle-aged woman said. "His motions hearing ran a little long this morning. I apologize. May I get you something to drink?"

"Water, please." Celeste perched in a chair at the middle of the conference room table.

"Flat or sparkling?"

"Flat is fine. But do you have lemon?"

"Of course. Let me get it for you. I'll be right back." The paralegal scurried from the room.

Celeste sighed. *Serving Celeste Solange flat water with lemon!* This was probably the highlight of the paralegal's day. Maybe her week. She'd have something to tell her family and friends, who would eagerly pick apart every inch of what Celeste wore, what she said, even how she smelled. Celeste knew it would be like this; she overheard other women in Beverly Hills (when they didn't realize the woman sitting next to them in a baseball cap and oversized sunglasses was one of the world's biggest stars) talking about their random celebrity run-ins. The way they carried on, it was as if royalty had descended from their throne or perhaps a god from the heavens. Didn't they realize she was just like everyone else?

Celeste heard a knock at the door and sighed. As if Howard's staff needed permission to enter their own conference room.

"Yes," she said. The paralegal tiptoed in, carrying a tray with flat water in a crystal glass and a plate full of freshly sliced lemon.

"I didn't know if you wanted ice, so I left it out." She set the tray down across from Celeste. "There's ice in the other glass. In case you want it."

"Thank you. Do you know what time it is?" Celeste asked.

The woman glanced at her watch.

"Ten after. The other parties won't be here for another twenty minutes, and Howard just pulled into the garage." She backed toward the door.

"Great," Celeste said, smiling. "Thanks again." At least, Celeste hoped, this woman's story would end on a positive note. *She smiled the most beautiful smile and told me thanks again. She really is just like us. So sweet, so down to earth.* That was the story Celeste wanted told. Not the catty *She was such a bitch; who does she think she is?* story. But after years of celebrity, Celeste had learned that it didn't really matter how the star actually behaved; the story ultimately told was always from the prism of the teller.

Celeste had just finished squeezing the lemon into her water (she'd decided against the ice; it made her crowns ache) when Howard burst through the conference room door.

"Cici! My darling. *You* are absolutely breathtaking."

Howard tossed the file marked *Solange* in front of Celeste and walked to the side table, grabbing a plastic bottle of water.

"I see you met Connie, my paralegal. She got you all squared away. My God, Celeste, how can a woman be so beautiful?"

Howard sat in the chair next to her.

"Thank you, Howard." Celeste leaned conspiratorially toward him. "You know I do have to try."

"Try? I doubt it. You are a natural beauty, my love."

Howard twisted open the top of the water bottle and took a swig.

"Now, are you nervous? Don't be nervous. You shouldn't be. This is just a settlement conference. No court reporters, no tape recorders. Just a dialogue between the parties—well, between their attorneys, to see if we can't complete this thing without going to court."

"What about the . . ." Celeste didn't want to say it. She let her sentence drift away, raising both her eyebrows.

"Yes, that. I made one copy. Just one, mind you, and I messengered it to Janice Rosenblatt just last night. That and a copy of the birth certificate. Told her it was imperative that she watch it before the conference today." Howard took another swig of water. "Of course, you know we have no idea where the DVD came from. You understand?"

Celeste smiled and nodded her head. She understood perfectly. Finally her prenup would be blown to bits. A thought that thrilled her. Not because of the money. She didn't need the money (although who was she to turn up her nose at a multimillion-dollar settlement), but she loved the idea of the tremendous pain it would cause Damien to part with so much of his precious currency. And (much like with his first wife, Amanda) for the simple fact that Damien couldn't keep his dick in his pants.

There was a knock on the conference room door, and the paralegal poked her head into the room.

"Howard, they're here."

"Great," Howard said. "Send them in." He leaned his head toward Celeste. "We should get their reaction to your directorial debut pretty quick."

Howard stood as Damien and his lawyer, who looked like an attack dog straining at the leash, entered the room. Janice Rosenblatt was six-foot-one and an overpriced Doberman bitch, trained to maul any woman who dared to divorce one of her celebrity clients. She wore a very expensive yet manly pantsuit and carried a Coach briefcase and bag. Very no-nonsense. She had represented Damien in his divorce proceedings with Amanda. Celeste was surprised that Damien was using Janice again; she hadn't gotten Damien a very good deal the last time.

Celeste looked at Damien. She felt indestructible. *Bring it on,* she thought as she sipped her water. Damien looked haggard and old. Older, perhaps, than the night just a few weeks before when Celeste and Bradford caught Brie Ellison's carnal devouring of Damien on film.

"Howard." Janice smiled as she sat in the chair across the table. "Ms. Solange." She gave Celeste a viperous look.

Celeste nodded her head toward Janice, acknowledging her presence but not deigning to speak to her, then turned her attention back to Damien as he made his way to the seat across from her. Her heart fluttered. His paunch was bigger, his hair grayer, and he did, in fact, walk like a very old man. The unkempt cheater with the sad eyes sitting across from her was not the behemoth take-no-prisoners Hollywood producer she'd married little more than a year ago. That man had been obsessive and vain, going so far as to keep a lint brush and roller in the glove compartment of each of his seven cars. This rumpled and unshaven Damien looked as if he'd neither slept nor eaten in the last three days.

"Shall we get started?" Howard asked.

"It won't take long," Janice said, pulling out her briefcase and bag.

"You received our settlement offer?" Howard opened his own file and rifled through the papers.

"I did. As well as Ms. Solange's attempt at blackmail." Janice smiled.

"Janice, I made this very clear. We have no idea who made this DVD. Or how. It came by U.S. mail. I even saved the envelope for you."

"How very kind of you, Howard. I am sure you did. However . . ." Janice pulled a file from her briefcase and flipped it open. "Your settlement offer is out of line with the prenup that your client signed before she married Mr. Bruckner."

Howard cleared his throat and leaned forward. "Janice, in light of the DVD, and the discovery of Ms. Ellison's birth certificate, I'm sure neither side wants a long, drawn-out process. We're talking about three very high-profile people here. Besides, who knows what could happen if the district attorney's office were to subpoena the DVD and the birth certificate."

Celeste looked at Damien across the table. He wouldn't meet her gaze. He leaned on his left hand, watching Janice and Howard as if watching a Wimbledon match.

"You know how the L.A. DA is. This is just the kind of slam-dunk celebrity case he'd love to try. If only for the publicity."

Janice glanced up from her file.

"Yes. This kind of publicity can be very bad for a career. Especially when you're a celebrity."

Janice pulled a DVD out of her briefcase and walked toward the television in the corner of the conference room.

"May I?" she asked. In one swift motion she pressed the power button and opened the DVD player.

"Of course. But Janice, we've all reviewed the DVD, and I don't think—"

"Howard, this is a *different* DVD." Janice smirked.

"Different?" Howard croaked.

"Yes, much older." Janice inserted the disc and stepped back from the television so that she and everyone else in the conference room had a clear view.

Celeste watched as the grainy picture slowly came into focus. She gasped as the camera panned across an open-aired cabana in an exotic local, the viewfinder landing on herself a few years earlier. There she was, in all her naked glory. Breasts, ass, and Argentinean muff. All of them exposed. She and another couple filled the screen (very lovely people, an actor and actress she'd worked with on the film set where she'd met Damien), all engaged in acts of sexual gluttony. While Damien, Celeste now remembered, worked the camera.

Celeste watched as she mounted the actor and kissed the actress. All had enjoyed the slow passion in the exotic South Caribbean locale. But Damien, ever-present Damien, was nowhere to be seen.

The entire saga came rushing back to her. Damien had begged for the foursome, tantalizing Celeste with the promise of marriage if she proved that they were sexually compatible. It had been the last night on set in the Caribbean, and most of the cast and all of the crew had flown back to the States that day. As producer, however, Damien had stayed behind to finalize details and to close up the set. Plus, he wanted another twenty-four hours alone with Celeste, or so he said. Celeste realized now that what she then believed to be an impromptu orgy was most likely planned by Damien down to the last orgasm.

Celeste watched as her body rocked back and forth astride the actor, her pelvis grinding away as the actress sucked on Celeste's left breast. Just as the moment of climax arrived, Celeste threw her head back and looked directly at the camera. A face contorted in passion, staring blindly at the lens. Janice Rosenblatt hit Pause. There the frozen image of an orgasmic Celeste Solange, megastar, the woman whom America adored, flickered on the television screen. The woman whom men lusted after and women wanted to be. Parents took their children to see her movies. With one frame of film, Celeste realized, her entire career would be destroyed.

Janice stared at Celeste, a sneer pasted on her lips.

"Images are very powerful things. And this image, I'd say, is worth almost ten million dollars. Or, very simply, the amount your settlement offer asks for above the terms of the prenup."

Celeste felt numb. Humiliation and betrayal: Her entire marriage to Damien had been founded on those two cornerstones. She glared at her soon-to-be ex-husband. This was lower than she thought even he was capable of sinking. He leaned forward, peering at the television, holding his head in his hands.

"Is this what you want?" Celeste hissed.

Damien turned his gaze away from the frozen image of Celeste and stared at the living image sitting across from him.

"This is what you brought on," he shot back.

"If we agree, how can we be sure this is the only copy?" Howard asked.

"Damien," Celeste said, her voice low, barely above a whisper, "is this how you choose to do this? In this deceitful, mean-spirited way?"

Celeste could feel the rage building in her body.

"You *know* the only reason I was even fucking that man was because *you* asked me to. Is this how you want to win?" Celeste asked, her voice growing louder.

"Celeste, I just—"

"Ms. Solange," Janice interrupted, "I'm going to ask you not to speak to my client directly. Please ask me or your attorney if you have questions for Mr. Bruckner."

"Your client, Ms. Rosenblatt, is still my husband," Celeste said. "Damien, after all that's happened, is this what you want to do? Ruin me? Ruin my career? Ruin everything? The image that everyone in America believes about me? Take it all away from me?"

Damien sat up and tugged on his shirt. "Celeste, I just want this finished. Whatever it takes, I want it over."

"Fine," Celeste said, and stood. She picked up her Prada purse. "You know, Damien, I know secrets about you, too, and if this ever gets out—"

"It won't," Janice Rosenblatt broke in.

"If it does, you can consider life as you know it over." Celeste glanced down at Howard. "I'm finished."

She turned and walked out of the fishbowl of a conference room. She'd suffered enough humiliation with Damien for a lifetime.

Celeste's Givenchy shoes clipped across the cement floor of the parking garage under Howard's building. She held her ticket out to the valet. She was humiliated. How had she ever loved such a snake? It was a cliché, she knew, but she'd given Damien the very best years of her life, both on film and in bed. She was pushing thirty (ahem, thirty-five). There weren't any good roles for thirty-year-old actresses. Teenage boys drove box-office ticket sales, and teenage boys did not want to see thirty-year-old breasts (no matter how firm). Thirty-year-old breasts, Celeste surmised, reminded them of their mothers. No, teenage boys wanted to see twenty-year-old breasts.

"Celeste, wait!"

Celeste turned. She couldn't believe Damien had the balls to follow her down here. She was angry enough to pluck out both his eyes with her bare hands. She scanned the parking garage. *Where was the valet with her car?*

Winded, Damien jogged toward Celeste but slowed down a safe distance away. She knew he remembered that she was a black belt in karate and jujitsu and did all her own stunts (action roles came in handy). And Damien knew from experience that she could kick his ass.

"Stay back!" Celeste threw up her right hand. "Not one step closer."

Damien stopped.

"Celeste, I didn't want it to end this way."

"What way, Damien? With you fucking a minor and film of me fucking a stranger? What way didn't you want it to end? Because it's ended in a repulsive pile of dog vomit."

"Janice said it was the only way around the district attorney pressing charges."

That was rich. As though Celeste would ever really give the tape and the birth certificate to the Los Angeles District Attorney's office. It was a bluff; was Damien so stupid that he didn't know that?

"So you humiliate me in front of Howard and that bitch?"

"Howard's seen worse. You should have seen the tapes Amanda had."

Celeste bristled. "How many tapes do you have, Damien? It seems you've managed to collect quite a video library of all your sexual trysts," she spat out. Her nerves were raw and her emotions frayed. *Where was the valet?*

"I would never show this to anyone. There are no copies."

"Really? How can you be sure? You don't think Janice's paralegal or secretary can't recognize a hot piece of merchandise? Anyone can burn a DVD. You know and I know the value of a celebrity sex tape."

"I have the only one. . . ."

Damien lifted his left hand. In it he held one DVD case with a clear cover. The fluorescent lights of the parking garage glinted off the reflective disc.

"How can I believe you, Damien?" Celeste shot back. "I don't believe anything you say anymore."

Damien stepped forward, holding the DVD in front of him, teasing her.

"It's true," he said, holding out the DVD case toward Celeste. "And I'm giving it to you."

Every fiber in Celeste wanted to snatch the DVD from Damien's hand, kick him in the balls, and run. But she restrained herself. She needed to be careful; where the DVD went, so went her career. That circular piece of plastic could ruin her forever.

Damien took two steps closer.

"Cici, just three things and it's yours. I swear there are no copies."

"What are they?"

"The prenup stays exactly as written, no district attorney, and I get the DVD of Brie and me. Fair?"

"*Fair* isn't the word I'd use, but it seems to be the only deal I can make."

"You played an excellent game, Celeste. I'd say we ended in a stalemate." He handed Celeste the DVD.

"Howard has the DVD of you and Brie. Plus the copy of her birth certificate."

"Yeah, although it looks like I have to marry her just to be on the safe side."

The valet revved Celeste's Porsche up to Celeste and Damien. *Finally.* The valet hopped out and held the door for her.

"So in a way, Celeste, even without the money you win."

Celeste climbed into her Boxster.

"How do you figure?"

Damien walked forward and leaned into the open coupe.

"Celeste, I'm finished. If *Borderland Blue* doesn't hit, I'm through. Summit isn't renewing my producing deal and I'm way too old to become an independent producer. Plus, I'm stuck with an eighteen-year-old child to raise, unless she divorces me or finds someone to run off with."

Celeste relaxed into the driver's seat of her car.

"I would have stayed married to you forever," she said.

Damien looked into Celeste's eyes.

"I know. But you know what, Celeste, I don't deserve you."

"Thanks, Damien," Celeste said.

"Got to get back upstairs," he called as he backed away from the Porsche. "You know that bitch charges me seven hundred fifty dollars an hour."

* * *

Celeste sat on the floor of her custom-made closet crying. She held the DVD Damien had given her as tears streamed down her face. She was alone. How pathetic. Celeste Solange, old and alone, in a giant house that terrified her. It hadn't been the money she'd wanted, it was the revenge. She hadn't gotten the money, and now she knew that revenge was useless. Seeing Damien withered and old. Admitting his career was over. Celeste now knew that there was no gratification in revenge. She had no emotions left inside her for Damien. She felt nothing but the embrace of sadness, knowing she'd spent so much energy and time obsessed with someone who meant nothing to her now. Someone who didn't know her and didn't love her. Damien had used her for his personal pleasure and then tossed her away. It was truly pathetic. How did she ever fall for that loser?

Celeste didn't know how long she'd been crying when her cell phone rang.

"Hello," she said, trying to keep the tears out of her voice.

"Cici, are you okay?"

Hearing that voice, his voice, made Celeste's bottom lip quiver.

"Yes." Her voice shook as sobs engulfed her body.

"Cici, are you at home?"

"Yes," she said, her voice muffled through her sobs.

"I'll be there in fifteen minutes, okay?"

"You will?" Celeste tried to gather herself.

"I got in this afternoon. I tried to call earlier but you didn't pick up."

"I was at Howard's."

"Your attorney?"

His voice was strong and soothing, as if he completely understood why she was upset.

"Please, Cici, let me come get you. I don't want you to be sad."

Such a simple statement, filled with so many promises for the future.

No quips. No jealousy. Just unconditional kindness. Celeste wiped away the tears on her cheeks. The old Celeste would have shot back a coy or smart remark, letting him know that she really didn't need him and that she was in complete control. But she did need him and she did want him. She hadn't been able to get him out of her mind. They'd been rendezvousing whenever he was in L.A. He didn't burst in with machismo and bravado, trying to let Celeste know (as all her past lovers had) how lucky she was to have him. No, in fact, he always made it clear how lucky he felt to have *her,* that he'd met this smart and beautiful woman who was sharing time with him.

It was disconcerting. It made her afraid. She'd never felt safe with a man, any man. But he wore her defenses down, with his consistent kindness and affection.

"Where do you want to go?" he asked her.

"I'm really not hungry," she said.

"No, beautiful. I have the jet waiting, and you could use the time after today. Where do you want to go?"

Celeste felt a smile creep over her face. The first true smile she'd experienced all day.

"Well," she said, "somewhere warm and private."

"Private? Why private?"

She heard a lascivious hint in his voice. He might be nice, but he wasn't a saint.

"We might enjoy the privacy."

"I like the way you think, lady. I know just the place. Get your toothbrush. We just turned onto Mulholland and we'll be at your place in five."

Celeste allowed herself another smile as she closed her phone. She looked at the DVD lying on the floor at her feet. Using her foot as a lever against the wood floor, she broke the offensive recording in two. No more smut, no more games, no more lies, no more Damien. That ugly part of herself and her life was dead, forever. With the snap of the DVD breaking, she knew it to be true.

Lydia Albright and Her Bottega Veneta Woven Leather Platform Pumps

LYDIA PULLED HER BLACK RANGE ROVER INTO THE GUEST PARKING SPACE IN front of Beverly Birnbaum's bungalow on the Summit Pictures lot. *Guest,* that's certainly what she was, having been banned from Worldwide. She'd been sharing space with Beverly for six weeks. Thank God Toddy had been compulsive about the daily downloading of Lydia's files to Lydia's laptop and BlackBerry. Toddy had managed to sneak into Lydia's old office the day after her expulsion and grab scripts and files before security showed up and escorted Toddy to the studio gates. Thanks to Toddy, they hadn't lost anything but office space. And Beverly Birnbaum was kind enough to give Lydia that, and a phone.

Lydia hadn't spoken to Zymar in five days. Tucked away in an editing bay in New Zealand, he was furiously finishing *Seven Minutes Past Midnight.* The composer, Derek Van Hausen (a close friend of Zymar's and a connoisseur of Balinese brothels), had agreed to finish the score without any guarantee of receiving full compensation. Lydia thought Zymar was a miracle worker; no one in this business worked for free. But Derek believed in the project and in Zymar. Besides, Worldwide had already cut Derek a check for the first half of his fee, and he felt confident he'd receive the other half. After watching Zymar's cut, he knew there was no way that Worldwide wouldn't release this film. And Derek's score, according to Zymar, was perfection.

Lydia passed Toddy, who sat outside Lydia's tiny closet of an office at the back of the Birnbaum bungalow. Lying on Lydia's desk was yet another ominous-looking envelope from Worldwide Business Affairs. This was the third she'd received. The others threatened jail time, monetary penalties, and lawsuits if the print for *Seven Minutes Past Midnight* wasn't immediately returned, and she was sure this one did the same. Of course, Lydia's entertainment attorney also received copies, as did Jessica. They were doing what any good team of representatives would do in this scenario: They were stalling. That and playing stupid.

"You are not to tell anyone where Zymar is," Jessica had told Lydia over the phone.

"Jess, everybody knows he's in New Zealand."

"Lydia, everyone but *you* knows he's in New Zealand. Got it? Right now it's the only way. And don't call him from your home or your cell. If this thing actually goes to trial, we do not want anything on your phone records. Use Bev's phone. Or borrow Mary Anne's. Do not leave a paper trail."

As a soldier in the screen trade, Lydia had conquered many opponents, but this war, the one with Arnold—this one seemed so personal.

"I miss him."

Jessica sighed. "I know. It's even more painful when you're in love. Changes the whole dynamic for the film."

Lydia bristled. *In love? Am I in love with Zymar?* Sure, he made her happy. She could barely sleep in her own bed without him. And she moped about the office pining for him. But also for her film.

"Jessica, I don't have time to be in love with Zymar," Lydia said, laughing. "I've got too many movies to make."

"Yeah, well, I don't have time to love Mike Fox, either, but I do. Don't worry, Lydia, no one is going to force you to quit film, stay at home, and make babies," Jessica said. "Okay, that's one of Arnold's henchmen on the other line, gotta jump." She released the line.

In that single conversation, Jessica had articulated every one of Lydia's fears. As a child, Lydia watched her frustrated mother (an actress by calling) marry a producer and leave her career behind. A semi-star, Sally Albright gave up Hollywood, bore three children, and drank herself into oblivion each night. It wasn't until Lydia was ten, when her father's career as a producer was peaking, that her mother's drinking got really bad. Sally would sit on the back veranda at night, staring at the pool, railing against the fate of her life. When Sally was particularly drunk, she wanted an audience for her sorrow, and because Lydia's father was always away on set and her two younger brothers were asleep in bed, it fell to Lydia to absorb the rants. How could Lydia have been so blind?

Lydia lifted the envelope from Worldwide off her desk and pulled it open. The tone was much more hostile, and instead of the signature of the president of Business Affairs at the bottom, Arnold himself had signed. *Somebody is getting desperate,* Lydia thought. She knew the longer she and Zymar kept the print away from Arnold, the bigger the fool he appeared to the Hollywood community.

"Zymar on line one," Toddy called out from her desk.

Lydia kicked off her Bottega Veneta woven leather platform pumps and settled into her office chair. One day ahead and seven hours back, that was the only way she could remember the time in New Zealand. She glanced at her watch; so it was two A.M. Saturday.

"Toddy, this one will be personal," she called, alerting her assistant to hop off the phone line.

"Hello, love," Lydia said.

"Lyd, you're in early. Tried the 'ouse but you'd already left." Zymar's voice crackled across the seven thousand miles.

Lydia paused. Even with satellites, there was a time delay whenever you had a phone conversation with someone on the other side of the globe.

"I miss you," Lydia said.

"Now, Lyd, 'ow could that be? You've got Arnold and 'is letters to keep you company."

Lydia grimaced and looked down at the new letter she held in her hands. "Just got another one this morning. This one signed by the leprechaun himself."

"'E must be getting serious, then, if 'e's signing them instead of 'is lackeys."

Lydia knew that post must be going well; he sounded chipper. But even Zymar's good mood couldn't pull her out of her funk. She felt like a wounded doe watching the wolves circle.

"I got one, too, today. My attorney forwarded it, some sort of legal paper demanding their print back. What a wanker. If I didn't love the film so much, I might shred the 'ole lot, fly back to L.A., and shove the 'ole damn thing up Arnold's ass."

"You sound happy," Lydia said.

"Three more days, Lyd, and it's finished."

"What? But I thought you needed at least two more weeks of post?"

"Little director trick: Always overestimate your timetable because then you look like a stud when you bring it in early."

"That's great news!" Lydia spun her chair around and looked out her window.

"The score is amazing. Van Hausen did a phenomenal job."

"Too bad I can't pay him."

"Oh, 'e'll get paid, Lydia. There's no way they're not releasing this film. No way."

Lydia wished she shared Zymar's conviction. She had, before the screening, but not now. She knew Arnold. He'd rather lose half a billion dollars than appear wrong in front of the world.

"I wish I was as confident. Three days, then what?"

"A screening."

"Don't joke," Lydia said. She wished she could fly to New Zealand to see the finished cut.

"I'm not."

"Zymar, stop it. You screen it here and Arnold will have us both in handcuffs."

"Lydia, 'aven't you been on your computer at all? Don't you watch television?"

"Not really. E-mails, letters . . . Why?"

"I built a site for the film, and this past week I've gotten a million 'its worldwide, and that number is growing. Go to defamer.com. They're clamoring to see this film. Then look at the Drudge Report. This little war we've got with Arnold is all over the Internet. The public wants to see *Seven Minutes*. Arnold can't stop it."

Lydia clicked over to defamer and was greeted by a big bold headline that read WHY IS MURPHY SO AFRAID OF MIDNIGHT? The article detailed (correctly) almost all of the ongoing battle between Arnold and Lydia. *Where do they get this stuff?* Lydia wondered. To the left were numbers from a poll; the choices were "Screen it" or "Let it die." Ninety-six percent of the people voting wanted to screen it.

"Zymar, it's one Web site. A bunch of computer geeks with nothing better to do can't force Arnold Murphy to schedule a distribution date."

"Lydia, these 'techno geeks' control the entertainment world. They spend millions of dollars on movie tickets. This movie, without a release date, is tracking higher than any other summer release. Click on the trailer."

"You cut a trailer?"

"Just click."

Music swelled from her speakers as sexy shots of a scantily clad Celeste filled Lydia's screen, intercut with a montage of breathtaking action sequences.

"Oh my God," Lydia said, caught between complete fear and jubilation. "You cut this and released the trailer on the Net, didn't you?"

"Nothing that can be proved, Lydia," Zymar said. She could hear the mischievous smile in his voice.

"Zymar, it's copyright infringement. Another felony. To edit is one thing, but to distribute . . . Arnold will throw us in jail for sure."

"Not if we get the spin out there first."

Lydia watched her screen as the trailer played again.

"Zymar, we can't—"

"Yes we can. I spoke to Jess and already 'ave the screening room locked in. Invite the distributors, the studio 'eads, the agents, the press. Invite Ted Robinoff, Arnold's boss. If 'e sees it, 'e'll know Arnold is wacko and 'e'll release the film for sure. Lydia, I promise, it's *that* good. It's worth the hype."

Lydia sat on the edge of her chair. She hadn't gotten anywhere in life by playing it safe. In fact, the first risk of her career many years before had involved Arnold Murphy. Back then it had taken every bit of her courage and resolve to tell Weston and Beverly Birnbaum when Arnold stole the script *Time's Up* from her.

Lydia and Arnold both had been working at Birnbaum Productions, she as a low-level development executive and he as a senior vice president. Treading water and desperately ambitious, he'd hated young Lydia and her pedigree from the start. Unable to take out his personal frustration on Weston or Beverly, since they were his bosses, he chose to abuse and humiliate Lydia instead. She'd been working with a "baby" writer on *Time's Up* for months, and just when she was ready to take the script to Weston, Beverly, and Worldwide, Arnold "found" the script on Lydia's desk and claimed it for himself. Arnold threatened Lydia and the writer, telling them both that no one would believe they'd developed the script, and that if Lydia or the writer went to the Birnbaums, Lydia's nascent career in the film trade would be dead. Lydia felt she had nowhere to turn, her father having died two years before. She didn't know whether Weston and Beverly would believe her or Arnold.

It was the writer who brought Arnold's deceit into public view. The writer told Weston, Beverly, and the president of production at Worldwide (with Arnold and Lydia both in the room) that it was Lydia who found the script, gave him great notes, and championed the project. Lydia remembered Arnold's eyes boring into her during the meeting. She'd stared at the table, unsure how to answer when the president of production asked her if what the writer was saying was true. But answer she did, and it was public humiliation for Arnold at the highest level. He lost his job and his reputation (although he quickly found another vice president gig at another production company), but he never forgot about the disgrace. Lydia stayed with the Birnbaums and developed a reputation for spotting great new writers and commercial material.

The bigger the risk, the bigger the reward.

"You're right; we need to leak the screening to the mainstream entertainment press," Lydia said. "There needs to be big buzz and big pressure within the community."

"Five days, Lyd. CTA screening room."

"If Arnold finds out when and where, he'll shut us down," Lydia said, knowing that she was, at this very moment, taking control of *Seven Minutes Past Midnight*'s destiny. She wouldn't sit by and watch Arnold shelve her film. "Okay, send Jessica the digital file for the trailer. It'll have to come from her or Kiki Dee. We leak the trailer, get the public clamoring for a release date. The screening is top secret. We'll invite the press and the studios."

"Exactly."

"When do you get in?"

"Commercial flight, through San Francisco, Burbank airport, arrives at three on Tuesday."

"We'll screen it on Thursday. Don't tell anyone. Not a soul. If your arrival leaks, Arnold will be there with the police and the FBI. He'll have you in cuffs and the print locked down or destroyed."

"Don't worry, Lyd."

"Okay. Okay. I need to go, we've got a lot to do," Lydia said, half to herself. Her mind was reeling.

"And Lydia," Zymar said. "I love you, too."

Lydia smiled as she heard the click on the other end of the line. Zymar didn't know it yet, but Lydia had decided this was the last trip he was ever taking alone.

29

Jessica Caulfield and Her
Silver Badgley Mischka Heels

JESSICA BENT OVER STEVEN BARTMEIER'S GOLD-PLATED TOILET AND VOMITED. She wiped her mouth with a piece of tissue, tossed it in the waste-basket, then turned and surveyed the damage in the mirror. She'd managed not to get any of the vomit in her auburn hair, down her Pucci gown, or on her silver Badgley Mischka heels. But her skin was a pasty gray. Perspiration collected at her hairline. Not enough to smudge her makeup, but enough to be noticed. *What was wrong with her?* The waves of nausea came at indiscriminate times, sometimes in the morning, sometimes in the evening, almost always at four P.M. She occasionally threw up when she had migraines, but there were no headaches accompanying these upset stomachs. Maybe bad sushi? (A sushi addict, tonight she couldn't even stand the thought.)

Searching under the sink, she found some mouthwash. This time alcohol had triggered it. One of the waiters had walked by with an especially strong bourbon. Jessica wrinkled her nose just remembering the smell; she rinsed and spit, getting the hor-rible taste out of her mouth. She pulled her Chanel red out of her bag and curved her lips. She prayed none of the other guests heard her. In a town where being thin was a competitive sport, the best bulimic was usually the winner, but that was a competi-tion Jessica had no desire to be involved in.

She dropped her lipstick into her evening bag and looked into the mirror. Jessica was confident no one would know what just happened. She spritzed the bathroom (just in case there was someone immediately behind her) and then pulled open the bathroom door. She had a lot of work to complete in one evening.

And she had to work quietly and quickly. Steven Bartmeier, one of the editors of *Variety,* was having a charity cocktail party at his palatial Bel Air spread, two thousand dollars just to get in the door. It was the perfect place to put "the spin" in motion. Jessica, Lydia, and Kiki Dee (nobody seemed to know where Cici was) had spent four hours in Jessica's office strategizing over their plan. They needed to have the "right" message about Lydia, Zymar, and *Seven Minutes Past Midnight*. They needed to get that message to the "right" people, and they had to accomplish all of it in five days. All this while never allowing Arnold to get the upper hand. Kiki was in charge of getting the word out to the mainstream media, *Entertainment Express, People, Us,* and *Star.* Jessica would work the inside of the entertainment community.

And having spent the last hour at Steven Bartmeier's, Jessica knew she'd struck gold; the guest list couldn't be more "inside."

Jessica walked toward the large atrium in the middle of Steven's home. It was the hub of the party. Old Hollywood. Not in age, but in power. The players, gathered at Steven's home, were the decision makers; they controlled the game. Producers, studio heads (surprisingly Arnold Murphy had yet to arrive), and celebrities schmoozed.

She needed to get a moment with Steven in order to set the *Seven Minutes Past Midnight* story in motion. Then Arnold and Worldwide would begin the spin game in the defensive position. She liked the idea of Arnold on the defensive. He'd have to refute every one of Jessica's claims that he was shelving a fantastic film and misusing the studio's money to play out a personal vendetta against Lydia. Obvious malfeasance by the head of a studio—that surely was worth a story on the editorial page of *Variety.*

Jessica looked forward to watching Arnold's decisions publicly scrutinized and questioned. A maniacal egoist with low self-esteem, he guarded his authority fiercely and didn't take probing well. He could barely contain his legendary temper in the most innocuous of settings, and she knew that any questions regarding *Seven Minutes* could set it off and help to destroy any glimmer of credibility for his arguments in favor of shelving the film.

Jessica spotted Steven Bartmeier across the room, chatting up, luckily for her, Mike Fox. (He'd been briefed on the plan; perhaps he was already whispering about *Seven Minutes Past Midnight* in Steven's ear.) Jessica walked with purpose toward the pair. She caught Mike saying, "The trailer is absolutely magnificent," as she approached.

"Jessica." Steven smiled at her. "We were just discussing one of your clients." He leaned forward and pecked Jessica on the cheek. "A very hot lady that is in the buzz right now, Lydia Albright."

Jessica gave Mike and Steven a knowing smile.

"Well, what can I say? I mean, it's just so obvious what Arnold is trying to do. This silly grudge he seems to have? It's a waste of the studio's money if you ask me. *Malfeasance* on Arnold's part. The public wants to see this film. And really, aren't ticket sales what it's all about, at least for the studios? Steven, you should take a look at the trailer. You can't believe the number of hits that the Drudge Report has gotten since someone stole a copy and uploaded the trailer to the site. Over a million in the last twenty-four hours and close to twenty million in the last seven days. You do the math— that's two hundred ten million in box office. Plus, it's an action film—they do amazing overseas. Can you even image what the international ticket sales will be? The DVD market alone will pay for the film."

Steven looked at Mike. "She's very impressive, isn't she?"

"I think so," Mike said, putting an arm around Jess.

Steven leaned in surreptitiously. "I hear there's going to be a screening."

"Now, Steven, you and I both know that would be illegal," Jessica said, taking a sip of her soda water.

"But a great way to get the community on board. Create some internal heat, some fire. Press Arnold from the inside."

His eyes sparkled. He was a member of the press, a reporter, and what reporter didn't love a secret?

Jessica glanced at Steven out of the corner of her eye. Slyly she titled her head. "Well, if something like that was to screen, I can think of no better place than CTA, and it would be a brilliant way to spend a Thursday afternoon, don't you agree? After lunch around three."

"That sounds ideal. Well, if something like that were to ever take place," he said, grinning, "you can count on my participation."

Jessica smiled. "Excellent. Now, should you hear other dates and times, you *ignore* them. Unless, of course, you hear it from me."

The plan included a disinformation campaign. It was inevitable that the news of a screening would spread like wildfire, but to ensure that there would be no unpleasant appearance by Arnold, Jessica and Kiki were floating a myriad of dates and times throughout the community. Only the people they needed at the screening would get the correct information. Unless they heard otherwise from Jessica, CTA at three on Thursday was the only place to be.

Jessica rested her head against the leather headrest in Mike's Aston Martin as he whipped around a turn on Laurel Canyon Drive. She'd done it; she'd passed along her verbal invite to everyone she was responsible for getting to the screening. There were no interruptions. Arnold Murphy had failed to appear. And Mike was an amazing asset. He'd worked the room with her. They made a fantastic team. Mike's humor softened Jessica's ever-present businesslike tone.

"Hey, so Will is having a party at his house tonight. It's not far from here. Want to stop by?"

Jessica glanced at the clock. It was only ten P.M., but she was tired and *famished*. A guilty little voice told her she should go. Missing celebrity parties, Jessica believed, was one of the reasons she'd lost Holden and Maurice. Plus, now she had Tolliver breathing down her neck.

"Can we get something to eat first?" Jessica asked.

Her hunger clawed at her insides. And she was horrified to admit, there was only one thing that would satisfy.

"Sure. Where you want to go? What are you hungry for?" Mike asked.

Jessica glanced sheepishly to her left.

"Well, you won't believe this. But I want a cheeseburger and fries."

Mike glanced over at Jess.

"Little overdressed, aren't we?" he kidded her.

He pulled to a stop at the light outside the Beverly Hills Hotel and reached out and touched Jessica's hand.

"A burger, huh?"

Jessica rested her head on his shoulder and nodded.

"Well, I know there's an Islands on Beverly. We'll go there."

Jessica smiled in satisfaction, knowing that her meal, and the chocolate shake she craved but failed to mention, was only moments away.

Jessica knew she should be on her feet working the room. An agent wasn't any good sitting down, a mantra she'd repeated to herself at every party she attended in the last seven years. A great agent continuously circled, meeting everyone, being everywhere, saying hello to every person at every party. You never knew when an opportunity might arise. And those opportunities definitely weren't going to come to you if you were sitting down with your feet up.

Like she was right now, tucked into a plush couch at Will's home with her feet resting on an ottoman. It was one A.M., and this party had just started to rock. DJ Jinx was warming up and the place was packed. Mike had disappeared an hour earlier, into a back room where there was some heavy-hitting poker game going on.

She chatted with Rachel Adamson, a young star repped by ACA, the competitive agency that had recently poached both

Holden and Maurice. Jessica supposed she could count this as work. She was, in a way, trying to obtain a new client for CTA. Rachel was in that perilous position that young female stars found themselves in after the first hit—what next? Actresses had such a small amount of time and few opportunities to make their mark. Jessica knew that if Rachel didn't "break out" in her next film, some new hot young thing would take Rachel's spot in line.

"So, Jess, do I go with the action film—it could be a franchise—or do I stick with the small character roles?"

"That's the million-dollar question, Rachel, figuratively as well as financially. What is your gut telling you? What do you want to do?"

"Well, Josh says I should go for the money, but my gut tells me that's shortsighted. Shouldn't it always be about the quality of the work?"

Jessica smiled. Not only was Rachel talented, she was also smart.

"I agree with you. When I advise my clients, I tell them it's got to be about the work. Now, if they don't care and only want the money, that's fine, and I'll negotiate the deal. But I know that part of what I need to give them for my ten percent isn't just my connections and negotiating skills, it's also my advice. The wisdom I've gathered over the last seven years."

Jessica's eyes drifted past Rachel toward the front door.

"Did you say your agent is Josh Dragatsis?" Jessica watched the little devil Josh stroll in with Holden, Maurice, and her former assistant (and now competitive agent) Kim.

"Yeah," Rachel said, turning her head to see what caught Jessica's attention. "I can't believe Josh convinced Holden to do *Booty Time 2*. And I thought he'd finally decided to become a legitimate actor."

Jessica could barely suppress her contempt. Her predictions about Josh and what he'd do to destroy Holden's career were already reality.

"That's what happens when it's all about the money for the agent," Jessica said. "Rachel, I'm going to find Mike. It's about time for me to go."

Rachel stood with Jessica and reached out to give her a hug.

"Thanks for all the advice, Jess."

"Of course. You know where I am. And you have all my numbers. If ever you're unhappy or just want to talk, please give me a call."

"I'm going to do that," Rachel said, eyeing Josh and Holden. "Let's get some lunch this week. I don't think I want to end up in *Booty Time Part 3*."

Jessica walked toward the private poker room knowing she'd just managed to take one of Josh Dragatsis's big clients. Three months ago, she'd have been thrilled, wanting vengeance against any competitive agent who even looked at one of her stars. But recently something had changed. The hunt and the kill were beginning to seem pointless to her. Jessica tried to shake these thoughts loose from her head. *What was she thinking?* Her rapport with stars paid for her lifestyle and had catapulted her to president of CTA. Such success had been her dream since she was pushing a mail cart a decade ago. She was definitely losing her edge.

Jessica could barely see through the thick haze of Cuban cigar smoke in the back room. The stench made her gag. She had to get Mike and leave quickly or she might vomit on the floor. She caught his eye and cocked her head toward the door. He nodded and held up one finger. She knew this would be his last hand. A pile of cash and chips lay in front of him, proving that the golden touch that made all his films turn to hits seemed to magically apply to poker as well. She'd never met anyone so adept at and also so comfortable with success. Never worried he might lose, Mike just kept on winning. *Why couldn't she be so sure of herself?*

Jessica stepped back and leaned against the wood-paneled wall. To be in this room, hanging out with the who's who of the entertainment universe, would have been any music or movie fan's dream. Young Hollywood, the next generation. Rappers, rockers, studio executives, actresses, and actors. These people were amazingly talented, but they were just people. When had she become so disinterested?

Jessica watched her former client Holden Humphrey enter the room through the French doors from the patio. She knew that as president of CTA and Holden's former agent, she should rush to him and schmooze him. Make sure that he knew he always had a home at CTA. But for the first time in her career, she didn't want to. She nodded her head in recognition, and to her surprise, Holden started walking toward her.

"Jess!" Holden said, with what sounded like relief in his voice. He leaned forward and pecked both her cheeks.

Jess gave him a little squeeze and a sincere smile. She wasn't angry anymore; she actually felt sorry for him.

"So, *Booty Time 2?*" Jessica asked.

Holden flushed and ducked his head.

"You heard?"

"Yeah. What happened with *Inside the Fire* and Tony Scott? I know he wanted you for that."

"I shit the bed," Holden said, using the age-old actors' expression for blowing an audition.

"Holden, how?" Jessica exclaimed. "You've been preparing for that audition. You and Moises worked on that role for weeks."

"I know, I know. Jess, it was a major cluster fuck. I just, well, I went out the night before. Josh had this major thing at his place."

"You did what?" Jessica could barely contain her anger. Opportunities like starring in a Tony Scott film didn't come often. In fact, most actors never got that type of chance in their entire careers.

"It's fucked up, I know," Holden said. He was obviously embarrassed. "They got it on tape, too. Plus, Tony was in the room."

Jessica knew that this was major damage. The only way around it would be for his agent to plead and beg for one more audition for Holden. Blame it on a death, the flu, a blow to Holden's head. Anything, as long as Holden got one more shot in front of the director.

"But you're going in to see Tony again, right?" Jessica asked.

"Nah. Josh said it wasn't worth it."

Jessica bit her lip so hard to stop herself from screaming that she tasted blood. *Be cool. He's not your client anymore,* Jessica thought.

"Besides, *Booty Time 2* will pay my full quote plus gross points."

"That's great." Jessica feigned pleasure. She knew, even if Holden didn't, that *Booty Time 2* would end his career.

"Hey, babe." Mike slid his arm around Jess's waist and kissed the top of her head. "Holden." Mike smiled at Holden. "How's it going at ACA?"

"You know, can't complain," Holden said, tipping the beer he held to his lips.

"Well, it looks like my girl is pooped. We're going to hit it," Mike said, steering Jessica toward the front door.

"See ya later, Jess," Holden called, smiling and giving Jessica a wink.

What had been a $20 million wink a month ago was soon to be worth absolutely zero in the marketplace.

"Later," Jess said, knowing that all her years of hard work for Holden Humphrey meant nothing at all.

30

Mary Anne Meyers and Her Adidas Running Shoes

Mary Anne felt like a spy. She wore dark oversized Gucci sun-glasses, a khaki trench coat, and Adidas running shoes (in case she needed to make a quick getaway). Her driver (Mitsy) stayed with the car while she paced in front of the arrival gate at the Burbank airport. The cryptic details that Toddy had given Mary Anne were sketchy. She was to pick someone up at the Burbank airport today. This someone would be on the three P.M. flight from San Francisco. According to Toddy, Mary Anne would know this person when she saw them.

It was all very cloak-and-dagger, something that made Mary Anne incredibly uncomfortable. A habitual rule follower, Mary Anne never enjoyed the frenzied adrenaline rush that accompanied illicit behavior. Her palms started sweating when she thought about making an illegal U-turn. Now she stood in the Burbank airport, waiting for something and someone she *knew* was illegal. Mary Anne just hoped it wasn't drugs. Surely Lydia wouldn't ever be into that scene. But Worldwide had frozen all of Lydia's films, and her lifestyle was very expensive. Mary Anne wondered if she'd have a legitimate defense when the police nabbed her. "I'm sorry, Officer, I didn't know that I was being used as a mule. I was just trying to help a friend."

Whoever this person was, Mary Anne was not helping them carry their bags. It was bad enough she was their chauffeur, but she wasn't becoming an accomplice, too. *But what if they got stopped in the car? And Mitsy! Why had she brought her mother?* Mitsy, even the new Mitsy, the one with a red wine obsession and a nicotine habit, wouldn't survive in the clink. Mary Anne inhaled and exhaled. *Be calm,* she told herself. They weren't going to get pinched. She'd make Mitsy drive. Who would ever suspect a fifty-six-year-old woman from Minnesota for a drug mule? Besides, this whole thing wouldn't take very long. She had strict orders to pick this person up and drop them at the Best Western three blocks from the Worldwide lot.

Mary Anne stood by the baggage carousel scanning the passengers of Flight 220 from San Francisco. She prayed that whoever this drug runner was, they hadn't checked their bag. *For God's sakes, surely they are smarter than that. I mean, this is L.A.; they have drug-sniffing dogs.* Mary Anne scanned the baggage claim area, searching for German shepherds or a SWAT team.

All she saw was one very big, very bald guy pretending to read a newspaper by the glass doors. Passengers trickled by, an elderly Asian couple and a group of twenty teenage girls carrying pillows and giggling. *Where was her connection?* She started to pace again. Of course she wanted to help Lydia. She'd do anything for Lydia. But serving time was not one of the things that Mary Anne ever thought Lydia might need.

Mary Anne suddenly stopped. *Pacing is suspicious,* she thought. Especially when you're whispering to yourself. *Calm down. It's not as if you have anything better to do.* It wasn't as if Mary Anne needed to get home and write. She wasn't on a deadline—at least not anymore. She'd gotten a call from Josanne Dorfman (or Jojo the monkey-faced girl, as Cici called her) two weeks before. Josanne was very abrupt; in fact, downright rude. She'd told Mary Anne to stop working on *The Sky's the Limit,* the script of Mary Anne's that Lydia had found in her slush pile months ago, the one that World-wide had purchased assuming it would be Lydia Albright's next film after *Seven Minutes Past Midnight* was complete.

"Mr. Murphy requested that I call," Josanne said, her tone implying that the fact that the call was at Arnold's request made it of the utmost importance. "We won't be moving forward on *The Sky's the Limit*."

Mary Anne was speechless. Still relatively new to the entire Hollywood film business, she wasn't sure what "not moving forward" meant.

"In fact," Josanne continued in her nasal voice, barely able to contain her glee, "we won't be moving forward on anything concerning Lydia Albright."

Josanne paused as if to let the meaning of this statement sink in with Mary Anne. "Except cleaning out her bungalow and shelving her film. That we *will* be doing," Josanne cackled.

But it was no joke. Mary Anne immediately phoned Jessica.

"It's a huge fucking mess," Jessica said, sounding irritated.

"What does it mean?" Mary Anne asked, hoping that all her hard work on both scripts wasn't for nothing.

"It means that Arnold Murphy is a huge prick," Jessica said, typing on her computer as she spoke to Mary Anne. "And that he's terrified of Lydia's success."

"But—"

"It seems that Arnold and Zymar had a huge fight at the screening. Arnold threatened to shelve the film, so Zymar stole the only print and went to New Zealand."

"What?!" Mary Anne was shocked. She'd spoken to Zymar the day before the rough-cut screening. He had been locked away in his editing suite on the Worldwide lot working feverishly on the film and had called to tell Mary Anne that she was a fantastic writer and how spot-on her dialogue was.

"Look." Jessica sighed. "This thing will work itself out; it always does. But for now, Lydia is banned from the Worldwide lot, and all the projects she's set up there, including *The Sky's the Limit*, are on hold."

"Can they do that?"

"They're the studio; they can do whatever they want. You remember that huge check that they gave you, the one with all the zeros? Well, they own *The Sky's the Limit*."

"Forever?"

Mary Anne's hopes were crushed. She loved *The Sky's the Limit*. The script was a character piece, very close to her heart. It was, Mary Anne believed, her first piece of truly beautiful writing.

"There is a reversion clause in the contract."

A glimmer of hope. "How long before I get it back?"

"Seven years. But please, trust me, it's not really dead. I've already started talking to Paul Peterson, the head of Summit, about Lydia getting an overall deal there."

"So . . ."

"Mary Anne, don't worry about this now. It won't take seven years. And don't worry about *Seven Minutes Past Midnight*, either. There are things that we are doing, I can't be specific, but Arnold has only won one battle, not the entire war," Jessica said, and then she belched!

Mary Anne giggled. The idea of the tightly controlled Jessica letting a burp slip was crazy funny.

"Oh my God, Mary Anne, excuse me." Jessica sounded horrified. "I'm so sorry. Dammit, I've been doing that ten times a day. I don't know what I ate, but this burping is just disgusting."

"Don't worry about it; happens to me all the time," Mary Anne lied.

"Thanks. Okay, now just continue working on *The Duo*. It's at Summit and Lydia will do it next if *The Sky's the Limit* gets pushed."

"I'm finished with it."

"What?" Jessica sounded surprised.

"Jess, I've done all the notes Lydia gave me. I handed it in to her three days ago. It's not like Lydia. She usually calls the day after I give her a script to read."

"Then I'm going to get you another assignment to keep you busy. Or do you have an idea for a film? I can get you mid, maybe high, six figures for an original."

"Well, I do have an idea that I've been working on. . . ." Mary Anne's voice drifted off. She'd been toying with an idea but didn't have the story hammered into a three-act structure yet.

"Great, come in and pitch it to me. Later this week. Lauren!"

Jessica yelled at her number one assistant. "Hop on this line and schedule a time for Mary Anne to come in and pitch to me."

"What happened to Kim?" Mary Anne asked. She'd gotten so used to dealing with Jessica's first assistant over the phone that she hadn't known the other two by name.

"Don't ask!" Jessica said, again typing away on her keyboard. "And don't be shocked if she calls you and asks you to lunch, either."

"She left?"

"Long story," Jessica said dismissively. "So how is everything going with your family?"

No matter how busy Jessica was, and Mary Anne knew she sometimes fielded up to three hundred phone calls in one day, Jessica always asked Mary Anne about Mitsy and Marvin. In fact, since Mitsy moved in with Mary Anne, Jessica had called several times just to check on Mary Anne's family status.

"Good. Not good. I don't know."

Mary Anne felt a pang of sadness surge through her.

"If you ever need someone professional to talk to, please, let me know. I know the most brilliant psychiatrist."

"Thanks, Jess. Maybe in a couple of weeks. Right now it just feels too fresh."

"I get it," Jessica said. Mary Anne could once again hear Jessica's fingers flying across her computer keyboard. Time to go. Mary Anne understood that every agent had ADD and that there was a maximum attention span of perhaps ten minutes.

"I'm going to take this other call. Lauren, are you on this line?" Jessica yelled out. "Mary Anne, Lauren is going to schedule a time for you to come into the office." And with that Jessica was gone. Jumping onto another call and spinning more business in the Hollywood phone web.

Now it was Tuesday and Mary Anne stood in the Burbank airport, waiting for a stranger. She glanced at her watch for the sixth time. According to the arrival board, the plane had landed almost seven minutes ago.

"You looking for someone, Miss?"

Mary Anne glanced up at a very tall man with a beard and a Dodgers baseball cap. He wore aviator sunglasses and a nondescript olive-colored jacket. But his voice sounded vaguely familiar. The stranger pulled his sunglasses down and peeked over the top, giving Mary Anne a wink and a great view of his stunning blue eyes. Zymar placed his index finger to his lips and shifted his eyes to the left and to the right.

Mary Anne cleared her throat and calmed herself. "Yes. Actually, uh, my roommate sent me to pick up a dear friend of hers, whom I've never met."

"Ah, you must be Mary Anne," Zymar said, extending his hand and continuing the charade.

"You must be . . . uh . . ."

"Patrick," Zymar said.

"Patrick, yes. So sorry. Well, *Patrick,* do you have luggage? Anything I can help you with?"

"No, just this."

Mary Anne glanced down at the rather large, hard plastic overnight bag Zymar rolled behind him.

"Well, shall we go, then? My car is right outside."

"Great," Zymar said.

Zymar glanced around the airport one more time. He walked beside Mary Anne, and under his breath, without moving his lips or removing his smile, said, "Mary Anne, 'as that big fellow over there pretending to read the paper been there the 'ole time?"

Mary Anne casually glanced to her right, where the big bald man with the newspaper still stood fifteen feet away. He glanced up, his eyes locking onto hers. Alarm bells within Mary Anne instantly went off. Whoever he was, that guy was not a nice man.

"Since I got here."

"Okay," Zymar said, still moving forward. "I need you to laugh like I've just whispered something very clever."

Mary Anne tipped her head to the side and gave Zymar what she believed was her most coquettish look. She tossed in some enthusiastic giggles and grabbed Zymar's arm.

"That was great. Now, when we're right in front of 'im, I need you to turn to me, tell me that you love me, and throw your arms around me."

"But Zy—" Mary Anne checked herself. "Patrick, you and my roommate are dating and I don't think that—"

"Mary Anne, this isn't about your roommate. This is about getting past this guy without 'im calling a goon squad. I don't 'ave time to explain. So please—"

And with that, Mary Anne threw herself into Zymar's arms, nearly knocking him to the ground.

"God, I've missed you. I love you so," Mary Anne said, giving Zymar a long, lingering kiss. She pulled away and blushed.

"Wow," Zymar said, putting his arm around Mary Anne's waist and grinning at the goon standing next to the door. "It's good to see you, too."

31

Celeste Solange Barefoot

IF YOU LIE NUDE ON A PRIVATE BEACH, YOU DON'T HAVE ANY TAN LINES, AND IF you make love on a private island for six days, you don't have any stress. A private beach, a private island, a private life, all in the middle of the Pacific with an exceptional man. What more could a superstar ask for? No shoes, no bags, no cell phones. Barefoot and wearing cotton sarongs. Fresh fruit for breakfast and grilled fish for dinner. It was, unquestionably, paradise. Celeste gazed out at the brilliant blue ocean in front of her. A warm tropical wind breezed through her hair. She was addicted to these early-morning walks, the only time she spent without him on the island. She savored these moments, the quiet joy of solitude, a gift that before this week she had never allowed herself.

Celeste turned and looked at the cottage that squatted forty feet back from and above the beach. It seemed to be an organic part of the island, sculpted to be an integral part of the view. The indoor-outdoor floor plan gave the impression that you were camping on the beach. The ever-present pounding of the surf felt like a heartbeat. An incredible private getaway. Celeste couldn't believe that he'd rarely used it, that he hadn't been to the house since his wife died years ago.

She'd learned about the wife and the rest of his life over the past six days, and shared her own journey. His story, a dramatic rise from poverty to become a millionaire five hundred times over. Hers, having fled from a trailer park in Tennessee to become one of the world's biggest film stars. Two different paths to success, but Celeste was surprised to discover that they bore similar battle scars from their relentless pursuit of it. A myopic and ever-present desire to succeed overshadowed the simple nuances of life.

He'd spent most of his children's childhoods chasing success. Money, a relentless taskmaster, kept him running about the globe. When finally he felt a sense of career achievement, his daughter was finishing graduate school and his son was college bound. Neither child really knew their father. Unforgivable, according to him, that he squandered that time.

Soon after, he recognized his folly and finally started spending more time with his family. Then his wife, after finding a medium-size lump in her breast, began a long and drawn-out battle with cancer. She'd been a great warrior, he told Celeste, his voice cracking. The death of his wife, he believed, closed his heart forever. Until he met Celeste.

At first he shrugged it off as a schoolboy crush on a larger-than-life fantasy. Every man in America adored Celeste Solange at one time or another. But then he'd *met* Celeste. His heart actually skipped, he said. His palms began to sweat, and, he remembered, he could barely speak. Celeste had a vague memory of their first meeting but nothing so steadfastly vivid.

"It was at that moment that I knew I had to get to know you," he told her the second night over snapper.

"That was years ago." Celeste smiled, sipping her wine. "Why didn't you get in touch?"

"I like to be sure about things. I'm methodical."

Celeste remembered very little about their early meetings. She had, however, spoken with him often over the phone, about various scripts his company had for films they wanted her to star in, and she had always found his tone endearing.

"People never understood when I told them you were always so sweet to me on the phone," Celeste said.

"Most people don't get that treatment, Celeste," he said, leaning back in his chair.

"I can't picture you being mean-spirited."

"Not mean, never mean. But tough. You can't succeed in business without being tough."

"But with me—"

"I don't have to be," he said, looking into Celeste's eyes. "Besides, I know you can be just as tough as me."

And there was the understanding between them. He'd never been the recipient of Celeste's hard edge nor she his, and their relationship nurtured the usually unexposed soft spots of their assertive personalities.

Celeste entered the bedroom from the beach. He lay on the luxurious seven-hundred-thread-count white sheets, his silver hair mussed but still beautiful. He was delicious in every way. She couldn't get over the fact that this was the first time in a life of luxury, stars, exclusive parties, and clubs that she felt happy and whole.

It was as if someone had wiped away a haze through which she'd viewed the world for her entire life and now there was clarity. Clarity, peace, and serenity. The past six days together, she'd embraced them.

Celeste lay down next to him and watched as his blue eyes opened, taking in her and their world. He reached his arm across the bed and pulled Celeste toward him. Without a word he kissed her eyes, her lips, her neck. She felt the joy and heat rising up from inside her, spreading through her body. His lips were moving expertly down her chest as his hands unwrapped the sarong she'd worn for her walk on the beach. They'd explored every inch of each other. She knew about the scar on the small of his back and the teenage DUI that went with it. He, of the welt on her upper back left thigh and the jagged piece of glass she'd fallen on at age nine.

Her lips parted as his tongue explored her mouth, his fingers massaging the wet between her legs. He nudged his knee between her legs, spreading them apart. Her body tingled, ready for him.

Wanting him. Desiring him to take her, to have her, to be his. His blue eyes stared at her as he entered her. Silently their bodies rocked to the rhythm of the waves outside their open door, the speed increasing as the rumbling of the surf engulfed them.

Celeste glanced at the clock. He'd been in the bathroom forever. He loved his long, hot showers. It was, perhaps, the only decadent moment each day that he allowed himself. She knew he was a man with amazing self-discipline. These six days together meant all the more because of his workaholic nature. They'd both turned off their phones on the plane. No computers, no television, and no radios. It was bliss. The entire world could be gone and they wouldn't know it.

But they were flying out today, back to civilization. Celeste glanced at her Chanel bag. She suddenly wanted to know what she'd missed. She reached in, pulled out her cell, and turned it on. *Forty-three messages!* Only ten people had the number to this, her most private line. She usually got only a couple of calls a day. Any business going on in her absence Jessica could easily handle. But as Celeste scrolled down the list of numbers, Jessica's turned up almost twenty times. Lydia was next with fifteen, and even her housekeeper, Mathilde, had tried to reach her a few times. *What was going on?* Celeste only needed to listen to four of the forty-three messages before the whole story unfolded.

"What are you doing, lady?" he asked in a playful voice as he emerged from the steaming bathroom. "We said no cell phones."

Celeste held up her hand and smiled at him, hoping not to annoy him. She was trying to catch the end of Mary Anne's impassioned plea for Celeste to call her.

Celeste flipped shut her phone and tossed it on the bed.

"We have to get back."

He smiled, watching her bounce across the room in a packing frenzy. "We're leaving in four hours."

"What time is it?"

"Nine A.M."

"No, love, not here, in L.A. What day and time is it in Los Angeles?"

"Let's see, we're seventeen hours ahead, so what, it's four P.M. on Wednesday?"

Celeste stopped and did the math in her head. "Hurry, we have to leave now!"

He smiled again. "Okay, beautiful, whatever you say. I'll call the pilots. We can be in the air in half an hour."

Celeste stopped throwing toiletries in her bag.

"I love you. You know that, right?"

He put the phone down and turned to Celeste. "Yes, beautiful. And I love you, too." His brilliant blue eyes flashed in the morning sun.

Celeste skipped out of the room into the bathroom.

"Hey," she called as she stepped under the hot water, "how fast can your plane fly?"

Lydia Albright Wearing Keds

THE SUPER-SECRET SCREENING OF *SEVEN MINUTES PAST MIDNIGHT* STARTED IN less than an hour and Lydia had yet to see Zymar or her film. Her director and the print were both safely tucked away, Lydia knew, in a Best Western in the Valley only three blocks from Arnold Murphy's executive suite. Hiding in plain sight. Thanks to Mary Anne's escort two days before.

Mitsy Meyers, surprisingly, was a godsend. Looking and sounding every bit the part of a Midwesterner on vacation in Hollywood, she'd been able to courier messages, food, and anything else Zymar desired to his hotel room without drawing attention. A guy with a beard, baseball cap, sunglasses, and a Eurotrash accent might collect some looks, but a middle-aged woman in khaki shorts and Keds over-pronouncing her o's at a Best Western in the Valley most definitely blended in.

Lydia had spoken with Zymar ten times in the last two days. He and Mitsy had hit it off famously. She was quite a hustler; in two days of gin rummy she'd cleaned Zymar out of all his cash and his watch. At least he wasn't bored or hungry. Having company, Lydia knew, calmed his nerves and most likely prevented him from making a foolish attempt to sneak over to Lydia's.

Lydia peeked out her upstairs bedroom window, the only one with a clear view to the street beyond her security gate. The black

Lincoln Town Car sedan with two goons inside sat parked next to the opposite curb, as it had been for the last two weeks.

Arnold was insane. He wasn't even attempting to be inconspicuous. There was only one reason for the black sedan that was tailing Lydia. Intimidation. But it wasn't working. Although she felt nervous about the plan and the film, Lydia wasn't scared.

She was Midwestern. That's what the mirror reflected, anyway. Her wig, specially designed by Celeste's stylist, Jonathan, was a perfect replica of Mitsy's brown helmet cut. The purple floral-print button-down shirt and Bermuda shorts that Jessica had purchased from Target.com, Mitsy assured Lydia, were duplicates of the clothes Mitsy would be wearing when she pulled into the gate.

Lydia glanced out the window. The fluorescent green Scion they'd rented for today finally came rolling up to her gate, the color intended to be especially conspicuous. The two goons in the car needed to get a good look at Mitsy and her ultra-bright car.

Mitsy pulled up and punched a button at the gate, causing the cordless phone Lydia held in her hand to ring.

"Hello," Lydia shouted.

She hoped the spies had their windows rolled down so they could overhear the exchange.

"Script delivery for Ms. Lydia Albright," Mitsy yelled into the speaker-box.

"Great!" Lydia yelled back. She pressed the number nine on her phone and watched as her security gate rumbled to life, lumbering backward into the drive. Lydia had parked her black Range Rover in front of her home so that the thugs would get a clear view of it parked safely on the drive.

Lydia waited at her bedroom window until the gate swung shut; she knew the goons couldn't see anything at the front door as long as the gate was closed. Carrying a white terry-cloth robe, she jogged down the stairs and pulled open her front door. There, standing across the threshold, was Mitsy Meyers, holding a script envelope and smiling. Their outfits and hair were identical.

"Mitsy, thank you so much," Lydia said, pulling her through the door. "You may have just saved my career, Zymar's career, and prevented both of us from spending years in prison."

Lydia threw the fluffy robe over Mitsy's outfit and grabbed the ten-dollar Kmart sunglasses Mitsy held out toward Lydia.

"My pleasure, dear, truly. I haven't had this much excitement in years."

"You'll stay away from the windows?" Lydia asked.

"And the doors."

"Vilma knows to tell anyone who calls or comes by that I'm sleeping."

"Great plan." Mitsy handed Lydia the keys to the frog-green Scion.

"Yes." Lydia smiled. "All because of you, a very great plan."

Jessica, Mary Anne, and Lydia had been stumped on how to get Lydia past Arnold's goons and to the screening at CTA. Their biggest fear was that Arnold would somehow manage to find out the correct date and time and prevent anyone from seeing the film. But then Mitsy had come up with the bait-and-switch idea.

The screening had become an open secret in town for the last three days. But thanks to Kiki with her PR firm and Jessica with her CTA agents barraging the industry with a variety of locales and dates, Arnold couldn't get a lock on the time and place. Only those guests specifically invited knew exactly when and where. And none of them would tell Arnold because they actually wanted to see the film.

The buzz in town was deafening.

Lydia put on Mitsy's sunglasses and glanced in the mirror. She never would have believed that she could pass for a fifty-six-year-old mother of three from Minnesota, but she could and she did. Her stomach tickled from the adrenaline at pulling off this little subterfuge.

"Okay, I think I'm ready."

"You certainly look like it," Mitsy said. "Good luck, dear. I know it'll be fantastic."

Mitsy pulled Lydia into a hug.

"Thank you for everything. You are simply the best. If this works, it's all because of you."

Lydia pulled open the front door and paused as the gate again pulled back into the drive. She wanted to make sure Worldwide's thugs got a clear shot of the frumpily dressed older woman who five minutes before had entered Ms. Albright's home. Lydia surreptitiously glanced at the black sedan parked across the street, then stepped toward the bright-green Scion and opened the door. As she drove past the gate, she purposely stopped and looked in both directions before turning right onto Mulholland. She wanted to make sure they both got a really good look at the cheap sunglasses and the very loud purple shirt with orange flowers.

Lydia drove cautiously, checking the black sedan in her rearview mirror for any sign of movement or alarm. She crested a hill and made the curve. Nothing. They weren't following her. Lydia let out a giggle of glee. Phase one was complete.

Lydia pulled the car into the underground parking garage at CTA. Already seven cars lined up at the valet. Per Jessica, the security guards were given strict orders to check the ID of everyone who entered the CTA building. Anyone not on the list didn't get in. Well, everyone except the middle-aged woman in the purple blouse driving the green Scion. The security guards had special guidelines for that car. As instructed, the guards waved her past the other cars, and Lydia zipped the Scion up one floor and into a prearranged spot. Lauren, Jessica's first assistant, stood waiting, her look of concern giving way to a slight smile.

"Thank God," Lauren said as Lydia emerged from the car. "She's been calling me every two minutes to see if you're here yet."

"Has Zymar made it?"

"Five minutes ago. He's upstairs in Jessica's office with the door closed," Lauren said. "This spy stuff looks fun in the movies, but it really wears me out."

"You and me both, sister," Lydia said.

* * *

Lydia walked into Jessica's office and all her eyes could see was Zymar. Beautiful, wonderful Zymar. Her heart fluttered. His scruffy beard tickled her face as he kissed her.

"Ahem." Jessica pretended to clear her throat. Lydia hadn't noticed that she was even in the room. "I know it's been six weeks, but come on, we've got a screening to do."

Lydia smiled at her friend. Jessica practically glowed.

"Go get changed, Lyd. You've only got five minutes. Security called and almost everyone's here."

"Cici?" Lydia asked, a hint of hope in her voice.

"Still no sign."

Lydia sighed.

"Need a bit of help in there, Lyd?" Zymar asked, a sexy smile dancing on his lips.

"No time for that," Jessica called from her desk.

Once inside Jessica's bathroom, Lydia began to shed her Midwestern costume. Mary Anne had packed Lydia's Armani pants, Donna Karan blouse, and Dior pumps, and left them in the trunk of the Scion. If only she'd been able to find and throw in Cici. It'd been seven days since anyone had seen or heard from her. They would have called in the FBI if she hadn't left a note with Mathilde. They knew she was on a private island some-where in the Pacific, but for how long?

Lydia tucked her white silk shirt into her black pants. She pulled off her wig and fluffed her chestnut brown hair. Jessica had finally received a garbled voice-mail message from Cici at nine A.M. this morning, something about landing in Hawaii, when Cici's phone completely cut out. With five minutes left, Lydia doubted that Cici would see this screening. She just hoped there'd be enough heat to ensure it wouldn't be the only one.

The screening room was full: seventy-five seats plus folding chairs in the aisles. Studio heads sat on the floor. *What a house!*

Lydia wondered if any film in Hollywood history had gotten a screening like this before. She suddenly felt panicked. She'd never seen the final cut. *What if this thing was a dog?* She looked at Zymar and felt a sudden pang of doubt. His last film had tanked. *What if this one was a stinker, too?* And in front of all her peers. They'd never forgive her for wasting their time for a crappy film. If Arnold shelved it, she was dead, and if it stunk, her career was finished. Well, better to go down swinging. The only path to success was to show the film. Lydia heard claps and she looked toward the screen. There stood Zymar, flapping his hands and asking the crowd to settle.

"Okay. I know this is a little unorthodox, the director speaking at a screening, but 'oo knows, this might be the only premiere and we need to get started before this party gets busted."

The crowd laughed, knowing full well that Arnold and Worldwide could pull the plug at any minute.

"Bring on the leprechaun!" Lydia heard someone yell.

Hoots and cheers followed.

"I just want to say thank you to the one person who made this 'ole thing possible—"

"Liideeeaaa!" Arnold's screech pierced the room.

Lydia's heart sank. She sighed and looked at the ceiling. She would now be beaten and led out in handcuffs in front of all of Hollywood. She turned, and there, standing at the back of the room with two oversized goons and what looked like attorneys or federal agents, was Arnold Murphy.

Boos and heckles rang out as Arnold squinted his eyes.

"There, there she is. I want her arrested. I want her jailed."

Lydia looked at Zymar, who looked as drained as she felt.

Jessica stood at Lydia's side. She leaned over and whispered, "This will be ugly. But stay strong. You've got the crowd on your side."

"Lauren, get security up here now!" Jessica hissed over to Lauren. "How the fuck did this prick get into the building?!"

"I have here a cease-and-desist order from a federal judge," Arnold bellowed. "Police are on the way. You, Lydia Albright, are a thief and a liar. And finally after years of fraud and slander, you are going to jail."

"Hey, Arnold, pipe down and show your film," an exec yelled from the first row.

"Yeah, Arnie, what are you so afraid of? That Lydia might actually be right?" another senior studio exec called.

"You think you'd want a film that made some money while you're running Worldwide," catcalled another. "Everything else you've released so far has tanked."

Jessica charged toward the leprechaun. "Arnold, this stops now. We are going to my office to discuss this."

"You, Jessica Caulfield, will be charged with conspiracy to commit fraud and a felony," he screeched. "Violation of copyright laws both domestic and international. Perhaps you two gal pals can be cell mates."

"I'm not kidding, Murphy," Jessica threatened. "*Now.* This is still my company, my building, and my screening room. So far all you've got proof of is a room full of people getting ready to watch a film. Do you even know what we're here to see?"

Arnold looked horrified.

"Yeah, Arnie, you're looking at the Peter O'Toole fan club. We're here to watch *Lawrence of Arabia*. Now get out."

"You won't get away with this," Arnold hissed as Jessica's security detail finally arrived at the screening room door.

"Come with me, Arnold," Jessica said. She grabbed his arm and pulled him back out the door.

"You two," Arnold said, pointing to his goons, "stay here. If they show anything but *Lawrence of Arabia*, come get me."

They nodded slowly.

Jessica nodded to the projectionist as she, Arnold, and his attorneys filed out of the room.

Lydia couldn't imagine how Jessica contained Arnold for two hours, but she did. Every time Lydia looked over her shoulder throughout the picture, the only people she saw by the screening room door were Arnold's henchmen. And they seemed to enjoy the film as much as the other ninety-seven people crammed into the screening room. As the credits rolled, with the closing score blaring from the speakers, Lydia overheard snippets of conversation.

"Huge."

"It'll break records."

"Amazing action sequence. I can't remember the last time I saw something like that on film."

"He's an idiot if he doesn't release this summer."

Lydia was thrilled. She received the kisses and handshakes of a conquering producer.

Zymar made his way through the crowd of well-wishers to Lydia's side.

"Oh Zy, it really is even better than I expected!" Lydia said, giving him a hug.

"Yeah, well, let's 'ope we get a release date," Zymar said.

"Well, if you don't, Arnold is a fool," said Jeff Blume, stretching out his hand to Zymar. "But then again, I worked for him, so I know that to be a fact.

"Hi, Lyd," he said, and gave her a hug. "Great job. It's amazing. Listen, if you don't get a release date from Worldwide, let me know. Galaxy has an option to pick up one of Worldwide's unreleased films. They owe us from way back. I don't think Arnold's aware of the deal; it predates him. But I want to make *Seven Minutes Past Midnight* a Galaxy release should Arnold be stupid enough not to distribute it."

"That's great news, Jeff," Lydia said.

Zymar placed his arm around her waist. At least part of the plan had worked: The public would get a chance to see the film. Lydia might not be able to make it to the premiere, as she'd be in federal prison, but at least the movie would be released.

Lydia walked into Jessica's office expecting police and federal marshals, but to her shock Arnold was gone. Waiting instead were Jessica and Cici. And Ted Robinoff.

"Lydia, it's *fantastic*!" Cici squealed, and sprang to her feet.

"You saw it?" Lydia asked, surprised to see her friend.

"We got there just as the opening credits closed," Cici gushed. "We saw the whole thing. Ted loved it!"

Lydia turned to look at Ted Robinoff, arguably one of the most powerful people in Hollywood. Definitely the most elusive. Lydia gave Jessica a knowing glance. They'd both suspected this love affair between Cici and Ted but had been unable to obtain confirmation from Cici or any of their other sources.

"So you liked the film?" Lydia asked.

"Very much," Ted said.

"Where's Arnold?" Lydia asked. "Sorry if I look a little panicked. I half expected to be arrested upon entering Jessica's office."

"Yes, Celeste told me about your ongoing problems with Arnold," Ted said. "It seems he's been less than helpful with this film."

It was an understatement but one Lydia chose not to comment on. She knew Cici well enough to know that if she hadn't already, she would fill Ted in on every one of Arnold's dirty tricks over the last nine months. A story that would be much more compelling for Ted coming from Cici.

"Well, that's finished now. All I want is a release date for my film. And not to go to jail," Lydia said, watching Ted Robinoff, wondering if he'd actually commit to anything at this moment.

"I need to go over to the studio," Ted said. "Arnold and I have a meeting at six. But Lydia, I can guarantee you that Worldwide won't be pressing any charges against you or Zymar."

He turned to Cici, his tone softening. "I'm going now. I'll see you around eight."

Lydia watched as Cici turned from tough über-star to sweet, soulful girl as she looked up and kissed Ted. She'd never seen her friend let herself be so emotionally vulnerable with a man, and she'd wager that stern, serious Ted was rarely so intimate with anyone on the planet.

Ted paused at the door to Jessica's office. "I wish I could give you a release date now, Lydia, but I need to meet with Arnold first. You have moxie and passion, and those are two qualities I admire in a person." He gave them a wave.

"Who is that guy?" Lydia said, dropping to the couch. "Is he for real?"

"Oh, he's for real," Cici said, "and he's mine."

"If we get out of this one, ladies, it will be a very good day," Jessica said.

A very good day indeed, Lydia thought.

Jessica Caulfield's Booties

JESSICA STARED AT THE DIGITAL CALENDAR ON HER FLAT-SCREEN MONITOR. SHE did the math for the third time in her head. *But . . .*

"Oh my GOD, I'm pregnant!" Jessica whispered aloud. "Lauren!" she yelled. "Call Dr. Crane and schedule an appointment for today if you can get it."

"But your annual isn't for another six weeks," Lauren said, standing in the doorway to Jess's office.

"Don't worry about it, just do it," Jessica said, and quickly minimized the calendar on her computer screen, even though there was no possible way Lauren could see it. Once Lauren returned to her desk, Jessica counted the days off on both hands for the fourth time.

"He can't see you until tomorrow," Lauren yelled out.

"Fine," Jessica called, "just book it."

Jessica didn't know if she was thrilled or terrified. Twenty-four hours was too long to wait. If her calculations were correct, she was almost eight weeks along. Eight weeks! That meant she'd be a mother in seven months. Jessica jumped from her chair and grabbed her Dior purse. There was a Save-On down the street. Normally she'd send one of her assistants or a trainee from the mailroom, but she didn't want speculation over her fertility filling the agency halls. There was enough gossip about her floating around already.

"I'll be right back," Jessica said, slipping quickly past her three assistants.

"Where are you going?" Lauren asked. "You have your weekly meeting with Jeremy and Tolliver in fifteen minutes."

Most of the time it was fantastic to have a brilliant obsessive-compulsive assistant like Lauren, but at this moment, Jess somehow felt as if she was being scolded by her mother.

"Back in ten," Jessica called. "I have to run out."

Lauren flashed a disapproving frown as Jessica hopped onto the executive elevator. Her heart pounded with excitement and fear. *What would Mike say?* He couldn't be surprised; they'd been less than zealous with their birth control. *Lackadaisical* was the word that came to mind.

The pharmacy next to the office was empty except for the clerk at the register and a blue-haired ninety-year-old woman in the birthday card section. Jessica grabbed three tests (all different brands just to be on the safe side) and bolted to the register. She slid up to a girl who looked to be no older than fourteen. The girl blew a huge bubble, then cracked her gum.

"That it?" she asked while listlessly passing the boxes in front of the bar code scanner.

"Yes, thank you."

"Sixty-three forty-nine," the girl said.

Jessica handed her a hundred. Parenthood was expensive and she didn't even know if she was pregnant yet.

She arrived back at her office with ten minutes to spare. *Just enough time to try one of my tests.* She slipped past Lauren and pulled shut her door (something she rarely did). In her executive bathroom she skimmed the instructions on test number one. She peed on the stick and waited, pacing in front of her executive toilet.

"Jessica?" She heard Lauren knocking on her office door. "Jeremy is on his way over."

Crap, Jessica thought as she scrambled to put all three pregnancy tests in the drawer next to the sink. No answers yet, and now she had to meet with Tolliver.

Jessica had lost a tremendous amount of respect for Jeremy recently, because he couldn't see through Tolliver's brownnosing, suck-up ways. Why Jeremy still believed that Tolliver was an asset to CTA was an utter mystery to her. His paycheck was enormous. The magic client list that Tolliver claimed he'd bring with him to CTA from his previous agency had never materialized. And he hadn't attracted any new talent, despite his touted skills. The man was expensive, had no clients, and brought in no business. *So why,* Jessica often wondered, *was he here?*

But Jeremy was completely enamored of him. Jessica believed that Jeremy, as an Americanized Brit who'd pulled himself up with hard work and a good marriage, was impressed with Tolliver's pedigree. Tolliver was related to two United States presidents and had a family lineage that could be traced back to the British royal family, or so he claimed. Jessica, however, doubted Tolliver's claims. She'd checked with some of the agents at his old shop, DTA. It wasn't that DTA couldn't make Tolliver's deal, but that they didn't *want* to make his deal. Tolliver hadn't met the bottom line. But now he had a new teat to suck off for at least three years. Jeremy was Tolliver's new sugar daddy, one who hadn't yet caught on to the scam.

This weekly meeting between the coheads of CTA was Jeremy's idea. He was trying to foster a feeling of collegiality and camaraderie between Jessica and Tolliver. So far, Jessica hadn't seen any kind of hard work that would make her want Tolliver as part of her team. He'd failed to close any deals or find work for any of CTA's clients. Most of the time he bounced from meeting to meeting coming up with grandiose plans and then never following through.

"Jeremy." Jessica rose from the chair across from her suede-covered sofa as Jeremy entered her office. Clean-cut and crisp, he always wore Michael Vartos (the company was custom-tailoring his clothes now). Jeremy kissed Jess on both cheeks.

"Jess, you look absolutely radiant," he said, taking a seat.

Little does he know, Jessica thought. *I may just be the very epitome of radiant, and glowing, and ripe.*

"Where's Tolliver?" Jessica asked. She peered through her open office door.

"Finishing up a call. He'll be down in a few moments. This gives me an opportunity to speak with you alone."

Radiant. What a word to choose. Jessica's mind drifted to names and baby carriages. *What color would she paint the nursery walls? Booties, she would get baby booties! Was it a boy or a girl? Which did Mike want?* She tried to imagine what a perfect combination of her and Mike's DNA would look like.

"Jess, what do you think?"

Jess broke from her reverie. She hadn't heard a word Jeremy said. "I'm sorry, I'm fighting a terrible cold and the medicine has me a little hazy. Would you repeat that last part?"

Jeremy didn't need to, as at that moment Tolliver entered Jessica's office. His brow was furrowed and his fists clenched. So tumultuous was his demeanor that he didn't bother to sit or greet either of them, choosing instead to pace in front of Jessica's desk.

"Well, Jess, it seems your screening yesterday put CTA in a very tenuous position," Tolliver said.

Jessica had little patience for Tolliver, anyway, and these dramatics irritated her. Keeping her disdain in check, she eyed him.

"How so? We didn't violate any copyright laws. Ultimately Ted Robinoff gave his consent to the screening."

"Yes, but it made Mr. Murphy very upset," Jeremy chimed in.

Jessica was surprised by Jeremy's response. The two men must have had a prior discussion about this matter. Jessica wondered what Tolliver was up to.

"It seems Tolliver has been working on a very important deal with Arnold and now, because of yesterday, it's in jeopardy."

"What deal?" Jessica asked, looking pointedly at Tolliver. She was skeptical. Aside from trying to sabotage Lydia's film, Arnold hadn't accomplished anything as president of Worldwide except losing money and pissing everyone off.

Tolliver flopped down on Jessica's couch, running his hand through his hair.

"Well, it's off now," he said. "It seems your little stunt yesterday cost CTA around seventy-five million."

"How can that be?" Jeremy asked, clearly upset by Tolliver's news.

Jessica furrowed her brow. If Jeremy believed that Tolliver had something brewing with Arnold, something that Jessica had somehow managed to swamp, she was really in trouble. Not because it was true, but because it meant that Jeremy was under the Svengali-type sway of Tolliver.

"Three full CTA packages. Before yesterday, Arnold was poised to purchase them from CTA, but now, thanks to the screening, all of it is off."

"How come this is the first I'm hearing of this?" Jessica snapped. It went against the very foundation of CTA that a senior agent, even a copresident, would be on the verge of something so big and fail to tell her and Jeremy.

"It was a very precarious negotiation," Tolliver said. "Made even more difficult, as you can imagine, by your involvement with Lydia Albright. With so much money on the line, I couldn't risk exposing the agency to this kind of loss until I was sure. The negative publicity around town if I failed to close such an enormous deal could be deadly."

Was Tolliver really this clever? Jessica hadn't given him nearly enough credit. There was no deal. She could feel it to her core. But what a brazen ploy, to claim such a huge deal and then blame the loss of it on her. *Bravo,* Jessica thought. She could think of no one else who had such a set of brass balls.

"Really? What were the film packages? Perhaps we can get Summit or Galaxy to pick them up," Jessica said, calling Tolliver's bluff.

"It's irrelevant now." He sniffed. "The packages were specific to Worldwide's needs, and I just finished what I assure you was a very unpleasant conversation with Arnold. And all three deals are off."

"Let me try to get Ted Robinoff." Jessica reached for the phone next to the sofa. "It's ultimately his decision on how the dollars are spent and—"

"No!" Tolliver exclaimed, nearly leaping from his chair.

Jessica eyed him. *Gotcha.* Now she was certain that Tolliver was lying about the whole ordeal. She looked to Jeremy to confirm that he had finally caught on to Tolliver's charade, but her friend and mentor was looking at the floor.

"This is very bad," Jeremy said, finally gazing at Tolliver and then Jessica.

Tolliver, seeming to sense that Jeremy still believed his tale, went for the kill.

"Bad? This isn't bad, Jeremy, this is a bloodbath. This and Jessica losing Holden and Maurice? CTA's lost over a hundred fifteen million in the last two months."

Tolliver studied Jeremy's reaction and continued. "According to Arnold, yesterday's screening may have made us vulnerable to federal prosecution for copyright violation."

Jessica seethed. What had started as a brazen attempt at a power grab by Tolliver was now turning into a circus.

"Tolliver, I can assure you that CTA is not at risk."

"Don't be so sure, Jessica," Tolliver spat out. "Had I not agreed to let Arnold into the screening yesterday, we'd all be in federal court today."

So Tolliver was the traitor. Jessica had wondered all of last night who had let Arnold and his thugs into the building. Her security team was impeccable; highly trained professionals with a spotless record. Lauren had even given each of the guards a picture of Arnold so they knew to detain him.

"*You* let Arnold into the building? I believe that my instructions regarding Arnold were explicit," Jessica said, her tone sharp. She turned her attention to her shell-shocked boss. "Jeremy, I spoke to Ted Robinoff today and he harbors no ill will toward CTA. There will be no legal action."

"For now," Tolliver shot back, fanning the flames. "But your little stunt was embarrassing and reckless."

"Reckless? It was quite well planned. In fact, even the CEO of Worldwide was here. I doubt that it would have been nearly as embarrassing for Arnold had my instructions been followed.

It's interesting to me, Tolliver, that I was on the phone with Ted Robinoff this morning and he made no mention of your seventy-five-million-dollar deal."

"Are you calling me a liar?"

"No, Tolliver, I did not use that word. However, ultimately Ted would have to approve of such a large expenditure. And if your deal was as imminent as you claim, then I'd think that Ted would be aware of it."

"You know, Jessica, Arnold warned me about you," Tolliver snarled. "Said there was a reason why someone as deceitful as Lydia Albright got along with you so well."

"I wish CTA had received a similar warning. It seems that neither I nor Jeremy were adequately briefed on your reputation or your earning potential."

"Reputation?" Tolliver spat out. "You, speak to me about reputation? You mean there are worse reputations than living with a gay man for four years, losing two A-list stars, plus whoring yourself out to a womanizing producer? Not to mention your former assistant absconding with CTA's most sensitive documents. And our Rolodex. Did you know that Josh Dragatsis calls all our top clients every day?"

Jessica was horrified. Tolliver had stepped way over the line. *You didn't get personal.* She had been in battles with agents before, but never one in which a colleague so blatantly lied and slandered her before the head of the company. Stunned, she looked at Jeremy, whom she expected to throw Tolliver out for such a rude outburst. But Jeremy sat frozen on the couch, his silence indicative of where his loyalty lay.

Jessica exhaled. "Well, Tolliver, I think you've made your opinions clear. And this meeting is finished," she said, gathering the shreds of her dignity.

Tolliver stood and exited without another word.

"Jess, I just don't know," Jeremy whispered. "If Tolliver's statements are accurate about the Worldwide deal . . ."

Jessica was rattled.

"Jeremy, I'm sure they aren't."

"That is a strong accusation against your copresident," Jeremy said.

"And yet so skillfully played by Tolliver, it is virtually impossible to confirm, isn't it?" Jessica hoped that Jeremy would see through the shell game. Throughout her tenure as president of CTA, she'd given Jeremy her unquestioning loyalty. At this moment, faced with this choice, she expected the same in return.

Jeremy rose from the couch, refusing to look Jessica in the eye.

"I don't see how this can continue much longer. You know what they say about a house divided. Distrust at this level, it will destroy CTA."

"I agree, Jeremy."

"Jess—"

"You really needn't say anything more." Jessica felt as though she should be angry. In fact, a minute ago she had been. She'd wanted to rage against Tolliver, his inaccurate claims and obvious lies. But something had snapped, and now somehow she didn't care. Jeremy, CTA, the title of copresident—it didn't matter to her anymore.

Jeremy turned toward Jessica's office door, both of them recognizing the finality of the moment yet neither prepared to acknowledge it.

"The attorneys, then," Jeremy said, reverting back to his stiff British manners.

"Yes," Jessica said.

"Right, then. Take your time, Jess, there's no rush. Not as though I'll be having security escort you out the door."

"Thank you, Jeremy. A couple of weeks, then. To exit gracefully."

"Certainly, of course. Anything you need."

And then he left.

Jessica let out a deep breath; she felt like a balloon had just been pricked by a pin. She was tired, whipped, and yet very calm. Not afraid or bereft, the way she'd always anticipated feeling if she got fired. Instead, a sense of calm empowerment surrounded her. The world, her time—all of it was now hers to fill.

*   *   *

Jessica sat on the couch in her living room waiting for Mike. She watched the headlights of his Aston Martin through the living-room windows as his car climbed the drive. She listened as the garage door opened and then closed. She heard Mike's footfalls as he made his way to the stairs. It was at that moment that he must have seen her. Sitting alone, in the dark, on her couch in the unused living room. She wondered what she must look like to him. Perhaps as though she'd just heard the news that someone had died?

"Jess?" he said, flipping on a soft light. He stood before her looking down, consternation on his face.

She tilted her head back, took in the sight of him in his shirt and Lucky jeans. Without saying a word she lifted the plastic stick to him, holding it out as if it were an offering. She'd retrieved it after Tolliver's tirade and Jeremy's betrayal. There was a quizzical look on Mike's face as he reached for the piece of plastic Jessica held in her hand. A look that gave way to shock and joyful surprise.

"Is this . . . ?" He didn't finish as a sly smile crept up his face.

Jessica nodded, watching his reaction. He scooped her up into his arms, twirling her with joy. He let out a sound like a whoop before they both collapsed breathless on the couch.

"I *knew* it!" Mike said, like the victor of a bet everyone told him he'd lose.

"Knew it? How? I didn't even know."

"Jess, come on! You're sick all the time, and tired, and"—he looked at her breasts—"your tits are huge."

Jessica playfully hit him on the shoulder. "Wish you would have told me."

"I thought you knew and wanted to surprise me. The other night completely sealed it, though."

Jessica gave him a questioning look.

"Jess, I've known you a long time. A cheeseburger? I've never even heard you mention a cheeseburger. And the way you plowed through those fries?" He leaned forward toward her tummy. "Someone must have been hungry," he said to her still-small belly.

"Don't forget the chocolate shake," Jessica said sheepishly, burying her head in his shoulder.

"Yeah, well, don't you forget the fruits and vegetables," Mike said in a protective tone. "We've got a baby to build. I think I'll hire a cook. How long do we have?"

"About seven months, give or take a week or two. I'm seeing the doctor tomorrow."

"Have you told Jeremy yet?" Mike asked.

"No, silly," Jess said playfully, "I thought the father should know first. Besides," she added, her face suddenly serious, "it won't be necessary to tell Jeremy."

"Oh yeah, why?" Mike leaned forward and brushed a strand of Jessica's auburn hair away from her eyes.

"Because I think I got fired today."

"You are on a roll, baby," Mike said, clearly relieved. "That place is the most toxic environment in town."

"Hey, that's my company," Jessica said with mock defensiveness.

"Was—no longer. I think it's great. You're way too smart for that place. And Tolliver? Who needs the pain?"

Jessica was relieved to hear Mike articulate all the thoughts that had run through her mind while driving home. *Who did need the pain?* She'd gotten into this business because she loved films and the people who made them, not because she liked battling people with no talent and huge egos.

"You can come back and work for me," Mike said coyly.

"Thanks, but no more bosses."

"Whatever you want." Mike put his arm around her and squeezed.

"Maybe my own management company. I'm going to think on it for a while, but I may go it alone."

Mike leaned forward and gave her a warm, languid kiss.

"Jess, you still don't get it." He smiled. "You're not ever going to be alone."

Mary Anne and Mitsy's Givenchy Shoes

TWENTY MINUTES LATE. IT WAS MITSY'S NEWEST AND MOST ANNOYING HABIT, always being late. Mary Anne glanced around the Coffee Bean patio and closed her laptop. She'd gotten a little further on the outline for her next script. But Mary Anne was hungry. She and Mitsy were going to have lunch and then buy Mitsy a car. It was her mother's second big purchase after her new Toluca Lake condominium, but the one that seemed to excite Mitsy the most. The recent spending spree had been made possible by the surprise sale of her three children's books to a large New York publisher. The size of Mitsy's advance surprised Mitsy, Mary Anne, and even Mitsy's new literary agent, Andrea (recommended by Jessica).

"What can I say, dear, people love buying books for their children. I know I always did," Mitsy said in her unassuming Midwestern way. It was the first money that Mitsy had ever earned—not that she needed it. According to her parents' separation agreement, half of their multitude of assets belonged to Mitsy, but it was the fact that Mitsy had earned the book advance, Mary Anne believed, that gave her mother a self-esteem boost.

Mitsy, the author, had informed the family that the condo was for winters. She made it very clear when she'd called Michael and Michelle (conferencing in Mary Anne) that she would be spending the spring, summer, and fall in St. Paul.

"I have to get my grandparenting time in, now, don't I?"

The final outcome of Marvin and Mitsy's marriage had yet to be determined. They still spoke three times a day, with Mitsy faxing task lists to Marvin's office of everything he needed to complete. Mary Anne did hear from her brother, Michael, that Marvin had decided it was best to end his relationship with Nancy MacIntosh. He helped her find a job in Bismark, closer to her family, something Mary Anne wished he had done years before.

"Sorry I'm late, dear," said Mitsy, breezing up in her white linen skirt and Givenchy shoes (another Los Angeles habit her mother seemed quite comfortable with: buying expensive shoes), "but I stopped in the most darling bookstore two doors down. They have a fabulous children's section and I started talking with the owner and it seems I now have my very first book signing."

Mary Anne marveled at the ease with which Mitsy seemed to plow through life. Mitsy's unflappability, a trait Mary Anne had been thoroughly annoyed with until recently, now struck awe in her. She hoped that someday she, too, would float through life's rapids confidently instead of flailing as if about to drown.

"Really? I've never noticed it," Mary Anne said.

"Well, let's stop in. It's on our way to lunch."

Mitsy pushed open the bookshop door and the bell above tinkled. The cool air was refreshing. Mary Anne inhaled, drinking in the familiar scent of paper, glue, and ink on the page. She looked around, glancing at her first childhood love: books. The shop was quaint with a warm atmosphere. *Well-loved* was the description that popped into Mary Anne's mind.

She wandered toward the fiction section, admiring the titles and the authors' names on each spine. It was a secret wish of Mary Anne's that she, like Mitsy, would write a book one day. Mitsy's laugh drew Mary Anne out of her bibliophilic reverie. She turned toward Mitsy, who now stood next to a gorgeous man.

"Mary Anne, I want you to meet Adam," Mitsy said, smiling at the tall man with glasses and curly dark hair.

"Hello," Mary Anne said. She extended her hand and hoped it wasn't shaking.

"I was just telling Adam about your newest script. It seems he's a writer, too," Mitsy said. "Adam, do you mind?" Mitsy asked, pointing toward the back of the shop.

"No, please. It's around the corner and to your left."

Mary Anne and Adam watched Mitsy's outline recede.

"Your mother is really something," Adam said. "I read a bio of her in *Publishers Weekly*. Amazing how she wrote her books years ago and just gave them away as gifts for years and years."

"Yes, we never knew just how talented she was."

"Well, talent seems to run in the family," Adam said, eyeing Mary Anne. "Your mother raves about you. She's very excited about your premiere."

Mary Anne blushed. *Was he flirting with her? Or just being friendly?* She wasn't good at reading those signs.

"Yes, it's all very exciting," Mary Anne said. The conversation seemed to stall.

"It's lovely, your shop," she blurted. "How long have you had it?"

"About five years," Adam said. "I was in New York before this, writing plays mostly. But my great-aunt left me the shop in her will, and I thought it had to be the perfect opportunity to make a change."

Mary Anne let her fingers drift along the spine of the book she'd been flipping through.

"*Skinny Dip*. Have you read it?" Adam inquired.

"No, but Hiaasen is one of my favorite authors."

"Brilliant, isn't he? You've heard they're turning it into a film?" Adam asked.

Mary Anne had heard. In fact, she was desperate to do the adaptation, but this one time decided to play dumb.

"Really?" she said.

"Yes. But Hiaasen is a tricky adaptation, don't you think? So difficult to capture his tone."

"You're right!" Mary Anne said, self-consciousness giving way to enthusiasm. "But every adaptation is about the essence of the book, the voice really, not just the plot."

Adam smiled. "If you like Hiaasen, you know what else you'll like?" With a twinkle in his eye he waved her forward, pulling a book from the shelves. "Now, give this a read, and then we should see the movie. Talk about a tricky adaptation."

Did he just ask me on a date? Mary Anne wondered.

"Mary Anne, we should go," Mitsy called from the front door. "We have the car dealership after lunch."

Mary Anne looked at her mother, wishing that she and Adam had another moment alone.

"Take it," Adam said, handing Mary Anne the book. "Just promise to see the movie with me as soon as you're finished."

Mary Anne blushed.

"I'd love to," Mary Anne said. *Please God, don't let me fall over anything,* Mary Anne begged as she backed toward the front of the shop. She followed Mitsy and gave Adam a quick wave and a smile as she pulled shut the door.

"He's a cute one," Mitsy said, grinning and putting on her sunglasses.

"Mother," Mary Anne said, not completely disagreeing this time with her mother's taste in men.

Celeste Solange

CELESTE GLANCED AROUND AT THE EMPTY REMAINS OF HER AND DAMIEN'S Hollywood Hills home. The house had sold quickly in L.A.'s hot real-estate market. (Telling people that Celeste Solange and Damien Bruckner slept there added a huge amount to the selling price.) The cleaners were thorough. All that remained was a pile of mail sitting on the kitchen counter and a pair of Prada flats next to the front door. She never wore flats, so it had to be a pair of her housekeeper's old shoes. Celeste lifted an official-looking envelope, the return address from Howard Abromawitz. Inside were the divorce papers. The prenup was still in place, and Celeste would receive all that had been negotiated between her and Damien prior to their marriage. That, and her freedom. She glanced through the documents. Yellow tabs pointed to the places she needed to sign. Happy to have this chapter in her life closed, she pulled a pen from her bag.

She put the papers in the already pre-addressed and prepaid envelope and sealed it. *Finished.* She picked up the rest of the mail and placed it in her purse. Turning to leave, she took one last look out the kitchen window. All of Los Angeles sprawled out beyond her pool. This was her final farewell to an unhappy home, a disastrous marriage, and a disheartening lifestyle.

Celeste would stay at the Four Seasons until after the *Seven Minutes Past Midnight* premiere. Then she and Ted were headed to New York. He'd convinced her to at least try his beloved Manhattan for a while. Nothing definite; she didn't have to stay. In fact, Ted had made it very clear he'd live wherever she chose. Just as long as they were together.

Walking toward the front door, Celeste spotted the *Enquirer* lying on the staircase. One of the cleaners must have forgotten their reading. She reached for the magazine and a giggle escaped her lips. There, plastered on the front page, was Brie Ellison, topless, groping a dark-haired, tattooed girl.

BRIE BUSTS OUT OF THE CLOSET, the headline read. The second page contained a salacious story about Damien walking in on Brie in a compromising position with her new assistant. Celeste surmised that the only way this could have offended Damien and ended their relationship was if the girls had no interest in his joining their affair. She wondered what Damien would do now. Brie had just fallen out of *Borderland Blue,* Damien's film, while it was in preproduction, and there wasn't anyone to take the role. Damien's movie was finished unless he found a star.

Celeste's phone rang as she pulled shut the front door for the last time. She walked to her Town Car, fished her phone from her purse, and glanced at the number.

"Jess, how are you feeling?" Celeste was thrilled that her former agent and now manager had finally decided to leave CTA. This change was, Celeste believed, the very best thing for Jessica's career.

"You will never believe who just called," Jessica said.

Celeste sat in the car's leather seat. She glanced at the *Enquirer* and smiled.

"Let me guess. Damien?" Celeste asked.

"How did you know? Did he call you first?"

"No. Have you seen the *Enquirer* today?"

"No," Jess said. "But it's all over *Variety* that Brie dropped out of the movie due to a family problem."

"If you call your female lover a family problem," Celeste said.

"You know what he wants," Jessica exhaled. "They'll meet your quote. It's twenty million dollars plus back-end gross."

"I just don't know," Celeste said, unsure that she wanted to spend the next three months on a movie set with her ex-husband.

"I told him it was a long shot. In fact, I was surprised that he even got Summit to make the offer. They've put Dennis in the other role and Bradford Madison has signed on for the third lead. It's a great script, Cici. I can't advise you to take it; you'd be stuck with Damien every day. But it's splashy and well written, and I know every A-list actress in town wants the part, now that Summit has stepped up with some real money for the role. They came to you first."

Celeste thought about it. She'd always loved the script and had desperately wanted to play the part. She knew she didn't have to ask Ted, but she wanted to speak with him before making her decision.

"I want to talk to Ted," Celeste said, twirling a lock of her blond hair in her fingers. "It shoots in New Zealand, right?"

"Actually Prague."

"Ugh, they have the worst food," Celeste said, "and they never wash their hands."

"Well, think about it. It's always good to have your next film booked before your last one premieres. We've got the offer to do the film from Summit for the next twenty-four hours. Speak to Ted and then let me know."

" 'Kay. Will I be seeing you and Mike tonight?"

"Of course. But I can't promise how late I'll be there. My ankles are huge. I swear I look like an elephant. You should see the shoes I have to wear. Flats! Can you believe it? No heels for the next four months. I guess my arches will love it."

"Not with all the extra weight." Celeste smiled.

She'd never seen Jessica look so beautiful nor be so happy.

"When do you fly to New York?" Jessica asked, a hint of sadness in her voice.

"Tomorrow evening. I have to tell you, I'm a little nervous, but Ted tells me I'll love it. Plus, he promises his jet can bring me back to L.A. whenever I want."

"It's perfect, Cici. Okay, I have to take this other call. So I'll see you tonight. And let me know. You have twenty-four hours to decide on this. Then Summit is moving on to Sandy. Production starts in three weeks. Talk to Ted."

Celeste watched as the Hollywood Hills rushed by her. She knew Ted wouldn't care if she went to Prague to do Damien's film. It really would, she knew, save Damien's career. Otherwise, he was dead, with this film falling apart and his last one tanking. And his finances weren't too bright, either, with all the alimony he shelled out to Amanda and now her. *Ugh. Why was she even thinking of being nice to that asshole? Because I am an actress. Good roles and great films are what I live for.* Well, that was the answer, then, she guessed. She'd have to do it. And Ted would just have to learn to love Prague.

Lydia Albright

LYDIA WALKED INTO HER BUNGALOW ON THE WORLDWIDE LOT. SHE LOOKED over at the tower of power, pleased that the executive suite was now vacant. She glanced at *Variety*. The headlines screamed her success: MIDNIGHT MINTS MONEY. Opening weekend, *Seven Minutes Past Midnight* bashed box-office records, pulling in a whopping $175 million over three days. Without qualification, that was a huge success. Lydia knew that on this Monday morning she was at the pinnacle of her success as a producer. The final numbers would be astounding. The film would run all summer in theaters and they still had the international releases. Never mind the DVD sales, which would be phenomenal.

Ted Robinoff had called Lydia Saturday night and asked her to produce the sequel. Of course she'd agreed. And Sunday, Worldwide Business Affairs had called Jessica to close deals for Lydia as producer, Mary Anne as writer, Cici to star, and once again Zymar to direct. It rarely happened that everyone came back for the sequel of a film, but they had, each of them, agreed to work together again. Lydia had spoken with Mary Anne yesterday. Already they had the kernel of an idea that would be a wallop of a sequel. Ted was pushing hard for a release next summer. With all the action sequences and effects, that meant they needed to get into production fast. Lydia wanted a start date in September

(Cici would have returned from shooting Damien's film in Prague), which gave Mary Anne enough time to complete at least two passes on the script.

Zymar was scheduled to meet with Mary Anne today. He'd been lazing by Lydia's pool when she left for the office that morning.

"Love how you directors live between films," Lydia teasingly called to him from their bedroom window.

"Got to enjoy success when it comes to you, Lyd. Never know what the next one's gonna bring." He smiled up to her as he sipped his coffee by the pool. "You producers work too much. Christina's already left for the office. 'Ow bout taking the day with me and driving up the coast in that fancy new car of yours?" He was referring to Lydia's new convertible Bentley.

A present from Ted Robinoff for all her hard work, as well as, Lydia believed and Cici confirmed, an apology for Arnold's behavior.

"This weekend," Lydia called back.

There wasn't anything that would keep her away from the office today. Today Lydia Albright, mega-producer, had all the juice in town. Any project she wanted, just tell the studio the title. Box-office records didn't often get blown to smithereens, but when they did, to the victor went the spoils. She knew that between this huge success, Ted feeling guilty, and Arnold no longer running Worldwide, she had a moment. A small window of time to get moving every project she was attached to produce. Lydia had an agenda, and she had the next five days to carry it out.

Lydia hit the door knowing that everyone would be calling or e-mailing her with congratulations. And indeed, she'd barely been able to enter her bungalow because of the half dozen huge bouquets lined up in the waiting room. But she needed to stay focused. Speak to each studio head who called, press them to move on all the films she had at each of their studios. Get them to make the big money offers to the stars she wanted.

"You've got a hundred and seventeen calls," Toddy said, "and that's just from last night."

All six lines were ringing. And Lydia's new second assistant was struggling to keep up.

"Help her," Lydia said to Toddy, walking into her office.

"I've got Ted Robinoff on line one," Toddy called out.

Lydia put on her headset. "Ted!" Lydia beamed. "So you're pleased with the numbers?" she asked coyly.

"*Pleased* isn't the word, Lydia. I'd say thrilled."

"Good. I can't wait for the next one. Mary Anne and I worked on it yesterday and I think it's going to be really good."

"I know it will be, Lydia; you have an instinct about these things." Ted paused. "Lydia, I have a rather unorthodox question for you. Something that I was toying with last night."

Lydia knew that meant he'd been picking Cici's brain about it.

"Would you ever consider—now stay with me on this, as it's a little unorthodox—would you ever consider running Worldwide?"

Lydia didn't know what to say. This wasn't a job she had ever considered. President of production? At a studio?

"Ted, this . . . I mean, this really . . . I'm caught a little off guard."

"I know, I know. It's unconventional and not something we'd discussed. But Lydia, you have amazing taste and instincts about what makes a great film. And not just with one genre like action or thriller or romantic comedy, but with it all. Everyone in town loves you, and your relationships are very impressive."

Lydia glanced down at *Variety*. It was all true. Except for one Arnold Murphy, who was now banished to the Siberia of entertainment, she was respected and well liked. She'd worked long and hard to establish her reputation and her career. It seemed as though there were no mountains left to climb, except maybe this one.

"Well, I have to ask the obvious question: What happens to my films?"

"Well, at Worldwide, we'd want you to stay on as producer for all your films. Give you sort of a hybrid deal. You could produce some films and be president of production, too."

Lydia realized that these deals had been done before, in rare circumstances where the producers were exceptionally adept. In some cases it was huge success, in others an abject failure.

"Do you mind if I think on it?"

"Of course. I didn't expect an answer today. But listen, I'd really like to sit down and speak with you about it. Over lunch? What about tomorrow at the Grill?"

"Aren't you in Prague?"

"Yes, but we're coming in tonight. Cici isn't on the shooting schedule and has the next three days off, and she wants to shop a little. Something about some new Louboutins? I don't know what those are, but she wants them."

Lydia stifled a laugh. *What a star.* Cici was stealing Ted's jet for a new pair of shoes.

"Tomorrow is great. I'll see you there at one."

"Fantastic, Lydia. And please don't make a decision at least until we talk."

"Sure thing. Thanks, Ted."

Lydia hung up the phone. She spun her chair around and gazed at the tower of power. Maybe the executive suite wouldn't be empty for long.

Jessica Caulfield

JESSICA CAULFIELD'S MOVE INTO THE SUITE OF SIX SMALL OFFICES IN BEVERLY Hills was finally complete. She'd been surprised by how many agents from CTA had begged to come with her. She'd taken two and told the rest that there just wasn't room. The same went for her clients. Jessica found herself in the enviable position of selecting those few clients from her A-list roster she wanted to take with her. As an agent, she'd juggled the careers of twenty to forty writers, directors, and actors at any given time. As a manager, she'd chosen a mere ten to be her clients. It was a more personal relationship, that of manager. She was to be their career guide, creative muse, spiritual guru, and motherly influence. Anything they needed to be able to perform at this hyper-competitive, high-stakes level. Her maternal instinct, having already begun to kick in based on her hormones, made her well suited to be the mother hen to an elite flock of ten.

Jessica waddled back to her office from the bathroom, a trip that was becoming increasingly familiar as the baby grew and rested ever more firmly upon her bladder.

"Holden Humphrey on line one," Lauren called out.

Jessica paused, catching her breath before lumbering across the hall to her office.

"Tell him it's going to be just a minute."

The baby had begun to slow her down, something that would have been completely unforgivable at CTA but that was just part of her existence at her own company. She was the boss; she made the rules.

Jessica settled weightily into her chair and reached for her headset. *Holden? Hmm.* She hadn't spoken to him since the night she'd bumped into him at Will's party. *Booty Time 2* had come and gone. As Jessica predicted, it was a complete disaster at the box office. She heard little more about Holden after that. The industry seemed to have moved on to the next big male star.

"Holden," Jessica said. "How are you?"

"Hi, Jess. It sure is good to hear your voice."

To her, he sounded forlorn.

"So tell me, what are you working on right now?" Jessica asked, curious to hear what, if anything, Josh Dragatsis had in the works.

"Well, you know . . . It's kind of quiet right now," Holden said with a hint of loneliness in his voice.

Jessica knew his career was cold. Casting was gearing up on a number of films, all of which had roles that were ideal for someone like Holden. If Dragatsis wasn't even getting Holden out for those roles, then it truly was frigid in the marketplace for him.

"So I hear you've got your own place now?" Holden asked.

"Yes I do," Jessica said, waiting for him to ask. She remembered that Holden had always been dismissive of her belief that he should take a manager. For the ten percent, she'd always thought another set of eyes and ears looking for opportunities for an actor could be well worth it. And of course, her belief was only stronger now.

"And a baby on the way, too."

"We're very excited," Jessica said.

If she was still an agent, she'd be trying to hide her pregnancy, keeping it from her competitors, who would see her upcoming maternity leave as the perfect opportunity to steal her clients. But as a manager, she didn't feel that way. There was an unspoken agreement among managers: no poaching. She was a more integral part of her clients' lives, and they hers. It was the type of relationship she'd tried to nurture with her clients as an agent but that was more suited to manager.

"So, Jess, I was wondering, do you remember a long time ago, when you told me to never be embarrassed to make the call?"

Jessica did remember a morning, what seemed like very long ago, when she'd cooked Holden a steaming plate of eggs.

"I do, in fact, remember," Jessica said, smiling not so much about Holden, but about her former self, her agent self, hyper-aggressive and competitive.

"So I'm making it. The call."

Jessica couldn't help but smile even wider. It was so sweet when they returned. Unlike a number of representatives, she never abused or humiliated her clients when they wanted to come back. And in this instance, with her change in position, and Holden's decline in the marketplace, it would be completely understandable should Jessica choose not to represent him again. She could easily beg off; her roster as a manager was in fact full. But she had a special spot in her heart for Holden, and she truly believed that with the right direction, he could be a huge star.

"Holden, I'm thrilled that you did. So why don't you come by the house tonight and we'll have some dinner and talk about what you want to do. Around eight?" Jessica asked, not missing a beat, nothing belying her sense of satisfaction at once again being right.

"Thanks, Jess," Holden said.

He was grateful and relieved. She could hear it in his voice. Jessica pushed the Release button on her phone.

"Lauren, can I get something to eat?" she called out to her assistant. "Let's order lunch early. Maybe a cheeseburger?"

"If I eat any more cheeseburgers, Jess, I am going to be as big as you, and that's without the pregnancy. How about a nice salad?" Lauren offered.

"Mike's paying you, isn't he? Are you keeping a diary for him of what I eat?"

"I'm calling La Scala. You love their turkey chop salad."

Jessica grimaced. A salad would have to do. Just as she thought about lunch, she felt it. A thud against the inside of her tummy.

"Wow!" Jessica yelled.

"What?!" Lauren screamed and rushed back into Jessica's office, her earpiece dangling.

"He just kicked me!" Jessica said, her face full of delight. "He must be hungry, too."

"See," said Lauren, "he's excited about the salad."

Jessica sat rubbing her tummy in the spot that her son had thumped her. Never before had she been so thrilled about being kicked by a man.

Mary Anne Meyers

MARY ANNE PATTERED ACROSS ADAM'S KITCHEN FLOOR. IT WAS EARLY. HER laptop sat open on the kitchen table. She'd been up writing since four A.M. She was so close to being finished. She had to figure out some tangles in the third act, and then it would be complete. Zymar would be thrilled. They'd finally hammered out the twist in the second act, where Cici's character appears to be a bad guy; of course, the audience finds out later it was all a ploy. It'd taken forever, but now this draft was almost ready. Just in time, as pre-production was a heartbeat away.

Mary Anne looked up to see Adam, freshly showered and dressed, walking into the kitchen. She sat at her computer with coffee breath and bed head, but it didn't seem to matter to him. He walked over and gave her a gentle kiss on the mouth.

"Good morning," he said, heading for the coffeepot. "How about some eggs?"

"Sure," Mary Anne said, making a move to get up from her chair.

Adam laughed. "I'll make them." He reached over and tousled her already messy hair.

She was still getting used to his laid-back ways. He kept surprising her with each kindness he bestowed. Last night, they'd spent the evening reading together, a silent joy for her. Adam's apartment was above his bookstore, a cozy two-bedroom with a deck and a view. He'd remodeled the space after he moved to Los Angeles. Originally his aunt used it as storage and an office, but there was enough storage downstairs. It was much smaller than Mary Anne's house in the Hills, but much cozier, too. Plus, it was like having your own personal library of all the newest books right downstairs. For two writers, it was heaven.

"I'm going to grab the paper before the eggs," Adam said, heading to the back staircase that led to the bookstore below.

Another perk: They received every major paper in America, and there was always one extra. She loved dating a man with a bookstore.

"Look what I found," Adam called, heading back up the stairs. He tore open a box.

Inside were four advance copies of Mitsy's first book.

"They're really cool," Adam said, handing one to Mary Anne.

She'd seen one before over at Mitsy's, but somehow this felt more real, holding a copy and knowing that every bookstore owner in America would receive Mitsy's book today. It was an exact replica of the first book Mary Anne ever read. The hand-drawn pictures were even the same.

"I'm so happy for her," Mary Anne said, flipping through the book. "And I'm happy for me, too." She looked at Adam.

With this gentle man, in this little bookshop away from the bright lights and celebrity of Hollywood and the movie business, she had finally found her haven. It wasn't quite Midwestern, but it wasn't very L.A., either.

"Hey, you figured out the third act," Adam said, bending over and skimming the screen of Mary Anne's laptop.

"I sure did," Mary Anne said, grinning.

"Bet you guys leave room for a sequel."

"There is always room for a sequel," Mary Anne said, turning back to her computer screen and typing two final words.

THE END

Ten Months Later

JESSICA SAT NURSING MAX. ONLY FIVE MONTHS OLD, HE'D SLEPT THROUGH THE Sunday afternoon premiere of Mike's newest film, *Sky Man*. She was thrilled. So was Mike. *Sky Man* would be a huge hit among the tiny-tot set. The premiere party was held in a tent that had been designed to be an exact replica of the cloud city Sky World that was home to Sky Man. Mike had worked so hard on getting this film made while starting parenthood. He'd even postponed production for six weeks after Max was born, almost losing his star. Jessica saved that deal, promising to get Matt a meeting with Zymar for *Fifteen Minutes Past Midnight,* if only he'd still do *Sky Man*.

Jessica glanced across the tent at Lydia working the room. She was the über-everything right now. Worldwide's box office, overall, had never been better. Jess didn't know how Lydia juggled it all—producing, president of production for Worldwide, Zymar. But she did, effortlessly and brilliantly. Unmitigated determination and belief in her projects, Jessica knew, drove Lydia forward. Besides, Lydia absolutely loved what she did.

"How we doing?" Mike asked, bending over to tickle Max's cheek.

"My little vampire is just about finished," Jess joked, removing her breast from Max's mouth.

"Oh, there's Cici!"

"Let me take him for a while," Mike offered. "You've had him all afternoon."

"Jess!" Celeste sang out, bouncing over to her and wrapping her in a huge hug. "You look beautiful. And look at my perfect little godson," Cici said, cooing over Max, the second favorite man in her life.

"You, as always, look stunning."

Celeste's megastar glow had only been enhanced with three successful films (each more so than the last) and the consistent love of Ted Robinoff.

"Where's Ted?" Jessica asked.

"Over with Lydia. Discussing their next big film, I'm sure. Have you seen Mary Anne yet? She brought her bookstore man. Soooo sexy. And smart. You know he quoted Whitman to me. I thought I might just die. Those two are perfect for each other."

Jessica had met Adam, and agreed with Celeste's analysis that Mary Anne had found her Mr. Right. Adam was smart and bookish, yet sophisticated.

"I hear, although she's not fessing up, that Max may have a playmate soon," Celeste said, giving credence to the rumor that Mary Anne's full face was not from the ten pounds most women gained when in a serious relationship.

"She'd be a great mom," Jessica said.

"And Mitsy would be thrilled," Celeste added.

Celeste now held Max in her arms. (having stolen him from Mike). Like most men, Max stared adoringly at Celeste, giggling at the funny faces she made.

Jessica scanned the crowd, watching her husband work the room. Lydia gestured enthusiastically to Ted about some project that was sure to be a tremendous hit. Mary Anne held Adam's arm as they made their way over to Celeste and Jess, weaving through the hectic tangle of celebrities and their children playing games and eating corn dogs. Agents and managers circled the outskirts of the tent, trying to make deals and poach stars. This Hollywood existence was, Jessica thought, surreal but it was for her, the ideal life.

Acknowledgments

THANK YOU FIRST AND FOREMOST TO MY BRILLIANT, BEAUTIFUL AGENT, ANDREA Barzvi. Without her vision and dedication, this manuscript would never have become a book. Andy is the best, and I am blessed to have her as my agent and my friend. Thank you to Emily Brotman and Jennifer Smith for their editing skills . . . and patience with my little *were* and *where* problem. I am grateful for Esther Newberg; she is a champion (the word *champion* to be used as both a noun and a verb in Esther's case). Also, to the handsome Nick Reed, my mentor and my friend (and perhaps the most fantastic motion picture literary agent in the world); thank you for giving a girl a chance.

Thank you to Shana Drehs, my amazing first editor. Her patience and passion for this manuscript were immeasurable. Her help was limitless. Thank you to Lindsey Moore, my second editor, for loving the manuscript and taking me on. Thank you to the whole team at Crown Publishers.

My gratitude to Paul Miloknay. I am thankful that he is my attorney. His advice and counsel on so many matters has been invaluable.

I am grateful for Rocky Mountain Fiction Writers, who long ago and far away helped me with my first manuscript; especially to Monica Poole, Tracy Abel, Johanna Gallers, and Linda Hulle.

Thank you to my friends, many of them original readers: Barbara Brumleve, Molly Carl, Leslie Ferguson, Carrie Jacob, Barbara Smith, Renie Oxley, Lauren Kisilevsky, Susanna Jolly, Swanna MacNair, Eric Levy, Pam Silverstein, Nicole Rocklin, and Lindsy Henderson.

Margaret Marr and Paula Glasscock were forever my cheering section, readers, and spell-checkers; thank you.

Nancy Orr, thank you for making all of it possible.

To my friends and colleagues at the mighty ICM, without whose support this book would not have been possible: Jeff Berg, Nancy Josephson, Ed Limato, Robert Newman, Nicole Clemens, Chris Andrews, Toni Howard, Martha Luttrell, Sloan Harris, Bob Levinson, Richard Abate, Kate Lee, Matt Solo, Nancy Etz, Carel Cutler, Steve Simons, Barbara Mandel, Babette Perry, Geoff Blaine, Eric Reid, Danny Wantland, and the magnificent Matt Olmon.

Thank you to my family: Linda Henderson, Bill Henderson, Nealie White, Craig White, Lauren White, Gavin White, David Glasscock, Elizabeth Leahy, Eloise Marr, Dixie Marr, Mark Henderson, Garrett Marr, and James Marr.

Finally, to Chad Henderson, Hayden, and Grace, the true believers in my life. With their love and support all things are possible. They are my every wish and my every dream come true.

About the Author

MAGGIE MARR WAS BORN AND RAISED IN ILLINOIS. AFTER PRACTICING LAW FOR four years, first as a guardian-ad-litem for abused children and then as a prosecutor in domestic violence, she made the move to Los Angeles with her husband, who is an actor. Her first job in entertainment was pushing the mail cart at ICM, where she eventually became a motion picture agent. She now splits her time between writing and producing. She is currently at work on her second Hollywood Girls Club novel and the television pilot *Pretty Is As Pretty Does*. Please visit her at www.maggiemarr.com.

RULE 1

There Are No Secrets in Hollywood
Kiki Dee, Publicist

Kiki Dee thought she knew where all the Hollywood bodies were buried—even the ones she had killed—because secrets were her business. Celebrity secrets. Kiki was a secret keeper. As a publicist, Kiki shifted the bright white spotlight away from everything her celebrity clients needed to hide. Their gratitude for her covering up their indiscretions took the form of a check, or cash, whichever they preferred. Kiki collected secrets the way some people collected diamonds or cars. Each naughty tidbit could potentially destroy Hollywood careers. And of course, along with the indiscretions came the clients. Kiki promised to lock the secret in "the vault," also known as her brain, for a weekly fee. Some called it extortion. Kiki called it commerce.

And Kiki didn't keep just one secret per client. She'd discovered that once a star accepted that she knew his most depraved act or hidden kink, suddenly all the crimes and misdemeanors came pouring out. Kiki listened to all her clients' confessions. It was good to have collateral.

But *this* secret, the one Kiki had just witnessed in Dr. Melnick's office . . . well, this secret was platinum. This secret had the potential to sink movie studios, destroy high-power industry marriages, and ruin one of the biggest celebrity careers in Hollywood. With this one very big and amazingly well-kept secret, Kiki and her publicity firm, KDP, which had suffered a precipitous slide into the abyss of B-list stars, would be back on top. This secret potentially affected dozens of Hollywood heavyweights. Not to mention the little lovely who was rapidly sleeping her way up the A-list. Kiki would sign two big stars based on this peccadillo. Failing to have her in their corner would result in the release of this salacious bit of gossip to the press. If the truth reached the masses, the two stars could kiss their careers and their paychecks good-bye.

Kiki had proof, and she figured it was worth at least seven figures. But Kiki cared little about the money. No, she desired prestige. The prestige obtained by representing the biggest stars in the world. Prestige and access were priceless commodities in Hollywood, and for Kiki prestige, access, and power made her job almost worthwhile.

Kiki would be thrilled . . . if she weren't so nauseated. Her discovery almost made the torture of her lipo, tummy tuck, and eye lift worth it. Almost. She gritted her teeth as the Lincoln Town Car came to a fast stop on Wilshire. How had *this* luscious deceit remained quiet? People must know. But Kiki had rummaged through celebrity lives for twenty (okay, twenty-five) years, and she had *never* sniffed a whiff of this treat. She carefully leaned back against the supple black leather of the backseat. It was a short four-block trip from Dr. Melnick's office to the Peninsula Hotel, but with stitches around her face and the super-tight spandex body glove around her stomach, the ride felt like miles. She knew from experience.

Although painful, the spandex body glove prevented her belly from rupturing. She turned her gauze-wrapped head toward the window and attempted to block from her mind the lipo procedure that Dr. Melnick had just completed, otherwise she'd be sick. She clutched the paper airsick bag that Dr. Melnick's receptionist (who herself had bovine-fat-enhanced lips and perfectly Botoxed brows) had handed her before the nurse wheeled her out the back exit of the office to her awaiting car and driver.

Boom Boom, Kiki's ever-faithful and ever-suffering assistant, sat in the backseat holding a BlackBerry in one hand and a cup of ice chips in the other.

"She said it was urgent," Boom Boom said and scrolled through the e-mails. "Here, look."

She held the BlackBerry within inches of Kiki's nose, but Kiki couldn't read it. *God, Boom Boom could be an idiot. You couldn't wear glasses right after an eye lift. Where did Boom Boom think they put the stitches?* Kiki leaned her head to the left. She could barely speak. Her lips were swollen (ass fat or bovine, she didn't even remember at this point), and her jaw hurt.

"Read it," Kiki mumbled, trying to move her lips as little as possible.

Boom Boom pulled an ice chip from the cup and managed to wedge it into Kiki's mouth. "Fine. It says, 'Kiki, my luv, we need to talk. Urgent news, don't want to e-mail, call me.'"

Kiki looked at Boom Boom. That was it? That was the e-mail Boom Boom appeared so worked up about? Kiki had worked the public relations gig for a long time, and *urgent* to one of her stars could mean a broken nail without a manicurist on set. This was nothing, especially compared with Kiki's recent discovery. But still, the e-mail had come from one of her biggest stars.

"When?" Kiki whispered then winced as the Town Car bounced over a pothole. She remembered that bump from the last face-lift, six months earlier.

"Three hours ago," Boom Boom said. She put on her headset. "Want to roll some calls? We've got twenty-five to return."

Kiki glared at her assistant. She felt doped up on morphine and hadn't yet taken her Vicodin.

"Lydia called. She needs an answer about press."

Kiki shook her head and motioned for the pad and pen resting on Boom Boom's lap.

"Jen wants to know about the CDF fund-raiser," Boom Boom continued. She handed Kiki the pen. "Also Natalie asked about your trip to the ashram, wants to know if it's one or two weeks?"

Kiki's head pounded. She put pen to paper.

"Galaxy just FedExed dailies from the *Take No Prisoners* set and wants you to let them know about the Oscar campaign."

Kiki finished writing and turned the monogrammed notebook toward her young, wrinkle-free servant. Boom Boom continued to chatter about appointments and calls. Kiki tapped on the pad, and then again with more force, finally requiring Boom Boom to silence her yammering and look at the paper.

A small gasp escaped Boom Boom's lips as she read Kiki's short but effective note.

"I'm just trying to be helpful. You don't have to get bitchy about it," Boom Boom said.

Kiki turned toward the window and tried ... ile—smiling wou... have torn at the stitches clamped to the ski... her ears. Busine... would have to wait until she was wrapped in e... red-thread-coun... sheets at the Peninsula. She relaxed as the lim... into the private entrance to the hotel, and glanced at the notep... r lap. Two very effective words were emblazoned across the pad: ... u.

...e s, life-threatening notes, secrets,

ries · ·

... at's life in Hollywood, where the right friend... ...ake or break...

Celest... ...battling everything and everyone from stalkers and wrinkles to the big egos of Hollywood's elite—all while juggling careers, clients, families, and Tinseltown's hottest actors. Can the four powerful movie mavens hold their lives together—and get a film made—amid all the craziness?

Find out in the dishy follow-up to *Hollywood Girls Club.*

Secrets of the Hollywood Girls Club
$23.95 hardcover (Canada: $27.95)
ISBN 978-0-307-34631-5

Available wherever books are sold.

After a successful career as a television writer and producer, working on such series as *A Touch of Frost*, *Midsomer Murders* and *Between the Lines*, **Michael Russell** decided to write what he had always wanted to: books. *The City in Darkness* is the third of his Stefan Gillespie stories of historical crime fiction, taking a sideways look at the Second World War through Irish eyes, and exploring some unexpected corners of the conflict, such as Danzig, New York and, in *The City in Darkness*, the cities of Franco's Spain. The first two Stefan Gillespie novels, *The City of Shadows* and *The City of Strangers*, were both shortlisted for Crime Writers' Association awards. Michael lives with his family in West Wicklow, in Ireland, not a million miles from Stefan Gillespie's home.

Website: michaelrussellforgottencities.com

Facebook: michaelrussellforgottencities

Twitter: @forgottencities